SHIVEREE

Sophie Dunbar

INTRIGUE
PRESS

For information, please contact Intrigue Press, P.O. Box 456, Angel
Fire, NM 87710, 505-377-3474.

ISBN 1-890768-11-1

First Printing 1999

This book is a work of fiction. Names, characters, places and incidents
either are the product of the author's imagination or are used fictitiously.
Any resemblance to actual events or persons living or dead is entirely
coincidental. Although the author and publisher have made every effort to
ensure the accuracy and completeness of information contained in this
book, we assume no responsibility for errors, inaccuracies, omissions, or any
inconsistency herein. Any slights of people, places or organizations are
unintentional.

Library of Congress Cataloging-in-Publication Data:

Dunbar, Sophie.
    Shiveree / Sophie Dunbar.
        p.   cm.
    ISBN 1-890768-11-1 (hardcover)
    I. Title.
    PS3554, U46337S55   1999
    813'.54—dc21   98-51073
                                                                        CIP

Merci beaucoup to the following:

Dwayne Savoy (no relation to Nectarine), Sommelier of the Windsor Court Hotel, New Orleans, for his superb wine selections for Foley and Charlotte's rehearsal dinner; to Mattie Allyn of Antique Guild Jewels, Los Angeles, re: blue sapphires, pink diamonds and black opals; to Jan Burke, for lending her wondrous hair to Esmé Barnes; to the real Opal Folsom, who introduced me to Red Velvet Cake and for allowing me to share her original recipe; to Barbara Hutnick, my special angel, who went even higher above and further beyond on this book; to Sylvan Markman, my fabulous husband, for taking that giant leap into the world of mystery.

A special hello to Beth (The Mystery Maven) Caswell, Joan Wunsch, Ruth, Bunnie, Colleen, Candace and all my girlfriends at Coffee, Tea & Mystery—Love you, ladies!

My deepest gratitude to the original Author and Finisher, Jesus Christ, for the gift of writing.

Also by Sophie Dunbar

Behind Eclaire's Doors
Redneck Riviera
A Bad Hair Day

This book is dedicated to Chris, my delightful and only son, who came along at exactly the right time.

SHIVEREE (shiv′e rē) *alt.* shivaree *n.* Uproarious serenade with tambourines, horns, cowbells, musical instruments and various noise-makers to celebrate the union of a newly married couple. (F. *charivari*)

FROM THE ATLANTA *JOURNAL-CONSTITUTION*,
Sunday, October 6:

DALTON-CALLANT

Mr. and Mrs. Emory Meredith Dalton of Buckhead, announce the engagement of their daughter, Amalie Charlotte, to Foley Preston Callant, Jr., a native of New Orleans, Louisiana.

Miss Dalton and Mr. Callant are to wed in a formal ceremony on Christmas Eve at the Peachtree First Baptist Church, after which transportation will be provided for guests attending the reception and dinner dance to be held at the Peachtree Chateau Hotel.

Miss Dalton, who graduated from Sweetbriar College with a degree in Journalism, was recently appointed Executive News Story Director of WBGZ Television in New Orleans. Mr. Callant, a graduate of Tulane University School of Law, is senior partner in the firm of Blanchard, Smithson, Callant and Claiborne.

The bride's mother is the former Daphne Lambert of Marietta. Her father, Emory M. Dalton, currently serves as Chairman of the Board for Peach Island Textiles. Parents of the groom, Foley Preston Callant, Sr. and the former Opal Key, are both deceased.

Following a wedding trip to Italy, the couple plans to make their home in New Orleans.

FROM THE ATLANTA *JOURNAL-CONSTITUTION*,
Sunday, November 17:

DALTON-CALLANT

Due to unforseen circumstances, Miss Charlotte Dalton and Mr. Foley P. Callant, Jr. will not be married at the Peachtree First Baptist Church as originally announced. Invited guests will be notified of the ceremony's New Orleans location at first opportunity. The date, December 24, has not been changed.

The Dalton and Callant families regret any inconvenience.

Mr. & Mrs. Emory Meredith Dalton

request the honor of your presence

at the marriage of their daughter

Amalie Charlotte

to

Foley Preston Callant, Jr.

in

The Crystal Ballroom

of

Riverside Manor Hotel

New Orleans, Louisiana

on

the twenty-fourth of December

at

seven o'clock in the evening.

RSVP   Reception immediately following the
Black Tie   ceremony at the River Queen Club

1

'Twas the night before Christmas when the groom and
the bride
Amid holly and mistletoe saw the knot tied.
With champagne we toasted the two newlyweds,
While honeymoon visions danced in their heads.
The cake it was cut, and the bouquet was thrown,
A flurry of rice, then the couple was gone.
But on the uppermost floor of that deluxe hotel,
Wedding guests were still stirring, set to raise merry hell.
So hearty they partied, like kids with new toys,
'Til who should arrive but the Shiveree Boys!
Roaming through corridors, cowbells aringing,
An ancient hillbilly tune they were singing:
Two hearts throbbing as one
form a union more sweet
yon lovers must mate
to the shiveree beat.
The Shiveree Boys thumped out a strange rhythm
That into the wee hours kept us awake with them.

Their serenade ended with one mighty crash;
Silence so golden descended at last.
Santa had just invited me onto his lap
(The better my first Christmas gift to unwrap),
When out in the hall there arose such a shout!
We sprang from our bed to see what it was about.
Eight men were gathered 'round a kicked-open door,
Staring at something that lay on the floor.
The big, noisy bunch stood docile and tame,
Scarce seeming to hear as Dan called them by name:
Tucker, Woody and Wes——stop playing rough.
Fenton and Huey, enough is enough.
Emory and Kyle, this racket's absurd.
But the Shiveree Boys answered nary a word.
Their leader Purcell (who looked like Slim Pickens)
Now turned a visage as grim as the dickens
Saying to Dan, "It ain't pretty, son.
Appears 'twasn't love, but vile murder done."
Then stepping aside he allowed us to see
What had suddenly halted that wild shiveree.
She'd been flung on the carpet in bizarrest of poses,
Decked out in garlands of blood and red roses.
Her forehead was marked with a bright crimson crescent
Diadem for the Ghost of Christmas present.

2

"Evangeline Claire Claiborne, I'm serious!" warned the bride-to-be. "You put down that hairspray can right this minute and let me look, or some lucky gator will dine on coonass du jour for lunch!"

I excused her tantrumette. After all, my best friend was a redhead on the edge, suffering intense job-related stress, due to her boss having been charged with murder in the first degree. The resulting increased workload had mandated shifting her elaborate formal Christmas Eve wedding from Atlanta's Peachtree First Baptist Church, to the just-opened Riverside Manor Hotel on the New Orleans waterfront. These days, Charlotte Dalton traveled with a cell phone clutched in each hand, designated Wedding and Work, respectively.

Next week, Daltons galore—from hick to high society—would descend upon us, eager to seize control of Operation Matrimony. Some of them weren't even waiting until then. Thirty minutes earlier, Charlotte's sister had called from Buckhead to demand a different color bridesmaid dress, claiming she looked like Mrs. Santa Claus in the custom-fitted, handsewn, paid-for, red satin grosgrain that her three cousins were wearing.

Me, I'd've been howling like a *loup-garou* by now.

Nevertheless, having spent nearly fourteen days wrestling with a truly demon-possessed auburn wig pinned to a Styrofoam head, creating Charlotte's hairstyle, I was not about to be hurried through the trial run.

"Sit still, *chère*," I ordered firmly, administering another spritz of lacquer to my masterpiece.

The bridal coiffure is an amazingly complex organism, requiring a mechanical structure engineered to achieve maximum aesthetic harmony with the ceremonial headdress, while flattering the face from every angle. And yet, once the veil is removed, this same hair must be able to rock and roll at the reception on its own merits.

But above all else, nuptial tresses should endow an everyday woman with a crown of glory, imparting mystical powers that transform her into—The Bride.

The latter element posed an even greater challenge in Charlotte's situation. As a television news reporter, her pale, piquant face and glossy, blunt chestnut mane were so familiar, some real razzmatazz was called for when at last she said, "I do!" to my husband Dan's pal and law partner, Foley Callant.

As owner of Eclaire, New Orleans' most delectable beauty parlor, I've designed hair for many high-pressure weddings, but never when I was also to be matron of honor. Dan, of course, would serve as Foley's best man, and one of the groomsmen—internationally famous hairmeister Marcel Barrineau—had been my tutor in the beautification business.

Therefore, acquiring the necessary personal and professional detachment had been difficult, but at the eleventh hour, I experienced what amounted to a hair epiphany. Upswept from a center part, then coiled and wrapped with a braid, it evoked the gamine yet austere, slightly menacing sensuality of a 1960s European fashion model.

Or, as Dan put it, "Darlin', that hair belongs on the child of James Bond and Holly Golightly!"

Now, I gave the thing a final pat, then swivelled Charlotte to face the mirror. She scrutinized her reflection tentatively, as if being introduced to someone she vaguely recalled having met before, then smiled uncertainly. "Claire," Charlotte whispered, "I . . . can't believe that fabulous creature is really me." And with that, promptly burst into tears.

"Oh, shoot! There I go again!" she sniffed, dabbing at her eyes with a Kleenex. "Foley's been threatening to slip a mood ring onto my finger, along with the more traditional wedding band."

What Mr. Callant actually had in mind when it came to jewelry were breathtakingly gorgeous, square-cut ruby and diamond earrings and a necklace to match Charlotte's engagement ring, but I was sworn to secrecy.

"Well, considering how I wrung myself to a rag over this hairdo, I'm immensely gratified you feel so strongly about it," I said, laughing. "But now—for the crucial test."

Early this morning, a fetching young UPS guy had trundled a load of packages—all from Atlanta's legendary Anne Barge for Brides—into my terra cotta, pine and tapestry reception area. When Charlotte arrived, we'd torn them open like excited little girls, scattering boxes, ribbons and tissue paper across the shop in gleeful abandon.

The largest parcel contained a wedding gown of white silk taffeta with an opalescent finish that shimmered like moonbeams on ice. Two slightly smaller ones held long, clingy sheaths of luscious, holly-green panne velvet, that both I and Nectarine Savoy (maid of honor, Marcel Barrineau's recent fiancée, and New Orleans Police detective) would be wearing.

There were also seductive little cocktail hats to go with—sleek green feathers and merest pouff of net—plus dyed-to-match Maude Frizon pumps, but those delights would have to be postponed. Somewhere, amid this glorious clutter, reposed the bridal veil.

The item turned up in a box behind my favorite cushion, upon which *Fais do-do, chère!* (Cajun for, "Party on, honey!") had been needle-pointed in elegant script by my assistant Renee's *Tante* Doux. I lifted the lid and there it was, looking like something that had drifted directly down from heaven.

The wide, crownless brim of snowy plumes was molded to frame Charlotte's face like a picture hat; misty chiffon attached to the bottom would trail dreamily around her shoulders and back, nearly touching the floor.

It felt almost alive in my hands as I carried it over to Charlotte, whose bright head drooped wearily under its unaccustomed heaviness, exposing her long, slender neck. I was reminded of a full-blown winter peony, swaying elegantly on its stem. Carefully, I adjusted the feathery wreath to fit snugly behind her ears, and arranged the gossamer chiffon. She looked so beautiful that this time both of us got weepy.

"Oh, Claire! I've never been so happy in my life! Nothing's going to spoil this for Foley and me. Nothing." A sudden strange sound, something between a sob and a giggle escaped her. "Sorry, this really isn't funny. But I was just thinking—at least nobody's likely to cash in their chips for a change. Right?"

It was a valid concern since during the past year, we—that is, Dan, myself, Foley and Charlotte—had been repeatedly sucked into one drama after another filled with larceny, heartbreak and murder.

Shaking off an unwelcome sense of foreboding, I gave Charlotte a hug. *"Fermé la bouche, chère,"* I commanded. "Everything's gonna be perfect, I garontee. The worst that could happen is your face breaks out in a great big *bouton* on your wedding day!

"No wait. The very worst is, you get *maladie de femme* on your wedding night!"

Her squeals of laughing protest almost drowned out the pitty-pat of little webbed goose feet, running across somebody's grave . . .

3

I was explaining Marcel's estimate for providing beauty services to the entire wedding party, when one of Charlotte's cell phones whirred.

"That's Wedding again," she announced, her ear as attuned to the nuances of each machine as a mother's to distinguish between the wails of identical twins. By now, even I was able to detect a certain petulant note in Wedding's ring.

But only hindsight revealed this call was a harbinger of calamity to come.

Tossing back filmy folds of veil, Charlotte put the phone to her ear. "Oh. Hello again, Lambie," she sighed, rolling her eyes at me. "Lambie" being the inevitable nickname bestowed upon Leanne Lambert Dalton, Charlotte's much younger, outrageously spoiled, sister.

Last week, Lambie had abruptly called off her engagement to kissing cousin Tucker John Dalton, thereby quenching what seemed to be the final flicker of hope for true peace between the Society Daltons and the Swamp Daltons.

During the post-Civil War Reconstruction era, Charlotte's ancestors had developed a scraggly, unappealing island off Georgia's Atlantic coast into the lucrative cotton and linen enterprise today known as Peach Island Textiles—a label synonymous with prestige household linens. Some Daltons grew and spun the fibers; others marketed the yardage.

They were completely dependent upon each other's specialized skills, yet over the years there'd come a rift between the growers and the merchants. These two camps began derogatorily calling each other "Swamp" or "Society," and those names had stuck to this day.

As time went by, occasional efforts were made to repair the breach, most notably fifty years ago when Society and Swamp cousins Imogene and Purcell had fallen madly in love. But then, Imogene got cold feet and threw Purcell over for a distant Society relative, and there'd very nearly been shots exchanged.

Although the factions had declared an armed truce for the sake of the one thing they could both agree on—Peach Island Textiles—they'd been aiming barbs at each other ever since.

Eventually, this family controversy degenerated into the caricature of a hillbilly feud. Swamp Daltons seemed to derive perverse pleasure from embarrassing "them snooty" Society Daltons. Charlotte once told me a hilarious story about a trio of Swamps performing a clog dance for their terrified captive audience in the glass elevator of a famous hotel.

But the last straw was at Charlotte's debutante ball when Uncle Fenton and Aunt Mamie took to the stage and belted out "The Butcher's Boy"—graphic, authentic lyrics and all. From that moment, Society Daltons had shunned any association with Swamp Daltons in public places.

However, Charlotte's wedding was one occasion where the twain must meet and, being genuinely fond of her more rustic relations, she'd managed to get both sides to sit down at the bargaining table. Truly a diplomatic coup since the fickle Imogene was none other than Charlotte's grandmother, and Purcell was still very much alive and kicking.

Things had been going fairly well, until Lambie up and repeated history by ditching Tucker John, Vice-President of Peach Island Textiles—and Purcell's grandson.

Lambie evidently had much to say, successfully foiling Charlotte's attempts to insert a comment. Finally, in exasperation she snapped,

"Shut up, Lambie! You jilted Tucker John, remember? He's got a perfect right to bring a date to the wedding if he wants to . . . no! I absolutely will not tell him he can't be a groomsman."

Suddenly, Charlotte sat bolt upright and screeched, "A WHAT?" Listening, she shook her head in disbelief, finally replying weakly, "Well, it's too late now. After all, I did promise Uncle Purcell he and the boys could sing whenever they wanted to."

Charlotte sighed again. "Okay, Lambie. Thanks for the warning— no, ma'am! That does not mean you get out of wearing the red dress!"

Flipping the phone shut, she turned to me with a glazed expression. "You won't believe this one, Claire. Poor Foley will positively croak!"

All Swamp Daltons were zealous preservationists of what they termed, "Dalton Cultural Heritage." It transpired that Great-Uncle Purcell, as their patriarch, had organized an authentic shiveree for Charlotte's wedding night. This charming backwoods mating rite involved friends (primarily male) of the newlyweds gathering outside the bridal chamber, cheering the pair on to consummation while singing, rattling tambourines, ringing cowbells, blowing noisemakers, and wreaking general havoc. One of the more ribald variations called for the Shiveree Boys to crash into the couple's room, surrounding their bed with shouts of congratulation, passing the cider jug to celebrate a job well done.

Foley would most certainly croak.

Even though Uncle Purcell had been less than candid with Charlotte, she wasn't about to go back on her word to him, especially not after what Lambie pulled on Tucker John.

"Anyhow, once his mind's made up, no mere mortal can stop him," Charlotte concluded listlessly. "You'll see." She fixed piteous green eyes on me. "Claire, remind me again why I chose to kill myself in this particular way?"

"Because you wanted your whole crazy family to share equally in the happiest moment of your life, whether they deserve it or not," I replied. "Anyway," I teased, "thanks to Uncle Purcell's wedding night shiveree, guess Dan and I can call off the big old twenty-one gun salute we'd planned in honor of that major sports event!"

Though Foley had been married before and Charlotte—well, let's just say she made a lot of wrong choices—this pair had endured smouldering months of celibacy and a stringent course of Full Gospel Baptist premarital counseling to make sure they'd be starting from scratch together.

Foley promised Charlotte she wouldn't regret it, because he'd built up quite a head of steam!

She smiled. "Ah, yes! That puts things back into perspective."

I glanced at the pewter clock on top of a tall pine armoire. "Listen, Charlotte. There's just enough time to slide into your dress before you leave to meet Foley and the sommelier at Riverside Manor. I want to get some Polaroids."

She frowned. "What on earth for?"

"Um . . . because I need a visual aid to help me reproduce the hair exactly as it looks now." Well, that was half the truth. "And, since the dress is already right here, why not? Then I can see whether everything's in balance, or if I need to modify."

Charlotte grumbled, but did as I requested. A few minutes later, she emerged from the powder room, and I caught my breath. She was suddenly someone out of a dream—unknown, yet eerily familiar. I fired off several shots, remembering to get a closeup of the hair to verify my cover story. These pictures were really a prelude to Dan's and my surprise wedding gift.

One day, while out for a leisurely drive, we'd stopped to poke around in a charming St. Francisville antique store. There, a huge, ornately carved mahogany frame Dan and I both loved, but had no place to put, had inspired us to commission Ambrose Xavier to paint a three-quarter, life-size oil portrait of Charlotte in her wedding gown. Ambrose is the same talented local artist who, every few months, hangs his new paintings of people wearing my hairstyles on the walls of Eclaire.

After I dismantled Charlotte's topknot and restored her hair to its normal state, she went off to change back into street clothes. While I was straightening up, a phone rang—mine, this time—but since it was Monday, when I'm officially closed, I let the machine answer. Then I heard Foley Callant's voice and quickly lifted the receiver. "I thought I told you never to call me here!"

"Well hell, Claire. What's a poor bridegroom to do? I tried Charlotte's wedding line earlier, but the damn thing's always busy and she won't even give me the number of her work phone." There was a pregnant pause. "She's not already on her way to meet me at the hotel, I hope?"

"Uh-oh, Foley. You-know-who is feeling very fragile today. Cancel that wine-tasting excursion at your own risk," I cautioned.

"But this is an emergency, Claire!" he protested. "Signet Oil's teetering on the brink of an offshore drilling strike. And Leighton claims he can't trust anybody else with our client's billions."

Leighton Blanchard, the most senior partner of Blanchard, Smithson, Callant and Claiborne, never hesitated to wield his considerable authority.

Just then, Charlotte returned in her grey cashmere pants suit. I made gestures to convey it was Foley, and passed the handset. "So, tell her I had to catch a plane to Lake Charles. Okay, Claire?" I could hear him whining cravenly. "And I'll call her tonight."

"Tell her yourself, you gutless gorilla!" Charlotte demanded sternly. She listened, then said, "Sure. I understand, Foley-pie. Uh-huh. Oil's more important than wine any day . . . what's that? You really mean it? Of course I can . . . I love you, too."

"Well that went a whole lot better than I frankly expected," I told her, after she hung up.

Charlotte feigned innocence. "I have no idea what you mean, Claire. Anyway, you know how Foley's been giving me chicken fits, poking his nose into every last living detail of the rehearsal dinner because he wants to impress Leighton? Well, he just now awarded me carte blanche to pick out the wine, of all things! I believe his exact words were, 'Surprise me, darlin'!'"

This wasn't the first occasion I'd been impressed with Foley's instinct for knowing exactly when to back off and give his high-strung filly her head.

At Charlotte's impromptu invitation to join the fun, I indicated my gold corduroy trousers, matching wool turtleneck and olive suede boots. "Only if the jacket that goes with this outfit will be dressy enough, since there's no time to change."

"Oh, Claire," she scolded, "don't always be such a prissy little clothespony." In haughty, mincing tones she continued, "Indeed, my deah. Your ensemble is most appropriate for an afternoon of serious spending."

"This wedding-o-rama of yours is going to give our economy such a boost, they'll probably present you and Foley with a key to the city," I predicted.

Among other things, Foley's largesse had extended to providing complimentary lodging for out-of-town family and friends, and he'd already paid a whopping, non-refundable deposit to reserve the hotel's entire top floor. Upon being informed that the originally scheduled seventy-two hour festivities had unaccountably snowballed into a virtual "Twelve Days of Christmas" bacchanal, he'd simply shrugged and observed philosophically, "Whaddya gonna do?"

Prospective bridegrooms as rich, generous and mellow as Foley Callant did not, needless to say, grow on trees—not even Christmas trees. No wonder Riverside Manor had chosen "Gloria in Excelsis Deo" for its holiday theme song!

"By the way," Charlotte confided, "I'm not showing Foley one single bill until after we get back from our honeymoon." She grinned. "See, I don't want to give him a heart attack before we've had a chance to consummate."

I laughed. "That's mighty considerate of you. After waiting this long to open the cookie jar, the poor man at least deserves to die happy!"

"Oh, he definitely will," Charlotte assured me, "because I intend to kill him with love in that great big old round bed up there on the twenty-first floor. Yes, ma'am. Our bridal suite is going to be the scene of the crime!"

We shared a rowdy little chuckle at her extravagant metaphor, blithely unaware it had been prophetic utterance.

Tragically, the real victim was not destined to die of love.

4

Dim lights flickering from mounted copper torchieres projected three shadows onto the wall, where they hovered with the distorted grace of a cave painting as Charlotte and I followed the woman down a narrow passage that ended abruptly at an arched doorway set into rough plaster.

The atmosphere was sexily gothic and about as subtle as the cover of a romance novel. And highly effective. At some point, I unconsciously slipped into a romping fantasy of a big, dark-haired, nearly-naked man crushing a small blonde against his broad, furry chest. His blue eyes flamed with passion as he gazed hungrily down at her exquisite, scantily-covered bosom that—!

Charlotte's explosive snort of impatience jolted me from bodice-ripper heaven with the mother of all anticlimaxes.

Our hostess was undaunted by any rude little hint to speed up the process, however. A pair of antique keys dangled from the long, heavy silver chain around her neck. She selected one, then turned it in the ornate brass lock with a provocative flourish. Slowly, she removed the key and favored Charlotte with a Giaconda smile.

"I believe you said you wanted something real special, Ms. Dalton?" her dusky murmur was the merest wisp of smoke drifting from a languid volcano, content for the moment to simply suggest hidden powers kindling beneath its surface.

"I *do* believe I *did*, Ms. Duffosat," Charlotte returned, in tones sweet as poisoned honey. "That *is* why we came along on this magical mystery tour? Because it's where you keep the special stuff?"

Montaigne Duffosat, Riverside Manor's beauteous sommelier, was supervising libations for all events connected with Foley and Charlotte's wedding.

In their case, the standard package of pre-wedding cocktail party, post-ceremony reception and morning-after brunch was augmented by a lingerie shower and tea, bridesmaids' luncheon, family mixer and a casual barbeque. So far, Montaigne's tip alone would undoubtedly yield a tidy nest egg, and the much-debated rehearsal dinner remained to be finalized. Small wonder she was absolutely determined to play her role to the hilt for this matinee. Even her uniform was fraught with drama. The knee-length fitted black wool crepe coat over matching tuxedo pants and chunky, expensive black lizard loafers, provided a stark backdrop for the keys on their silver chain. The priestess.

Montaigne's script had called for an expedition down to Riverside Manor's nether regions, where we now stood contemplating the most gloriously tacky wine cellar in the whole wide world.

Fitted with an airtight door of mahogany behind a grill of scrolled brass, this was where the wines, brandies, cognacs and ports of rare and distinguished *noblesse* were secreted, as opposed to the high-tech storage adjacent to Montaigne's second-floor office. There, more frequently-requested labels reposed within easy reach.

The brass grill scraped across the slate floor as Montaigne pulled it open. She twisted the second key on her chain in the mahogany door (salvaged from a church in Sao Paolo, we were informed) then pushed. It swung inward with a hissing noise that barely masked Charlotte's own fretful sigh.

"Can't the woman move any faster?" she muttered irritably.

"You hush and be nice," I ordered, keeping my voice down. "She's only trying to give you your considerable money's worth."

Charlotte made a contrite grimace and whispered, "Blame my bridal hormones."

When Montaigne glanced back quizzically, Charlotte summoned an apologetic smile. "Lead on, Ms. Duffosat," she invited, with a sweeping gesture.

"As you wish, Ms. Dalton," Montaigne replied, gracefully inclining her head.

"Oh, and by the way," added Charlotte. "Please. Call me Charlotte."

"Thank you, Charlotte," said Montaigne. "And you may call me—Ms. Duffosat." Her face broke into a friendly smile. "Just kidding!"

On this amicable note, we entered the tasting room and discovered the stage had been carefully set.

A long cypress refectory board, surrounded by matching ecclesiastical, throne-like chairs (from a convent in Normandy), hanging tapestries and massive pillars of beeswax impaled upon towering wrought iron candlesticks, created a most impressive tableau.

The candles were already burning brightly, emitting the faintest tinge of honey as their reflected flames danced off a vast pewter tray, which contained several wine bottles in a variety of alluring shapes. Each costly label shimmered seductively, whispering of unimaginable delights to be attained . . . for a price.

Montaigne ensured Charlotte and I were comfortably settled on our respective thrones, then a silvery glissando of Hildegarde of Bingen music (*Feather on the Breath of God* by Emma Kirkby and the Gothic Voices) cascaded into the chamber from a myriad of concealed speakers, thus achieving maximum medievality.

For nearly an hour, Montaigne tantalized us with scant, teasing sips of her most precious wines, splashing them into cut crystal goblets like liquid jewels. Each tasting was accompanied by a condensed but impressive pedigree, plus carefully documented provenance concerning the lone case of 1949 Chateau Latour at $2,000 a bottle. (Purchased from the estate of a famous movie star after his 1955 suicide.)

Gradually, under the sommelier's artful ministrations, even Charlotte managed to relax. Or, possibly we were both induced into a hypnotic state by the wine and music, because we found ourselves seriously considering a bottle of Chateau d'Yquem, 1967. Fortunately, I remembered that none of us ever drank dessert wine, so there was no way we could justify spending $1,200, even for this undeniably celestial nectar.

By the end of the session, Charlotte was docile as a lamb, pontificating about "first growth" and "appellation" as if she actually had a clue. Draining the last drops of something red, velvety and exceedingly pricy, she waved languid acquiescence as Montaigne verified our final selections:

1985 Mouton Rothschild First Growth Bordeaux——6 @ $400 ea.
Corton Charlemagne 1989 (Louis Jadot)————-3 @ $150 ea.
1985 Chateau Pichon Lalonde————————-3 @ $160 ea.

Montaigne didn't bother to conceal the deep purr of satisfaction in her voice as she recited the list, and why should she? The girl had worked hard for her money.

"Well, between settling up with Belinda, and this wedding to you, poor Foley will never be able to afford to get married *or* divorced again!" I laughed, watching Charlotte scrawl her initials sloppily across the invoice.

She arched a sly brow. "Good point, Claire. Hey, Montaigne! How about throwing in a couple of those Chateau Latours while you're at it?"

"Oh, Charlotte. I'm sorry, but I can't." Montaigne's minky lashes fluttered regretfully. "See, we only recently acquired that case, plus four single bottles we're using very sparingly as samples. The manager's still holding out for sale of the entire case, and he's not ready to let me start breaking it up just yet."

However, before we could escape the wine cellar, Montaigne had one last card to play. "Now. About liqueurs . . ."

5

Forty-five minutes later, borne upon the fumes of a very senior citizen Remy XO, we emerged from the hotel's Poydras Street exit. A damp, chilly mist drifting off the river enveloped us.

Shivering, I turned up the collar and tightened the sash of my long, army green cashmere coat, a most fortuitous last minute decision. Charlotte snuggled deeper into what was actually an exquisite faux fur she'd dubbed her "fink," but looked enough like a full-length Blackglama mink to incite a tongue-lashing from the occasional fur protestor. Didn't she feel awful about the poor, defenseless creatures who'd died for her coat?

To which Charlotte would whine, "I might, if I didn't know for an absolute fact that not one of those eighty-five teddy bears suffered a moment's pain!"

"Well, it's almost three-thirty. Are you going back to work now?" I asked Charlotte.

She started to shake her head negatively, then stopped in mid-motion. "Oops, better not do that again. Drat that wine-mongering courtesan, anyway!"

"You wouldn't be referring to Montaigne?"

"I would so too," Charlotte contradicted. "That's one sloe-eyed vixen on the make, Claire. You mark my words." She grinned reminiscently. "But that hussy sure do know her wine, don't she?"

"Uh-huh. While we just know what we like," I said. "And we liked just about everything. Maybe we ought to share a cab."

"No thanks, Claire. Fashion Bouquet's got some samples ready for me to look at, and you know how Trevor is. If I'm not careful, he'll talk me into carrying a partridge in a pear tree down the aisle. Right now, I'm feeling feisty enough to stand up to him."

Fashion Bouquet was located just around the corner in the Art District. When we reached Camp Street, Charlotte turned left and I continued walking along Poydras.

The wind had picked up, causing some posters tacked to a wooden construction barrier to flap sharply as I passed. Vaguely, I noticed all the posters were identical, featuring a beautiful naked woman in an impossible position, with thorny rose vines growing out of and around her body, scattering droplets of blood here and there.

It was advertising the Thorton Gallery's upcoming exhibit of contemporary Navajo art by Sam Stormshadow. Why that name should ring a distant bell, I didn't know. For that matter, the contorted woman looked disturbingly familiar. Probably because I'd been sitting in a basement drinking wine for two hours.

Still basking in the afterglow of that recent adventure, I kept my pace to a stroll, letting the crowd surge around me, making no effort to flag a cab, until I reached the corner of St. Charles Avenue. Across the street, the Signet Oil building preened, resplendent in its holiday finery, and I became aware of what my subconscious had known all along was my destination.

Signet Oil, on whose behalf Foley had been dispatched to face down a band of discontented drillers aboard an offshore rig, was one of Blanchard, Smithson, Callant & Claiborne's top five clients. Because the ever-fluctuating environmental and foreign political complexities and perils of the oil business put greater demands upon the time and expertise of its legal advisors, Blanchard, Smithson—after nearly forty years on Baronne Street—had recently moved into sumptuous new offices atop Signet's corporate headquarters.

Signet's logo, unmodified since 1948, was a tough-looking, full-frontal swan—or cygnet—artfully punning its corporate identity. My father-in-law, Dave Louis, now "of counsel" in the firm he helped found, told an amusing story about "Siggy" and some activists back in the late sixties. The group's literature featured a picture of Siggy as a pitiful oil spill victim, his splendid white feathers matted with black crude.

Not only was Signet able to sue for libel, since no Signet tanker had ever been guilty of an oil spill, but also for copyright and trademark infringement, because the protestors had altered the actual artwork of Signet's registered corporate symbol!

I stepped through Signet's revolving brass door into the warm, busy lobby where a massive, glittering Christmas tree soared majestically, and Handel's "Messiah" rang out in glorious surround sound.

As the first exultant chords of the "Hallelujah Chorus" crashed victoriously into the atmosphere, I felt the quick sting of tears and for a fleeting instant, caught a glimpse of something far beyond myself.

I thought of poor Handel, rejected, impoverished, desperate, suddenly caught up into the supernatural thirty-six day trance during which he produced the masterpiece that would establish him forever. And e-e-ver.

Mingled fragrances of cappucino and fresh-baked cinnamon rolls wafted enticingly from Beanie's Coffee Car. I swerved in and purchased a double Mocha-Melt to go, then resumed my journey across the vast marble acres, bypassing the general elevator bank.

Aware my every move was being tracked by video security, I rounded a corner to the private car and entered Dan's access code on the adjacent keypad. The doors had no sooner whooshed shut behind me than I was on the thirty-fifth floor. My cappucino was still steaming. It's a wonder there wasn't a sonic boom.

Blanchard, Smithson's stunning reception area had natural sheared wool carpeting that cut curving swathes through a gleaming floor laid out in intricate diamonds of rich woods—cypress, teak and pear.

There were soft leather sofas the shade of fading summer leaves; wide, down-stuffed chairs upholstered in mushroom-colored shantung. Teak tables displayed raku vases and bowls shaped like shells or rocks by ceramacist Mas Ojima, and upon the textured khaki walls hung

"Magnolias" and "Wrought Iron," two series of oils by California artist
Connie Engel, commissioned exclusively for Blanchard, Smithson.

Behind a tall mahogany switchboard, incoming calls chirped discreetly, skillfully relayed by a bevy of operators.

This splendor was dominated by a semi-circular teak desk in the
center of the floor with its own separate switchboard, through which all
phone calls to the senior partners were filtered. Presiding at the desk
was Patricia Dobson, an icy blonde who was referred to behind her back
as "Ms. Doberman." "Dobie" for short.

Patricia observed my approach with a frown. "Good afternoon,
Mrs. Claiborne," she barked, disapprovingly. "I wasn't informed you
were expected."

"Possibly because I'm not," I replied, soothingly. *Down, girl.*

Patricia's frown deepened, taking in my wind-tousled hair and
Styrofoam Beanie's cup. "I see. Well, in that case, I'll ring Mr. Claiborne to ask if he can fit you in," she said, doubtfully.

"Oh, I'd much rather you didn't," I told her firmly. "I want to
surprise him."

With a tight little smile she reached for the phone. "How sweet.
Nevertheless, it's company policy."

"I'm sure my husband will be pleased to hear just how vigorously
you enforce company policy," I remarked casually. Taking a sip of
cappuccino, I watched her get the message. I hated to pull rank, but if
you didn't stand up to Dobie, she'd gnaw your leg off.

Patricia put down the phone with visible reluctance. "Go right in,
Mrs. Claiborne," she conceded grudgingly, and buzzed me through a
mahogany door into the inner sanctum.

Treading carefully, so as not to spill coffee onto the thick ivory
Berber carpet, I arrived at Dan's lair. The door was closed, but Esmé
Barnes, his paralegal assistant, was just coming out of her office.

"My goodness, Claire!" she exclaimed. "How'd you ever get past
Dobie?"

I looked demure. "Oh, I have my little ways."

Esmé laughed. "I'm sure you do."

I found Esmé Barnes a very intriguing character. Lean and equine
as a thoroughbred mare, she almost always dressed in tones of wine,
taupe, violet or magenta, because of what those colors did for her hair,

which contained permutations of silver and bronze that no tint mixing or weaving technique on earth had ever achieved. She wore it pulled straight back into a bun, the perfect foil for the clear amethyst frames of her retro specs.

Esmé was the type of woman in old movies who would remove her glasses and shake out her hair while some dumbfounded male squawked, "G-golly, Miss Barnes. You-you're beautiful!"

Esmé's once-prominent father had lost everything in some investment fiasco twenty years ago, which forced her to drop out of Newcomb College and go to work in the Blanchard, Smithson typing pool. She'd been with the firm ever since.

Depending on whom you spoke to, Esmé had been romantically linked with Leighton Blanchard, the deceased Buzzy Smithson, and possibly offered occasional solace to Foley Callant during those miserable years he'd been married to Belinda.

Some of the rumors about her may have even been true, but every now and then I'd caught a hint of heartbreak in the fine grey eyes. I often wondered what Esmé's side of the story was, but if that secretive lady ever felt the need to unburden herself, she'd hardly choose her boss's wife for a confidante.

Esmé indicated Dan's closed door. "Does he know you're here?"

"Not yet. It's not a bad time, I hope?"

She gave me a knowing look. "Something tells me there's no such thing where you're concerned, Claire. Well, if you'll excuse me, I have a meeting in five minutes." And, in a flash of lavender Armani gabardine, was gone.

I opened the door to Dan's office just wide enough to stick my head in. "Knock, knock," I called softly.

He glanced up from the file he was studying in surprise. "Well! Hey there, baby!" Rising from his leather swivel chair, Dan came out from behind an enormous messy desk to meet me.

"Why don't you just bring the rest of your fine little self on in here?" Shutting the door behind us, he helped me off with my coat and steered me to a sofa.

"Now, to what do I owe the pleasure?" he inquired, proceeding to make short work of the remaining cappuccino.

Leaning back on the sofa, I gazed up at Dan standing over me in suspenders and loosened tie. The sleeves of his fine cotton shirt were rolled up, exposing darkly furred forearms, and there was plenty more everywhere else. As always, the sheer maleness of him made me quiver. "*Au contraire*, Dan Louis. The pleasure is definitely all mine," I murmured.

The Beanie's container paused in mid-air, and Dan's blue eyes glinted as he stooped down to take a closer look. "Why, you little rascal! What have you been up to?"

He listened with amusement while I related my experiences as Foley's surrogate on the wine tour. "But I'm fine, Dan. Really." I assured him. "And since I was so close, I couldn't resist dropping in on you."

"Well, I'm glad you did, darlin'," he said, planting a coffee-scented kiss on my forehead. "In fact, if you don't mind waiting around for a half-hour or so while I finish up, we could have an early dinner together. I missed lunch today and I'm getting hungry. You in the mood for some Emeril's?"

"That sounds like a good plan," I agreed.

He went back to work and I relaxed, sinking deeper into the sofa's buttery leather depths. Through floor-to-ceiling windows behind Dan's desk, city lights began to twinkle in the gathering dusk. From out on the river came the faint echo of tugboats, braying like little donkeys as they nudged a bulky freighter to its dock.

I loved Dan's new office, which he had designed himself, confining the color scheme to browns and greys evocative of smoke drifting from fine cigars, like the Dominican currently clamped between his teeth.

Watching him scribble notes on a yellow legal pad, I was caught up in the movement of his large hand, wanting to nibble his fingers. For starters, that is. I fantasized about his right ear for awhile, and worked my way down the cheek. I'd just begun on his neck when he growled, "Evangeline Claire! You are messing up my concentration, sitting there lusting after me like that! Fortunately, I'm nearly done. I still need to sort through the mail though, so come on over here and make yourself useful."

I took a chair in front of his desk, and started organizing things into neat stacks by the categories he specified. Something on the throwaway pile caught my eye. It was a formal invitation to Sam Stormshadow's opening at the Thorton Gallery, featuring the same painfully rose-entwined woman I'd noticed on the posters.

Picking it up for a closer look, I experienced another stir of recognition. "Sam Stormshadow," I mused aloud. "That name sounds so familiar."

Dan grunted. "Well, it ought to, Claire. That's the Indian artist Foley caught Belinda with!"

While there are undoubtedly eight million naked stories in the Crescent City, few could rival the night longsuffering Foley Callant had returned home early from a business trip, and discovered his art groupie wife re-enacting that famous potter's wheel scene from *Ghost* with her studley Navajo ceramics instructor, while the Righteous Brothers wailed "Unchained Melody" at top volume.

"And Belinda actually sent you an invitation?" I asked, unbelievingly.

Dan stood up and stretched. "No, darlin'. Not even Belinda would be that brazen. I don't think. I'm on the Thorton's mailing list."

I continued to study the painting. "Strange as it may sound, I think I recognize this model, Dan."

He came around the desk and took the invitation from my hand. "Not too strange, considering it's Belinda," he commented.

With a shock, I realized he was right. If one picture was worth a thousand words, what in heaven's name did this one say about Sam and Belinda?

Dan flicked it expertly into the trash. "Forget about it," he advised. "Belinda and her art show are totally irrelevant to us. That woman is out of all our lives forever, thank God!"

He pulled me out of my chair and into his arms. "And now, I am very interested to hear what you were thinking about from across the room awhile ago. Be sure not to leave anything out."

As I began to talk, he slid his hands beneath my sweater, stroking and caressing until my head started to whirl.

"What's the matter, baby?" he whispered insistently, when my voice faded. "Cat got your tongue all of a sudden?"

"Uh-huh. A great big furry cat's got my tongue" I demonstrated. "See there?"

"Oh yeah," he breathed, with some difficulty.

I slipped the suspenders down from his broad shoulders, untucked his shirt, then teasingly fiddled with the trouser buttons, only to run my fingers around his bare waist instead.

Dan laughed softly. "You must go on and play your little tricks, babydoll. Daddy's got a few of his own."

Daddy was ever so right about that.

But he couldn't have been more wrong when he said we'd seen the last of Belinda Callant.

The Dalton-Callant
"Welcome To Our Family"
Mixer

December 17
The Castle Pub
Riverside Manor Hotel
New Orleans, Louisiana

MENU
"Fish In The Chips"
Seared sliced filet of salmon on roasted potato rounds
with sour cream and caviar.

"Pig's Wings"
Glazed boneless chicken wings stuffed with spicy ground roast pork.

"French Bangers"
Grilled Strasbourg goose sausage on toasted baguette
with English mustard sauce.

6

The following weekend, I packed Renee off to Houma for the holidays, then closed down Eclaire until after New Year's, allowing the contractors plenty of time to do some much-needed painting and refurbishing. Dan decided it would be silly not to have our upstairs living quarters spruced while they were at it, so we accepted Foley's gracious offer of a suite on Riverside Manor's top floor for the duration.

All eighteen rooms displayed either breathtaking views of the Mississippi, or choice Canal Street and Vieux Carré cityscapes. Only the swanky River Queen Club one level higher, where the wedding reception would be held, boasted more panoramic vistas.

Twenty-one was laid out in a kind of Z-shape, with the honeymoon fireplace suite self-contained in the upper bar, thus ensuring complete privacy. Sixteen mini-suites opened on either side of the diagonal, while another enclosed fireplace unit was located in the attenuated lower bar. Foley insisted that Dan and I establish residence in the latter because otherwise, there would be a knock-down drag-out battle for occupancy of those particular premises.

With so much advance bad press, we'd steeled ourselves for total chaos when the kinfolk began checking in. Instead, faint gurgles of plumbing and occasional muffled voices were all that betrayed the presence of others. Dan mentioned the possibility of overkill.

"Don't be lulled," Charlotte warned darkly. "I know these people. They're just conserving their strength."

As a precautionary measure, Riverside Manor's busy Castle Pub had been selected for tonight's kickoff wedding event, the Dalton-Callant family mixer. Hopefully, everybody would behave themselves better surrounded by ale-drinking dart players and rosy serving wenches in peasant costume than they might in a private room.

The pub was a good choice I felt, cozy but not too small, picturesque enough to provide a neutral topic of conversation. A merry blaze crackled in the stone fireplace, its walnut mantel festooned in tartan-bowed cedar garlands and whimsical Christmas stockings. On the wall above hung a large oil portrait of Princess Diana, draped in black mourning.

Now, I raised my goblet of Pouilly-Fuisse to her in a tearful salute, thinking for the thousandth time how impossible she was really gone.

Earlier, Dan had called from Baton Rouge to say his meeting was running about an hour behind schedule, which meant he should be arriving soon. A serving wench freshened my wine, and I settled down in a leather chair close to the fireplace to wait for him, glad I'd worn my comfortable butterscotch-colored chenille pantsuit. Festive touches were quilted gold flats and the emerald earrings and pendant Dan had given me for Eclaire's grand opening.

From my vantage point, I observed Foley and Charlotte circulating among their relatives. What a fabulous couple they made, and how lucky for Dan and me that our two best friends had fallen so in love with each other.

Charlotte glowed in a mid-calf suede skirt and jacket of that dusty pink which does such wonderful things for redheads. Foley looked like the rich, successful lawyer he was in a three-piece charcoal wool suit and silk tie exquisitely patterned with green holly leaves and red berries.

A surreptitious head count revealed there were around thirty-five people sporting the little mistletoe boutonnieres entitling them to eat and drink at Foley's expense.

Of these, Daltons held the definite majority, outnumbering Callants by nearly seven to one. Charlotte, though as yet without portfolio, was clearly weighing in as a Callant, not leaving Foley's side for more than a minute at a time. In fact, the Callant department was even thinner than it seemed at first because I learned neither of Foley's two widowed aunts were Callants themselves but Keys, sisters of his late mother, Opal.

The only actual Callants besides Foley were a group of cousins, insurance attorneys from Lafayette, who currently displayed little interest in mixing with Daltons or anybody else, intent as they were on getting through as many free drinks as possible.

When Montaigne Duffosat glided past the big oak table around which they and their wives were clustered, the booze meter clickety-clicking behind her Mona Lisa smile was practically audible.

Knowing Dan was already acquainted with Foley's relatives, I took stock of the numerous Daltons I'd met so I could fill him in. Except for Charlotte's twin cousins, Woody and Wes—twenty-five, tall, red-headed and impossible for a casual observer to tell apart—I was fairly certain I had all their identities straight.

That tiny, fluffy blonde with wide green eyes was none other than Lambie. She took after her mother Daphne's side of the family, while Charlotte favored Emory, their father.

Grandmother Imogene was the quintessential Southern matron, one of the rare auburns who'd faded without looking like somebody left her out in the rain.

Emory's brother and sister-in-law, Stafford and Alicia, were the parents of Wes and Woody, as well as sultry brunette Cecille. Cecille was married to Reggie Worth, a dissipatedly handsome lounge-lizard with an Errol Flynn mustache.

The legendary Great-Uncle Purcell bore a remarkable resemblance to the late Slim Pickens, and he had four grandchildren. Jolene and Bobette were the progeny of eldest son Fenton. Mamie, Fenton's lusty wife, had a 1950s rich hillbilly haircut and cats-eye glasses. She referred to earrings as "earbobs." She and Fenton were the pair who'd regaled the crowd with graphic song at Charlotte's debutante ball.

Purcell's other boy, Huey, was a widower, fairly attractive with a needy, "please-take-care-of-me" look that equally attracted both the most dominating and the most motherly of females. Huey's two sons were, respectively, Kyle (divorced, randy, and something in Research and Development at Peach Island) and Tucker John—Lambie's jilted fiancé.

Tucker John Dalton did not look like a happy man, despite the striking Fawn Goldfeather, whom he'd defiantly imposed upon us. A Creek Indian artist, Fawn had recently been hired as a textile designer at Peach Island for their new line of pure linen sheets currently in development.

And Fawn herself was positively not acting like a gal wild enough about her man to commit such a serious social faux pas. Instead, her rather malicious black eyes seemed to stray just a little too often in the direction of Reggie Worth. At one point, when Montaigne Duffosat paused to greet Reggie and Cecille, Fawn gazed at our sommelier with such burning hostility, it might've caused her to spontaneously combust, if she'd happened to notice.

Now what, I wondered, was that all about?

Tucker John, for his part, couldn't keep his own eyes off Lambie, who was pointedly determined not to look at him.

And naturally, everybody else covertly watched the three of them, waiting for something to happen.

Oh, dear.

"Hey, Claire!" Foley called, leading Charlotte over to join me. "Danbo better hurry up and get here or he'll miss the whole party."

"How's it going?" I asked.

Charlotte sighed. "So far, so good. Personally, though, I think they're all still jet-lagged. Don't forget, we've got eleven more days to go."

"Just a cockeyed pessimist, aren't you, darlin'?" teased Foley.

"I would so love to be wrong, Foley-pie," Charlotte said earnestly. "But I'm not."

"Oh, there you are, Foley!" exclaimed a twittery voice. "Sister and I couldn't think what became of you."

Foley laughed down at the little round woman who'd spoken. "Aunt Pearl. Did you really have to scold Charlotte's Aunt Alicia about her diamonds being dirty?"

Aunt Pearl sniffed. "Well, they are very good diamonds and it's shameful to see them neglected so. Stones are alive, you know, in their own way."

Foley's aunts, Pearl and Topaz, were jewelers. Upon attaining widowhood, each had reclaimed her maiden name of Key, then together taken over their father's shop in Alexandria after his death. It was they who had designed the ruby and diamond earrings and necklace which were to be Foley's wedding gift to Charlotte.

I smiled, imagining her face when she opened the box.

Pearl was filling Charlotte in on some family history.

"See, our dear daddy was just so crazy about Ruby—that was our mamma's name—he decided to call all his girls after precious stones. Which is a real sweet idea, when you think about it." Aunt Pearl had been wearing her frosty blue hair set in the same tight society waves for upwards of fifty years, but her laughter was free and warm.

"First came our sister Opal—Foley's mamma, God rest her soul," she added, with a damp blue glance at her nephew. "Then there was me, Pearl. I'm the middle one."

"And last, but definitely not least, is Topaz," boomed the tall, rangy, freckled female approaching us. Triumphantly snatching a pewter tankard of ale in each fist from the tray of a passing serving wench, Topaz thrust one of these at her sister. "Here. Drink up, Pearlie. You've probably been talking so much you're bound to need to wet your whistle."

Aunt Topaz was appealing in her own rugged, hearty way, with Eton-cropped hair of a rather virulent gold she frankly admitted was dyed "Topaz Blonde" on purpose. Her eccentric evening attire of red riding jacket, long brown taffeta skirt, and Wellington boots was strangely (and, I would bet, totally coincidentally) appropriate to these surroundings.

"One good thing about Daddy's fixation though," Topaz remarked. "When each of his girls turned sixteen, he gave us rings set with our namestones." She displayed a hefty round topaz kunckleduster. "Show them yours, Pearlie."

Pearl fluttered a soft, plump right paw upon which gleamed a giant, lustrous silver-blue baroque pearl set in platinum filigree.

"Some oyster, eh?" guffawed Topaz.

Foley, scotch in hand, was observing his future wife's sincere pleasure in Pearl and Topaz, an expression of tender pride upon his handsome face. I found it unbelievable that the slutty Belinda had treated him so badly. How unfortunate her return to New Orleans should coincide with his wedding. Oh, well. This may be a small town, but it's still plenty big enough to avoid people you don't want to see.

Foley had given Belinda a far greater divorce settlement than she was legally or, more to the point, morally entitled to. There wasn't the slightest necessity for their paths to cross . . .

"Those are such lovely emeralds, my dear." Pearl's breathy warble came as a welcome distraction from shadowy thoughts.

"Why, thank you. My husband gave them to me," I replied, granting her permission to lift the pendant for closer inspection. I really wasn't terribly surprised when she popped a jeweler's loup into one eye.

Foley was, however. "Aunt Pearl!" he expostulated.

"It's okay, Foley," I assured him, laughing. "Just the other day, Dan was saying we should have the stones reappraised."

Meanwhile, Aunt Pearl was squinting through her glass at my emeralds. "Mmmm, very fine, very fine indeed. Excellent quality," she cooed lovingly. "Your husband certainly knows how to give a good stone, my dear."

"Now Pearl, don't go getting ribald," admonished Topaz with a wink at the rest of us. "Anyway, long as you've got your loup out, why not check and see if any stones in Charlotte's ring are loose?"

Pearl took Charlotte's left hand and gazed down at the concentric circle of pigeonblood Burmese rubies and South African diamonds. Again, tears misted her faded blue eyes. "Many a time Daddy told us how he went specially to Burma to get these rubies. Nothing but the best would do for his Ruby, he said, and there was only one place to go, far as he was concerned."

"Yes, and damn near died of malaria doing it," Topaz put in gruffly. "Not to mention how some natives attacked him just as he was leaving the mining office. Miners or missionaries, they were all fair game. Tried to kill him and get the stones, but Daddy wasn't about to let that happen, not after all the trouble he'd gone to! Fought 'em off like a tiger, and won!"

Aunt Pearl screwed in her glass again, carefully examining Charlotte's ring for wobblers.

Charlotte gazed up at Foley. "Hmmm. Grandpa sounds like quite a hunka-hunka man," she commented. "I wonder if that family DNA is still going strong?"

Foley grinned wickedly. "You'll be finding out before you're too much older, darlin'."

Charlotte looked skeptical. "Uh-huh."

Neither of them noticed when Pearl finished her inspection and pronounced the ring fit for matrimonial duty. As she returned the loup to her velvet bag, the beautiful pearl ring caught my eye, and I spoke impulsively.

"Wait a minute! Why does Charlotte have Foley's grandmother Ruby's rubies, instead of Foley's mother Opal's opals?"

I was unprepared for their extreme reaction to such an innocuous question. Pearl seized one arm, Topaz the other, and they pulled me aside.

With a grim expression Topaz said, "Sorry to be so rough, Claire, but we don't want Foley or Charlotte to hear you. Fortunately," she added wryly, "they weren't paying a hell of a lot of attention."

"The thing is, dear," Pearl said seriously, "Opal's ring was stolen. It was a stunning thing, wasn't it, Topaz? A perfect black opal from the mythical Lightning Ridge mines in Australia, with a fire inside that looked like an atomic explosion when struck by the light."

I remarked I'd never seen a black opal before, but it sounded fabulous.

"Chances are you have without realizing it, Claire," Pearl said, in an odd tone. "*This particular* black opal isn't *entirely* black at all, but a very intense blue. Rather flashy, in fact."

"Our sister's ring was quite large—a six-carat marquis cut, flanked on either side by pink baguette diamonds," finished Topaz. She looked at me hard. "Are you sure you've never seen a ring like that, Claire?"

In my mind's eye there appeared a picture, of a slender, spoiled-looking hand with long, pastel nails, adorned with—

Topaz sensed recognition dawning and nodded. "Exactly!" she grated, through clenched teeth.

"But—" I glanced over at Pearl, who stood with folded arms, no longer the twittering, blue-haired little old lady from Alexandria, "you said the ring was stolen?"

"That's right, Claire," Topaz snapped. "Stolen by the sneaking harlot Foley was married to. You see, that ring wasn't just a piece of community property. It's a priceless heirloom, one of a kind. But her sleazy lawyer managed to finagle the judge into ruling it was a gift, since Foley had indeed given it to her as an engagement ring."

"And we," announced Pearl, "are on a mission to get it back!"

I looked from one sister to the other, curious as to whether they knew their quarry was due to arrive in town any day now. If not, I certainly wasn't going to mention it. Not that Belinda didn't thoroughly deserve to have the Jewel Sisters nipping at her round heels. I just didn't want these aging avengers causing a fuss and spoiling the wedding. We already had enough potential trouble brewing with the Daltons.

"Well," I told them, "having once been acquainted with the lady"— Topaz snorted gustily—"in question, I can definitely understand your sentiments. However, I'm sure, given its recent history, neither Foley nor Charlotte would want anything to do with that ring. At least, not now."

Two identical pairs of blue eyes regarded me with astonishment. "Bless your heart, Claire!" exclaimed Pearl. "Of course they wouldn't. But we do!"

"Damn straight," concurred Topaz. "And I'm going to get it off that floozy's hand if I have to chop off her finger!"

Pearl gave a quick, scandalized little cackle. "Now, Sister! Tell Claire you don't really mean that!"

But garrulous Topaz, thoughtfully twisting her own namestone ring around a knobby joint, for once had nothing to say.

7

Bong, bong, bong . . .

The bar clock, a scale model of Big Ben, began to strike nine, signaling a change in shifts. Dart players tallied up scores; other customers paid their tabs, preparing to leave.

Bong, bong, bong . . .

I escaped from Kyle Dalton, who'd backed me into a corner and poured out the entire seamy story of his failed marriage to an aerobics instructor named Darby, insisting I greatly resembled her. Except, of course, I was much nicer and not nearly such a tramp.

Unfortunately, Kyle had consumed enough alcohol to give him delusions that I actually *was* Darby, repentant and returning to his waiting arms. Only an adroitly wielded knee persuaded him it was a case of mistaken identity.

Bong, bong, bong.

Safely back in my chair before the fireplace, Di gazed down at me pensively. *Ask not for whom the bell tolls, ducky.*

As the last chime of the clock reverberated, the party hung suspended between life and death. Then, the opening chord of "Winter Wonderland" rippled into the leaden atmosphere.

It was Reggie Worth, accompanying himself on the pub's baby grand. As he sang, others began to cluster around the piano. Even the Callant cousins and Fawn Goldfeather gravitated closer.

Beside Reggie on the bench, Cecille swayed in time to the music, wearing a possessive, doting smile.

Poor Reggie, I thought. Not only does he look like a gigolo out of an old Hollywood movie, he's even singing for his supper like one. But then, Reggie *was* a gigolo.

Charlotte told me Reggie's father, curator of a famous museum, had been the inside man on a huge art robbery, then murdered by the other thieves for his trouble. This immediately put the quench on Reggie's career—he'd been working for an important art gallery in New York at the time.

To pay the bills, Reggie turned himself into an *objet d'art* for a series of enormously wealthy women, one or two of whom were foolish enough to marry him briefly. Reggie, alas, was a gambling man. He thought he'd hit the jackpot with third wife Cecille Dalton, who not only came in for a juicy slice of the Peach Island pie, but also inherited several million from one of her mother Alicia's relatives.

But Reggie had met his waterloo. Lovestruck as she was, Cecille loved her money more and fenced it in with barbed wire before they were wed so Reggie couldn't get near it. Then, after the honeymoon, she offered him a job as her own private art broker, to scout for new artists and buy their work as an investment. During their four years of marriage, Reggie's unerring instincts had paid off quite handsomely— for Cecille. Ironically, he'd simply added to the pile of dough he couldn't touch.

Although, Charlotte hastened to assure me, Cecille did remunerate her husband with a generous salary.

From time to time, Reggie would rebel against his fate by vanishing to have himself a gambling fling, usually shacking up with some beautiful young artist for a lucky charm. But Cecille always knew just when to yank his leash. And Reggie always knew just when to heel.

The fact that he had been the one to bring Fawn Goldfeather's talents to Peach Island's attention possibly explained both Fawn's bored attitude toward Tucker John, and why she'd used him as her ticket to New Orleans.

Noting Cecille's sharp, determined chin, and Reggie's comparatively weak one, I didn't see much joy in store for Ms. Goldfeather.

But whatever his faults, Reggie was a marvelous piano player with a wonderful voice. Just about everybody joined in on "Silver Bells" and "Jingle Bell Rock," then Mamie and Fenton harmonized on "White Christmas," sounding like a countrified Bing and Rosemary.

It was during "Let It Snow" that I felt a definitely masculine form press in close behind me. Thankfully it wasn't Kyle, him having thrown me over for one of the serving wenches who he decided looked much more like Darby than I did. Therefore, I surrendered to the strong arms enveloping me in a rear embrace with total confidence. Dan bent to kiss my cheek, then said in my ear, "Did I miss anything exciting?"

I shook my head negatively, figuring the news that Belinda Callant now had a price on her head—on her ring finger, anyway—didn't count.

The secular holiday songs began melting into Christmas carols. I loved listening to Dan, alternating between bass and baritone depending on the key. He did a solo turn on "Emmanuel" that brought down the house.

I had to hand it to Reggie. He'd certainly rescued this little affair from an early grave. The family that sings together, clings together?

Whatever, the ambience was far more festive now, and Reggie was rewarded with enthusiastic applause after signing off with "Chestnuts Roasting on an Open Fire," aka "The Christmas Song."

"I sure didn't plan on being this late, baby," Dan apologized, accepting a glass of Merlot from a saucy waitress. She blushed when he thanked her with a smile. "The traffic from Baton Rouge was just plain hell. When I finally rolled into the garage, I was so damn grubby and rumpled, I had to get out of my suit and have a quick shower."

"If I'd known that, you probably wouldn't have gotten down here at all," I told him, approving of his navy blazer and burgundy cashmere V-neck vest over shirt and tie.

He grinned down at me. "You just keep on being a good little girl, and Santa's going to bring you something very nice indeed."

"Well," I said, "he'd better, because I've got some very nice things for Santa." I planned to surprise Dan with several pairs of risqué men's Christmas underwear on various nights during the holidays. My favorite, which I was saving for Christmas Eve, was a pair of black silk boxers with a big red ribbon on the fly and the words, *Your real present comes later!* At the sight of these, Charlotte had gone into hysterics, demanding to be told where I'd found them. I was the only other person who knew what Foley would be wearing on Christmas Eve.

Thinking of this, I couldn't help laughing, earning a distrustful look from Dan. Charlotte and Foley picked that moment to join us.

"What's so funny?" Foley asked.

Dan shook his head. "I'm almost afraid to find out. I think Claire's got some kind of trick Christmas present lined up."

"I guess you could say that," I agreed, struggling against a fresh wave of giggles without success. For Charlotte's benefit, I sketched a bow in the air below my waist, and she got it instantly. Then we were both off.

"Now, don't you feel left out, Foley-pie!" Charlotte managed to say. "Ms. Claus didn't forget you!"

Dan and Foley stood there watching us with nearly identical expressions of arousal and suspicion, but we were spared cross-examination by the Callant cousins. Having quaffed their fill, they were now showing signs of sociability.

With Jack Daniels-inspired sentiment, the cousins hailed Dan as a long-lost friend, then sought to draw him and Foley into giving a free legal opinion on a certain abrogation dispute their Lafayette firm was involved with.

Charlotte and I exchanged superficial chitchat with their superficial wives, whose first names escaped me as quickly as did those of their husbands. These pushy ladies kept dropping heavy hints that Foley should abandon his other guests for the honor of taking them all out to dinner at Antoine's within the hour, as they were just starving for some real (expensive) New Orleans cuisine.

Unsurprisingly, they hadn't much noticed the delicious and substantial edibles provided by their host, having been so focused on the drinkables.

When E.Z. 3, the popular jazz trio, began tuning up for their first set, Foley, Charlotte, Dan and I used the diversion to slip away from the clutch of Callants before they realized there wasn't gonna be no Antoine's, and turned ugly.

After dancing the first two numbers with Charlotte and me, Foley and Dan went off to do their duty as Southern gentlemen, making sure every woman that wished to dance got the opportunity.

Charlotte's father, Emory, came to claim his daughter for a turn on the floor to "Chances Are," and I felt doubly flattered to find myself whirled determinedly into the arms of one of the two youngest males present—either Woody or Wes—and then to have the other—either Wes or Woody—cut in.

After that, I was in constant demand as a partner, and congratulated myself on having opted for my comfy Chanel flats.

The dance floor was small, forming a kind of TV screen for the series of vignettes I witnessed, *en passant*.

Tucker John and Fawn rhumbaing without once looking at each other . . . Lambie, telling a still-ambulatory Kyle no, it definitely was *not* God's will for them to be together because Darby left him and she'd broken up with his brother . . . Cecille, keeping a tight rein on Reggie, while making sure he noticed how very much she enjoyed her dances with Dan and Foley . . . and the evening's showstopper, Imogene and Purcell, doing a stately foxtrot to "Night and Day," an unmistakable signal to all Daltons that a cease-fire had been declared.

I know I danced with nearly every man present, except for a couple of Callants, Kyle Dalton (whom I avoided), Tucker John (who, following that lone spin with Fawn, avoided everybody) and Reggie Worth (who was probably too afraid to dance with anybody but Cecille).

When E.Z. 3 took a break, Dan joined me at the bar, where we got better acquainted with more Daltons. Foley and Charlotte came in at the end of Fenton and Mamie's hilarious tale of Peach Island's ill-fated attempt to raise goats for mohair, so they had to tell it over again.

Amid the laughter, Imogene marched up, the very picture of outrage. Charlotte was justifiably leery. With this family, anything could happen. "Gran, what on earth's wrong?" she asked, bracing herself.

"Charlotte, dear. I'm afraid I've got terrible news!" moaned Imogene. "Ten minutes ago, I was summoned to the telephone for an emergency long-distance call from Atlanta. And who do you suppose it was?"

Charlotte shook her head numbly.

Imogene took a deep, quavering breath. "It was that lily-livered Reverend Brock, informing me, at this late date mind you, he will regrettably be unable to fly in to officiate at your wedding ceremony. And do you know why? Because he had previously obligated himself to a full calendar of Christmas activities at the church, and our Board of Deacons voted unanimously against his absence on Christmas Eve! Can you imagine?"

Mamie hooted. "I always did say that church was deacon possessed!"

Charlotte had been fearing God-knows-what horrible tidings, and her shoulders sagged with relief. "Gran, you can't really blame his own church for wanting their pastor on Christmas Eve," she said gently. "It was different when we were getting married there. Reverend Brock was able to squeeze us in before the 11:00 P.M. candlelight service."

Imogene planted a fist on each hip. "Be that as it may," she huffed, "I shall seriously consider transferring my membership elsewhere."

Foley patted his future grandmother-in-law's stiff back. "Now, don't you worry, Immy darlin'. Our own spiritual leader will be more than happy to fill in."

Dan started to laugh, but quickly transformed it into a cough when Imogene swivelled a gimlet eye first in his direction, then back to Foley. "Y'all haven't gone and gotten mixed up with that New Age stuff, have you?" she demanded suspiciously.

Foley looked shocked. "Of course not, Immy! Would I lead your granddaughter astray?"

"Relax, Gran," Charlotte soothed. "We're not licking crystals, or anything like that."

"Well . . ." Imogene wasn't quite convinced.

Dan put in, "Mrs. Dalton, I played football with their pastor at Tulane, and I can personally vouch for Saint."

Imogene recoiled. "Mercy! I am hardly insisting upon a saint to perform my dear Charlotte's wedding ceremony, Mr. Claiborne. Merely a Baptist."

"Oh, Saint's just his nickname," Foley explained. "His actual title is the Reverend Percival St. Dennis, and he's definitely a card-carrying Baptist. Right, Danbo?"

"And then some," Dan agreed, fixing his gaze on the dish of roasted almonds atop the bar. His lips twitched.

There were two major things about Reverend Saint that distinguished him from the typical Baptist preacher people such as the Daltons were accustomed to. One was that he Spoke in Tongues, which, upon reflection was likely enough to send Imogene over the edge. The other—

Just then, the band swung into a sizzling arrangement of "They Can't Take That Away From Me," and Dan hustled me onto the floor.

"Dan, what's going to happen when the others find out Saint's not only a holy roller, but—"

He cut me off with a kiss. "Hush, darlin'. I've had enough Dalton squirreliness for one night. They'll just have to deal with it, is all."

Dan twirled us around a few times, then held me tight, humming along as the band segued into "Cheek to Cheek." I drifted to the music in my husband's arms with closed eyes, gradually becoming aware of an intrusive sibilance unrelated to the caress of wire brush upon brass cymbal.

Peeking through my lashes, I saw a couple inches away on the crowded floor engaged in whispered—but heated—disagreement.

The woman's voice rose to a vehement mutter, ". . . a total waste of time!"

"Well, don't blame me, baby!" snarled the man softly. "It was your big idea. I had no way of knowing . . . " Dan waltzed me away before I could hear any more of their argument.

It appeared that Reggie Worth had risked incurring jealous Cecille's certain wrath by dancing with yet another angry woman. Fawn Goldfeather.

Lingerie Shower And Tea
For Miss Amalie Charlotte Dalton

December 18
The Fountain Terrace, Riverside Manor Hotel

Appetizers
Relish tray with winter vegetables
Sautéed oysters and shrimp on toast rounds with jalapeño jelly

Grilled Tea Sandwiches
Breast of Muscovy Duck on roasted garlic bread
Medallion of lamb on Gruyere cheese mini-baguette
Individual eggplant and Parmigiana Reggiano bruschetta

Dessert
Chocolate Chestnut Torte with Marrons Glacé Ice Cream
Sour Lemon Tart   Cha-Cha Cocktails

Teas
Lapsang Soucong   Chinese Gunpowder   Ceylon

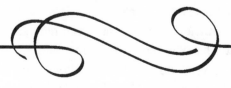

8

I'm convinced there's an evil force assigned exclusively to scramble communications between people and their contractors. No matter how clear everything seems before work begins, signals invariably become crossed.

The next morning, I drove uptown to see how things were progressing at Eclaire. Instead, Mr. Barushka, the foreman, proudly escorted me upstairs where a painter was putting final touches on the living room.

He couldn't understand why I was so upset. Had not the daring new celadon glaze come out magnificently? Didn't the apricotta wash fill my kitchen with the rich, golden-red glow I'd envisioned? And the black and grey marbleizing of the bathroom walls looked authentic enough to have been quarried in Tuscany itself, did it not?

My attempts to explain to Mr. Barushka that, while I was enraptured by such consummate artistry on the part of his crew in an unbelievably short time, nevertheless, the work had occurred in reverse sequence to our agreement. This only served to confuse him.

Finally, I gave it up and simply allowed myself to savor the transformation he'd wrought. I hadn't anticipated to what extent custom paint and dark-stained hardwood floors would make our living space look so much grander.

My heartfelt praise revived the emotional Mr. Barushka, who'd been blowing his nose on a blue bandana to hide the moisture in his soulful brown eyes. He accompanied me downstairs to Eclaire and appeared to listen studiously as I reiterated a few points I thought might get overlooked, but whether I made any impression would only be evident in the finished product.

On the way back to Riverside Manor, I stopped by my favorite boutique, Fancy's Finery, to pick up the present I'd ordered from Paris for Charlotte's lingerie shower this afternoon.

Fancy herself, Fanchon Theriot, was enthroned on her trademark leopard chaise lounge, drinking coffee and bullying a customer. "No, you can't try on that yellow suit!" she barked at a pallid young matron. "You'll look like a sick fish and blame it on me. It comes also in rose, however. You will at least look like a happy, healthy fish. Tell Irma I said to bring it to your dressing room. Go, now."

Fish Woman thanked her and swam off obediently.

Fancy was full-blown, fiftyish, and extremely colorful—that is to say, gaudy. Yet she carried only the most exclusive, elegantly simple clothing in town. Things she wouldn't dream of attempting to wear herself.

"Ah! Good morning, Claire," Fancy greeted me warmly. "Marie just went into the back to wrap Charlotte's gift. Would you like to see it first? I think you'll be very pleased."

When I said I would, Fancy rose from the leopard chaise, stuffed her fat little feet into a pair of ornate, expensively trashy gold mules, and clattered toward the rear of the shop, beckoning me to follow.

The handmade brassiere and panties were obtainable only via *Soie Suzette* through a limited number of U.S. retailers. Because each delicate garment was custom made, a remarkable number of precise— and extremely intimate—measurements were required. Conveniently, Fancy had access to Charlotte's since she was a regular client.

My selection had been based on a full-page photograph in the catalogue, of a pale, auburn-haired model wearing a bra and panties of the finest silk lace in a color described as "Champagne d'nud." Only a second look disclosed the elegant brassiere featured sheer mesh inserts at each nipple, and a two-inch wide swathe of the same from belly button to small of back on the deceptively modest panties. If those undies lived up to their picture, they most likely would not survive beyond their initial mission.

"Marie!" screeched Fancy, flinging aside the heavy leopard velvet draperies separating shop from the utilitarian work area and storeroom. "Don't wrap those Suzettes until Mrs. Caliborne sees them."

Tiny, autocratic Marie looked up from the work table piled with gilded tissue, leopard grosgrain ribbon and beige, suede-textured boxes of various dimensions. "All right, but make it fast," she commanded. "I've got several more packages to wrap and have delivered in time for Miss Dalton's shower, as well. Oh, don't be concerned, Mrs. Claiborne," Marie added, "nobody else ordered anything from *Catalogue Soie Suzette.*"

She unfolded a layer of tissue paper to reveal the lingerie, even more provocative in the flesh(tone). I was in love. Imagining Dan's reaction to those little numbers, I decided I had to have some, too.

Fancy knew the signs. "But not in that color, Claire. Hold your hand next to it. You see? It is much too pink for your skin. You will look like a boiled shrimp." Her metaphors were running entirely to the piscatory today.

"This style comes also in 'Amor d'or', however," she said kindly, flipping through a copy of *Soie Suzette* to the color chart. "Ah, here we are. Put your hand next to this, please. Yes, your skin in 'Amor d'or' will look dusted with gold."

Though she didn't actually say gold*fish*, we both knew I was hooked.

Back in the shop, I poked through the sale rack while Marie finished wrapping Charlotte's parcel, and discovered a three-piece outfit of rich, winter-white wool—turtleneck sweater, cuffed trousers and long coat—in my size. "How did you let me miss this before?" I asked Fancy, now reclining on her leopard chaise to rest after writing up my order for the "Amor d'or" items.

She waved a red-nailed hand, disclaiming any responsibility for the oversight. "There is also the little suede beret with a darling gold angel—"

Much later, I staggered dazedly to the car, laden with leopard shopping bags. In addition to the beret, there had also been the little suede shoulder bag with a darling gold angel clasp, and the little suede shoes with a darling gold angel on each vamp. The amount of the check I'd written was a merciful blur.

The dashboard clock read 2:45, which meant I had just over an hour to drive back to the hotel, bathe and dress for the shower at four. Fortunately, I already knew what I was going to wear.

Back in our suite, I rang up Dan to apprise him of Mr. Barushka's dyslexic approach to our project.

At first, he expressed mild irritation, but then said since everything had turned out so well, we wouldn't risk disrupting Mr. Barushka's creative flow, even if it was flowing in the opposite direction. "I'll try to run over before he leaves and take a look," Dan concluded. "Now. Remind me again what you're up to this afternoon, Claire? I've lost track. Somebody ought to print a souvenir program for this thing."

I told him it was Charlotte's lingerie shower, for which I would be late if I didn't hurry. "But don't worry, Dan. There's nothing scheduled for tonight, thank goodness."

"Amen to that!" he concurred.

After we hung up, I whirled through my fluff and puff routine, slid into my new clothes, which fit like they'd been made for me, and was on the elevator down by 3:57.

Imogene and Daphne Dalton were hosting the shower and tea at the Fountain Terrace of Riverside Manor, located on the mezzanine overlooking the main lobby.

Fountain Terrace's indoor garden setting was lovely, with hanging baskets of ferns, skylights, and patio of rough Mexican pavers. Luxuriant greenery and flowers bloomed in large, terra cotta planters placed strategically among groups of green wrought iron tables and chairs cushioned with fern-printed chintz.

Beside the *verde* marble waterfall fountain, whence the room was named, our group of forty females was seated around four tables of ten each, partially screened by a row of banana trees. The water splashed soothingly into a pool paved with coins, countless wishes, many of which would never come true.

Trevor of Fashion Bouquet had outdone himself on the decorations. For centerpieces, he'd transformed garage sale jewelry boxes in random shapes and sizes into works of art with a crackle-glazed ivory finish and gold leaf. Each open container rested on an antiqued mirror oval, and was filled with fragrant tea roses and gardenias, surrounded by cascades of lace, ribbons and chiffon.

The gold-banded, eggshell china was set on placemats of large crocheted doilies, teadipped to match the serviettes, which were bound with lace garters. Each name was inscribed in Victorian script upon placecards held by miniature lace teddy bears, stuffed with gardenia potpourri.

An old-fashioned kidney-shaped vanity table with a glass top and flouncy lace skirt held a growing pile of stylishly-wrapped gifts.

There was much oohing and cooing over the lavish presentation, as people began finding their teddy bear-designated seats. Around my table—hosted by Charlotte—were Nectarine Savoy, Cecille Worth, Pearl and Topaz, Jolene and Bobette, Leighton Blanchard's wife, Kitty, and Fawn Goldfeather.

"Ohhh!" sighed buxom Jolene Dalton, fanning her napkin. "This looks just like a fairytale, Charlotte! You know what? It flat makes me want to run right out and get married." She turned to her sister. "C'mon, Bobette. Let's put on our hunting caps and find us a couple of New Orleans husbands. We're here for almost two blessed weeks. Shouldn't take much longer than that."

Bobette dimpled. "I might, if Russell Mayhew doesn't get on the stick and produce an engagement ring real soon. Except Mamma says most New Orleans men are profligate adulterers and drunkards."

"Oh, the poor things can't help it," drawled a husky voice to my right. "It's the humidity, you see." Dark, beautiful Kitty Blanchard seemed coolly amused as Bobette's merry face clouded with a pink blush of dismay.

"Goodness! I-I'm real sorry, Mrs. Blanchard," she stammered. "I didn't mean to imply anything derogatory about Mr. Blanchard."

Kitty's red lips curved in a smile. "Of course you didn't, Bobette. At any rate, Leighton is fully capable of implicating himself."

Ouch. Was Kitty just being playful with her claws, or had stuffy Leighton actually misbehaved? Her aristocratic profile was inscrutable.

It was all I could do to refrain from turning my head toward the table presided over by Daphne Dalton, where Esmé Barnes was seated in orchid wool crepe.

Cecille Worth laughed. "You are truly naive if you think the sins of adultery and drunkenness are confined to the males of New Orleans, Bobette. Even in Georgia, there are any number of foolish sluts who are vain enough to believe they will be the one to permanently lure that simple-minded, wayward husband into a divorce from his wife."

Zing. Cecille laughed again, looking directly at Fawn Goldfeather, who pretended not to notice.

"I absolutely adore your outfit, Claire. It suits you perfectly," said Kitty, distracting me from the swirling undercurrents.

"Why thank you, Kitty," I replied. "That little red knit and satin number you're wearing isn't too shabby, either."

We discussed clothes for awhile, then the talk got around, as it always did with Kitty, to some of the upcoming fund-raising events she was involved with. This was kind of a ticklish subject for me, since I was currently the only wife of a Blanchard, Smithson senior partner who worked, and therefore not free to plunge headlong into all the popular society charities.

Of course, Foley's marrying Charlotte would up the count to two, but nobody would expect her to neglect television journalism to help plan a benefit ball. In comparison, hairdressing was perceived as a toy career, and though I'd served on the occasional committee, it never seemed to be enough. Kitty, while not actually applying pressure, knew just how to imply it.

That's why I tuned out most of her monologue, until I became aware she was gazing at me expectantly.

"I'm sorry, Kitty. I didn't quite catch that last part."

A little vertical crease of irritation appeared between her perfectly arched black brows, but she smoothed it out. "I said," she repeated, "don't you think Belinda's timing for the Thorton exhibit is too bizarre?"

Quickly, I glanced across at Pearl and Topaz to see if they'd overheard, but both aunts were evidently engrossed in lecturing Nectarine about the hallmark characteristics of a truly desirable sapphire. After presenting her with a gorgeous emerald engagement ring in the most romantic way, Marcel had no sooner put it on her finger than he'd decided she must instead have a sapphire to match her beautiful blue eyes. As yet, no suitable replacement had been found.

Leaning closer to Kitty I murmured, "For reasons I can't get into right now, please don't mention the B-word at this table. Okay?"

Kitty shrugged. "Fine by me. She's not worth mentioning, anyhow." Then she turned to speak to Fawn Goldfeather, seated at her right.

The buzz of gossip subsided as waiters began serving tea and sandwiches. The hot food smelled so delicious, I took two of everything.

For awhile, nobody said much, other than to exclaim over the unique menu, and wonder aloud if we got seconds. But when Kitty excused herself to visit the Ladies', I noticed Fawn's plate was practically untouched, and her teacup stood upside down in its saucer. She was making rather a point of drinking bottled water.

Bobette took notice of this and remarked ingenuously, "Oh, Fawn! You're not drinking your tea. Are you a Mormon or something?"

Fawn's quick response indicated she'd been waiting to be asked. "A Mormon! Certainly not! I boycott tea because of the Boston Tea Party."

Looking perplexed, Bobette said, "S'cuse me?"

Fawn tossed her short dark hair. "Surely you've heard of the Boston Tea Party? When the so-called founding fathers of this nation raided a British merchant ship and dumped all the tea overboard to protest English taxing on the Colonies without representation?

"What I, as a Native American, object to is that those great white warriors disguised themselves as Indians to pull the heist."

"I always did think that was pretty chickenshit of them!" Topaz declared, while unabashedly pouring herself another cup of Lapsang Souchong.

Fawn didn't look all that pleased when Topaz's sentiments elicited general support from around our table. "Yes, well," she said ungraciously. "My point is, people masquerade as Indians whenever it's to their advantage. Whether it's whites hoping to get them blamed for their own actions, or a bunch of fractionated breeds, trying to get certified so they can horn in on the gambling money."

It simply wasn't Bobette's day. Bewildered at the avalanche her simple question had triggered, she cast a beseeching look in Charlotte's direction.

"You've raised a very interesting issue, Fawn," Charlotte told her. "In fact, it would make a great in-depth news story for WBGZ. Do you have a card? I'd like to contact you about this when I get back."

Fawn shook her head. "It's already been done. By much bigger-name reporters, Charlotte. Phoney white limo liberals sneering behind their microphones at savages squabbling over the wampum."

Before Charlotte could react to this slap in the face, a waiter appeared, balancing a hefty silver tray on each palm.

"Ladies, if I might have your attention for just a moment, I'd like to show you our two wonderful desserts." He lowered one tray to reveal something so sensuous, moist and chocolatey, it was very nearly soft porn. This was described as chocolate chestnut torte, which would be served warm with chestnut ice cream, studded with marrons glacé.

"Ooh!" squealed Jolene lustfully. "I might as well go ahead and sit on that because that's where it's gonna end up, but I've absolutely got to have some!"

The other tray proved to contain my personal weakness, an ultra-tangy lemon tart.

Pearl dithered. "Oh, dear. They both look so good, I just can't decide."

"So why not have some of each?" tempted the waiter.

Kitty returned to her seat, with only the merest whiff of tobacco smoke to betray she'd sneaked out for a ciggy. "Ah, just in time for the cellulite course!" she exclaimed. Complacently aware nary a bulge nor bump lurked beneath her tight red knit suit, she ordered a "tiny sliver" of each sweet.

When the waiter went away to fill our orders, Montaigne came forward rolling a cart bearing Chambord and white-flowered bottles of Perrier Jouet Champagne, ingredients for Cha-Cha Cocktails, the house specialty.

Montaigne poured each flute one-quarter full of the rich, dark raspberry liqueur, swirling it around to coat the inside. Then, she added the champagne, which immediately burst into a brilliant purple mist.

Charlotte announced she waived her right to a toast, saying that Cha-Chas are best savored when fresh, so everybody drink up.

My first cautious sip produced a sensation nothing short of magical. It was the perfect accompaniment to the chocolate and lemon desserts.

"Mmm," purred Kitty Blanchard, "me for more Cha-Chas."

Fawn refused a cocktail because she boycotted alcohol on general principles, though personally not a victim of the theorized genetic enzyme deficiency to metabolize liquor afflicting a large percentage of Native Americans, which the white U.S. government had taken shameful advantage of to immobilize the Indian nations.

Jolene, emboldened by Cha-Chas and fed up with Fawn's self-righteous attitude, delivered herself of a loud mock snore, and Bobette tried to stifle a giggle. Fawn glared.

Charlotte intervened diplomatically. "Reggie Worth tells me you're quite an artist, Fawn."

"How interesting!" chimed in Nectarine, following Charlotte's lead. "I always wished I could draw and paint."

Kitty, midway through her third Cha-Cha, surfaced to inquire, "What mediums do you prefer to work in?"

Fawn never had a chance against the three-pronged attack of social flattery. While expressing gratitude to Reggie for recommending her to Peach Island's textile design department, she of course was eager to break into the big-time art world with her serious oils on canvas, which she claimed raised the bar for Native American artists. All she needed was the right representation.

"As a matter of fact, Charlotte," Fawn continued, "one of the people greatly responsible for the commercial success of Indian artists is also named Callant. Belinda Callant. Is she any relation to Foley?"

Next to me, I felt Charlotte stiffen.

Topaz rushed into the lethal little pause. "Not anymore, thank God!" she boomed cheerfully, waving to get Montaigne's attention. "Belinda is Foley's ex-wife."

"*X-rated*, you mean," muttered Kitty, with such feeling that I turned to look at her curiously. Had Belinda hit on Leighton, too? It was definitely conceivable.

"Oh, well." Fawn looked rueful. "I was afraid it might be something like that. I just wish there was a way to get Belinda Callant interested in me."

"There is. Dress up like an Indian *man!*" advised Pearl, with a titter.

"That'll do, Pearlie!" Topaz admonished.

Charlotte nudged me and whispered, "Don't worry, Claire. I'm fine."

I squeezed her hand. "Good."

Montaigne, who hadn't heard Fawn's dissertation on alcohol, again offered her a Cha-Cha. "Are you sure you won't have one, Miss Goldfeather? They're my own invention, and very good, if I do say so."

Fawn eyed her with that same puzzling hostility I'd noticed the night before. Then she spoke so softly, only Kitty and myself overheard. "How now, half-breed?"

Montaigne's expressive face went totally blank, and she quickly wheeled the cart away.

Kitty looked at me and arched her eyebrows. "Well!" she murmured.

Just then, the women at Daphne's table started tapping their water glasses with knives for silence. When this was more or less achieved, Daphne rose from her chair. "Ladies, gather 'round!" she called. "It's time for the bride to open her presents!"

There was a spatter of applause, followed by the scraping of chairs as everyone began converging toward the vanity table, heaped high with beautifully wrapped packages.

Close by, I overheard Jolene grumble to Lambie, "Serious art, my hind foot! Acts like she's better than the rest of us, locking herself up in her studio all day. Meanwhile, Daddy says nobody's seen so much as a pillowcase border design from her drawing board."

Flushed with anticipation, Charlotte took her place on the flounced stool at the vanity. Nectarine volunteered to record the list of who gave what, and the games began in earnest.

With every new garter belt, teddy, negligee and bustier displayed, the gals got naughtier. Biggest hits were a sheer leopard thong teddy from Fancy's, trimmed in mink, and a bra and panties that were little more than three green silk fig leaves.

As the bright clouds of wrapping paper and ribbons dulled into merely bothersome trash that needed to be picked up, most of the local invitees began taking their leave.

"Don't anybody forget your teddy bears!" called Lambie.

Nectarine and I helped Charlotte pack away the undies. It was a slow business because we kept stopping to inspect various items. Charlotte held up what I'd bought her. "Claire, this is probably the most elegantly decadent ensemble I've ever seen. Thanks, honey."

"While mine is just plain decadent!" chuckled Nectarine, wiggle-waggling the baby blue rhumba panties—named for the copious rows of lace ruffles on the rear—so that they seemed to dance. "I don't know what came over me when I walked into Down Undie. You're lucky I didn't get you that crotchless red and black number, Charlotte."

Grinning, Charlotte said, "Make a note, Claire. Now we know what to buy Policewoman for her honeymoon."

Nectarine's smooth cinnamon cheeks turned rosy. "I suspect Marcel's tastes run more to tailored silk charmeuse pyjamas, à la Katherine Hepburn. As do my own, ordinarily."

"All the more reason to wear something extraordinary for that monumental occasion," Charlotte told her.

"She's right, Nectarine," I agreed. "Go ahead—blow his fastidious little mind right out of the top of his sleek, every-silver-hair-in-place head!"

Nectarine smiled mischievously. "I'll do it! I saw some other things, too."

All at once, there was a commotion on the stairs. Then a masculine voice bellowed, "Listen up, ladies! This is a panty raid."

Charlotte, Nectarine and I hurriedly tried to conceal the lingerie as Foley, Dan, Marcel, two or three Dalton boys, and Reggie Worth barged into the area, eliciting pleasurable female shrieks and giggles.

"Hey! There's the loot!" shouted Dan, spotting the dressing table. He put his head down for a football charge.

"No! Don't let him get anything, Claire!" Charlotte cried.

But Dan had already scooped up a gold box and thrown it for a completed pass to Foley, who just managed a peek before Nectarine retrieved it.

While I was distracted by the scrimmage, Marcel did an end-around and snatched the leopard teddy from my grasp. As I gave chase, he waved it over his head like a banner. "I perceive this is a most sexually-explicit garment, Foley," Marcel observed, flipping it across to him.

Foley held it up and goggled. "I'll say!"

"Whoo! Whoo!" Dan laughed so hard he had tears in his eyes. "But that little touch of mink gives it some class!"

The next few minutes were hilarious pandemonium, as the women tried to defend the lingerie from the men. I tackled Dan around the waist from behind. "You bad boy!" I scolded. "I'll bet this panty raid was your idea!"

Effortlessly, he detached my arms and swung me around. "So what?" He grinned down into my eyes. "Tell the truth. Didn't you love it?"

"Okay. It was fun," I admitted.

"That's the idea. Now, we're all going down to the Court Lounge in the lobby before dinner. Then I thought we could take Foley and Charlotte and Marcel and Nectarine to eat at Bayonna's. Get away from this wedding stuff for a few hours."

I told him I was sure Charlotte, especially, would appreciate that.

Almost all the guests had gone by now. Lambie, Imogene, Daphne and some of the other relatives stayed behind to supervise the repacking of gifts. Dan and I started down the stairs with Foley and Charlotte, followed by Marcel, Nectarine, Pearl, and Topaz.

About halfway down, Pearl exclaimed, "Sister! Be careful!"

Turning, I saw Topaz leaning over the railing, staring into the lobby below. Ignoring Pearl, Topaz reached forward and gripped Foley's shoulder in her strong, bony hand. "Before you take another step, Foley, there's something you should know."

Foley looked around at her with a bewildered expression. "Huh?"

Topaz pointed downward to the woman wearing a rose-colored suit, standing at the registration desk. A brass trolley piled with expensive luggage was parked nearby.

When the desk clerk looked up from his computer and shook his head negatively, the woman pounded the marble counter with her gloved fist and tossed long hair that gleamed like burnished bronze. Her angrily raised voice carried clearly.

"What do you mean there's no reservation in the name of Belinda Callant, you idiot!"

9

For a few seconds, we all just stood there like we'd been flash frozen.

Dan growled something unintelligible. Behind me, I could sense Pearl quivering with emotion, though Topaz, after that initial reaction, was now maintaining her cool.

I knew both aunts were experiencing great frustration because Belinda had on gloves and they couldn't see if she was wearing the opal ring.

If the sight of Belinda had given the rest of us such a nasty shock, I hated to think what effect it must be having on Foley and Charlotte. That tall beauty with her cheating little heart represented eleven years of misery and shame from Foley's past. She wouldn't think twice about throwing a monkeywrench into his future.

Dan said quietly to Foley, "There's two ways we can play this. Shift into reverse and take the fire stairs up to the next floor. Or—"

"Or," Foley interrupted, "I can walk down those steps with the love of my life and confront whatever needs to be confronted." He looked at Charlotte. "It's your call, honey."

Charlotte smiled. "Then I vote confront, Foley-pie. That 'love-of-my-life' speech swung me over."

In any case, the decision was taken out of our hands when the persecuted desk clerk glanced up and spotted Foley. A tide of relief washed over his earnest features.

"I'm sure we can get this straightened out right away, Mrs. Callant. Here comes Mr. Callant now!"

Belinda spun around on one spike heel so fast, her long hair swatted the clerk right in his chubby face.

It took her a few beats to recover. Then, with mocking brown eyes she surveyed our group. "I suppose it's too much to hope that I'm having an exceptionally bad dream?"

"I'd be delighted to pinch you, just so you'll know for sure," Pearl offered.

"Dear Pearl," murmured Belinda. "And Topaz, too. How is everything down at Zircons R Us?"

Foley intervened. "What's this all about, Belinda?"

For the first time, she looked directly at him, standing large, handsome and solid, one arm wrapped protectively around Charlotte's shoulders. I imagined I caught just the faintest shadow of regret brushing across her face. If so, it was quickly replaced by an impish expression. Moving nearer, she slid a rose-sleeved arm through Foley's free one.

"Well, darling. While there seems to be an abnormal preponderance of Callants in the computer, there is no Belinda listed. This despite the fact I produced a confirmation which proves a suite was reserved in my name two months ago."

The clerk spoke up. "I think I know what happened, Mr. Callant. When you booked the twenty-first floor in your name, and listed several other Callants as your guests, I'm afraid that the person handling your account assumed that Mrs. Callant was included and, um, well, canceled her previous rooms. We accept full responsibility, of course."

Dropping Foley's arm, Belinda stalked over to the counter. "Very noble, since you *are* responsible!" she snapped. "So just give me a suite and have done with it."

"Well, uh, I'm sorry, but that's impossible Mrs. Callant," quavered the clerk, who'd been clattering frantically away on his keyboard all the while. His brow was moist with anxiety. "We're booked solid straight through New Year's Day—the Sugar Bowl, you know—and there's not one vacant room available tonight."

He cringed away from Belinda's scowl crying, "It's the truth! I checked for any holdbacks and I swear, there's not even so much as a closet! If there were, I'd give it to you, for Mr. Callant's sake."

Belinda leaned in closer. "Then you better get busy, little man, and find me a decent room elsewhere, or they'll be serving your testicles for calamari. Understand?"

"Yes, ma'am, yes, ma'am," he gabbled, clicking desperately at the keyboard.

She swung around to Foley with a curious stare. "And just when did you get knighted Lord of Riverside Manor?" she demanded. "All this bowing and scraping like you owned the place, or something."

The clerk momentarily forgot his plight. "Oh, the entire hotel's excited about Mr. Callant's wedding to Miss Dalton on Christmas Eve . . . Mrs. Callant." Comprehension dawned. "Ohhhhh!" he breathed, diving back into cyberspace.

Belinda folded her arms. "Well, well! The plot thickens. And I suppose this is the lucky girl?"

Foley smiled at Charlotte. "I don't know how lucky she feels right now, but yes, Belinda. This is Charlotte Dalton, my betrothed."

"How do you do," Charlotte said politely.

Belinda nodded curtly, her raking glance assessing Charlotte from head to toe. "Oh, yes. I remember you now. You're Claire's reporter friend."

She sauntered back over to us, her bronze mane and apricot skin glistening in the light, looking absolutely lovely. Belinda was like a female Dorian Grey. Somewhere, there had to exist a picture of her, exposing all the cruelty, selfishness and depravity I knew she had committed.

"Hail, hail, the gang's all here!" Belinda laughed. "Dan, honey. You look more edible than ever. And little Claire seems to have been clutched by an angel."

Marcel beat her to the punch. "Good evening, Belinda. I, too, have acquired a fiancée."

"Ah, well! Maybe the third time will be the charm for you, Marcel. But where is she?" Belinda hadn't yet noticed Nectarine, obscured from view as she was by Foley's height and breadth. "I've simply got to meet the woman who caused you to trade in your little black book for a ball and chain!"

"The portion of that particular metaphor which referred to fetters is more aptly chosen than you realize, Belinda," Marcel returned smoothly. "And I am delighted to immediately grant your request to make the lady's acquaintance."

Few can withstand a blast from Marcel's verbal stun gun, and Belinda was no exception. While she was temporarily dazed into silence, Marcel asked Foley to step aside. Belinda's eyes widened.

Taking Nectarine's hand, Marcel said, "My darling, perhaps the only benefit to be derived from this rather awkward encounter is that Foley's former wife will have the privilege of meeting my future bride."

Nectarine, elegant in a saffron silk coatdress that almost matched her long ringlets, gazed imperially at Belinda. "Good evening."

Belinda gaped. "But—she's . . . she's . . . ."

"She's *what*?" Marcel inquired.

"She's Nectarine Savoy, the fashion model!" Belinda finished weakly.

"Was," Nectarine corrected. Flipping up one golden lapel, she displayed a badge. "Now Detective Sergeant Savoy of the New Orleans Police Department."

Belinda still hadn't pulled herself together when the desk clerk piped up timidly, "Oh, Mrs. Callant! I finally located a no-show at the Marriott. They promised to hold it for thirty minutes."

"The *Marriott*!" Belinda wrinkled her nose.

"Better grab it," Dan advised. "This town's booked fuller than Bethlehem on Christmas Eve."

Belinda looked sulky. "But I had a reservation."

Pearl was still feeling her Cha-Chas. "First it was just one little Indian. And now, it's a whole reservation!" she observed loudly, fending off Topaz's efforts to shush her.

Right on cue, up walked a very good-looking Indian man with long, sexy braids, wearing a black leather jacket. He was carrying a cell phone and a Walgreen's bag.

"Sam, what took you so long?" Belinda sounded relieved.

"Hey, you knew I'd have to wait until the pharmacy contacted your doctor in Santa Fe before they'd give you a refill," the man replied calmly. Noticing us he added, "What's up, a party?"

"More like an emergency," drawled Belinda. "By the way, Sam. Do you remember Foley?"

Belatedly, Sam recognized the Wronged Husband and dropped the hand he'd been about to offer. Foley, however, seized it and pumped heartily. "Sam Stormshadow! Good to see you again!" he said, throwing the other man into total confusion.

Sam turned dark inquiring eyes upon Belinda, who explained how Foley's wedding arrangements had fouled up their reservation. "And now," she whined, "we've got to rush over to the Marriott before they give away whatever pitiful hole they've got."

The desk clerk assured the couple they would be notified the moment a room at Riverside Manor became available. If it did. And of course the Manor would pick up the tab for their Marriott accommodations.

"You certainly will!" Belinda snarled. "Meanwhile, we're leaving our luggage here, just in case. I shall hold you—what *is* your name, incidentally?"

"Darren, ma'am," the little clerk replied timidly.

"I shall hold you, *Darren*, personally responsible for this luggage. We'll have it sent over later. If the room is satisfactory, that is. You can at least manage that much?"

"Yes, ma'am," Darren squeaked. "I've got a taxi waiting out front for you ma'am."

Belinda ignored him. "This is all your fault!" she accused Foley, then swept off with Sam.

Foley studied Charlotte anxiously. "Are you okay, darlin'? I'm sorry you had to go through that."

"Goodness, Foley!" Charlotte protested. "I'm fine. What about you though?"

He laughed and gave her a hug. "Couldn't be better," he declared. "Anyway, it's all over now."

"No it isn't, no it isn't!" moaned Darren, slumped over his counter like a spilled glass of water. "The Marriott just called. Remember that no-show? Well, they showed up five minutes ago. Their connecting flight was delayed in Dallas."

He raised a stricken face to us. "You know what this means, don't you? She'll be ba-ack!"

10

Riverside Manor's Court Lounge was strategically positioned to the oblique right of the reception desk, affording an entertaining view of lobby traffic. Curved sofas and deep swivel chairs around low tables created a warm, comfortable atmosphere, which romantic couples and convivial groups found equally inviting.

Our particular group wasn't feeling quite as romantic or convivial as it had prior to the Belinda sighting, but after being installed at a corner table and supplied with drinks, olives and mixed nuts, we were on the road to recovery.

Topaz was currently holding forth on the subject of sapphires to Marcel. "As I was telling Nectarine earlier, you mustn't be misled by the cliché notion that the darker the blue, the better the stone. A truly dark sapphire has almost no play of light. Or 'dance,' as we say in the trade." She waved a dismissal of dark blue sapphires. "Far as I'm concerned, you might as well settle for an onyx and save yourself several grand."

Pearl sighed dreamily. "I can see you are a man who treasures the rare and beautiful," she told Marcel. "My father was the same way. Such a pity that the perfect sapphire for your stunning fiancée is unavailable."

Naturally, this piqued Marcel's interest. "In what sense is this most remarkable stone you mentioned unavailable?" he demanded. "Certainly if it exists at all, it is subject to being acquired by some means, no matter how extreme."

"Pearl is referring to the glorious sapphires obtained exclusively from the Kashmir mines of India," Topaz said, "which were totally depleted in the early 1900s. Obviously, Kashmir sapphires still exist. The question is, where? They've been scattered to the four winds for many, many years. If, by some miracle, you were to find one, it almost definitely would not be a loose stone, but set into an important piece of jewelry."

"So why are these Kashmir sapphires all that special?" Nectarine wanted to know. "And how would you recognize one if you saw it?"

"If you'd never seen one before, you probably wouldn't," Pearl said frankly. "Gemology, I confess, can be very subjective. However, our father had good friends from India, the grandson of some rajah or other and his wife. Upon their marriage, the old rajah presented the bride with an unquestionably authentic Kashmir sapphire, of the most heavenly, dazzling cornflower blue—just the color of your eyes, Nectarine—five carats, as I recall.

"Patek—that was our father's friend's name—traveled all the way from London to have Daddy set the stone into a ring, and we girls got to hold it and hear all about Kashmir sapphires. Daddy made a fabulous platinum ring, didn't he, Topaz? I'll never forget Patek's expression when he saw it. The stone itself was cut in that cushion shape so popular up to the 20s. It was a very sexy look. I hope somebody brings it back into style."

"And surrounded by old mine cut diamonds—that means the round cut used between 1890 and 1910," finished Topaz. "Pearl's right, Marcel. A Kashmir sapphire would have been perfect for Nectarine."

Marcel drew himself up. "Would have been? I say, she shall have it! What's more, I want this cushion shape and mine cut you spoke of!"

Nectarine glowed with pleasure.

Foley laughed. "And just how do you plan to lay your hands on such a thing, Marcel?"

"But, of course, I would not attempt to conduct the search myself," Marcel said, "I shall hire qualified experts." Turning to the aunts he added, "It is agreed then? You will endeavor to locate for me a Kashmir sapphire ring as you described?"

Pearl and Topaz looked at each other. "I don't know, Sister," Pearl demurred. "It's a very tall order. What if we should fail?"

"Nonsense!" brayed Topaz. "Are we our father's daughters, or not?"

Pear blotted a tear. "Indeed we are!" she declared. "And well able to accomplish the task."

Good, I thought. This new project would divert them from Operation Belinda until Foley's wedding was over.

Topaz addressed Marcel. "All right, we'll do it. Now, about our commission . . . "

The four of them went into a huddle, leaving Foley, Charlotte, Dan and me to discuss the thing uppermost on our minds.

Dan began. "Look everybody. The hotel situation being what it is, we all know there's going to be big trouble with Belinda before this night is done."

"But she's got any number of rich, artsy friends in town," I reminded him. "Why can't she just stay with one of them?"

Foley smiled sardonically. "Probably because none of the women want to wake up in the middle of the night and find their husbands in bed with her. Again."

Well, that was understandable. Not even our famous Southern hospitality extends that far.

"Hey, Danbo!" Foley said suddenly. "Couldn't we park them at your parents' place for awhile?"

My in-laws, Rae Ellen and Dave Louis, were temporarily residing in Austin, Texas, where D.L. had experienced a miraculous cure for degenerative kidney disease through Dr. Miguel Jesus, a holistic physician. D.L. was now helping Dr. Jesus to cut a path through the hostile medical and legal jungle to establish a clinic of alternative medicine.

Now Dan said, "I'm sorry, Foley. Didn't I mention that they leased their house to a Hollywood producer for a year? I gather he's getting ready to shoot another of those legal thrillers."

"Oh, well." Foley shrugged. "That's showbiz. By the way, D.L. faxed me they couldn't make it in for the wedding after all. Said they had to be at an herbal therapy conference in Palm Springs."

"Next thing we know, he'll be publishing a newsletter!" laughed Dan. "I'm sure glad he and Mamma are having so much fun with this."

"Reluctantly bringing us back to the subject of Belinda," I said. "Why has where she stays become our problem?"

"Because I don't think it quite sunk in that Foley is landlord pro tem of the twenty-first floor, Claire," Dan replied. "But when it does—"

He was right. It didn't bear thinking about. We were still cudgeling our brains for a solution when various members of the wedding brigade started to trickle into the Court Lounge.

First came Imogene, who made a beeline for our corner. Pearl and Topaz scooted apart on their sofa to make room, and Imogene sank gratefully down between them. "Thank you, dears," she said. "Another minute on these feet and Charlotte would've had to get somebody to wheel Granny down the aisle!"

Charlotte made a rude noise. "That'll be the day! Don't anybody start feeling sorry for her. She's tough as an old alligator. And by the way, Gran. Thank you for that scrumptious shower. It was perfect." She blew Imogene a kiss.

With twitching lips, her grandmother attempted to fix Foley with a stern glare. "Well it was. Even that so-called panty raid didn't spoil it."

Marcel cleared his throat. "Foley is not responsible, Mrs. Dalton. I must confess to being the culprit who instigated that somewhat juvenile prank."

While Imogene, Pearl and Topaz awarded Marcel an indulgent chuckle, Nectarine, Charlotte and I gaped at each other in disbelief. Who'da thunk Marcel capable of such frisky hijinks?

Our waiter pulled over two swivel chairs for Reggie and Cecille Worth, who simply took their welcome for granted. With a winsome smile, Reggie offered a fistful of cigars around, which our menfolk accepted with alacrity.

"While I am not at liberty to divulge where these come from gentlemen," he drawled, "I will say they are a great favorite among certain dictators."

"Oh, has Cecille taken up cigar smoking?" a poker-faced Imogene asked Reggie, who smiled uncertainly.

"You're a riot, Imogene," Cecille informed her great-aunt. "A real riot."

Foley puffed on his stogie and frowned at the aunts, as if suspecting them of putting Imogene up to mischief.

I noticed Reggie's face brighten and followed his line of vision to see Tucker John Dalton and Fawn Goldfeather approaching. Cecille affected languid disinterest, but every line of her body went taut.

More chairs were brought for the newcomers. When the waiter had received their order for bottled water and Jack Daniels Black on the rocks, Cecille spoke. "Now tell us what you two lovebirds have been getting up to!" she caroled archly.

T.J. glowered and slid lower in his chair. "Nothing to speak of, Cece," he mumbled.

Cecille turned to Fawn. "Uh-oh! Do I detect trouble in paradise? Well, don't worry, Fawn dear. Reggie and I fight all the time, just to experience the delicious pleasure of making up again." Shifting her chair closer to Reggie's, she gazed at him adoringly. "Isn't it delicious, darling?"

"Delicious, darling," echoed Reggie dutifully, avoiding Fawn's stony black stare.

"Actually, Tucker John and I just came from visiting several art galleries on Royal Street," Fawn said then.

Cecille half-hid a yawn. "Please! I hear enough about art from Reggie as it is."

Fawn went right on. "As I expected, Native American painters are shamefully unrepresented."

"Oh, for God's sake, Fawn!" T.J. groaned. "Get off your soap box for five minutes, will you?"

She bristled. "I beg your pardon? After looking at windows full of blue dogs, red cats and such, foisted off upon the public as art?"

Reggie mentioned two notable galleries that specialized in Native American work.

Fawn scoffed. "Where Indians are stereotyped as incapable of anything beyond basket weaving, rugs and fringed moccasins. Oh, I almost forgot! Turquoise jewelry.

"There isn't one oil painting on their walls that wasn't perpetrated by a paleface or Hispanic culture thief."

"I'm not kidding, Fawn," T.J. warned. "I've had enough."

Fawn raised a disdainful shoulder. "Nobody is forcing you to stay."

"Fine by me. I'm outta here!" T.J. announced. He half-rose from his chair, but sank back when he spotted Lambie entering the hotel from Poydras Street.

Lambie's cheeks were pink from the cold, and her round green eyes sparkled up at the man whose arm she clung to. They were laughing.

The man was Kyle Dalton. When T.J. saw Lambie and his brother together, he uttered a few succinct words I can't repeat.

Lambie greeted us with a benign, "Hey, y'all!" and we shifted to squeeze in the two additional chairs which our waiter magically produced, along with another round of olives and nuts.

I nudged Dan to let him know I was getting hungry. He nudged me back to let me know the message had been received, but we were stuck here until an opportune moment.

"Oh, Charlotte!" Lambie exclaimed. "Kyle and I had the best, best time! We took that Riverfront streetcar all the way down to Farmer's Market and back." She turned a limpid gaze upon T.J. and Fawn. "You two really should go on that ride. It's very romantic."

T.J. steamed silently.

Charlotte caught my eye and grinned. Lambie's technique might be old as the hills, but she was working it well. She definitely had T.J. off balance.

Kyle brushed back his longish, dark red hair. He was surprisingly attractive when sober and not suffering from Darby hallucinations. "I was going to take Lambie on over to Pat O'Brien's, but then I remembered we had to rehearse tonight. Right, T.J.?"

At the realization his brother wouldn't be spending any more time with Lambie, T.J. perked up. "Hey, yeah," he agreed, checking his watch. "We've still got fifteen minutes, though."

Foley looked puzzled. "But the wedding rehearsal's not until Sunday afternoon?"

"No, Foley!" Kyle laughed. "This rehearsal is for your genuine hillbilly wedding night shiveree! Remember?"

"Amazing as it sounds, I had managed to put it out of my mind. Until now, that is." Foley's tone was hollow.

Charlotte sighed. "I hadn't."

"Aw, c'mon. Be a sport, you guys!" urged T.J. "Grandpa's gone to a whole lot of trouble to organize this thing. You should feel honored. It'll be fun!"

Kyle grinned. "For some of us, anyway."

Charlotte wriggled with embarrassment. "Since when do you have to rehearse beating on pie pans and shaking tambourines?"

"Oh, Charlotte. There's so much more to it than mere noise," Imogene reproved. "Every community who practiced shiveree-ing developed their own style. Some phrases of the older country-western love songs can be traced back to specific shiverees."

"Spoken like the true Swamp Dalton you almost became, Aunt Imogene," Cecille jibed lightly.

Kyle touched Imogene's arm. "Grandpa's been working on our harmonies for 'Two Hearts'," he said meaningfully.

Imogene gave a soft gasp and put her hands to her face. I caught the glint of tears. "How nice!" she managed to squeeze out, finally.

"That's the song my great-grandpa dug out of the archives for Grandpa and Imogene's shiveree," T.J. explained. "Only, it never happened."

Giving Imogene a chance to recover, Topaz said, "Pearl and I overheard a shiveree once when we were very young. We didn't know what it was, of course. Mamma gave us the G-rated explanation, that everybody was so happy those two people got married, they were having an extra-special celebration."

"When Charlotte mentioned the shiveree, I looked it up in this funny old book about courtship and marriage customs," Nectarine said. "Apparently, the shiveree has been practiced in some form by every culture in recorded history. Certainly the Israelis and the Africans made quite a thing of it."

"*Charavari*, as my particular ancestors called it, was reserved for the marriage of two extremely ugly people," Marcel contributed. "The goal, I believe, was to create such havoc and distraction as to render the pair powerless to consummate their physical union, thereby postponing, however temporarily, the reproduction of their inevitably ugly off-spring!"

This earned a round of laughter. Marcel went on. "When it was discovered that, quite to the contrary, the intense noise exercised an aphrodisiac effect upon the couple, the practice was recognized as useless for its intended purpose and eventually abandoned."

"In Cajun, the word is also *charavari*," I volunteered. "Except the ceremony was limited to the wedding of two previously widowed people."

Fawn sneered. "Your so-called *charavari* is yet another example of culture theft. It was originally a totally female ritual, when the wise women would take the young bride into the ceremonial wigwam. There, the girl would deflower herself on a wooden phallus while the older women beat drums and chanted."

"How disgustingly barbaric!" Cecille grimaced. "And what did they do if the poor girl wasn't a virgin? Skin her alive?"

"In certain cases, both she and the man responsible were hided," Fawn answered unfeelingly.

Lambie whimpered at the mental picture.

T.J. stood abruptly, looking down at Fawn with distaste. "Shut the hell up, Fawn!" he ordered angrily.

So shocked was she, she complied.

"Hear, hear!" Kyle seconded his brother. "Listen, T.J., we better get going. I've still got to tune my banjo."

As the brothers walked off toward the elevators together, Lambie smiled gently to herself.

"Well," Foley told Charlotte, "nothing I've heard so far is making me look any more forward to that percussion serenade than I did before."

"Me neither," Charlotte commiserated.

"Although," Marcel mused aloud, "the ritual is not entirely without its primitive appeal."

"Yeah, well. You're not the guy who's going to be up there on the receiving end," Foley retorted.

Dan snapped his fingers. "I think I just solved your problem, Foley."

"Which one would that be, genius?" Foley inquired.

"Both," Dan said, with a grin. "But hold on a minute. If anybody else gets wind of this plan, it's useless."

"What are you people whispering about over there?" Cecille sounded fretful.

Charlotte replied, "We're just trying to figure how to break up the party without being rude, Cuz. We've got dinner reservations at 8:30."

"Oh." Cecille looked at Reggie expectantly. "And where are you going to take me tonight, Reggie-ums?" she demanded, stroking his little mustache.

Reggie-ums was caught off-guard. "Er, I though perhaps Galatoire's would be pleasant, dear," he improvised hastily.

Cecille clapped her hands girlishly. "Goody!"

Topaz, Pearl and Imogene took their leave, having decided on the spur of the moment to go see Al Hirt at the Jumbo Room.

Lambie looked at Fawn, who'd been slugging down her second bottle of water like it was blended whiskey. The woman must've had a sphincter of steel.

"I guess that leaves just you and me," Lambie said wryly. "I'm game if you are. We could walk over to Riverside Cafe for some Creole food."

"I'm not hungry," Fawn snapped.

Lambie rose and stretched. "In that case, it's me for jammies and room service." She kissed Charlotte and Foley. "Goodnight, y'all. Don't worry Foley. I won't order anything too expensive."

In the wake of Lambie's departure, Reggie said he'd better go call Galatoire's, and Cecille excused herself to visit the powder room.

A minute or so later, Fawn, whose superior bladder had finally reached maximum capacity, followed suit. But she left her purse behind, which meant we still couldn't just get up and go.

Noting that it was nearly eight-thirty, Marcel and Nectarine volunteered to head on over to Bayonna's and stake out our table before the maitre d' gave it away to some hungry tourists.

After they'd gone, Dan outlined his idea to answer both Belinda's housing shortage and Foley and Charlotte's desire for a shiveree-free marriage bed.

After explaining how Mr. Barushka had reversed the order of our redecorating, he said, "I took a run over there this afternoon to check things out. Incidentally, Claire, it looks great. Anyhow, Foley, the house will be ready for us to move back in by the twenty-third.

"My first thought was for you and Charlotte to take our present rooms, and let Belinda and Sam have the bridal suite."

Foley laughed. "Bubba, I love it!"

"You're forgetting one tiny thing," Charlotte objected. "We'll still be here in the hotel. When Uncle Purcell and company discover the switch, it won't take them two minutes to ferret out our new location. I'd be a nervous wreck."

Dan nodded. "I said that was my first thought. But my second thought was better. They'll never find you at our house."

Foley wrinkled his brow. "I don't quite follow you, Danbo."

"Dan and Claire are offering us their place for our first night together as man and wife, Foley-pie," Charlotte explained.

I disclaimed any credit. "This is the first I've heard of it myself, but I think it's a brilliant idea!"

My mind was already racing ahead. Juanita, our housekeeper, and I would have to get together and plan lots of special little touches to make everything perfect for them.

Then I pulled up short. "Wait, Dan. Aren't we just taking it for granted the arrangement appeals to Foley and Charlotte?"

"Take it for granted, please!" Foley urged. He looked at Charlotte. "Right, darlin'?"

My emotional friend dabbed at her eyes with a cocktail napkin. "You two are the best," she sniffled.

Dan laughed. "It's unanimous, then."

"Belinda still has to buy into the conspiracy," I reminded them.

"If the woman wants a roof over her head, she'll swear not to breathe a word about this to anybody," Dan said flatly. "Also, we'll simply allow her to think Foley and Charlotte will be in our suite. That way, she won't know where they are, either."

Charlotte held up a restraining palm. "No, wait. Forget it. Belinda's not going to stall a bunch of drunken hillbillies caterwauling outside her door, just to protect our privacy."

Dan looked gleeful. "Now who said she would know one blessed thing about that? Ahead of time, I mean."

"Oh, you are bad, Danbo!" Foley roared appreciatively.

The success of Dan's plot depended upon Belinda and Sam sustaining the illusion they were staying in the same area as Foley's other guests, though such a room did not exist.

At no time must they allow anybody on the twenty-first floor to spot them entering or leaving the supposedly unoccupied bridal suite. The only people aware of this scheme besides ourselves would be Darren, and the bellboy who took up their luggage.

Foley and Charlotte decided they didn't even want Marcel and Nectarine knowing they would be spending the night at our house, so we agreed to keep the double-bluff a secret just between the four of us.

A critical decision, as it turned out.

Charlotte glanced over toward the entrance. "Whoops, thar she blows, folks!"

Belinda was bearing furiously down upon the registration counter. Sam, talking on his cell phone, trailed a few steps behind, consort fashion. Foley hurried to intercept his ex-wife before she could inflict further damage to Darren's fragile psyche.

The necessary arrangements were made in short order. When Foley rejoined us, he was accompanied by a mollified Belinda and Sam. Their arrival coincided with the return of Reggie and Cecille. Right on their heels came Fawn. I suspected her of lying in wait.

Introductions were performed all around. When Belinda removed her glove to shake hands, the big black opal ring winked coquettishly. I was thankful the aunts were safely occupied with Al Hirt.

Starry-eyed at such extraordinary serendipity, Fawn proceeded to positively gush over Belinda, while ignoring Sam Stormshadow.

Belinda seemed much more interested in Reggie Worth, however, and they immediately began to talk shop. Cecille was thoroughly put out, but there was nothing she could do. After all, Belinda Callant was one of the prime movers and shakers in the art world, and the more connections Reggie made, the more money Cecille made. She hovered over their exchange like a hawk though.

Neglected by their respective patrons, the two natives grew restless. When Sam ordered a margarita, Fawn attacked him for drinking the white man's firewater.

"What's it to you, squaw bitch?" flared Sam.

Fawn then demanded to know his position on enforcing rigid standards to insure the integrity of Native American art.

Sam replied indifferently that if Native American artists practiced personal integrity, the art would take care of itself.

This did not satisfy Fawn. Soon, Reggie, Belinda and even Cecille were drawn into their dispute, and the art babble began to erupt in great profusion.

None of them noticed when we made our break for freedom and, more importantly, food.

The last thing we heard was Fawn Goldfeather's jeering voice calling Sam Stormshadow an Uncle Tom-Tom.

11

I had two stops to make before the bridesmaids' luncheon, so I swung by Juanita's place first, knowing she would be up. By the time we'd finished dinner last night, it had been much too late to call her and discuss preparations for Foley and Charlotte's fleeting but momentous stay beneath our roof.

The skinny pink stucco house with its brace of matching flamingos and glass block windows was something of an anomaly in the old Victorian neighborhood near South Peters and Elysian Fields.

Its former owner had gone rather overboard during the fifties craze of the mid-eighties, installing salt-and-pepper carpeting, bubble light fixtures, mint-green Formica kitchen counters and so forth with a lavish hand. The house was warm, colorful, nostalgic and exactly right for Juanita and Carlos Valle. They'd bought it soon after their marriage nearly ten years ago, and never altered so much as a linoleum tile since.

Juanita, who'd just seen Carlos off on his gardening rounds, greeted me with her shiny black hair still in two waist-length ponytails, wearing a flowered cotton housecoat beneath which her unharnessed, mind-boggling breasts cavorted like porpoises.

I sat in the chrome and red vinyl breakfast nook while Juanita bustled around her time-warp kitchen making fresh coffee, clucking delightedly as I explained the situation.

"I must come before church to prepare the wedding breakfast for them!" she declared, plunking down a cup of strong black fluid in front of me. Pouring another for herself, Juanita slid into the opposite side of the booth, nodding vigorously.

"Señor Foley loves my *churros* with honey. Then, of course, he must have plenty of protein to build up his strength again," she added, her soft brown eyes dancing with mischief."Something *muy especial.* Perhaps my hash *con pollo*."

"Hold on, Juanita! Aren't you forgetting that's going to be Christmas morning? What's more, they'll need a taxi for 6:30 in order to catch their 8:00 flight to New York."

"*De nada!*" Juanita protested. "It will be no trouble at all. Besides, I have been trying and trying to think of a worthy gift for Señor Foley and Señorita Charlotte. Now, I know."

"God bless you then," I said, reaching across the table and squeezing her hand. "But just remember—as of December 25, Charlotte will be Señora Charlotte. Doesn't she rate something *muy* on your breakfast menu, as well?"

Juanita's earthy laughter caused her bosom to thud merrily upon the tabletop, setting our cups rattling in their saucers. "Now, *niña*," she reproved. "You know I would never forget the bride! She shall have sliced bananas with fresh ricotta and cinnamon."

Next, we tackled the subject of which bedroom the couple should occupy. While the guest room was nearly large as the master suite, the fireplace was smaller and it had but a connecting half-bath. Since the main bathroom could only be entered through our bedroom, it seemed more logical and convenient for them to stay there.

However, it was kind of weird to think of Foley and Charlotte in Dan's and my bed. Close as we were, that was getting just a tad too intimate for comfort.

Juanita settled the issue by reminding me that the guest bed was not only king size, but had never yet been slept in. Which meant my unopened pale yellow Porthault sheets would fit. Then and there, I decided those sheets would make a poetic little extra wedding present, as well as adding a dash of variety to all that Peach Island bedding they'd be obligated to use from now on.

Between us, we finished off the pot of coffee, working out a schedule to ensure the newlyweds would find the refrigerator filled with tempting snacks, a bottle of Cristal '81 on ice, the fire ready to light, the bed turned down, and mints on the pillow.

The most important item, though, was Ambrose Xavier's portrait of Charlotte in her wedding dress. Dan and I were hopeful the artist would have the painting finished in time to hang above the fireplace in the bridal chamber. It would be the first thing the couple saw when they entered.

Despite his awesome talent, Ambrose hadn't yet had his big breakthrough; consequently, his finances rocketed wildly between flush and bust. One always knew when Ambrose was having a dry spell, because his phone would be disconnected.

It had been disconnected when I tried him this morning, which is why, after leaving Juanita's, I was crawling through the narrow maze of French Quarter streets in rush hour traffic, trying to reach the Monteleone Hotel garage before all its public parking spaces were filled.

To paraphrase our late local comedian Billy Holliday, getting a parking ticket in the French quarter was really a medal of honor, because it meant you had actually found a place to park!

Emerging victorious from the garage, I cut diagonally across Iberville to Exchange Place. Ambrose's fourth floor walk-up was in a house about halfway down the alley to my left. Although Ambrose insisted that Dave Ferry had occupied his exact apartment during the alleged plotting of the JFK conspiracy, at least two other houses on Exchange laid claim to harboring that dubious tenant.

There was no intercom. I pushed the bell marked AX and waited. With artists, one never knew. Ambrose could either still be sound asleep, or already hard at work, catching as much precious winter daylight as possible. I was relieved when the buzzer rattled a prompt response. At least I didn't have a cranky, half-awake painter to contend with.

Eight long, steep flights of stairs later, I arrived at 4-A to find Ambrose lounging in his doorway. A sable brush tipped with white pigment was parked behind one ear. A good sign. His handsome face lit up when he saw me.

"Hey, Claire! Where y'aat, doilin?" We must be tuned to the same channel, or somethin'. I was gonna ring you down by a pay phone."

Ceremoniously, Ambrose ushered me inside, where priceless antiques rubbed comfortable shoulders with found objects—"road kill" as he called them—in illogical but perfect harmony.

I declined his offer of coffee. That pot I'd helped Juanita put away was beginning to make me feel like I had a big rubber band twanging between my eyes.

Ambrose transferred a tall bronze candlelabra, slightly dented at its base, from a needlepoint chair to the top of an ornate birdcage, and invited me to sit.

"Thanks, but I can't stay long, Ax," I told him. "By the way, you said you were going to call me. What about?"

"Oh. That." His silvery eyes dropped away. He slid the brush from behind his ear and threaded it between large, paint-spattered, curiously unartistic-looking fingers.

I felt a twinge of alarm. "Ax! Don't tell me you haven't started on Charlotte's portrait yet?"

He jerked a startled glance up at me. "No way, Claire! I been on a roll with that, in fact." Ambrose waved the brush. "I'm seeing this as one very major spiritual picture, like. Those white feathers and red hair are really trippy."

My relief was so evident that Ambrose hastened to add, "Hey, you know I'd never let you down, doilin'. If it wasn't for you, well." He saw no need to elaborate.

"Then what's the problem, Ax?"

He looked uncomfortable again. "Okay. Because I been all involved in your feather thing, I let some C.O.D. stuff for an ad agency slide. Translated, I don't get paid until they get the art. So I kinda thought—"

Ambrose braked in mid-sentence and stared at me as if realizing for the first time I was actually present in the flesh. "Intermission, Jack! Since when do you come calling on me at the crack of dawn?"

From the beginning of our relationship, I had made it a point never to acknowledge Ambrose's extremely iffy monetary situation, always treating him as a talented artist who deserved to be handsomely remunerated for his work. I had seen too many local painters, some more gifted than others, slip into a needy, handout lifestyle which quickly eroded both their self-esteem and creative identity.

That's why I ignored the fact that for the first time ever, Ambrose had very nearly asked me for another payment on Charlotte's portrait, responding instead to his question about why I was there.

"Well, I had such a big favor to ask you, I decided I'd better take a chance you were here and do it in person," I said, as if I didn't know his phone was disconnected.

His face cleared. "Hey! Anything, doilin'. You know that."

Without divulging why, I explained that we needed the framed portrait delivered to our house by the twenty-third, a mere four days away. Was that at all possible? Naturally, we were prepared to pay a substantial bonus. Up front. I mentioned a figure.

By the expression on his face, Christmas had just come early for Ambrose Xavier, and not one minute too soon. He was delighted to inform me that he was already basically done, save for a few vital finishing touches.

Ambrose tucked the check into the pocket of his paint rag of a shirt, patting it a few times as if to reassure himself it was really there. He studied me a moment, then asked suddenly, "Claire, do you want to see her?"

Personally, I don't even like clients looking at their hair in the mirror until I'm good and ready. For this artist to entrust the sight of his unfinished work to me was such a gift, I almost wept.

Silently, Ambrose held out his hand and I took it. As he slowly led me through the dining room and kitchen, I knew he was fully aware of what he was bestowing, and how much it was costing him. But at the door to his studio, Ambrose didn't hesitate. Opening it, he gave me a gentle push across the threshold.

At once I was engulfed in a not-unpleasant haze of oil paint, turpentine and varnish. The phalanx of floor-to-ceiling windows revealed a Mary Poppins-esque infinity of French Quarter rooftops and chimneys.

There were two long tables supporting some of Ambrose's finds in various stages of refurbishing; a row of paintings on the floor was turned to face the wall. A bit farther along, the great mahogany frame waited patiently to receive its new tenant, making even the expanse of bare wall it enclosed look interesting.

But I only had eyes for a tall, solitary easel shrouded in muslin standing beneath the skylight at the end of the room. As I began to move toward it, Ambrose called out, "Stay where you are, Claire. And don't look until I say so."

Obediently, I closed my eyes.

A minute or two later Ambrose said, "Now."

Even so, I was totally unprepared. I gasped and took an involuntary step backward, because Charlotte actually appeared to be moving straight at me. This illusion of momentum was so intense, the gossamer veil seemed to swirl and the snowy feathers to flutter as if yearning to take flight.

With amber and copper and sepia, Ambrose had infused the backdrop with a mystical, medieval burnish against which Charlotte's pale skin and white dress shimmered ethereally.

Her green eyes were deep wells filled with love, and her soft pink lips were slightly parted in a breathless half-smile.

She was Queen of the Angels, about to enter into the presence of her Divine Bridegroom.

This, to quote Ambrose, was indeed "one major spiritual picture."

It was also major museum quality.

In that instant, I knew beyond all question that Ambrose had not neglected his other paying assignments simply to go off on some self-indulgent jag, zoning out on white feathers and red hair as he'd so casually implied. No. This portrait was the result of an all-consuming, gut-wrenching, passionate inspiration that had kept him working from first beam of daylight until last.

I thought of Handel again.

I didn't even know I was crying, until I felt tears on my cheeks.

Ambrose didn't ask what I thought. He didn't have to.

There was nothing else to say. I kissed his cheek and left him standing there, still gazing at the portrait.

On my way down those endless stairs, I started to cry again because I realized Ambrose had fallen hopelessly in love with the dream woman he'd painted.

In my emotional distraction, I exited the hotel garage onto Bienville and failed to turn left on Royal. Since all French Quarter streets are one way, this error meant I had to get to Conti before I could re-access Royal, a far greater challenge than it sounds in mid-morning.

This maneuver put me into Royal's snail's pace traffic a block above where I'd started. I glanced at the dashboard clock. It was going to be another close call and this time, I hadn't the perfect outfit conveniently at hand.

Throngs of pedestrians strolled leisurely from one side to the other between the idling cars. They knew we weren't going anywhere.

A dark, striking woman in a yellow wool suit crossed directly in front of me. Not until she'd reached the sidewalk on my right did I recognize Montaigne Duffosat, defrocked of her usual priestess black. Mildly curious, I watched in the rearview mirror.

She halted in front of a shop just behind my car. There was brown paper taped over its windows. She pressed the buzzer.

I twisted and ducked gymnastically, trying to make out what was printed on the shop's red awning. No sooner had I deciphered "Thorton Gallery" when the door was opened by an attractive man. With what seemed to me a furtive glance in either direction, he took Montaigne's hand and swiftly drew her inside. The door closed behind them.

The whole drama was over in a flash, but it had lasted long enough for me to identify the man. Sam Stormshadow was pretty much unmistakable, after all.

I wondered how on earth Sam and Montaigne had ever gotten together. And I couldn't imagine why he'd chosen the Thorton for a rendezvous spot. Particularly right in the midst of arranging his exhibit and Belinda liable to show up at any moment.

Unless he wanted to get caught?

Well, if so, his wish was about to be granted. A tall, willowy figure with long bronze hair, wearing a long bronze mink to match, was striding briskly toward the gallery. She passed close by without noticing me.

Again I observed through the rearview mirror, holding my breath, waiting to see what would happen. Of course, the traffic finally began to move just as she reached the gallery door. A chorus of impatient horns blasted their displeasure at my tardy response.

As I accelerated, I glimpsed two eccentric characters skulking along the sidewalk some distance in Belinda's wake.

Though Pearl and Topaz might have appeared comical to some, I didn't think there was anything at all funny about their vow to repossess their beloved sister's Lightning Ridge black opal ring.

Bridesmaids' Luncheon

December 19
Restaurant Regina
Riverside Manor Hotel

MENU
Cream of Mussel Bisque with Saffron

Sweet and Sour Baby Beet & Buffalo Mozzarella Salad

Sauteed Chicken Wishbones with Citrus Glaze
and Dirty Rice

Green Beans

Individual Blackberry Cobblers
with Fresh Vanilla Bean Ice Cream

12

"Oof!" grunted Jolene, as her sister struggled to zip up the back of her bridesmaid's dress. "I guess we shoulda tried these on before lunch!"

"Okay, Jo. Suck it in again," Bobette ordered.

Cecille Worth lifted a slim, disdainful shoulder. "Well, Jolene. After the amount of chicken you consumed, I am frankly amazed you can even get into the thing at all."

Jolene exhaled, causing the zipper to surrender what few centimeters it had attained above the waist. "For pity's sake, Jo!" squealed Bobette. "I almost had you over the hump."

"But it wasn't just any old chicken!" panted Jolene defensively. "See, when we were little girls, Bobette and me used to fight over the pulleybone, there being only one per bird. But then Mamma discovered Colonel Sanders and quit frying her own chicken. It was like pulleybones all at once became extinct, or something."

Jolene shook her head. "Do you realize," she marveled, "there's a whole generation of kids out there who have no idea how they're being deprived by those chicken places?

"Of course, I never expected a fancy restaurant like Regina to serve up genuine pulleybones, except they called them wishbones on the menu." Her eyes took on a reminiscent glow. "Just oodles of them, right there for the taking. I suppose I lost my head."

"Not to mention your waistline," Cecille jabbed. "But you Swamp Dalton girls eventually run to fat, anyway."

"One, two, three. Suck in, Jolene!" Bobette's sharp command deflected her sister's angry retort. To Cecille she added, "Can't you be nice for more than three minutes at a time?"

"Probably, if I tried real hard," Cecille laughed. "But seeing as how it's only you, why bother?"

Though the bridesmaids' luncheon was a great success, the bridesmaids themselves, with the exception of Nectarine Savoy, who'd had to report back to headquarters and would be along later, were experiencing severe post-prandial depression. It was nothing but bitch, bicker and moan from the instant they'd entered Daphne and Emory's suite for final gown fittings with Mrs. Cahoon from Anne Barge for Brides.

Charlotte had gone off Christmas shopping with Daphne, Imogene and assorted aunts, saying she was counting on me to keep these females from torturing poor Mrs. Cahoon beyond all endurance.

Her concern was entirely misplaced.

That deceptively benign-looking, oxford-wearing seamstress was in fact a highly outspoken Scotswoman, tough as they come after twenty-five years on the Southern society wedding circuit. And not, I suspected, above administering a judicious pinprick whenever she deemed it necessary.

Jolene's observation that the fittings should've taken place before lunch was well-founded. The fare, while sumptuous, could hardly be classified as dainty. Nor the accompanying wines, which had possibly flowed a bit too freely from the hand of Montaigne Duffosat.

During the serving, I'd covertly studied Montaigne, who'd resumed her neo-ecclesiastical garments, for some lingering mark of her odd little tryst with Sam Stormshadow, but could detect nothing beyond perhaps a slightly more pronounced curve to her enigmatic smile.

Charlotte's gift to each of her attendants had been concealed beneath paper lace nosegays of miniature roses lying upon our plates—exquisite gold watch-fob bracelets from Adler's adorned with a heart-shaped charm inscribed *Foley and Charlotte, December 24*, and the individual bridesmaid's name on the reverse.

We were all wearing them now, but not even their festive 18-karat jingle could lighten the atmosphere and enhance the digestive process like yesterday's surprise panty raid.

Bobette's sudden whoop of victory at having finally coerced Jolene's reluctant zipper to do its duty was greeted with applause. The full skirt billowed as Jolene executed a triumphant pirouette; so did her full cleavage, oozing over the too-tight strapless top like melted marshmellows.

Lambie giggled. "Oh, Jolene! One more bite of anything and everybody's going to see *your* pulleybone!"

Mrs. Cahoon marched over to survey the damage, tape measure in hand. "Tsk! I really don't know if there will be sufficient seam to let out, Miss Dalton," she informed an abashed Jolene. "It's quite possible I shall have to insert a gusset. I must say, however, you do look rather bonnie in the dress, my dear," she added kindly.

Jolene brightened. "Well then, Mrs. Cahoon. Long as you're at it, go ahead and insert me a little extra margin for error. That way I can party now and worry later. Like after New Year's."

"Just call 1-800-IMSOFAT!" chanted Cecille.

"Oh, stop picking on her, Cecille," Lambie said wearily. "It's not Jolene's fault Reggie's been playing 'Playboy and Indian'."

Cecille flared. "Look who's talking! I seem to recall you lost a perfectly good fiancé, Swamp Dalton though he was, to Princess Pocahontas."

"No, Cecille." Lambie shook her fleecy blonde curls negatively. "She had nothing to do with that."

"I'll just bet," Cecille sneered.

"Well, I can't for the life of me understand what's so special about that Fawn Goldfeather," sniffed Bobette. "I mean, she's attractive enough, I guess. But my goodness! No matter how nice you try to be, she'll find some way to pervert it into a racial insult. But you've all seen how she acts."

Jolene added, "And the way she's got it in for white men? Honey, if I were one I'd be flat terrified to you-know-what with her, lest I wake up to discover she had removed my vital necessities!"

"That's right," agreed Bobette. "Hey, Lambie! Maybe you and Cecille should inspect your troops, just to make sure they've still got a three-piece set!"

I glanced quickly over at Mrs. Cahoon, who was kneeling to pin up Lambie's hem, and saw her shoulders quiver in silent mirth.

"Anyhow," Bobette went on in a complaining tone, "I don't think there's one sexy thing about her."

"I suppose it must be the art, Bobette," Lambie replied pensively. "T.J. said her portfolio is fabulous."

Cecille sighed. "I hate to admit, it is. Reggie brought the book home to show me right after they'd met. He was so excited about her talent."

This remark was greeted with heavy silence. "But it's true!" she insisted. "Listen, the only thing on this earth Reggie's not a fool about is art. Fawn Goldfeather's paintings express a wild, extravagant beauty and generosity she is clearly incapable of communicating any other way.

"There were two in particular I badly wanted to buy, but she absolutely refused to sell. Reggie says Fawn's strategy is to use her book strictly to get commissions, and create an entirely new body of work from scratch. In the meantime, she's going to hang onto every original canvas until after her premier exhibit, which is bound to succeed, then offer a showing of those first works to whatever gallery is the highest bidder."

I remarked that Fawn Goldfeather seemed to have her career path aggressively mapped out.

Cecille, who'd presented her back for Mrs. Cahoon's attentions to a slightly bunched gather at the waistline said over her shoulder, "Oh, I know it sounds commercial and unromantic, Claire. But so many talented artists lose out because they simply have no idea how to market themselves."

I thought about Ambrose Xavier and had to agree.

"Turn to your right if you please, Mrs. Worth," mumbled Mrs. Cahoon, through a mouthful of pins.

Cecille complied, then continued, "Reggie, however, has strongly advised Fawn to sell two or three paintings from the first lot to carefully selected buyers. Just enough to start whetting the critics' appetites and create a buzz, as they say in Hollywood, that would continue to build and carry over into her debut."

"May I see the left side, Mrs. Worth?" requested Mrs. Cahoon.

Cecille darted a quick glance at me. "Last night, Reggie persuaded Belinda Callant to look at Fawn's book as soon as she gets a chance. And should Belinda decide she wants to sponsor an exhibit composed solely of those first canvasses, as I'm certain she will, Fawn can't possibly afford to turn her down."

With a laugh, Cecille added, "But two certain paintings in that exhibit will be wearing a 'sold' sticker. Mark my words, Fawn Gold-feather is going to be very big."

All the while Cecille was talking so animatedly, I'd been listening with a strange sensation of unreality. On one hand, she was a fierce and protective tigress about her husband Reggie-ums. Yet she was capable of achieving sufficient detachment to rave about the talent of her employee Reggie's mistress, and tacitly acknowledge the probable necessity of said employee Reggie to make himself available on an ongoing basis for the delectation of an influential, notoriously lusty, art promoter.

I found such a schizophrenic relationship horrifying in the extreme.

Now Bobette, who enjoyed a little more freedom of movement in her dress than did Jolene, shrugged. "Maybe you know what you're talking about, Cecille. But you and Reggie and T.J. are the only living souls I've heard of who've ever seen anything Fawn's painted. She even got T.J. to install an electric lock on her studio door, and nobody knows the code but her. Can you beat that?"

Cecille fluttered a dismissive hand. "The textile industry is an entirely different arena for a real artist, Bobette. Perhaps she's concerned about her designs being stolen."

Bobette's creamy skin from face to bosom flooded with an angry red. "By who, Cecille Dalton? Me? Jolene? Mamma? Your *family*, though you don't like to own us.

"And what do you mean, 'real artist'? We've all won international awards for Peach Island with our designs, remember? You should. You were right there in Paris cozying around Ralph Lauren and the rest of them when you've never lifted one blessed finger for our company except to clip your coupons and count your money and chase after your poor excuse for a husband!

"And now you have the brazen gall to hint Fawn Goldfeather needs to worry about us stealing her pitiful sheet decorations?"

Bobette clenched a serious-looking fist, and Cecille drew back in surprised alarm.

The knock on the door was a most welcome interruption. I hastened to fling it open, heedless of whether some stray bellboy would witness a gaggle of belles in assorted stages of dishabille.

Fortunately, it was Nectarine Savoy.

"Hello, Claire. Sorry I couldn't make it back sooner. A couple of things came down at the station."

"Well, that's crime for you," I said, ushering her inside. "We were just hovering on the brink of needing a peacekeeper ourselves. Weren't we, ladies?"

"Oh?" Nectarine's eyes circled the large room like a pair of brilliant blue hawks. "What's the problem?"

Jolene and Bobette fidgeted uneasily. Cecille said nothing. Mrs. Cahoon stood by demurely, hands clasped over her stomach, the large, bristling pincushion strapped to her wrist like an outlandish bracelet.

Lambie, a veritable Christmas angel who bore not the slightest resemblance to Mrs. Santa Claus in her long red dress and fluffy blonde hair, drifted forward. "I'm afraid we got ourselves all worked up over that woman my—former fiancé brought with him to the wedding. You know, Fawn Goldfeather?"

She stretched a little white hand appealingly toward Nectarine. "See, T.J. asked Fawn to come along to get back at me, because we broke up and all. But wouldn't you just know it, he had to be the only person at Peach Island who didn't have a notion she was shacking up with Cousin Cecille's husband. You know, Reggie?"

Nectarine nodded. "I can definitely understand how that would create a lot of tension."

Jolene put in. "And the woman can't even carry on a civil conversation. She's always on a tirade about culture thieves, whatever that's supposed to mean, and white folks and—oh!"

"Don't worry, Jolene," Nectarine laughed. "I got an earful from her, too. Maybe even more because she considered me a fellow woman of color, if just barely."

She turned as Mrs. Cahoon deferentially approached, carrying a long box. "Ah, is this mine?"

"Yes, Miss Savoy," Mrs. Cahoon replied. "I do sincerely hope you'll be pleased. I don't often have the opportunity to dress a model of your caliber, you know."

Nectarine smiled. "Former model, Mrs. Cahoon," she corrected gently. "But thank you, all the same." She lifted the lid and drew out the shimmering green panne velvet. "Oh, it's beautiful!"

Mrs. Cahoon turned pink to the roots of her iron-grey Maggie Thatcher helmet. "My pleasure, I'm sure."

As Nectarine shed her chalk-striped suit jacket, Bobette asked curiously, "Is there any reason you can't tell us what Fawn said to you?"

Nectarine stepped out of her skirt and considered. "No, not really. But I'll have to talk while I dress. Marcel's coming up here in about twenty minutes, remember?"

This announcement was met with squeaks of dismay, one of them mine. I had completely forgotten to notify the others.

"I'm sorry, it's my fault," I apologized.

"But why does he have to see us in our dresses?" demanded Cecille. "He's only going to do our hair, for heaven's sake."

"Don't ever let him hear you say that," I advised her. "Marcel designs hairstyles from the toes up, particularly when it's a special occasion. He is, after all, an *artist*."

"Touché," Cecille muttered, with an unwilling half-smile.

The story Fawn told Nectarine was something straight out of a daytime talk show.

Fawn's father had been one of those unfortunate alcoholic Indians she so despised. He'd deserted her mother, who soon remarried—to a white man. She'd had another daughter by him, and, for whatever reasons, Fawn grew up feeling inferior to her half-white, half-sister.

A year ago, the mother and half-sister were killed in an automobile accident along the Virginia coast. Fawn had no contact with either her real or adopted fathers and claimed she desired none.

It was, as Nectarine observed, at least a partial explanation—but no excuse—for Fawn's bad attitude.

I thought privately that it also explained her vicious behavior toward Montaigne Duffosat, who definitely carried quite a bit of Indian blood. Maybe she reminded Fawn of that hated sister.

Nectarine stood majestically in the long spill of clingy fabric as Mrs. Cahoon fussed around with every fold, cooing, "Lovely. Simply lovely!"

"And then," Nectarine concluded, "after Fawn had totally dissed Indian men, she got started on white men. That's when I decided I'd had enough.

"I pointed out that there was an extremely large percentage of cream in my coffee, in case she'd missed it, and most of my best friends, coincidently, happen to be at least partially white. Moreover, I was engaged to a very white man whose old New Orleans French family had undeniably kept slaves and no doubt contributed generously to the gene pool from whence I eventually sprang."

"Ooh! I'll bet that shut her up!" Bobette chortled.

I said, "Nectarine, you've been hanging around with Marcel so long, you're getting to sound just like him. Maybe you are related, at that!"

Mrs. Cahoon directed her attention to me. "Mrs. Claiborne, would you be good enough to put on your dress?"

It was nothing short of a minor miracle that she managed to whip her ragged band of recruits into the semblance of a crack bridal unit by the time Marcel Barrineau tapped on the door.

After declaring himself enchanted with the gowns, he said, "Claire, I am beginning to hatch a marvelous inspiration. But, of course, I will first need to know exactly what you have created for Charlotte to ensure we are in accord."

"That's easy," I told him. "Meet me at my shop in an hour, and you can take it home with you."

He threw Nectarine a sizzling look, kissed Mrs. Cahoon's hands, assuring her with unconscious arrogance, that her beautiful dresses were certain to set off his hair arrangements to perfection, and breezed out.

Though Marcel was convinced the choice of hairstyles could make or break a wedding, he never imagined they could also be a matter of life and death.

13

About forty-five minutes later, I turned into our street, passing the caravan of Mr. Barushka's workers, through for the day, wheeling toward St. Charles.

I pretended not to notice when Mr. Barushka himself, at the helm of a putty-colored Chevy flatbed, did a startled doubletake in my direction. Had his expression been one of alarm, or mere surprise? Whichever, it was useless to fret.

As dear *Tante* Jeanette, who'd raised me from a baby after my parents died, used to advise: "Can't be worrying about those things you can change, *chère*, because you can change them. And don't be worrying about those things you can't change, because you can't change them, no."

Nevertheless, based on my recent experience with Mr. Barushka, it was with some misgiving that I mounted the steps leading to my shop's entrance. I paused to wipe flecks of plaster dust from the antique bronze angel doorknocker, a gift from Dan upon Eclaire's opening, which, despite its unwitting role in the demise of a manicurist, had become my logo.

But after all, when I unlocked the door and stepped into the foyer, I encountered nothing beyond the normal chaos of remodeling, which was only to be expected.

The four tall pine armoires, too heavy to be moved out, were instead parked in the middle of the floor, shrouded with thick canvas tarpaulins. In one of these reposed the Styrofoam head crowned with Charlotte's marriage hair, but which? There was no help for it; unless I got lucky the first time, I'd have to check each one.

More tarps were spread to protect the terra cotta tile floors while the ceiling was being repaired. Fallen plaster crackled beneath my feet as I crossed for a sneak preview of the only major alteration, the addition of a private suite exclusively for my clients.

Hitherto, Eclaire had been a one-chair beauty boutique. Part of my Christmas gift to my assistant, Renee Vermilion, was to put her in charge of the outer salon, while I withdrew to the inner sanctum.

Mr. Barushka had created an arch between the nail salon and the kitchen. A short hallway led into what would be a sunny lounge with French doors opening onto the herb garden and swimming pool, where clients could relax comfortably while waiting for their appointments or processing curls and color. A separate powder room was being added for their convenience.

But just now, with the dank odor of moist cement permeating everything, it was yet a far cry from the glorious space of stone, suede, mahogany, damask and leaded glass I'd envisioned.

Another archway framed my rounded workroom, where a skylight had already been set into the domed ceiling. Positioned directly beneath it would be a circular mahogany station, allowing me to attend two clients at once. In an alcove to the left were installed a pair of ergonomically correct shampoo bowls; on the walls, chalked arrows and measurements indicated the placement of curved mahogany storage cabinets with leaded glass fronts.

I felt a tingle of excitement. This soon would be my art studio where I would wield brushes filled with color upon the most challenging, unpredictable canvas of all.

A distant pounding roused me from my daydream. I retraced my steps to investigate and discovered an impatient Marcel waiting at the door.

"When one keeps an appointment, one expects to be admitted promptly, Claire," he grumbled, treading gingerly through the debris in his lustrous black Italian loafers. "As my repeated ringing of your bell failed to produce results, I concluded the apparatus had been disconnected."

He was right. An inspection revealed several colored wires dangling limply down the wall.

"I'm sorry, Marcel. I didn't think to check. And I would've heard you sooner if I hadn't been in the back, fantasizing about my new aerie."

Marcel untied the belt of his black cashmere trenchcoat and stuck his hands in the pockets, instant *GQ* cover. "Well? Am I permitted to see these premises in their embryonic state? I need not, of course, point out that the unique and thorough training at my side, which produced the excellent stylist you now are, is directly responsible for the necessity of such construction."

"No, you needn't," I agreed, smiling, "but since you did—walk this way, please." I beckoned and Marcel followed, complaining about the mess with every step.

But upon our arrival, as I explained the configuration of the lounging area and powder room, he lapsed into uncharacteristic monosyllables. I began to wonder what he didn't like.

At his continued lack of response, I felt hesitant to show him my studio, but he went right on in without waiting for an escort. I entered to find him standing under the skylight, looking up, then around.

Mechanically, I recited the various features, and pointed out this and that. Still, he said very little. I was starting to feel hurt and angry when he remarked finally, "But Claire, this is most astounding! I personally know many famous stylists who naturally maintain a work area separate and apart from the rest of their salons. But few, if any, have had the foresight to create an entire apartment, so to speak, which allows the client to remain in total privacy."

Marcel strolled back into the first room to take a survey. "It is comparable to waiting in the first class lounge before takeoff," was his verdict. "I congratulate you, Claire. And I must have the name of the genius responsible for this concept. There is a possible project which he or she will find most interesting."

"Come on, Marcel!" I laughed. "You don't have to go that far to make me feel good. I'm just glad you like it."

Marcel looked at me. "One moment, Claire. My compliments were quite sincere but I assure you uncalculated to elevate your self-esteem. Am I to understand that you are responsible for the design of this space?"

"Well, if you mean did I draw rough sketches and tell Mr. Baruskha what I wanted, yes. But that's all."

"All?" echoed Marcel. "Evidently, Claire, you fail to grasp the essence of my observations. I have recently been apprised of the imminent availability of a prime location in the French Quarter.

"But, should I undertake such an endeavor, I shall require it to be completely different from my other establishments. I would be most open to entertain whatever suggestions you care to put forth."

Certainly I was flattered at such high praise from the maestro, but it was not without reason Marcel had acquired a reputation for having whims of iron. "Anytime, Marcel. Just let me know. But I thought you came here to pick up some hair."

With a show of reluctance, he allowed himself to be coaxed back into the main salon, leaving me to awkwardly maneuver the weighty canvas from the door of an armoire while he stood well aloof from flying dust. After all that, Charlotte's hairdo wasn't inside, but fortunately, it was in the next one.

Marcel took the wig stand from me and revolved it like a globe, not missing a nuance of angle. A slight smile played upon his lips. "I had not previously discerned to what extent you received an impartation of my gift, Claire," he commented. "This is something that could have been created by myself years ago as a young man in Paris."

Indicating the center parting and the braid wrapped around the coil, he added, "Here we see two perfect notes with which to compose our theme. You and Nectarine shall have the top half of your hair parted in the center and pulled back into a ponytail which will be bound by a braid. The remaining hair will flow loosely to your shoulders."

I told him that sounded wonderful, and would work perfectly with our little green feather hats.

"And now," he mused, holding the head aloft and squinting, "for the bridesmaids. Yes, I see a coronet of braids, swept from a center part and threaded through with narrow, red velvet ribbon. Most unusual, and quite perfect."

The fact that all the bridesmaids had shortish hair presented no problem. Marcel would augment with high-quality, dyed-to-match tresses culled from his private herd of human hair growers. And guess who was assigned to shear a lock from each woman to ensure the perfect tone was achieved.

"Why not get Nectarine to do it?" I inquired sardonically. "Collecting hair samples is part of her job description. She's already got all those cute little plastic bags to seal it in and everything."

Marcel looked amused. "But alas, she would not know where to cut without leaving a most distressing gap. And I must confess to some surprise at your lack of enthusiasm, Claire."

"Oh, Marcel," I sighed. "Of course I'll be glad to help you. It's just that every time I get a few days off, I end up working twice as hard."

I changed the subject. "Anyway, how is the sapphire ring search coming along? Any progress?"

It was his turn to sigh. "As yet, nothing but a vague rumor of a remote possibility in Belgium. It is most mysterious and frustrating when one considers there must have been thousands of those stones mined and not, in the scheme of time and space; so terribly long ago.

"I do, however, place the utmost confidence in *les soeurs* Key." He paused. "Based on appearances, one would never suspect them of maintaining impressive connections within global jewel circles. At any rate, I feel certain they will locate my beloved's ring in time for our wedding—" He stopped suddenly and I pounced.

"Marcel! You've set the date! When?" I demanded.

"Now, Claire," he said urgently, "you must keep this to yourself as it will not be announced until after the new year, nor have any arrangements whatever been made. But, at the risk of appearing rather overly sentimental, we have selected February 14 to exchange our vows."

"Valentine's Day!" I exclaimed tearily. "How beautiful, Marcel. How truly wonderful."

He looked at me seriously. "It is, without doubt, the most important decision, and the most difficult, I have ever made in my life, Claire."

A little later, he took his leave, the Styrofoam head tucked under one arm like Ichabod Crane's nemesis.

I locked up and drove back down St. Charles Avenue, now dense with Christmas shopping traffic. Since there was no wedding event scheduled for this evening, I could actually enjoy the opportunity, enforced by frequent stops and starts, to view the beautifully decorated and lighted mansions .

Back at Riverside Manor, I was heading for the elevator when I spotted Fawn Goldfeather pacing the lobby, hugging a black leather portfolio to her chest. At first, I couldn't figure out what seemed different about her, then I realized—Fawn's new-looking ensemble featured an overtly Indian motif.

Both her ochre buckskin jacket and matching ankle moccasins dripped with fringe. A leather belt beaded in the thunderbird pattern cinched the waist of her jeans. Long, elaborate earrings that appeared, as best as I could tell from where I stood, composed of feathers, leather, silver and—could that be the despised turquoise?—swung and flashed beneath her dark hair as she turned to scan first one entrance, then the other.

Ironically, Fawn looked even less like a Native American than she ordinarily did. On her, that drugstore Indian getup was a costume she couldn't quite pull off.

I realized Fawn hadn't yet noticed me. Acting on impulse, I slipped behind a marble pillar to observe her, pretending to be searching for something in my bag lest I appear to lurk.

All at once, Fawn smiled a welcome. Reggie Worth had entered through the revolving doors and was moving in her direction. Stealthily, I glided behind the next pillar, the better to eavesdrop.

When I looked again, Fawn's smile had become an angry glower as Reggie protested, "There was absolutely nothing I could do. An art critic from the *Times-Picayune* asked Belinda to give a joint interview with Sam. He brought along a photographer. Trust me, it was not the moment to remind her of her meeting with us to look at your book."

"But she promised," Fawn griped.

"Don't worry, baby. I can positively guarantee you Belinda Callant will see your work," Reggie stated with such assurance, Fawn's eyes flashed suspiciously.

"Yeah? Well, you just better deliver on that, Reggie. We wouldn't want dear old Cecille to find out how you've been inflating art prices so you can skim a cut off the top, would we?"

A wave of anger washed over Reggie's weak, handsome face, but he said smoothly, "Now, Fawn. Is that any way to talk to the man who's going to make you a star?"

"I'm sorry." Fawn's apology was grudging. "It's just a big disappointment. After I got all dressed up, too."

"And very nice you look," Reggie soothed. "But it doesn't have to go to waste, you know. Cecille's got a seven o'clock appointment in the health club for a sauna and massage. She'll be gone for at least two hours. And I'll be so lonely."

Fawn was tempted. "I do miss you," she admitted. "But where can we go? Even though T.J. has been bunking with Kyle, he could barge in at any time and you know what would happen."

"Then I guess it'll have to be my place," said Reggie. "One stolen moment so sweet, and then off you must flee on swift, silent feet."

"Oh, I'll be there!" It was the first time I could remember hearing Fawn's laugh, which sounded rusty from disuse. "You do like to live dangerously, Reggie."

Reggie smiled bitterly. "Do you call this living?"

14

Our hotel suite, while not precisely home, was where we were hanging our hats, and it was good to be back. It got even better when I heard splashing and rumbling noises emanating from the bathroom.

A haze of steam, redolent with rich tobacco and D'Adventur cologne surrounded me as I entered to discover Dan, stretched out in the oversized tub with the Jacuzzi churning and foaming at full throttle. His eyes were closed, and there was a glowing cigar clamped between his teeth. An ashtray and a half-finished glass of white wine stood on the marble ledge. He looked like a great big tropical fish in an exotic tank.

I savored his submerged furry body for a moment, then observed, "Well, if that's not the picture of perfect bliss!"

Dan opened one lazy blue eye. "Not quite perfect, babylove," he mumbled around the cigar. "But now you're here, it could be."

"If that's an invitation, you don't need to ask me twice," I told him. "Make some room while I go get out of these clothes."

"Bring along what's left of that Pinot Grigio while you're at it, Claire," he called after me.

In the bedroom, I peeled everything off and stuffed it into the hotel dry cleaning bag for tomorrow's pickup. My black suede and lace pumps, after their excursion through the construction site, were misted with white plaster and would probably have to be sent out for rehab.

The pale aqua satin robe with a terrycloth lining felt wonderful, just the right combination of sleek and snuggly. Quickly, I twisted my hair into a topknot, then retrieved the bottle of wine from the kitchenette refrigerator.

"You were gone too long," Dan complained when I returned.

"Oh, dear. Has the moment passed?" I wondered, letting the robe slip to the floor.

His eyes struck and flared like matches across my body. "Well, if it did, there's another one right behind it, darlin'," he promised.

I stepped down into the swirling water, and Dan poured the wine. "Hey, baby. You forgot to bring another glass."

"No, I didn't. I'm just basically all wined—and dined—out for one day. I don't want to end up like Jolene." Dan chuckled at my account of the buxom bridesmaid dripping out of her dress like a two super-scoop ice cream cone.

"I'm feeling a tad overfed myself," he remarked, smacking his corrugated abs. "Maybe we'll wander down to the pub later on and split a sandwich."

I slid lower to allow one of the water jets to pound the center of my back. "Ummm. Meanwhile, this feels so good."

Dan moved closer. "How about . . . this?" he wanted to know.

What with *this*, and that, not to mention the other, we actually had an appetite by the time we rolled into the Castle Pub. The Thursday night crowd was thin, compared to our previous visit, and we were speedily presented with both the Beck's beer Dan had ordered, and a wooden platter bearing what looked like half a tri-tip roast on a baguette the size of a concrete block.

"How'd they ever cut this thing in two?" I marveled. "With a chainsaw?"

"Well, the menu did say their sandwiches were kingsize," Dan reminded me. "It merely neglected to identify the king as Henry VIII."

While we ate, I filled Dan in on my day, from Juanita and Ambrose, to Nectarine's sketchy history of Fawn's background, to Fawn's black-mail-spiced reference to Reggie's creative accounting practices, finishing with the rendezvous I'd overhead them arrange for seven o'clock in Reggie and Cecille's room.

Dan looked disturbed. He checked his watch against the Big Ben clock behind the bar. "It's about 8:20 now. This sounds like a very unhealthy situation, Claire. Did you get the impression they want to get caught?"

I ruminated on that as I pecked at a manageable portion of sandwich. "Not exactly," I said finally. "I think Fawn was kind of jazzed by the risky element, but I don't believe she wants an open showdown at all. Her main agenda is to break into the big-time art scene, and for that she needs Reggie to maintain his status quo with Cecille.

"However," I added, "Reggie almost sounded like he just didn't give a damn anymore. I wonder why? Charlotte told me that Cecille rules. And Reggie obeys."

Dan raised his Beck's bottle to our waitress, indicating a refill, then commented, "It occurs to me that Reggie might have an agenda of his own."

"Like what?" I demanded. "As of now, he lives in luxury in a great big Buckhead mansion with a beautiful woman who puts up with his gambling and adultery and, don't forget, pays him lots of money to do something he actually loves.

"And while that sounds like my personal idea of a marriage made in hell, he's been a willing co-conspirator for going on five years. Why would he trash that, and for what? Rather, for whom? If Reggie leaves Cecille, Charlotte says it's an ironclad fact, well-known to all and sundry, that he takes nothing with him.

"Even if Fawn makes it big overnight, she won't ever be able to keep Reggie in the manner to which he's been accustomed. Nor, from what I've seen, does she have the slightest desire to do so."

"Well," Dan said, when I'd run down, "I wasn't thinking of Fawn."

Before I could question him further, two things happened simultaneously. Big Ben struck the half-hour, and Fawn Goldfeather, without portfolio, walked in and sat down at the bar.

Dan nodded. "You were right, Claire. Reggie told her they'd have at least two hours, but evidently, neither of them was willing to cut it that close."

15

Though Dan had made impressive inroads on the sandwich, he at last admitted defeat and allowed a waitress to remove it. At her arch ribbing about his eyes being bigger than his stomach, Fawn glanced in our direction. We both called out hello, but she barely acknowledged the greeting.

When the bartender brought her drink, I was astonished to see him deliver instead of bottled water, a frosted mug of ice and a red can of Classic Coke.

"Looks like she's all set to tie one on," I murmured. Dan chuckled.

Next to arrive was a member of a warring tribe, Sam Stormshadow. He paused by our table. "Uh—you're Don and, no don't tell me, Chloe, right?"

"Almost, but not quite." Dan stood, offering his hand, which Sam accepted. "Dan Claiborne. And this is Claire, my wife."

Sam shook his head in self-deprecation, causing dark braids to snake silkily over the shoulders of his black leather jacket. "I'm sorry. Although, that's pretty good for me after three margaritas. Which is what I'm told I put away the other night when we met."

"Sit down, Sam," Dan invited, drawing out a chair.

Sam looked at me. "I don't want to impose."

"Not at all," I replied, striving for a poker face. If only he knew how much we wanted to ask him!

Dan cleared his throat, a signal to let him lead off. "Claire and I didn't notice you overindulging, Sam. Anyway, three margaritas? That sounds about average—if not downright low—when it comes to margaritas."

"To a Mexican, or even a white guy, maybe!" Sam laughed. "But I recently discovered I've got a form of that Indian low-alcohol tolerance thing."

"Oh, the missing enzyme to metabolize it, or something," I said, remembering Fawn's dissertation.

"Or something," Sam agreed. "Right now, more researchers are leaning to the enzyme deficiency theory. In my particular case, for the last year or so, I know I can drink two average drinks—makes no difference whether it's wine or hard liquor—and no more. After that, it's like *The Lost Weekend*. Blackouts, the works."

He frowned. "When people tell me things I've done in that condition, I can't even relate. They could be talking about a crazy stranger, and one I frankly wouldn't care to meet."

Dan asked bluntly, "Would you say then, when you exceed your two-drink maximum, you do so deliberately, with full knowledge of the possible consequences?"

"Hey!" Sam raised his hands in mock surrender. "That's a loaded question, Dan. You sound like a lawyer."

"If it sounds like a lawyer, it's probably a lawyer," Dan replied. "I happen to be with the firm of Blanchard, Smithson."

The bell rang. "Callant and Claiborne," finished Sam slowly. "Oh, God. That's right, you're Foley's friend. Then you know about—" Sam was still fumbling for a euphemism to describe his clay-smeared debauchery with Foley's wife when our waitress bounced up.

"Can I bring you something from the bar, sir?" she chirped.

"Great timing, honey," Sam laughed. "Well, why not? Make it a Jack Daniels Black, on the rocks." As she bounced off again, Sam glared at Dan. "You got a problem with that?" he challenged.

Dan said gently, "I may be a lawyer, Sam, but I'm not your judge, jury and executioner. I think you're wearing all three of those hats yourself."

Sam's dark Indian gaze locked with Dan's steady blue one for an emotion-charged second, then dropped down to his large, strong hands. They were incongruously smooth and well-kept for a sculptor who consistently wrestled secrets from hearts of wood, stone and clay. His secrets?

When Sam failed to speak, Dan said kindly, "To answer the question you didn't ask, yes. We know what happened at Belinda and Foley's house that night. In fact, I'd say virtually all the people invited to your opening know about it too, and that's just why they'll come when otherwise they'd let it slide by because of Christmas."

Dan stopped when the waitress delivered Sam's whiskey, then resumed. "What's more, since New Orleans art buyers tend to become personally involved with their purchases, I predict the Thorton event will be a near sellout—especially the big, expensive pieces—for the very reason they can tell folks the inside scandal about the artist when they show them off."

Sam turned his untouched glass in interlocking circles upon the oak tabletop. "I hope so," he muttered. "I don't ever want to see that shit again! Oh, that shocks you?" he demanded, intercepting my swift, startled look at Dan. "Well, it sure as hell shocks me. Months of my life working day and night. I couldn't stop. God! I never knew I had such stuff inside me.

"Belinda made me feel primitive, barbaric, savage. Everything I'd done before seemed tame and pastel and small. And then"—he took the first sip of his drink—"then, this little Indian boy woke up and it's been a living nightmare ever since."

The very bones in his beautiful face suddenly seemed suffused with pain and self-loathing. Unbidden, he continued to talk. It was like a slowly leaking dam that, instead of bursting open, had inexorably eroded to the point of crumbling softly away.

Shorn of the emotion with which he told it, Sam's narrative was an exotic variation on the basic theme of wealthy-patron-takes-over-entire-life-of-talented-artist.

Though Sam Stormshdow had been nationally acclaimed before getting mixed up with Belinda, he'd encountered a lot of resistance from powerful people in the art world who decided he was too non-traditional. One important critic in particular had mercilessly trashed him for not adhering exclusively to native themes and techniques—even colors—the very thing that same critic previously denounced other Native American artists for doing, declaring them stuck in a time warp!

Also, Sam had discovered that being a successful minority artist made you fair game for national politicians who, in turn, were under pressure from special interest groups proclaiming themselves as the final authority on what did or did not legitimately represent the art of their particular minority.

Small wonder then, that beautiful, rich, reckless Belinda had seemed to him a breath of fresh air, instead of the toxic gas she actually was.

She'd sparked insane fantasies, then pushed him to translate them into form. Not even the humiliation of Foley catching them rolling naked in clay all over her concrete studio floor had been sufficient to jolt him from his hypnotic state. In fact, he remembered almost nothing about that fateful night.

And after Belinda moved into his Santa Fe home, her flagrant infidelities with her other artist clients only served to turn up the flame of his passion. For her, and for his work.

At first, their stormy partnership seemed to pay off. Since the "art-farts," as Belinda called them, dictated that Native American artists function as sacred cows, her very clever publicity campaign hyped Sam Stormshadow as a paradigm shatterer. This tactic forced the critics to concede the same creative latitude to the Indian artist as they had to the Hispanic, or be branded as bigots.

As a result, the premier exhibit of this particular work, held at the Los Angeles Museum of Art just a couple of weeks ago, had been the hottest ticket in town.

But ironically, that's precisely when he'd snapped out of his trance and realized he was living in hell with a she-devil.

Dan interrupted. "What do you feel triggered that revelation?"

"That's easy," Sam answered, twirling the ice in his empty glass. "I saw—I mean, really saw—my recent work for the very first time."

The way it had happened was this. Because of the time factor, Belinda dispatched Sam on his round of local television appearances and newspaper and magazine interviews, while she and the museum people set up the exhibit. They'd arranged to meet there about an hour prior to the opening, but she was late. Nobody else was around when he arrived, so Sam walked into the exhibit alone.

The first thing he'd seen was a naked terra cotta female, laughing as she thrust a silver and turquoise knife into her vagina, which spilled forth blood and thorny red roses. Rose vines were wrapped around her breasts, their thorns gouging blood from the nipples. Her hair was long, except for the raw, bloody crescent-shaped patch where she'd been ritually scalped. More blood trickled down her face.

He'd nearly thrown up.

Everywhere he looked, this woman loomed before him, partially scalped and impaled with sharp weapons, protruding briary vines, dripping blood and roses.

He shuddered. "It was monstrous. Vile. Horrible. And I had done it with these hands." Sam looked down at them wonderingly. "I wanted to scream at the top of my lungs. For one split second, I literally thought I was going to lose my mind."

Then, Belinda had come in, smelling of wine, with a handsome museum official. Sam had hated her in that moment, because he'd finally recognized her as she really was, as his spirit had known all along she was; a beautiful rose, corrupted and polluted by her own blood, whom he'd been replicating in painting and sculpture for months on end.

I recalled my conviction that Belinda was a Dorian Grey. Evidently, it had required a lot more than one picture to expose the full range of her depravity.

Sam took a deep breath. "And the most frightening thing of all is those L.A. sickos gave the show rave reviews. What were they thinking?"

One more fact emerged from our conversation. The reason Sam could barely recall the night Foley had surprised him *en flagrante* with Belinda was that he'd drunk most of a magnum of champagne earlier.

"I never responded to your question about whether I violated my limit deliberately, knowing it could be to my peril," Sam reminded Dan.

"The answer of course, is yes. It was then, and it is now." He waggled his empty glass at the serving wench. "But for entirely different reasons."

16

Both Dan and I were pretty well wrung to rags after Sam finished his tale of terror.

We were glad when, shortly after obtaining his refill, he excused himself and slouched down to the end of the bar. Nobody was playing darts just then, so Sam helped himself to a handful from the bucket on the counter top, and began to hurl them forcefully at the target. His technique may have lacked elegance, but not accuracy; all but a couple of the feathered missiles landed on the bull's-eye, or within the next two rings.

I couldn't help but wonder if he'd ever utilized darts to puncture one of his Belinda effigies.

Until Fawn Goldfeather slid from her stool to join him, uninvited, I'd nearly forgotten she'd been here all along.

"Well, Sam Stormshadow. How does it feel to have prostituted your work in order to become house injun for a bunch of rich white people?"

Sam whirled on her, dart in hand, and she drew back. "Have you ever seen my work, bitch?" he snarled.

"Oh, who hasn't? That Thorton poster's all over the place."

"Uh-uh. That's not what I asked you," Sam said. "Since 1987, when I began showing professionally, have you ever, at any time, attended an exhibit, gallery opening, or even glanced at a catalog of my work?"

Fawn looked scornful. "That's not the point."

"Oh, but it is!" Sam took another threatening step forward. He still hadn't lowered the dart. "Unless you've seen my art with your own eyes and hated it, you've got no right to pass judgment. Because you know what that makes you, Fawn Goldfeather? It makes you both a hypocrite, and a Judas to your own race."

Taken offguard by Sam's counter, Fawn blinked first. Sam pressed his advantage.

"And while we're on the subject, just what denomination of Creek are you? Were your ancestors Tamathil, Hitchiti, Chiaha, Oconee, Tocatocuru, or what? Tell me, have you traced the *itaiwa* where your old ones kindled the Sacred Fire at the Busk of Green Corn on the *pascova*?"

Even on less than two drinks, Sam looked truly demented. Fawn tried to back away, but he kept coming.

"Where is the modern capital of the Creek Nation? Do you have a theory as to the significance of the dogwood flower design on Swift Creek paddle pottery?"

Maybe we should have intervened but, shameful as it is to confess, were kind of enjoying watching Fawn being forced to swallow a big dose of her own medicine. Sam, a Navajo, knew more about the Creeks than she did herself!

He was just getting started on something—or someone—called a *Mico Apokta* when Fawn managed to croak, "Okmulgee."

Sam stopped in mid-sentence. "What?"

"Okmulgee," Fawn repeated angrily. "Okmulgee, Oklahoma is the capitol of the Creek Nation."

"Oh, who wouldn't know that?" Sam mocked.

At some point, Montaigne Duffosat had drifted into the pub. When Sam noticed her, his expression softened. "Oh, hello there!" he called.

Fawn turned to see who had distracted his attention. At the sight of Montaigne, a nearly visible mist of hatred swirled around her head.

Without another word, she pivoted on her heel and left. Sam didn't even realize she was gone.

Dan toyed with his empty beer bottle. "Baby, I'm torn. Should we leave? Or should I have another beer while we stick around for the next act?"

"That'd be your third, wouldn't it? Well, okay. But only if you promise to remember any wild and crazy things you might do, just in case they bear repeating."

"Now, darlin'. Don't I always?" He grinned. "Anyway, I'll skip the beer. But I do think maybe we ought to stay a little longer, for Foley and Charlotte's sake. I don't much care for all these undercurrents."

I agreed, so he ordered Cokes for us both.

Sam and Montaigne were still leaning against the bar, talking softly. The close proximity of his face to Montaigne's acted as a magnet to draw out her own primeval Indian-ness. Viewed in profile, their heads were like matching bookends.

Into this quiet interlude swept Belinda Callant with surprise escort, Kyle Dalton, in tow.

I'd never seen him so well-groomed, and he looked frankly yummy, with his neck-length mahogany hair sleekly under control, and a fine navy blazer custom-tailored to his muscular torso. Belinda whispered in his ear, and the green Dalton eyes blazed dangerously, giving him the air of an aristocrat raised in the jungle by savages. Of Lambie's streetcar-riding companion, or T.J.'s amiable elder brother—even the horny drunk—there was no sign. Tonight, this mercurial man was intoxicated to the point of no return—with Belinda.

I seriously began to question whether Kyle was quite right in the head. Perhaps all those generations of Dalton inbreeding were exacting their toll. Certainly he was a fine physical specimen, but genetic aberrations didn't necessarily always manifest externally.

I tried to recall what his job was at Peach Island. Something out in the fields, Charlotte had said. Oh, yes. He supervised the precutting from various growths of flax and cotton in sufficient quantities to process, weave and inspect before final harvesting. I personally wouldn't want to be anywhere near Kyle Dalton with a knife in his hand.

Charlotte also mentioned that his obsession was to develop a perfect natural blue cotton that would require no indigo dye, worth millions if he should succeed.

Belinda twined a serpentine arm through his, pressing close to his side. The groaning ache in him for her was so strong, it could be felt clear across the room. She laughed, loving the effect she had on him, egging him on.

Though Belinda didn't in the least resemble any of the females Kyle in his cups confused with trampy Darby, she was definitely Darby's spiritual twin. Which just goes to show you.

We thought there might be trouble if Belinda and Kyle joined Sam and Montaigne at the bar, but no. Sam saw the couple approach and waved them over.

Kyle wasn't pleased but, being attached to Belinda, had no choice but to trail along. His response to Sam's hello was little better than a warning growl of one territorial male to another over a bitch in heat, unaware that Sam wouldn't lift a finger to fight for her.

Belinda deliberately turned up the fire under Kyle by coyly twisting one of Sam's braids around her finger. Was the gesture intended to be symbolic, or just coincidental? No matter. It had the desired effect on Kyle. He seethed.

Montaigne observed this bit of byplay with an ironic expression directed at Sam, who neatly wiggled off the hook by turning away to pick up his drink, thus pulling the braid from Belinda's grasp.

It was so subtle, Belinda didn't catch on, but it sent a coded signal to Montaigne. *You see? I'm breaking loose.*

"Well, did you two finally get everything settled?" Belinda asked, looking from Sam to Montaigne.

"I think so, Mrs. Callant," replied Montaigne. "Chilean red and Argentinian white are my recommendation for the wines.

"I have arranged a tasting for you and Mr. Stormshadow tomorrow in the wine cellar. Around noon, if that's convenient?"

Belinda waved the hand not clutching Kyle. The hand wearing the black opal. "Oh, do we really need to go through all that? I'm sure whatever you decide will be fine, dear."

It wasn't entirely clear whether that patronizing "dear" had been addressed to Montaigne or Sam.

Unperturbed, Montaigne continued. "As to the menu, I've discussed several possibilities with the chef. Our goal is to adhere to the authentic flavor and color of the Southwest without digressing totally into Mexican. If you and Mr. Stormshadow will accompany me to the kitchen, I'll have one of the cooks heat up the samples Chef has prepared for you to choose from."

"You don't mean now?" Belinda protested. "Kyle and I just came from dinner. I couldn't eat another bite. We were on our way to the lounge for a cognac. Sam, you pick the food. It's your opening, after all."

I gave Dan a meaningful look. If those two had been discussing nothing but food and wine earlier, we were Don and Chloe.

Sam was careful to avoid Montaigne's eye as he said casually, "Sure, Belinda, I'll take care of it. And the wine tasting tomorrow too, if you'd rather not bother."

"Whatever," Belinda was growing restless. Glancing around she noticed us for the first time.

"Dan! Just the man I need to see. Hello, Claire," she added. "You've met Kyle Dalton, haven't you?" Obviously forgetting that he was a close relative of the bride with whose wedding to her own ex-husband we were deeply involved.

Belinda sat without being asked, pulling Kyle down into the chair beside her. "Kyle's been telling me about the blue cotton he's working on, and how eventually he wants to develop a whole spectrum of naturally-colored cottons."

She patted Kyle's pale cheek. "Isn't he such an artist? And then he said the most amazing thing. Tell Dan the amazing thing you said, Kyle."

Kyle, who had been planning on having a whole other kind of discussion, was at first reluctant, but allowed Belinda to persuade him.

"We were just talking about art and painting. And I happened to mention that canvas is made from heavy cotton fibers. Several painters I know say they use up too much expensive paint on the background— that stark white canvas just sucks it up. Well, I began thinking in terms of pre-colored canvas—yellow, blue, beige, grey, green—even black.

"I guess what it actually is is a colored primer, not intended as a substitute for creativity, but to let the artist choose a tone which would cut down on the amount of paint required to get all that white canvas out of the picture, so to speak."

Belinda laughed. "Who cares if they substitute it for creativity? Certainly not I, after seeing what some people come up with on their own. My point is, I think we've got a major money-making idea here. So, how do we copyright it, Lawyer Dan?"

I saw on Dan's face that he hadn't missed that "we" Belinda was using so freely. He spoke directly to Kyle. "You could be onto something. I think it's definitely worth pursuing." He took out his wallet and extracted a business card. "Give me a call before you leave town, but not until after the wedding, please! We'll talk."

"Didn't I tell you?" Belinda asked rhetorically. As she stood, Kyle rose with her like a remora tracking its shark. "Thanks, Dan. 'Bye now, Claire. Come on, Kyle. Let's have that cognac."

When they'd swum off, Dan remarked, "Just one more minute of that bloodsucking female and I wouldn't have been responsible."

"Well, you're such a gentlemen, it didn't show a bit," I assured him. "Anyway, you've got to hand it to Belinda. She spotted Kyle's pipe dream for solid gold. She sure does know how to pick a winner."

Dan looked angry. "Uh-huh. And she wastes no time trying to turn them into losers. If Foley had been a weaker man, she'd have either totally destroyed him or he'd be on death row for murdering her. And you heard what Sam said."

"Yes, but I think she's about to lose her grip on him, courtesy of Montaigne."

The space at the bar where Sam and Montaigne had been standing was now deserted. Presumably, they were in the kitchen tasting Southwest hors d'oeuvres.

All at once, Dan laughed. "I wonder what's going to happen tomorrow down in that wine cellar if Sam consumes more than two drinks?"

"Ah, but Montaigne's got the keys!" I reminded him.

17

"This makes me feel so violated," whined Lambie Dalton.

"And you'll look it, too, if you don't stop squirming around," I advised, combing through her cloudy blonde curls, searching for the exact spot to snip. "Just relax and trust me, okay?"

"I guess I have no choice."

"No," I agreed. "Not when Monsieur Marcel Barrineau himself has ordained that your hair shall be braided into a retro coronet, and your hair's not long enough. But not just any old prosthetic braids will do. No, ma'am. Your braids must be of top quality, virgin human hair from Marcel's stable of virgins, colored to match your own hair to perfection."

"Oh. Well, do we get to keep them after?" she wanted to know.

"Of course. They're part of the deal, and you don't want me to tell you what it cost your sister."

"Oh!" squeaked Lambie in surprise, as I dangled the lock of hair I'd taken without her realizing. She scampered over to the dresser and looked anxiously in the mirror.

"Why, I can't even tell! Hey, Claire. You're good!"

"I've got the quickest scissor finger in the South, honey," I bragged, twirling my shears like a pistol.

Lambie smiled. "Oh, isn't this going to be the most beautiful wedding, Claire? I'm so happy for Charlotte, she's got such a wonderful man."

It was just too ripe an opportunity to pass up for a little more snooping. But I deposited her hair sample in a small plastic bag, secured it with a twist tie, stuck a round peel-off dot on the outside and marked it with "L.D." before observing, "The problem is, Lambie, wonderful is nowhere near perfect. And sometimes, you unfortunately have got to lose something before you realize just how right it was for you. Believe me, I speak from sad experience."

Lambie flushed. "You mean me and Tucker John, don't you? Oh, I know everybody's been speculating. Is she a snob with cold feet like her Grandma Imogene? Did she catch T.J. with another woman? Does she have another man waiting in the wings? Well, don't believe anything you hear, Claire. None of it's true."

I looked at her. "It certainly isn't. Because you are totally in love with Tucker John, and fully intend to marry him. Am I right?"

Lambie's big eyes widened. "I didn't realize I was being so obvious."

"Oh, you're not," I said. "Remember, nobody else thinks that. I guess I picked up on it because of what I went through with my husband, but that's another story, and much too long to tell right now."

Sweeping scissors, plastic bags and stick-on dots into my leather carryall, I was prepared to leave when Lambie stopped me.

"Since you've already guessed so much, Claire, I'll tell you the rest, if you want to know. Only, you've got to promise to keep it a total secret. From *everybody*."

I slung the bag over my shoulder and tried not to look too eager. "Sure, I've got a minute."

Lambie began to pace. "See, I've been in love—I mean, really in love—with Tucker John since I was a little girl. He's the only boy I've ever cared about."

Though Tucker John was seven years older than Lambie, the two of them, along with Woody and Wes, were always thrown together at family gatherings because they were the youngest.

Having made up her mind, Lambie began going along with her father on his frequent trips to Peach Island, always making sure she saw Tucker John, who treated her like his spoiled little sister. Eventually, he developed the habit of confiding in her. She knew all his likes and dislikes, his girlfriend problems—just about everything there was to know about her man.

As she talked, I tried to picture the beautiful, fairylike child she must have been, solemnly absorbing and filing information for her future with the clueless Tucker John.

What amazing—and somewhat alarming—determination and single-mindedness!

When Tucker John at last began to notice Lambie as a woman, it just seemed to him like the natural, comfortable thing to do to get engaged to her.

And that was exactly the problem.

Lambie wanted far more than a buddy-buddy marriage; she wanted fire, excitement and passion. But the little creature was far too wise to discuss her real feelings with him. What was needed, she decided, was a wake-up call, a shock to the system.

So she'd taken the biggest gamble of all and canceled their engagement.

"I'm an all or nothing-at-all kind of girl, Claire," Lambie concluded. "If I can't have Tucker John the way I want him, then I don't want him." She clenched her little fists. "But I don't want anybody else to have him either. If another woman tried to take T.J., I think I'd kill her!"

Being all for true love triumphing in the end, I was glad that the breakup had acted like a bucket of cold water flung in T.J.'s face. But as I knocked on Jolene and Bobette's door, I was feeling rather unsettled by the discovery that Lambie Dalton really was a wily little vixen in sheep's clothing.

I was admitted by a tousle-headed Bobette, still in her peach chenille bathrobe. "Jolene and I were just having breakfast."

I followed her into the small sitting room, where Jolene lounged in a pair of flannel pyjamas and matching robe decorated with chocolate cupcakes and other assorted pastries, intently watching a weight-loss infomercial while eating a beignet.

On the coffee table, two plates of the French doughnuts sprawled lasciviously beneath their blankets of powdered sugar.

"Bobette, we got to order us some of this stuff," she declared. "Look, see how it just sucks the fat right up? They call it 'liposuction in a jar'."

Jolene noticed me. "Oh, hey Claire. Have a beignet. We met some people last night who said Morning Call had the best ones. But then we heard no, Café du Monde. So, we ordered a bag of each."

"Which is which?" I asked. Café du Monde was my own personal preference, but I'd never turn down a Morning Call.

The girls looked at each other in consternation, then giggled. "Oops, we can't remember!" Merrily, Bobette twirled a forefinger at her temple in a cuckoo gesture.

"Oh, shoot! Now I expect we'll have to eat them all!" chortled Jolene.

Their good humor was infectious and welcome, after my intense session with Lambie. While I ate a beignet (Morning Call—I have a secret way of telling) I explained my errand.

"I just got one little question," said Jolene. "What's a coronet?"

"Well, it's a braided style that was considered to be the height of soignée in the thirties, then briefly revived in the late forties. But it never really caught on because it was a) very difficult for the average house-wife to do herself, and b) it took a woman who was already soignée to pull it off successfully."

"Uh-huh," said Jolene. "But what does it look like?"

"The best way I can describe it is as a braided crescent crown," I replied. "It's similar in shape to Charlotte's bridal headpiece, which is one of the reasons Marcel selected it. Coronet is a type of crown."

"Groovy!" Jolene struck a pose. "I keep telling you I'm a queen, Bobette. Real swan-yay."

"You mean real Swan-nee!" laughed her sister. "Braids are a type of pigtail, Jolene."

Like Lambie, Jolene and Bobette wondered if they got to keep their braids, post-wedding, and were delighted to find they did.

"But you only need to take one sample, Claire," Jolene told me. "Bobette and I were born with the exact same natural color."

"Now that's where you're wrong, Jolene. You're kind of a cinnamon tone, but Bobette's more nutmeggy."

Bobette hooted. "Hey, Jolene! Now we can call ourselves the Spice Girls!"

The two sisters immediately went into an entertaining impression of the singers, making it hard to reconcile that only yesterday, one of them had been ready to punch the living daylights out of her cousin Cecille.

Mission accomplished, they urged another beignet on me before I left. I accepted, but, messy as I knew it would be, wrapped it in a napkin to go. This job was taking much longer than I'd thought. I still had to get Cecille's hair, then deliver everything to Marcel before noon.

Fortunately, I caught Cecille just as she was going out.

Despite her previous evening of sauna and massage, she looked haggard, but elegant, in a black Valentino suit.

Of all the bridesmaids, she alone had the innate style to wear a coronet of braids the way it should be worn.

"I think the whole thing's ridiculous!" Cecille snapped after hearing me out. "But since I have nothing to say about it, just hurry and get it over with, please. I've got an appointment."

She stalked into the kitchenette and sat on a counter stool while I carefully sectioned her wealthy Southern matron pouff. "Don't worry, I'll put everything back just the way it was," I promised.

"Nobody can," Cecille stated flatly. She looked up at me with bleak eyes. "I'm not talking about the hair, of course."

"I'm sorry," I murmured. Not knowing what else to say, I changed the subject. "You know what, Cecille? In this light, I see your hair has kind of a minky brown underglow. This color reminds me of—" I could have bitten my tongue.

Cecille uttered a harsh little cackle. "Of Fawn Goldfeather's hair, you mean. Well, you're right. There's quite a touch of the tomahawk, so to speak, in my mother's bloodline. I just happen to be the only one in two generations to actually look the part."

She smiled painfully. "You'd think one Indian would be enough for any man, wouldn't you?"

We left together, but while Cecille went on to the elevator, I stopped in the hallway to fish the room key from my carryall. This shouldn't have taken more than a minute. However, the overhead lights were purposely dim for ambience, and my bag was big and deep with way too much stuff in it.

"What are you doing?"

Fawn Goldfeather's sudden appearance startled me so, I gasped and dropped the bag. Everything spilled out onto the floor.

"Fawn! You must've known I didn't hear you coming. Why sneak up on me like that?"

She didn't apologize. "Can I help it if I walk like an Indian?"

On swift, silent feet.

"We both know there's no correct answer to that question," I retorted, getting down on my knees. "But I'm running late. Maybe you could help me out here?"

"Why should I?" asked Fawn, but she deigned to join me on the carpet. She picked up the plastic bag containing Lambie's hair, then noticed the others.

"What's all this hair for? Hey, are you into voodoo?" Fawn peered at me with new interest.

"Not hardly. Jesus wouldn't like it." Then, feeling maybe I'd been too abrupt, I briefly explained the braids. "But why on earth did you immediately assume voodoo?" I asked, remembering just in time not to put the room key back into my bag.

Fawn rose from the floor. "Because I know its practitioners use hair for casting spells. To possess the hair of one's enemies is believed to exercise power over them." Dusting off her hands, she added, "Of course, the island peoples took that from the Indians."

Down Home Barbeque

December 20
The Manor Promenade

Barbeque
Rack of Lamb
Baby Back Ribs
Beef Ribs
Free Range Chicken
Potato Salad   Deviled Eggs   Boiled Peanuts

Desserts
Pecan Pie   Banana Pudding
Chocolate Coffee Cake
Homemade Butter Pecan Ice Cream

Sangria
Beer
Ice Tea

18

The Manor Promenade wrapped a Mississippi River view halfway around the exterior of the hotel's mezzanine level.

Retractable, mango-colored awnings and portable butane torch heaters made it an ideal venue for outdoor festivities in all but the most inclement weather conditions. Tonight, while crisp, was clear and dry, perfect for this informal occasion which allowed Foley and Charlotte to include everybody from their respective workplaces they weren't able to invite to the actual ceremony and reception.

Kitty, Charlotte and myself were circulating through the crowd with Leighton, Foley and Dan, helping to stroke the egos of important Signet Oil clients, and greeting the more junior members and staff of Blanchard, Smithson, Callant & Claiborne.

A large, festive group from the law firm was gathered in honor of Foley's impending marriage. Even Dobie had relaxed her guard dog demeanor for the event.

And there was mysterious Esmé Barnes, svelte in a heavy blue-grey sweater and matching ribbed wool leggings. Her iridescent hair, instead of being confined to its customary bun, dangled in a long braid down her back.

I reflected it was probably a good thing Marcel and Nectarine were previously obligated for the evening. Once Marcel met Esmé and saw her hair, I wasn't sure he could be trusted around that pigtail.

When we six encountered the vivacious group where Esmé stood chatting, I made it a point to watch her and Leighton and Kitty Blanchard very closely.

Leighton, with his thick shock of white hair and mustache, verged on a caricature of the powerful, successful Southern lawyer. He was a trifle too well-fed perhaps, but sleek, nonetheless.

It was difficult to envision this somewhat bombastic personage committing hanky-panky with Belinda Callant, as Kitty had implied; slightly less so to consider the possibility of a long-term liaison between him and Esmé.

And yet, Leighton had been married to Kitty, a classic Louisiana beauty of the type you see in old portraits, for nearly thirty years. There were no children, just the two of them and a household staff in the big, historical mansion out on River Road that had belonged to the Blanchards for centuries.

I wondered what the real story of their marriage was. Dan almost certainly knew. Something, however, cautioned me not to ask him about them. It was probably the only subject we never discussed.

All this was running through my mind while we were talking to Esmé and her friends. But either Kitty, Leighton and Esmé had knit their social act to seamless perfection, or there was simply no truth to the faint whispers.

Still, what of Kitty herself, taking quick little jabs at her husband during the lingerie shower? Was it just the Cha-Chas talking?

Or did Kitty have very good reasons for being so everlastingly wrapped up in her charity work? Did Leighton have good reasons of his own for conducting a discreet affair? What secret sadness cast that shadow over Esmé's narrow, lovely face?

Only one thing was certain—nobody ever knew what went on behind other people's closed doors.

I was glad when the rounds were over and Dan and I were free to break away from the Blanchards.

A sudden flurry of musical instruments tuning up announced that the band was about to begin their first set. And who could be more appropriate on this night of unity between the Swamp Daltons and the Society Daltons than Bubba Smoke and the Swamp Society? Foley had booked the Cajun group, who'd played at Dan's and my wedding, for obvious reasons.

Dan suggested a little stroll along the promenade. "You sure do look cute in that fuzzy thing, baby, but are you going to be warm enough?"

I convinced him that I would be quite snug in my cuddly twinset of yellow mohair, by demonstrating how the inner sweater's cowl collar converted into a hood.

Strictly to be polite, we accepted stemmed glasses of Sangria from a waiter who told us it had been concocted to Montaigne Duffosat's specifications. Dan took a cautious sip, then smiled. "Well, I know what I'm drinking tonight. Go ahead and try it, Claire."

He was right. But then, I should've known Montaigne was incapable of stirring up just any old ordinary batch of punch.

We sampled from long tables piled high with food Charlotte described as "Georgia on my behind." Every dish had been prepared by Riverside Manor's catering staff, using authentic Dalton family recipes.

The various meats sizzling on big gas grills were drenched in Emory's own special sauces. As far as he was concerned, there was absolutely no argument as to whether or not baptism by total immersion (in sauce) was necessary to obtain true Southern barbeque.

Imogene staunchly maintained no Swamp Dalton could even come close to achieving her supreme deviled eggs, but conceded Society Daltons were basically useless at boiled peanuts. That particular project was assigned to Huey and sons, but Kyle and Tucker John had deserted their posts early on.

Now Huey, wrapped in a big white apron, stood alone, tending the oil drum where the goobers were simmering in brine, looking cute and flushed and forlorn. Iris Henry, a reluctant divorcée from Blanchard, Smithson's research department, was finding him irresistible.

Fenton and Mamie claimed credit for the potato salad, pecan pie (made with dark Karo syrup only), hushpuppies and cracklin' cornbread.

The chocolate coffee cake recipe contributed by Cecille's mother Alicia, was just that—a rich, luscious chocolate cake with a texture both smooth and crunchy from adding strong brewed coffee and freshly ground beans to the batter.

Great-Uncle Purcell had jealously guarded his banana pudding and butter pecan ice cream recipes for fifty years, divulging them now solely because he was physically incapable of producing sufficient quantities to serve two hundred-plus guests.

This fact, however, did not prevent Purcell from having two of his ancient, hand-cranked ice cream makers FedExed to the hotel in time for the barbeque. He had loaded them with the necessary ingredients and was issuing loud challenges to any "real men" who wanted to test their strength at a deceptively simple chore.

"Guess you New Orleans boys just ain't got what it takes!" he'd taunt, as one by one, the local jocks went down in defeat.

Dan and Foley's opportunity didn't come until the end, when those cranks were virtually impossible to turn.

"Come on, Foley-pie! You can do it!" urged Charlotte, triggering a chorus of rowdy jesting from the onlookers.

I was pleased and proud when Dan was able to crank the handle three whole times, but Foley, red-faced and grunting, managed five complete turns before flexing a triumphant bicep, then collapsing.

"Ain't nothing like cranking ice cream to separate the men from the boys!" Purcell declared. "Now, let's just see what we got here."

With exaggerated ceremony, he opened the machine Foley had been working, and inserted a spoon. A loud cheer went up when he lifted it in the air to display solid ice cream.

"Ohh! That's a real good sign, Charlotte!" shrieked Bobette.

After such flagrant symbolism, Dan and I were both mightily relieved when his machine also proved to contain the finished product.

From that point, the party really started to heat up. Everybody ate, drank Sangria à la Duffosat, and danced to Bubba and the band wailing their way, Cajun style, through the Country Top Forty. I noticed Dobie was cutting loose with Huey Dalton, of all people! Tenderhearted, nurturing Iris Henry never had a chance with him against that dominatrix.

And Fawn Goldfeather, in another new leather jacket—plain black this time—didn't protest when someone jerked her into a line dance.

But best of all, Lambie and T.J. were dancing together. T.J. was looking down at the girl in his arms as if seeing her for the first time. Way to go, Lambie!

I was glad for Charlotte's sake that this joint venture between the relatives was turning out so well. Maybe now their silly feud would end forever.

The first hint of impending trouble occurred after Dan excused himself to visit the gents'. I was leaning back against the wrought iron railing, enjoying the antics of Jolene and Bobette with two young Blanchard, Smithson attorneys, when I became aware of Kyle Dalton's presence nearby.

The dark expression on his face warned me that Belinda Callant was somewhere about. Well, if he'd invited her, he was paying for it now because she and Reggie Worth were out on the floor, dancing slow and close.

Reflexively, I scanned around for Cecille, surprised not to see her hovering over Reggie as usual. Where was she when we really needed her to swoop down and pluck Reggie from Belinda's clutches? Kyle looked about ready to blow. I felt positive Belinda knew it, too.

Searching for Cecille, I plunged through the swaying bodies, momentarily delayed by Woody or Wes, who wanted to make it a *dans à trois*, to the extreme displeasure of his partner.

I finally located Cecille, two-stepping with a fairly attractive man I'd never seen before. She wasn't at all happy to be interrupted, but agreed to accompany me to a relatively quiet spot when I insisted it was important.

The unknown man followed us off the dance floor to a vacant bench along the railing, and Cecille did nothing to stop him.

"If you'll excuse us, this is private business," I said.

The man smiled pleasantly, causing his brown eyes to crinkle at the corners. "Cecille's private business *is* my business," he replied.

Cecille laughed at my confusion. "Claire Claiborne, meet Maumus Tulley. My attorney. Mo flew in today from Atlanta."

So that was the appointment she'd rushed off to keep after I collected her hair sample.

"Hello, Mr. Tulley. How nice you were able to make it in for the wedding," I fished.

Mo Tulley smiled and Cecille laughed again. "Oh, that was very subtle, Claire. But let's not beat around the bush, okay? Mo's here for the divorce, not the wedding."

Naturally I was curious as to what had been the last straw to break this particular camel's back. Cecille had already put up with so much from Reggie, I couldn't imagine why she'd just all of a sudden stop.

Unless somehow she'd gotten wind of Reggie's scheme for creating a little extra cash flow?

"Reggie doesn't know I'm in town yet," Mo cautioned me. "We don't want to put him on his guard until I've had time to figure out whether Cecille can afford to go through with a divorce."

"But Charlotte told me there was some fool-proof, booby-trapped prenuptial thing," I said to Cecille.

She nodded. "Mo and I rigged it like *The Last Crusade*, honey. Under ordinary circumstances, Reggie wouldn't have a prayer if we divorced. Ironically, the only way he'll get anything at all is if we're still married when I die. In that unlikely event, he'd inherit just about everything. Except now there's a complication. Tell her, Mo."

He looked at Cecille. "Are you sure you want to get into that right now?"

"Oh, for heaven's sake. Why not? The more people who gossip about it, the better. Just in case Reggie is tempted to become a widower when he gets the bad news."

What made the situation extraordinary, Mo explained, was the phenomenal appreciation of the art assets Reggie acquired for Cecille, technically acting as her employee, while concurrently being legally married to her.

"Reggie's success on Cecille's behalf will make it extremely difficult to justify and enforce the original agreement," Mo concluded. "With a halfway decent lawyer he could clean up. That's something neither of us could have anticipated four years ago."

Since it didn't sound like they'd yet discovered Reggie had been juggling art prices, I certainly wasn't going to be the one to suggest that line of investigation.

"Well, in view of what you've told me, you probably won't care, but I think you should know Reggie and Belinda are dancing plastered together like white on rice, and your cousin Kyle is on the verge of committing mayhem," I reported.

At the mention of Belinda's name, Cecille's face sharpened to that same old hawklike possessiveness I'd grown accustomed to seeing her display over Reggie.

"Oh, is that right?" she growled. "Well, if he thinks—" without bothering to finish, she stalked off in search of her errant spouse.

Mo gave an angry snort. "God! When I think of how hard I tried to keep Cecille from marrying him! But it was no use. Her mind was made up. 'Don't worry, Mo. I know I'm buying damaged merchandise. But I want him. Just fix it so he can't bleed me dry.'"

He shook his head angrily. "And now I seem to have failed to do even that."

Oh, my.

"How long have you been in love with her, Mr. Tulley— Mo?" I asked softly.

He didn't appear to resent my question. "Ever since high school. I never felt like I had a chance, she was so beautiful. And so very rich."

Unwilling to risk rejection as a lover, Mo Tulley had settled for the role of trusted friend and advisor to Cecille for years. Would he take the risk now, when it looked like he might have another chance?

Since Mo and Cecille had told me everything except what I really wanted to know, I just came right out and asked him why Cecille had suddenly taken a notion to pull the plug on Reggie.

As he understood it from Cecille, matters had come to a head since they'd arrived in New Orleans. One morning, she simply woke up and decided enough was enough, but how to get rid of Reggie as cheaply as possible? Surely catching him in the act of adultery would help win the courts to her side, she reasoned.

To this end, Cecille proceeded to set a trap for Reggie, telling him she had a massage appointment for seven o'clock, and would be back around eight-fifteen.

I stifled an exclamation. I'd personally overhead Reggie tell Fawn they could count on Cecille being gone until at least nine o'clock! Dan and I had seen her come into the pub at exactly eight-thirty, concluding they were playing it safe.

But what had actually happened sounded like a French farce.

For reasons unknown, Fawn failed to show up at Reggie's room until nearly eight o'clock, just as Cecille was stealthily entering. Instead of Cecille catching Reggie in a compromising position with Fawn, Fawn had caught Cecille in the act of attempting to entrap Reggie, though neither she nor Reggie recognized the episode for what it was.

Of course, the pair claimed they'd merely intended to discuss business.

Cecille had jumped the gun, and it backfired. However, having once made the decision to get out, she was determined to find a way. And so, Mo Tulley had been summoned to New Orleans.

Now I understood what Cecille was trying to accomplish.

What I didn't understand was why Reggie had lied to Fawn about how much time they'd have together before Cecille's return.

19

Well, who would believe it / here we are again
But something is different this time
We're just not the same / as we were way back then
We're together again for the first time . . .

What started off as a pity dance with Mo Tulley because Cecille failed to rejoin us and I didn't have the heart to abandon him, had turned into a pleasant interlude.

Mo was that rare animal, a man with a sense of rhythm and an ear for lyrical nuances, as well.

Long gone are the children / who hurt each other so
It's a man and a woman this time
Why did it take so long / for us to grow
Together again for the first time . . .

The song held special significance for Dan and me; we'd danced the first dance at our wedding reception to Bubba smoothly crooning those same poignant phrases that were now evidently speaking volumes to Mo regarding him and Cecille.

There's a first time for everything / even this
Getting together again
Two different people have shared their first kiss
And the difference is perfectly plain . . .

I wondered if Mo had ever kissed Cecille, other than in his wildest fantasies. If not, shame on them both. He was good looking, cultured and well-built. Cecille could certainly have done worse. And had, as a matter of fact.

Well, who could've guessed / life would take this turn
Or had it been planned all the time
How our separate roads / led us to return
Together again for the first time.

When the song ended, there was still no sign of Cecille. Mo declined my offer to help him find her, saying his body clock was still keeping Eastern time, and he would take a taxi to the Lakefront where he was staying with friends.

"She knows the number," he concluded. "I think I'll let her find me, for a change."

"Atta boy, Mo!" I approved.

Quickly, he bent and pecked my cheek. "Thanks for that, Claire. And the dance." With another of his special crinkly smiles and a wave, he melted from view.

"Just who the hell was that and where have you been?"

My husband's tone of voice was definitely irate. He caught hold of my arm just a bit more roughly than usual, and his eyes shot off tingling blue sparks of jealousy.

The music began again, and Dan gathered me tightly into his arms. "I ought to paddle your little behind, making me hunt all over the place for you like that," he complained.

I tilted my head back to look up at him. "Were you planning to use your bare hand, or what?" I inquired interestedly.

His gaze kindled again. "Hey, better be careful, little girl."

"Empty threats!" I scoffed.

"Oh, yeah?" he retorted.

Suddenly, Dan spun me out, then jerked me back hard against him. For the next few bars of "Lovesick," he outlined, in explicit detail, the fate that awaited me in our room.

This information left me so limp and breathless, a restorative drop of Sangria was definitely called for. When sufficiently recovered, I apprised Dan that Cecille had sent for Maumus Tulley, and why.

"It's a damn shame, but I think she's doing the right thing," was Dan's response.

"*If* she actually goes through with it," I said. "I have my doubts. One minute, Cecille's whistling for good old reliable Mo, who instantly drops everything—at Christmas time, mind you—and comes galloping in from Atlanta on the redeye to plot her divorce.

"The very next minute, upon hearing that Belinda and Reggie are dirty dancing, she's charging off to break it up. Explain that," I challenged.

Dan nodded. "Okay, try this. Remember when I said I thought Reggie might have a hidden agenda of his own that had nothing to do with Fawn?"

"Yes. In the pub. And we never got around to discussing what you meant."

"Well, don't you see, Claire? Everything Mo told you confirms it. Cecille set a trap for Reggie, hoping to catch him in the act of adultery with Fawn. The trap failed, but only because Fawn showed up so late.

"What we didn't know until now was that Reggie deliberately gave Fawn the wrong time frame. Which means Reggie planned for Cecille to find him in bed with Fawn, because he wanted to force the issue. Never realizing Cecille had the same thing in mind herself."

"How ironic they'd be so totally in synch on this," I said. "But what's really odd is Reggie's apparent willingness to sacrifice Fawn to gain his freedom, after he's already invested so much in their relationship, if you can call it that."

Dan agreed but added, "Odder still, seems like Cecille built her entrapment scheme entirely around Fawn and nobody else. Because when Belinda looked like having snared Reggie on the rebound, Cecille immediately rushed to put out the fire, abandoning faithful Mo in midstream."

"So what are you saying, Dan? That Cecille was all set to hand Reggie down to Fawn Goldfeather, but not Belinda Callant? That's way too deep for me."

"It makes perfect sense, baby," Dan insisted. "Look. Cecille is all about control—of her marriage, and especially her money. She tolerated Reggie's little ways until she was finally good and ready to call the whole thing off.

"Only, instead of simply putting her cards on the table, she decided the marriage was going to end precisely how and when she wanted— even to the point of who Reggie would be with when it happened."

I put in, "And Mo did say Cecille wrote that particular scenario to try to put Reggie in the worst possible light if they ended up having to go to court."

"And then what happened?" Dan asked rhetorically.

"Her timing is off by a mile and Reggie winds up in the arms of rich, influential Belinda Callant, instead of an unknown wannabe artist."

I mulled that over. Yes, upon further reflection, Dan's take did make sense. It was one thing to discard a husband to a woman you considered your social inferior, rather like donating a bag of old clothes to charity; quite another for a successful woman who was your peer to go after that same husband without even knowing you were planning to dump him.

Dan was right. If somebody like Belinda considered Reggie Worth a trophy, Cecille could not afford to let her win him.

And what of poor Maumus Tulley, waiting by the phone for his instructions? Would Cecille even remember he was in town?

"I'll lay you odds," Dan offered, "once Cecille is back in the saddle, she'll still go through with the divorce. Meanwhile, I expect she'll put Mo to work on changing her will."

I'd forgotten that Reggie's reward for staying married to Cecille and outliving her would have been to inherit the whole pile. Obviously, though he'd concluded it wasn't worth sticking around for on the off-chance, and had been prepared to kiss it all goodbye. Dan thought for Belinda, but my feeling was Reggie had certainly circled the block too many times to succumb to Belinda's poisonous charms.

"Dan Louis, could we not talk about this anymore? It's so depressing."

"You're right, darlin'. How about another dance or two? And then—" he waggled his eyebrows at me meaningfully.

Instantly, the heaviness lifted and I laughed as he led me back onto the jammed dance floor.

Bubba Smoke had strapped on his vintage accordion, and the band was pelting out intense Zydeco. This is not easy music to dance to, but once you catch the groove, the energy is comparable to that of *Riverdance*.

The tempo and volume increased. It felt like everybody at the party was spinning, whirling and stomping as one. I saw Sam Stormshadow swing Montaigne Duffosat completely off her feet. Their faces were glowing.

As if by a giant magnet, Dan and I were gradually drawn to the very center of the floor, where Belinda Callant was dancing first with Kyle, then with Reggie, back and forth, back and forth, flinging her long, bright hair, taunting, teasing, seducing.

Both men were sweating profusely, scarcely seeming to be aware of each other, their eyes locked with burning lust upon Belinda, who swayed between them like a beautiful cobra.

She virtually had them hypnotized, and I was astonished that hardly anybody else appeared to grasp there was something abnormal going on here.

Fawn Goldfeather was paying attention, though. She'd attained a vantage point by climbing onto the wide border of a large, rectangular cement planter filled with ivy. From this distance, her expression was undecipherable.

Sam and Montaigne were twirling in our direction, until Sam noticed Belinda. With a look of disgust, he spun his partner away.

Through the swirling clutch of gyrating bodies, I glimpsed Cecille, whose gaunt face was pinched with fury.

Leighton and Kitty Blanchard danced over to us before they realized what they'd strayed into. By then, however, there was no escape.

"Uh-oh!" Dan muttered into my ear.

Belinda spotted Leighton and, in a flash, slithered between him and Kitty. Throwing her arms around his neck, she planted a big, wet kiss beneath his white mustache.

"Ohhh! Leighton, honey!" she cried. "I missed you sooo much, my big old daddy bear!"

Leighton flushed scarlet and vainly attempted to extricate himself from her epoxy-like embrace. "Why-uh—hello, there, Belinda," he stammered. "Yes, it's been a long time, hasn't it?"

Belinda gazed at him soulfully. "A mighty long time, Leighton. Too long."

I didn't dare trust myself to look at Kitty, who hadn't spoken a word. Instead, I glanced over at Kyle and Reggie. They were emerging from their trances in some confusion.

Leighton Blanchard was not the head of one of the South's biggest law firms for nothing. Recovering his aplomb, he pulled out his handkerchief and wiped his lips. "So nice to have seen you again," he said stuffily, emphasizing the past tense.

Dan thought it was time to step in. "Oh, there you are Leighton!" he exclaimed loudly. "Claire and I were wondering where you and Kitty had gotten to."

Kitty looked at me. Her dark eyes gave nothing away.

At the sound of Dan's voice, Belinda turned with a glad little cry. "Dan! I've been saving a real special dance just for you. Claire doesn't mind, do you, Claire?"

Confirming that Leighton and Kitty had availed themselves of the opportunity to flee the scene, Dan answered for me. "In fact she would mind, seeing as how I promised her the next three dances. And I always keep my promises to Claire."

He aimed a thumb back toward Kyle and Reggie. "Besides, I notice you've already got two other partners waiting for you over there."

Belinda pouted. "The more, the merrier, darling."

What I saw was more trouble headed our way, and frantically tried to wave Charlotte and Foley into a detour, but they mistook my signals for a welcome, and kept coming.

When Belinda noticed the bridal pair, her eyes glistened with an unholy light.

"Here *comes* the groom!" she trilled gaily. "Oh, Charlotte. You are one lucky girl, indeed. Only I don't know whether you're going to be enough woman for him, honey. My Foley is definitely all man and a yard long!" She giggled. "Or damn close."

Foley and Charlotte stared at Belinda, unable to believe their ears. She'd been talking nonstop at warp speed. I all at once recalled the prescription Sam filled for her at Walgreen's. Could some drug or other account for her outrageous behavior?

Before Foley was able to get Charlotte away, Belinda said, "Maybe we ought to have us a girl talk? I could give you some valuable pointers on the special things he likes."

She gave Charlotte a rude little push and moved closer to Foley. "Do you remember when we were the only two passengers in First Class on that flight to London?"

Foley winced with anger and distaste at the memory she'd conjured up.

Suddenly, Charlotte spoke. "Shut your vile mouth and get out of here, you filthy slut!"

Dan's eyes popped. He'd never heard Charlotte talk like that. Nor, very often, had I.

Belinda flashed dangerously. "How dare you order me around!" she snarled, and gave Charlotte another of those irritating little pushes.

That did it.

Next thing we knew, Belinda and Charlotte were kicking, slapping, and yanking each other's hair.

Shouts of, "Cat fight! Cat fight!" began to draw the crowd into a circle around the two women.

Bubba Smoke and company launched into a stirring rendition of "The Battle of New Orleans."

Not to be outdone, Kyle and Reggie began trading punches, inspiring several other self-designated studs to do the same.

Foley and Dan attempted to separate Charlotte and Belinda, but the bad blood was running too hot.

"Shit!" yelled Dan, taking a flying high-heeled kick in his right shin.

The music grew louder and wilder, as the fight became more vicious. Belinda now sported a bloody scratch on her neck, and one of Charlotte's sleeves was gone.

Their struggle carried them forward, cleaving a path through the spectators. Gaining an advantage, Belinda forced Charlotte back against the iron railing, but in a surprise move, Charlotte slid her legs between Belinda's then heaved upwards with all her strength. This maneuver threw the other woman off balance, and sent her flying over the railing into the oily water below.

Unfortunately, the same momentum caused Charlotte's heels to flip over her head, and the first splash was quickly echoed by a second.

Pausing only long enough to shed his coat and shoes, Foley plunged over the railing.

A sudden dark shadow streaked past us. It, too, dove into the water.

"Was that who I think it was?" I asked Dan.

He grinned. "Right on!"

Imogene, Daphne, Emory, Lambie and Tucker John had managed to push their way to the forefront. Now, they hurried to peer over the edge.

"My baby!" Daphne wailed.

Emory called down anxiously, "Foley! Have you got her yet, son?"

There was no answer.

T.J. administered comforting pats to Lambie's back, while she wrung doll-sized hands.

Imogene stood slightly apart in icy, affronted silence.

Riverside Manor's security had activated high beam lights set into the stone below the guardrails. There were four narrow little ladders attached at intervals to the bottom of the Promenade. For just such an occasion as this, no doubt. One security guard called out directions on a bullhorn.

A storm of applause greeted Foley's dripping head as it emerged into view. Security rushed to help him lift Charlotte over the rails and down onto the deck.

They soon had her wrapped in blankets, while the family fussed around. I knelt beside her and she clung to my hand.

"I feel like such an idiot!" she quavered weakly. "I'm sorry, everybody."

Foley stroked her clammy forehead. "That was some slick Wrestling Queen move, baby. Did I ever tell you you're my hero?"

Charlotte smiled faintly. "Don't make me laugh, Foley-pie," she whispered. "I'm liable to start spewing up a bunch of Mississippi slime."

This galvanized Imogene into action. "Has somebody called an ambulance?" she demanded imperiously. "We've got to get Charlotte's stomach pumped out immediately! God knows what she might have swallowed!"

"Right away, ma'am," piped one of the security people. "Do you want Touro or Baptist?"

Amazed anyone would even have to ask, she retorted crisply, "Why, Baptist of course."

Another cheer heralded the second rescuer, hauling the sodden Belinda. After delivering her to the blanket team, he squished across the Promenade toward us. Beads of water gleamed like tiny diamonds upon his tight, black curls. Amusement, disappointment and concern vied for prominence upon the dark, handsome face.

He sat down on the floor next to Charlotte and Foley in silence. When at last he spoke, his voice was deep and rich with an Island lilt. "Well, my brother and sister. I do believe the Lord Jesus would be appreciating an apology from you right about now."

The other Daltons present looked embarrassed and mystified at this unexpected turn of events.

Catching Dan's eye, Imogene asked, "Are you by any chance acquainted with that extremely large black gentlemen who appears to be engaged in some sort of ritual with Charlotte and Foley?"

Dan smiled. "Why yes, ma'am," he answered blandly. "That's the Reverend Percival St. Dennis. He'll be performing your granddaughter's wedding ceremony."

Imogene recovered her voice. "I . . . see. Well, I suppose we must count ourselves fortunate to have someone of our own denomination willing to step in at the last minute . . . "

"*Kerashona nofronda kehalo!*" Saint boomed suddenly, startling us all.

"I don't know, Aunt Imogene," said Tucker John doubtfully. "That sure doesn't sound like any Baptist I ever heard!"

20

One of the reasons that some of us in the South are still speaking to each other, and certain politicians keep getting reelected, is our unwritten code of social penance: The bigger the *faux pas*, the grander the compensatory *beau geste* required.

This extremely simplistic—but highly demanding—*comme il faute* has the distinct advantage of being absolutely clear, even without a rudimentary grasp of French. If you wish to make amends, it must be done in such a way that everyone involved understands what is being accomplished, yet on such a grand scale that no one is made to feel uncomfortable at your humility.

Whatever her motives, Belinda Callant had instigated this procedure.

Members of the wedding party awoke to find ivory envelopes had been slipped beneath their doors. Each contained a thick, matching formal note of charming apology, written in Belinda's own hand, for her role in last evening's melodrama, and a VIP invitation to tonight's reception for Sam Stormshadow at the Thorton Gallery, followed by dinner at Antoine's.

Yet, Belinda had done many far worse things and never before sought to atone. The question was, why this time?

The only people asking it, however, were Foley, Charlotte, Dan and myself, since nobody else concerned—save Pearl and Topaz—knew her history. Therefore, it was highly unlikely any of them would pass up that enticing offer of dinner at Antoine's—especially not Jolene and Bobette.

Foley, of course, had graciously—without a word of reproach—declined for both himself and Charlotte from her hospital room at Southern Baptist, not that she could've eaten anything after having endured a stomach wash, poor darling.

And, not that Belinda seriously expected (much less wanted) them to come, but the gesture, as mentioned previously, was mandatory.

So it was that Saturday night found Dan and me all dressed up at the Thorton Gallery, instead of hurling our sweat-suited selves into the mall madness of last-minute Christmas shopping like we planned.

Somehow, we'd felt obliged to chaperone this absurd little field trip, if for no other reason than to supervise the aunts, whose indecently speedy RSVP of acceptance was as suspect as Belinda's own extension of what appeared to be an olive branch.

As it happened, not everyone had come along on the junket. Numbered among the missing was Huey Dalton, whom nobody had seen hide nor hair of since last night. Perhaps Dobie had dragged him off by the scruff of his neck to her cave. Unsurprisingly, Daphne, Emory and Imogene were absent; also Stafford, Alicia, Woody and Wes.

That left ourselves, Pearl, Topaz, Jolene, Bobette, Fenton, Mamie, Tucker John, Lambie, Reggie and Cecille, with Kyle and Fawn bringing up the rear as jokers wild.

Outside the Thorton's Royal Street entrance, two officious young persons checked our group's invitations against their master list before allowing us beyond the veil to rub shoulders with New Orleans' arterati.

Once inside, we were greeted by the shrill wail of wooden flutes, accompanied by the monotonous thump of a tom-tom. Mingled fragrances of birch and piñon incense hung in the rather chilly air.

Huge screens blocked off immediate access to the gallery, creating a kind of anteroom where three portable bars had been set up. Waiters circulated among the crowd, bearing large silver trays of esoteric

Southwestern hors d'oeuvres. The chunks of grilled chicken and sirloin marinated in tequila, lime and jalapeños, and roasted corn patties with chipolete salsa tasted marvelously unique.

The event had been orchestrated to begin at a bar, then subsequently flow into a reception line before passing through to the exhibit.

Beneath a banner proclaiming "The Beautiful Woman of Blood and Roses—An Obsession," stood Belinda, an Hermés scarf concealing the gouge on her throat inflicted by Charlotte, evidently suffering no ill effects whatever from the quart or so of river sludge she'd ingested. This despite her adamant refusal of the stomach pump. Dan speculated maybe because the stuff had felt right at home after she swallowed it.

Next to her, looking like he'd rather be anywhere else in the universe, a glum Sam Stormshadow mechanically greeted the guests. Occasionally, Belinda tossed him an impatient, questioning glance, as if finally sensing he was no longer the same man she'd left Santa Fe with.

Montaigne was nowhere in sight.

Kyle Dalton, strung tighter than a Cajun fiddle, had managed to press ahead of several people in line. When he reached Belinda, he seized her hand possessively, and leaned forward to speak urgently into her ear.

Whatever Kyle said caused Belinda's airy, mocking laughter to pop and fizz above the noise like champagne over the rim of a goblet. "Don't be ridiculous, darling!" she chided. "You better run along now and see the art."

Belinda reached past him to shake hands with the next person, and Kyle swung blindly around, not quite seeming to realize where he was. His cinnamon eyes were like two burnt holes in the pale Dalton face.

It took him a few seconds to get his bearings, then he lurched behind the screen barrier guarding the display. Sam observed his departure with pity.

Dan and I hung back to keep an eye on Pearl and Topaz until they were safely past Belinda and inside the exhibit room. That's how we happened to witness the encounter between Belinda and T.J. and Lambie.

Belinda took a long, slow look at Tucker John, and behaved as if she'd never seen him before. "Well, now. You've got to be Kyle Dalton's little brother, don't you?"

T.J. admitted it, then attempted to introduce Lambie, but Belinda continued to speak only to him. "Maybe you can help me out with some ...genetic research, baby brother." She moved closer to him. "You see, I'm very interested in finding out whether certain ... traits ... run in your family."

Sam, realizing her direct hit had temporarily rendered T.J. incapacitated, came to the rescue. "Belinda, there's still a lot of people waiting," he pointed out.

The couple moved on. T.J. looked dazed, outraged, and yes, aroused, all at once. Lambie's face was blank as an ivory figurine's.

"Claire!" Dan said suddenly. "Where did Pearl and Topaz go?"

A large number of guests were now bypassing the reception line and going straight through to the exhibit. Possibly the aunts joined them, I suggested.

He was unconvinced. "I wouldn't be surprised if those two characters figured out we were keeping tabs on them and decided to give us the slip!" Dan laughed. "Anyway, let's go ahead and check to see if they are back there. I feel accountable to Foley."

We hurried behind the screens into the main room, not in the least prepared, despite Sam Stormshadow's warning, for what we were about to behold.

The large space was completely dark, except for the illuminated statues and paintings. Beneath various colored spotlights beaming down, or lit from below, the Beautiful Woman of Blood and Roses with Belinda's face performed her grotesque, profane rituals of self-mutilation.

Though there were many people about, the conversation was subdued to an intense hum. Prospective buyers clustered around the sculptures, consulting their programs. In the eerie light, faces were distorted and decadent; eyes glittered with unspeakable thoughts as they gazed upon the images of a woman transported with the worship of erotic pain.

What we didn't realize, until closer inspection, was that the weapons were actual silver and turquoise daggers, knives, swords, spears, large rusty nails, arrows and razors, each of which slid into and out of its very own, custom-carved wound. My question about whether Sam had ever employed darts was answered when we rounded a corner where loomed a statue that had one plunged so deeply into each nipple, only the feathered shafts were showing.

Dan felt me shudder, and put an arm around my waist. "Welcome to hell's finest museum," he murmured.

Continuing the tour, we saw Fawn Goldfeather gaping up at the giant canvas from which the posters had been reproduced. Farther along, Kyle Dalton wandered stunned among the objects, while Reggie and Cecille made a brisk, professional circuit of the display as they must have done at other shows so many times before.

But of Pearl and Topaz, there was no sign.

Bobette's voice erupted into the oppressive atmosphere like a breath of fresh air. "Well, now I know why they call it the Thorton Gallery!" she declared. "It looks like old Billy Bob cut loose in here with his slingblade!"

An expensively dressed woman glared at Bobette, scandalized. "Shush!" she commanded.

Jolene bounced up to defend her sister. "Hey! Why can't she talk if she wants to? We aren't in church or a library or anything."

"But you are in the presence of Art," snapped the woman.

"Oh, no! I know Art and that ain't him!" Fenton called across from where he and Mamie, in appalled disbelief, contemplated the woman straddling a large barrel cactus, earning a communal, "SSSH!"

Mamie had donned the cats-eye glasses hanging from a gold lavalier around her neck, apparently to make sure she wasn't hallucinating, when Jolene and Bobette joined their parents. Solemnly, the sisters scrutinized the cactus- impaled woman, then broke into horrified giggles and whispers.

Mamie planted a fist on each printed silk hip and treated her daughters to a cats-eyed glare. "If you two don't hush up that trash this minute, I'm going to march you straight to the bathroom and wash out your sanctified mouths with soap!" she threatened.

Jolene and Bobette subsided with demure, "Yes, Mammas," but continued to elbow each other in the ribs.

"Come on, Claire. We still need to find Foley's aunts," Dan reminded me.

I went reluctantly, not liking to miss whatever other nuggets Jolene and Bobette might deliver to further outrage that pretentious audience.

On the way out, we passed Lambie and T.J., sitting on a bench. "But you heard the whole thing, Lambie! You know it was her! I didn't do anything!" T.J. was protesting strenuously, too dense to realize that was exactly what Lambie was so mad about. He hadn't done anything to stop Belinda from making a pass at him.

21

Ascertaining that Pearl and Topaz were nowhere in the Thorton Gallery, nor in any of the nearby small jewelry shops that might've captured their attention, Dan and I set off for Rue St. Louis, just in case they'd already gone on to Antoine's in order to lay some kind of trap for Belinda.

At the restaurant, however, there was no sign of the aunts. We were informed that Mrs. Callant had reserved the 1840 Room (named for the year Antoine's was founded) for her party at ten o'clock, which left us with around an hour to kill.

Believe it or not, when one has lived in New Orleans for any length of time, it is possible to grow jaded to the charms of this unique city. As an antidote, Dan and I occasionally like to play tourist, just to get a fresh perspective. The problem is, we rarely have time to do so.

Now, presented with an unexpected opportunity, we voted to take Lambie's suggestion and ride the red Riverfront Streetcar, something we had never done. Before departing, Dan persuaded the bartender to make us a couple of Antoine's famous French 75 cocktails to go. The ingredients are gin, lemon juice, syrup and champagne, sort of an adult Sno-Cone and therefore perfect for a nighttime adventure.

We walked from St. Louis to Toulouse and down to the old Jax Brewery. Since we were already a little past midpoint on the line, we climbed aboard a car going toward Esplanade, at the far end of the French Quarter, planning on riding back to Toulouse. The rest of the route—from Toulouse to Canal Street—would have to wait.

Our conductor clanged his bell and we were off, jostling down tracks between the French Quarter on one side, and the Mississippi River on the other. At that hour, and from that vantage point, those familiar sights and sounds took on an entirely different aspect.

Gusts of music and laughter were carried by the breeze from brightly-lit excursion and gambling boats out on the water. Delicious aromas wafted from restaurants in the French Market, which looked foreign and mysterious.

When the car stopped at Ursulines on our way back, we were astonished to see Pearl and Topaz among the embarking passengers. Both were carrying bulging shopping bags from Aunt Sally's Praline Shop. The sisters looked equally surprised to see us and, I thought, a tad furtive. But maybe that was just my imagination.

Dan greeted them with a smile. "What have you ladies been up to?" he inquired casually.

"Oh, Pearl here got a sudden yen for pralines!" boomed Topaz, as they took the seat opposite. "Right, Pearlie? And of course it had to be Aunt Sally's or nothing at all."

"Looks like you stocked up for some time to come," I remarked. All four bags were crammed with boxes of pralines, plus copious handfuls of individually wrapped pieces of the confection, convenient for snacking.

Pearl clutched the handles of her bags more firmly. "They will keep very well in the freezer," she chirped. "Who knows when we will return to the Crescent City? Sister and I both have such a sweet tooth."

Topaz then asked about Sam's exhibit. Upon hearing our (edited) report, she declared herelf delighted that she and Pearl had opted for the praline expedition instead. "You can call me an old reactionary, but seems like the nastier it is, the quicker people will jump and defend it as art," Topaz sniffed.

"Oh my, yes!" Pearl agreed. "So much filth is foisted upon the public beneath the banner of free expression."

"Sam didn't intend to create filth," I told her, "much less have it applauded, as has happened. At this juncture, he wishes the whole thing had been destroyed by an earthquake at the Los Angeles show."

"I thought the boy looked most unhappy tonight," Pearl said. "Didn't you, Sister?"

Topaz pursed her lips. "Anybody who spends much time around that trollop is bound to look unhappy. Remember how miserable Foley was?"

"Indeed I do!" cried Pearl. "Oh, at first it seemed like such a good match. She was from a very fine old family, you know, the Hartleys of Lafayette. Orphaned at only seventeen, and left an heiress. So beautiful, too. Foley was simply head over heels. You remember, Dan. But then, we started noticing certain . . . ah . . . things. Dear Opal was worried but Foley just wouldn't listen."

She sighed. "Of course, none of us ever imagined it would turn out quite so dreadfully."

"Nonsense, Pearl!" Topaz reproved. "After all, Foley is going to marry his wonderful Charlotte in a few short days."

Pearl dabbed at her eyes with an old-fashioned lace hanky she magically produced from somewhere on her person. "He told us that Charlotte is the love of his life. Nothing must be allowed to spoil this wedding for them."

"Seems to me," Dan observed, "if last night's scuffle didn't do it, nothing will."

"Of course it won't," Topaz said stoutly. "After Charlotte's safety, my only concern was that Belinda wouldn't lose our opal ring in the water. It was the first thing I checked when that amazing Reverend St. Dennis hauled her in."

"Even in her weakened condition, she laughed at us about that," Pearl quavered indignantly. "Said she'd had the ring sized directly on her finger so it could never come off accidentally."

Dan said frankly, "As long as we're on the subject, there's something I don't understand. Since you feel like you do about Belinda, why did you accept her invitation to dinner tonight?"

Topaz looked at him like he didn't have good sense. "My dear young man, if nothing else, she did the right thing for once. We felt duty-bound to respond in kind." Grinning impishly, she added, "Besides, who in their right mind would turn down dinner at Antoine's."

"And there might not be another such auspicious occasion to present our proposition—" Pearl broke off at Topaz's fierce headshake.

"Toulouse Street. Tooooou-loouse!" announced the driver.

"Here's our stop," Dan said. "Let me help you with those bags."

"Thank you very kindly, but we're not invalids," snapped Topaz. "You and Claire go along, we're right behind you."

Dan slipped his hand around my forearm and we walked the short distance to Antoine's in the pleasant afterglow of our French 75s. Pearl and Topaz trotted briskly behind, the Aunt Sally's shopping bags bumping noisily against their bodies with every step.

Our arrival at the restaurant coincided with that of Reggie and Cecille. Things looked pretty much back to normal there, no matter Dan had bet she still planned to go through with the divorce.

Poor Mo Tulley.

Once inside, a solicitous maitre d' attempted to divest the aunts of their praline supply, without success. Giving it up, he escorted us to the elegant 1840 Room, where Belinda presided at the head of a long table laid for sixteen, with a noticeably cheerier Sam at her right. A busboy was squeezing in an extra place setting.

"I asked Montaigne to join us since she did such a good job on the reception," Belinda explained patronizingly. "Won't it be nice to get waited on yourself for a change?" she added to Montaigne.

Montaigne's eyes flickered briefly, but she merely smiled and said, "Thank you, Mrs. Callant."

"Oh, call me Belinda. Everyone else does."

Another of those smiles was all Montaigne permitted herself as she took the chair at Sam's right. This move thwarted Fawn Goldfeather, who had been maneuvering for that spot, probably because it was the closest available to Belinda. Unless she'd developed a sudden crush on Sam.

With poor grace, Fawn plopped down beside Montaigne. But she and Sam were so discreetly absorbed in each other, neither of them acknowledged Fawn's presence. Miffed, Fawn turned away and snatched up a menu.

Belinda didn't much seem to care who sat where, except for putting Reggie on her left and consigning Kyle down to the foot of the table, thereby ensuring he'd have a clear view for drooling over her all night, but so far away he couldn't touch her.

The rest of us were left to sort ourselves out among the remaining places. Dan hooked the two chairs next to Cecille for us.

When everybody was more or less settled in, Belinda tapped on her water glass with a knife handle for silence. The black opal glittered. "I want to thank you all for doing me the honor of coming tonight," she told us charmingly.

"It means a great deal to Sam and myself to know we're among friends, especially when there's such a wonderful announcement to make."

Montaigne lobbed a startled glance at Sam that plainly demanded exactly what kind of announcement Belinda intended to make? Sam's confused expression clearly indicated he had no idea.

Belinda continued. "As of tonight, practically every piece of sculpture, and most of the paintings, have been spoken for. Our New Orleans show has been far more successful than we ever dreamed!"

This was greeted with polite applause, and Sam's visible relief. Perhaps he'd been afraid the unpredictable Belinda had taken it into her head to say they were getting married.

Personally, I felt chilled at the revelation there were so many people willing and able to spend multiple thousands of dollars for those pieces.

What's more, the statues were life-sized—some even bigger—not small obscenities for secret delectation to be easily swept out of sight into a drawer. Where on earth could anybody display such an object?

The bedroom, of course.

Although if I were single and some guy who owned a *Beautiful Woman* managed to lure me that far into his den, the minute I laid eyes on the thing I'd disappear so fast he'd wonder if I was ever really there in the first place.

At least it was good news for Sam. The sooner the *Blood and Roses* inventory was disposed of, the sooner he'd be done with Belinda.

But Belinda hadn't finished her speech. "Sam doesn't know this yet, but tonight there was a ferocious bidding war between two gentlemen over *Woman #1*, which reached six figures!"

There was another dutiful spatter of clapping. Except for Reggie and Cecille, we were way out of our depth.

"But the very best part of all," Belinda continued, looking exalted, is that the loser in that contest wants Sam to create an almost identical *Woman*—a sister, we'll call her, to *Woman #1*—for a price equal to his top bid for the original.

"And—I have accepted his check for the deposit! Isn't that fabulous news, everybody?"

Sam never raised his head to acknowledge the crackle of applause. His anguished eyes remained fixed upon the charger in front of him, as if it contained the head of John the Baptist.

Dan whispered, "You know which statue that is, don't you, darlin'?"

I nodded. *Woman #1* was the figure Sam had seen in the Los Angeles museum that had shocked him into total revulsion for his own work.

And for the model, as well.

Now, in cosmic irony, one had committed him to producing a clone of the other, just when he thought he was almost free of them both.

Dinner At Antoine's

Hosted by Belinda Callant

Hors d'oeuvres
Huitres en Coquille à La Rockefeller
Avocat Crevettes Garibaldi   Canapé Rothschild

Salade
Fonds d'Artichauts Bayard

Entrées
Filet de Truite Meunière   Pompano en Papillote
Crabes Mous Grilles   Pigeonneaux Paradis
Tips de Filet en Brochette Médicis

Legumes
Pommes de Terre Soufflées   Epinards Sauce Crème

Desserts
Cerises Jubilée   Crêpes Suzette
Omelette Alaska Antoine

22

The rest of the evening passed in a blur of Antoine's finest, many of the same dishes they'd been serving for over a hundred and fifty years.

Dan and I did our fair share of the eating. Except for Montaigne's Sangria, a deviled egg and some potato salad, topped with a handful of boiled peanuts, we'd missed out on last night's barbeque, thanks to that impromptu water ballet performed by the past and future Mrs. Callants.

Looking back, I realize that this dinner was the catalyst in a murderer's decision to kill. At the time, however, I was too caught up in the delicious food and drink, and the warm, deliberate pressure of my husband's thigh against mine, to bother with much else.

Even now, all I can recall are vague impressions. Of Bobette and Jolene, giggling over their second helpings of everything . . . Cecille, fully in control of herself, contributing intelligent (I supposed) comments to Belinda and Reggie's art talk . . . Sam Stormshadow, allowing a waiter to fill his glass for the third time . . . Montaigne's sleepy, noncommittal smile . . . Fawn's unsuccessful efforts to hold Belinda's or Sam's attention . . . Lambie, still making Tucker John pay . . . Belinda, catching T.J.'s straying gaze in her velvet web . . . Kyle Dalton, drinking too much, eating too little, never taking his dark, burning eyes off the woman opposite him.

And through it all, beautiful Belinda herself, laughing, flirting, twirling the flowing ends of the Hermés scarf like a tassel tosser, reveling in her power over so many men at once, indifferent to any suffering she might be causing.

When the waiters judged us to be properly stuffed, they came to clear away and receive our orders for coffee and liqueurs. Dessert had already been decided upon—enough Cherries Jubilee, Baked Alaska and Crepes Suzette for all at the table to taste some of each. Almost everybody took advantage of the break to get up and stretch, or visit the restrooms. I opted for the latter.

When I came out of the stall, Belinda was sitting at the dressing table, touching up her face, listening with apparent interest to Fawn's eager pitch.

"Yes, Reggie Worth's very high on your work," she told Fawn. "I promised him I'd look at your portfolio and I will. There's just been so little time, you know."

"Oh, that's all right, Belinda! I totally understand," Fawn lied brightly.

Belinda backcombed the long lock of hair calculated to dip over one eye. "Now let's see," she mused, "when can we do this . . . ?"

I left them coordinating their schedules. Well, at least Fawn was finally going to get what she wanted.

Back in the 1840 Room, all the men except Kyle and Sam were gently puffing on cigars.

Dan pulled me down beside him. "Hey, baby. I missed you," he said.

"Can I have a puff?" I asked, reaching for his cigar.

He pulled it back. "Now, darlin'. You know what happens to me when I watch you do that."

"Of course. Why else do you think I do it?"

"In that case." He passed the cigar to me, and I made the most of it. I really had him going good when a sudden crash shattered the mood.

Kyle, who'd been leaning his chair back on two legs, had taken a hard spill. Unfortunately for him, Belinda happened to return at just that moment.

When she saw Kyle lying in a drunken heap, Belinda bent over him in mock sympathy, her long hair swinging across his face. "Oh, you poor baby! I think we'll put you in a taxi, honey, and send you home. We don't want you to hurt yourself."

Kyle growled something incoherent, then reached up and seized a fistful of the dangling hair. He began to pull.

At first, Belinda laughed, but when he wouldn't let go, she became alarmed.

"You idiot!" she shrieked. "That hurts!"

"Good!" Kyle wheezed thickly. "Want it to hurt."

It took T.J., Fenton and a waiter to force Kyle to loosen his grip of steel on Belinda's hair.

"Come on, Kyle," T.J. urged. "Lambie and I will take you back. Okay?"

"Lambie? Where's Lambie?" Kyle moaned.

"Here I am, Kyle," she said calmly. "Listen, we'll have dessert together back at the hotel. Just the three of us. How's that sound?"

"You're so sweet, Lambie," sobbed Kyle. "Not like Darby. And not like"—he shot a black look at Belinda—"her. You're a damn lucky sonofabitch, T.J., you know that?" Kyle inquired as his brother helped him struggle to his feet. "You don't deserve sweet lil' Lambie."

When the trio had departed, Belinda smoothed down her tousled hair and flung the ends of the scarf jauntily over one shoulder. "Well, another night, another drama!" she laughed. "I think we could all use some dessert after that."

The waiters sprung into action and in no time, big skillets filled with cherries or crepes were flaming tableside. Then, another waiter entered flourishing a tray upon which reposed the majestic Baked Alaska.

Jolene and Bobette oohed and aahed and loosened their already strained waistbands in preparation for the grand finale.

Since people kept getting up and moving around, the waiters served informally, placing a small portion of each dessert on every plate, then leaving them on the table.

Dan and I were joined by Fenton and Mamie, who kept us laughing with more stories of projects gone wrong at Peach Island. Like what happened to Hamid, the Egyptian they'd hired to test-grow a stand of pure Egyptian cotton on Georgia soil.

U.S. Customs at first suspected the cotton seedlings of being drugs. But when somebody from the Department of Agriculture verified they were indeed cotton, the inspectors dumped the priceless little plants from their trays to ensure Hamid wasn't smuggling opium.

Hamid was so incensed at such treatment, he immediately flew back to Egypt and refused all pleas to return.

When we finished dessert, it was after two o'clock in the morning. Dan suggested we make a circuit around the dining room to say goodnight to everyone.

But while Montaigne was chatting with Reggie and Cecille, Sam Stormshadow pulled Dan aside, saying he had a confidential legal question.

I moved on to the sated Jolene and Bobette, who had finally met their match in Antoine's. Then, I noticed Pearl and Topaz had backed Belinda into the far corner. Seeing Dan was still occupied with Sam, I strolled casually around the table, pretending to nibble from one of the remaining dessert plates until I could hear them behind me.

" . . . got to be joking!" Belinda was saying, her voice edged with derisive amusement. "It must be worth twice that."

"But nobody's offering you twice that, are they?" Topaz pointed out.

"And we're prepared to pay cash. Right this minute," declared Pearl.

Belinda snorted. "Where is it, then? Not even you look hippy enough to have $35,000 cash stuffed into your drawers, Pearl. Anyway, even if I wanted to sell the ring—which I don't—do you think I'm so stupid I'd just hand it over to you before seeing the money?"

"Oh," Topaz said smugly, "it's here, all right. In this very room."

"Ha! I'll believe it when I see it," Belinda laughed.

"Okay, Pearlie. Show her da money," Topaz ordered.

"Righty-o, Sister," Pearl agreed.

She fluttered into my line of sight, over to where she and Topaz had been sitting. I almost lost it when she hauled up one of the Aunt Sally's bags from beneath the table. No wonder all those loose pralines were scattered around! Pearl and Topaz had bought enough boxes of candy to empty out and stuff full of cash.

Talk about your sweet deals!

A sudden intake of breath betrayed that Belinda had seen what was really inside that colorful box decorated with the quaint, kerchiefed head of Aunt Sally.

She was all business now. "If I agree, the ring will have to be cut off."

"That can be easily arranged, dear," Pearl twittered happily. "We have all the tools of the trade with us."

"Understand, I'm not promising anything," Belinda warned.

I began to sidle away, a little concerned at how good I was getting at eavesdropping, and bumped right into Dan.

He looked at my prop dessert plate incredulously. "You can't be serious, darlin'! Put that down and let's get out of here, I've had it."

Sam and Montaigne were now sitting together, and he wasn't bothering to conceal his true feelings. He reached for her left hand, his strong sculptor's thumb stroking the inside of her delicate wrist.

Fawn Goldfeather watched them, literally vibrating with rage. Maybe she'd tumbled for Sam after all, poor thing.

Although we knew the artist had well exceeded his known limit tonight, it seemed to have turned him into a pussycat. That is, until Belinda stalked up to the couple. It had belatedly dawned upon her that Sam was seriously beguiled by Montaigne.

Without acknowledging the other woman's presence, she drilled out a command. "Sam! I want to leave. Right now!"

Sam gave Montaigne a tender smile. "Will you excuse me, please?" he requested politely. He rose leisurely from his chair and faced Belinda.

Right in the midst of her triumphant smirk at Montaigne, without the slightest warning, Sam grabbed the ends of her long scarf and spun her like a top until she hit the wall. Hard.

As Belinda slid to the floor, Sam snarled, "So leave, bitch!"

23

I opened my eyes Sunday morning to be confronted with the bedside clock's pulsing red numerals advising that it was almost noon.

This tardy chambering had not been deliberate wantonness, but was the result of a bedtime delayed until 5:00 A.M.

Upon witnessing Sam's violent assault on Belinda, an Antoine's waiter, in deepest gratitude for that four-figure tab she'd run up, called the police.

Since the French Quarter station house is literally right around the corner from Antoine's, two plainclothes cops arrived almost at once. They handcuffed Sam and discreetly escorted him away through the side alley from whence they came. Patrons still lingering in the main dining room had no idea there'd been an incident.

As the only attorney on the premises, Dan felt duty-bound to offer assistance to Sam, even though defense work is not remotely his area. When the criminal lawyer—an old Tulane buddy—he called to consult had gotten over his ire at being roused from a blameless sleep, he told Dan that nothing could be done until a formal charge was made and bail had been set. After giving Dan the name of a reliable bondsman, he hung up.

Save for the waiters and busboys clearing away evidence of our dissipation, no one was in the 1840 Room when Dan finished telephoning from Antoine's office.

We emerged from the restaurant into a chilly, pre-dawn dampness, and made our way to the police station.

There, we found Belinda refusing to press charges of aggravated battery against Sam. "This is all just a ridiculous misunderstanding," she insisted to the senior arresting officer. "My boyfriend had too much to drink and lost his temper. End of story. He's never treated me like that before. Has he, Dan?" she appealed.

"I've certainly never seen him," Dan replied truthfully.

No, I thought. He usually just makes statues of you and rips them to pieces.

The officer gave an angry sigh. "Okay, lady. It's your funeral."

"Thank you so much," Belinda retorted icily. "Would you please release him now?"

"Can't, ma'am." The officer shook his head, looking happier. "He passed out cold when we threw him in the tank. You can come collect him tomorrow morning."

There was no way we could avoid sharing a taxi back to Riverside Manor with Belinda. Dan solved the awkward seating challenge by riding up front with the driver. Nobody spoke until we were buzzing down Canal Street.

"Thanks for your help, Dan," Belinda said finally.

"Let me set the record straight, Belinda," Dan replied. "I'm glad you weren't injured, but whatever help I have to offer is for Sam."

She brushed back the long comma of hair from her forehead. "I see. Well, if that's how it is, fine by me. Sam Stormshadow's the most valuable asset I own right now, so whatever helps him winds up being good for me, too."

"Excuse me. Sam's the most valuable asset you *own*?" Dan asked in disbelief.

"Maybe you should take a look at his contract, Dan, since that's your specialty. It says fifty percent of anything that can be defined as a work of art, be it Sam's smallest doodle on a note pad to the biggest canvas, pot or statue in his studio, that he executed or even conceived while under my management, belongs to me."

"A fifty percent management fee?" Dan echoed incredulously. "That's not only exorbitant, Belinda, but some judges might even consider it extortion."

Belinda twitched her minkclad shoulders impatiently. "Nobody forced him to sign it, Dan. Sam knew he had cost me my marriage, my home, my place in New Orleans society, and he wanted to make it up to me somehow."

"And naturally you did nothing to disabuse him of the notion that you had never cheated on Foley until he came along."

A streetlight shone through the dirty cab window, catching a gleam of perfect white teeth as she smiled. "Naturally."

I'd kept quiet as long as I could "But why, Belinda? You've got plenty of money, so it can't be that."

She looked at me. "Can't it, Claire? Just how much money is plenty? But no, it's not the money, as such. It's the respect I get because I know how to make real art pay off, big time. Very few people are able to do that, particularly with Native American artists, who've got so many stereotypes to break.

"For some reason, I'm able to look at their work and pick out exactly which intrinsic elements they must focus on to put them over the top and into the year 2000. I've never been wrong, either. I've got five other Indian artists under contract besides Sam. Four have broken into major money because I showed them how to appeal to the big spenders like entertainers and other high-profile types without going totally commercial."

"Well, that's not a shabby track record," Dan commented. "One bust out of six."

"On the contrary, Dan," Belinda said. "The sixth would've been at least as big as Sam, if death hadn't intervened. Even posthumously if the paintings, in which I own a half-interest, had been shipped to me first. Unfortunately, they are languishing in some unknown location and the useless insurance investigator from Lloyd's of London hasn't been able to track them down."

Belinda broodingly twisted her long front lock around a forefinger. "Oh, well, water under the bridge. Anyway, I'm giving you fair warning, Dan. I'll fight down and dirty to keep what's mine, including Sam Stormshadow and all his works.

"Even if we break up, I'll still own half of everything he does for the next seven years because I can prove I'm responsible for his highest level of success."

"It's an approach," Dan conceded. "But hypothetically—what will you do if he refuses to sculpt that variation on *Woman #1*?"

She didn't have to stop and think about it. "Sue him!" she shot back instantly. "For the amount of the commission plus damages to my professional reputation, and everything else my attorney wants to tack on. I'll keep him so tied up in court that he won't be able to think about anything else, much less work."

Belinda laughed. "And that goes for anybody who tries to do me out of anything or put something over on me. I'll blow the whistle so fast and so loud, they won't know what happened."

She laughed again. "You can't very well claim I've ever shied away from scandal, can you? The only difference now is, I get to be the accuser instead of the accusee."

I finished playing my mental video and lay still so as not to disturb Dan. Belinda had made it abundantly clear that she would shrink at nothing to retain anything she considered hers, be it money, respect or a man's soul.

But what if she were to lock horns with another woman who felt the same way? Someone like Cecille Dalton Worth, for instance? Curious how similar their attitudes were toward the men in their lives. It's not over until the thin lady sings.

Belinda might be getting up to her usual tricks with studs like Kyle Dalton, but only a man such as Reggie Worth, with his skill and breeding, would be suitable as a husband. And it sounded like that was her ultimate goal. Her ruminations upon the loss of respectability, her marriage, her home and a place in society were more revealing than she intended.

Cecille, I was convinced, had finally recognized Mo Tulley's true value and had been ready to give Reggie his walking papers until she realized Belinda was seriously interested in him.

Belinda was totally nonchalant about Sam until she discerned he was feeling things for Montaigne he'd never felt for her.

It would be interesting to see how those two women would solve their need to control the men they no longer wanted, without depriving themselves of the ones they did.

Reggie had been hot for Fawn Goldfeather, until he'd met Belinda. Now it looked like he'd attempted to use Fawn to force Cecille's hand.

And Fawn herself had either genuinely fallen for Sam Stormshadow, or she merely wanted to defeat her dead—but still hated—half-sister in the person of Montaigne Duffosat.

Oh, why did all this convoluted mess have to happen at our best friends' wedding? It was supposed to be a happy time.

Suddenly, I was being cuddled from behind against a big, bare, furry chest.

"Hey there, baby," Dan greeted me, his voice still rough with sleep. "What time is it?"

I checked the clock. "12:30."

He groaned. "You're kidding. My God, what a night!"

Obviously, it was way too late to go to church. Also, we'd missed all our favorite Pentecostal TV preachers like Jesse Duplantis, Rod Parsley, Creflo Dollar and Clarence McClendon. Dan channel-surfed, but all he could find were dry-as-dust mainstream denominational services.

He pointed the remote and clicked off. "You know it wasn't our fault this time, Lord," he told the ceiling.

I put my head on his shoulder and ran my fingers through his soft chest hair. "We should at least try to squeeze some Christmas shopping in before the rehearsal at five o'clock," I recommended. "Otherwise, we'll have to do everything tomorrow because Tuesday's Christmas Eve and the wedding."

"Can't do too much tomorrow, either," Dan said. "Foley's bachelor party starts at six, remember?"

"I remember." Of course I did. Dan was hosting it, along with Leighton, at a French Quarter bar and grill called the Legal Limit, owned by yet another old Tulane law school buddy.

"You better behave yourself," I warned.

His eyes twinkled mischievously. "Now darlin'. It's just going to be a little innocent boy fun."

"Uh-huh. Well, I expect you not to hire anybody to do anything you wouldn't want me to do in front of a roomful of strange men."

Dan looked somewhat taken aback at this and I thought I'd spiked his guns. Until he grinned and said, "In that case, you're going to have to show me exactly what you mean. Or I won't know."

"All right. I will!"

Jumping out of bed, I switched on the radio, and found some slow funky blues.

"I'll be right back," I told him.

Hurriedly, I fished a pair of black thigh-high lace-topped stockings from a drawer and slipped them on. Then I stuck my feet into the tallest heels I'd brought along, making sure the shoes didn't show beneath my long satin nightgown.

As a woman singer began to wail about her mean ol' man, jest as mean as he could be, I returned to the bedroom, bumping and strutting to the throbbing beat.

In the beginning, Dan was laughing, but by the time the singer was moaning how sweet her mean old man could love, and I was down to nothing but my bikini panties, the stockings and the high heels, he was sitting on the edge of the bed, and he wasn't laughing anymore. Definitely.

I shimmied over to him and started high kicking. "Mean ol', sweet ol' loving man," I crooned along with the radio.

He reached up and grabbed my ankle in midair.

It was the most inappropriate moment possible for the tormented face of Kyle Dalton to pop into my head. I remembered his schemes for natural blue cotton and color-primed canvasses. Could Belinda Callant have possibly induced him to sign one of her famous fifty-fifty contracts?

I didn't wonder about that for more than a couple of seconds, however.

Dan pulled me by the leg onto his lap. "Come here, baby."

'Cause my mean ol' man
Oh! How he makes such swee-ee-eet love to me . . .

24

Decorating hotel ballrooms for weddings is a tricky business. Nothing can be done very far in advance, because the designated facility could conceivably turn over two or three times during one twenty-four hour period.

Christmas, with its countless seasonal festivities, only serves to compound the logistical problems of a hotel wedding. At Riverside Manor, for example, the Crystal Ballroom alone had so far today hosted a breakfast, a luncheon, and an agoraphobic's dream come true—one of those traveling seminars about how to create vast wealth without ever leaving home. Well, except to attend the seminar.

Tonight, immediately following the wedding rehearsal, a hotel catering team would appear to set up for a "Friends of the New Orleans Opera" dinner.

Though Trevor of Fashion Bouquet had done preliminary sketches for Charlotte's wedding weeks ago, this was the first time he'd been able to coordinate his already rushed holiday floral schedule with the ballroom being momentarily empty, to take actual nuts and bolts measurements.

When we began wandering in for rehearsal at five o'clock, Trevor was perched atop a tall metal hotel ladder, snapping birds-eye Polaroids. Below, two of his minions darted about with notebooks and tape measures.

"We're not finished yet!" he shrieked down at us, in near-hysteria.

"It's okay, Trevor," Charlotte called soothingly. "Take your time."

But Charlotte's calming effect on Trevor was undone by the arrival of Sally Holt, a big, blonde, senior wedding coordinator from Anne Barge for Brides. She'd flown in from Atlanta this morning, having victoriously pulled off last night's complicated nuptials of an important, thrice-divorced politician, and she wanted up on that ladder *now*.

Sally fretted and tapped her large, black patent leather pump impatiently until Trevor finished shooting the roll of film and descended.

After informing Charlotte he'd gotten what he needed to begin work in earnest, Trevor aimed a parting zinger at Sally Holt, assuring her that the ladder was guaranteed to support up to 500 pounds of pressure.

Sally had come equipped with a portable CD player, and put everybody through their paces to generic wedding-type music, not what would actually be playing at the ceremony, but sufficient for the task.

Dan and I filled our own roles as best man and matron of honor, then stood in for Foley and Charlotte. As I waited outside the ballroom entrance on her father Emory's arm, a wave of nostalgia swept over me at the familiar strains of "The Wedding March."

Emory and I paused, as Sally directed, in the doorway, the idea being to give the groom that first, unobstructed glimpse of his bride, and she of him.

When I saw Dan standing where the altar would be, facing me, I felt the tears welling up. Even in my long, petunia pink angora sheath, I felt like a bride in white again. With every slow, measured tread, I flashed back to our own wedding of the previous August, and all the heartbreak, turmoil and danger that had gone before, and come afterward.

Life had never seemed to me so unbearably precious and fragile as it did now, drawing closer to Dan with each step, until I was drowning in his blue, blue eyes.

I barely heard Saint rumble, "Who giveth this woman in marriage?" or Emory's cultured Southern tones answering, "Her mother and I."

Dan stepped forward and took my hand. I saw there were tears on his own cheeks. Behind us, I could hear sniffling among the onlookers.

"Dearly Beloved," intoned Saint, "we are gathered together this day in the sight of God, et cetera . . . "

I let my mind wander and my gaze drift around the semi-circle of attendants. On my left, the bridesmaids were succumbing to misty-eyed sentiment. Even Cecille. Was she remembering the past? Her wedding to Reggie when love was fresh and she thought she could get the leopard to change his spots? Or was she envisioning a future with Mo Tulley, who'd marry her if she didn't have a nickel, and would worship her forever?

To my right, Leighton looked like a ponderously solemn stuffed owl; Marcel contemplated Nectarine with an unfathomable expression; Tucker John anxiously watched Lambie for some further sign of relenting; and Woody and Wes appeared equally overwhelmed by the proceedings, their mouths hanging slightly open in identical gapes.

Maybe it was due to Saint's mellow, Caribbean cadences, but I got the impression everyone was listening especially intently as he recited the simple words of that ancient, much-maligned, distorted, and generally dishonored marriage covenant.

Saint paused to inquire whether there would be a child ringbearer. Upon receiving a negative reply, that Dan and I would be carrying the wedding bands for our friends, he beamed approvingly. "Very wise. Even the most precocious of tots are prone to stage fright at the critical moment. Such a charming idea, but one that rarely works out as planned.

"I'll never forget one dear little fellow who absolutely refused to surrender the rings as requested. The ceremony ground to a complete and embarrassing halt while his mother chased him all over the church!"

There was laughter and a perceptible release of tension at Saint's anecdote.

He called Foley and Charlotte up front so they could observe more closely as he instructed Dan and me to demonstrate how they would be receiving Holy Communion.

Next came the candle lighting, then the exchange of vows and rings.

"I now pronounce you man and wife!" thundered Saint finally. "Now you may kiss your bride, et cetera, et cetera."

Dan took me into his arms. "Just so you'll know, Claire. I'd do this whole rigamarole all over again in a heartbeat," he whispered against my lips.

"Hey! Who's getting married around here anyway?" Foley joked. "Good job, Danbo. Thanks."

Charlotte was pale but radiant in a dinner suit of lime satin that turned her eyes luminous green. "You and Dan were beautiful, Claire. I just hope we look as good as you did!"

"Don't be ridiculous," I told her, with a hug.

Sally punched on her CD and the triumphant strains of the recessional march blasted forth.

"I want each gentleman to make a slight bow to his lady before he offers her his arm!" Sally yelled.

This sounded corny, but was in fact rather elegant in execution, once we got it down after five or six attempts.

We weren't done with the rehearsal a minute too soon. The "Friends of the New Orleans Opera" dinner crew swarmed in right on our heels, and already had three round tables set up before Sally could get down from her ladder.

As we passed the concierge's desk en route to the elevator, Foley and Charlotte asked us to have a quiet drink with them in the private lounge of the Tapestry Room, where dinner would be served. I was surprised when Dan declined. "Thanks, but we can't right now. There's something I need to show Claire up in our suite."

Foley awarded his friend a look of disbelieving admiration. "You just never stop, do you?"

"No, no!" Dan protested. "It's nothing like that."

"Sure," Foley retorted skeptically. He looked at his watch. "It is now six o'clock. Cocktails will be served at six-thirty."

"We'll be there," promised Dan.

In the elevator I asked him, "What's going on, *chér*?"

"Nothing, really," he said. "Except that when we got back from the mall, remember how we just threw our bags all over the place because we were in such a hurry to get ready? That wasn't very smart of us."

Now he had me concerned. Amazingly, we'd managed to find almost all the gifts on our lists. Some were extravagant and rather costly. We really should've taken time to store them out of sight in the closet so as not to flaunt temptation right in the face of any hotel employee who might be weak in that area.

I thought of the lush Goldpfeil wallet with a hundred dollar bill tucked inside waiting to be wrapped for Ambrose.

We raced from the elevator to our room. Dan fumbled around with the card key (I detest those things) but finally the green light blinked on.

Within, all appeared to be just as we left it, except for a towering Christmas tree already strung with myriads of twinkling lights, standing in front of the tall windows looking out onto the river.

"Oh, Dan!" More tears spilled over. This certainly was my weepy day.

Although I hadn't mentioned it, I'd been feeling a little sad about not being home and having a tree for our first Christmas together. Technically, it was our second Christmas being married, but the other didn't count since we were separated at the time.

He laughed. "I was worried they might not have finished yet, but Victor, the concierge, gave me the high sign when we passed his desk just now."

Indicating two large shopping bags, he said, "While you were zoning out in Victoria's Secret, I was looking for ornaments. At this late date, the pickings were pretty slim, but I expect they'll do."

I walked over and put my arms around his waist. "Dan Louis, I know you're not perfect, but you sure come close."

"Well, we're family, Claire. Even if it's just the two of us for now. So this is going to be our little family tradition. No matter where we are for Christmas, we will always have our own tree."

"Can we play carols and decorate it after dinner?" I asked.

"That was my plan. Providing the stressed-out brides, conniving long-haired nymphomaniacs, jewel-hunting aunts and Indians on the warpath will give us a night off."

Rehearsal Dinner

Hosted by
Miss Charlotte Dalton and
Mr. Foley Callant

December 22, The Tapestry Room
Riverside Manor Hotel

White Corn Soup with Roasted Pimento

Salad of Arugula, Mushrooms, and
Garlic-Stuffed Olives with
Olive Oil and Fresh Lime Dressing

Baked Pheasant Under Glass with
Poire William and Rosemary Sauce

Turnip Mousse
Sauteed Okra

Lemon Mirror Cake
Godiva Chocolates

25

This was the dinner Foley and Charlotte had put so much effort into planning, and it was perfect. Light enough not to be daunting after all that heavy food we'd been having, but sufficiently rich to impress the senior-most member of Blanchard, Smithson, Callant and Claiborne, who fancied himself quite the gastronome.

Of course, those wines Charlotte and I had been so adroitly maneuvered into selecting had plenty to contribute.

Speaking of our sommelier, Montaigne Duffosat had withdrawn into her shell once more, professional, polished and strictly business. Undoubtedly, she felt humiliated by the events of last night, particularly when she'd allowed herself to be witnessed responding to Sam's gentle wooing, only to have him morph into a violent abuser of women right before her eyes.

We were all seated around a large circular table, its centerpiece a wide shallow bowl of cut crystal, filled with white roses and leaves of green and white holly.

The atmosphere was considerably brighter, possibly due to the absence of Fawn, Sam, Belinda, Kyle, Pearl and Topaz.

I was between Dan and Kitty Blanchard, who, though not in the wedding party, had to be invited because of Leighton. Which in turn meant Reggie was included because of Cecille, Leighton's partner for the ceremony.

Kitty was again acting like the blithe, sophisticated matron I'd always supposed her to be, laughing and gossiping with Imogene across Leighton about the head of a national charity they both knew.

Tucker John looked much happier, because Lambie had allowed him to put an arm along the back of her chair. And when one of his hands strayed upward to toy with a wispy blonde curl, she didn't protest.

At the far curve, the Dalton youngsters—Woody, Wes, Jolene and Bobette—had their variegated red heads together, probably plotting a fast getaway to experience some real New Orleans nightlife.

Reggie and Cecille acted civil enough toward each other, but both seemed preoccupied.

This was the first time I'd seen Marcel and Nectarine be so affectionate in public. I wasn't about to speculate on what they might do in private. My relationship with Marcel was too longstanding and complex for such delving.

I did wonder how the quest for Nectarine's Kashmir sapphire was progressing. Surely Pearl and Topaz weren't spending all their time concocting schemes to wrest the black opal away from Belinda. Hopefully, she would accept their sugar-coated cash and be done with it.

Because Foley and Charlotte were honeymooning in Italy, Leighton took it for granted they wished to hear—in great detail—about his and Kitty's one trip to that country some fifteen years before. Eventually, we all had to listen. Leighton possessed one of those moist, resonant voices that can extinguish any auxiliary conversation without ever being raised.

In no way did he permit this filibuster to interfere with his eating and drinking pleasure.

It took Kitty and Imogene to set his captive audience free.

Kitty interrupted a convoluted description of a ruined villa in Tuscany. "Excuse me, Leighton honey. But Imogene here has kindly invited us to spend a week this summer at her place on Peach Island."

I knew from Charlotte that Imogene's modest-sounding "summer place" was a West Indies-style plantation house surrounded by four landscaped acres.

Leighton was delighted. Ever since Foley got engaged to Charlotte, he'd been casting a covetous gaze eastward to the Peach Island Textiles legal business.

Dollar signs flashed in his eyes as he said heartily, "Well, thank you very much, Imogene. But first, you must come stay with us this spring. New Orleans is at its finest in May, you know."

Daphne and Emory, having previously ascertained that the Blanchards were accomplished equestrians, chimed in with an invitation to the annual foxhunt given by their Buckhead riding club.

Southern hospitality continued to ooze.

Kitty reminded Leighton about the New Orleans Yacht Club Regatta, and didn't he think Daphne and Emory would enjoy that?

Dates were discussed, and, pending conflict with prior commitments, invitations accepted.

If we Southerners always have places to go and people to see, it's because we're usually disposed to obligate ourselves socially on the spot, and stick to it. I've heard that some people in Los Angeles can actually take a whole year to agree to have lunch together.

When the waiters came to remove our plates before dessert, Kitty hissed, "Claire! You, me and Charlotte. In the sandbox. Now!"

Charlotte caught my signal, and the three of us excused ourselves.

The powder room was sybaritic—black marble, gleaming brass, and dusty rose carpet. Kitty checked the stalls for feet, then sat on a black and rose-striped stool, crossed elegant legs sheathed in holiday-sparkled black stockings, and lit a cigarette.

She exhaled, closing her eyes blissfully.

Charlotte regarded her with exasperated affection. "Okay, Kitty. Let's hear the big secret. I know you didn't haul Claire and me in here simply to share your secondhand smoke."

"Anybody can tell you're an investigative reporter, Charlotte," Kitty teased, opening her eyes. "So, how'd you like to investigate behind the scenes of a real live bachelor party?"

Charlotte dropped onto the next stool. "You don't mean—?"

"Oh, don't I?" drawled Kitty.

"I find the idea strangely appealing," I told her. "Only, how do you propose we accomplish this? They're going to be holed up in the Back Room of the Legal Limit."

Kitty flicked a careless ash into a brass wastebasket and smiled. "Let's just say Griffin Jones owes me a great big favor?"

Griffin, who owned the Legal Limit, was a good ten years younger than Kitty Blanchard.

Charlotte held up a restraining hand. "I'm sure I speak for Claire when I say we won't ask, so don't you dare tell us. I just want to know the plan."

Kitty looked from Charlotte to me. "You're in, then?" she said, out of the corner of her scarlet mouth. You'd think we were planning a heist.

Her arrangement with Griffin was very simple. We were to wait in a nearby bar until he alerted Kitty via her cell phone that the "entertainment" was about to begin.

Then we would proceed through an alley to the rear of the building. Griffin would admit us through the fire door and sneak us backstage, where we could watch from the wings.

Immediately when it was over, he would hustle us out the same way. The boys would never know we were there.

With a husky chuckle, Kitty ground out her cigarette. "Doesn't that sound like delicious fun?"

"To me, yes," agreed Charlotte. "But I frankly never would've suspected you could dream up such a naughty escapade, Kitty Blanchard!"

Kitty looked pleased. "There's a lot you and Claire don't know about me, Charlotte."

We arranged to meet at Napoleon House the following evening at seven, then availed ourselves of the facilities before returning to the dining room.

"It's not that I don't trust my Foley-pie," Charlotte remarked pensively, freshening her bright coral lipstick. "But it would be enlightening to see how he behaves when he thinks I'm not around."

I said I felt the same way about Dan. I did not mention the private show I'd put on for him earlier.

Kitty fluffed out her shiny black hair. "Well, I wish I could say Leighton was above reproach, but that wouldn't exactly be true.

"Oh, now why did you get so quiet on me all of a sudden?" She laughed. "I don't mean he goes out deliberately trolling for pussy, or anything. But, let's face it, should said pussy throw itself at him, he's way too pompous and egotistical to know how to extricate himself.

"The only real problems we've ever had were situations like that. I bet you didn't know about that twenty-year old secretary who gave a whole new meaning to the words 'desk-set.' She actually expected Leighton to divorce me and marry her! Did you ever?"

Wordlessly, Charlotte and I shook our heads. That was one nugget Dan and Foley had successfully kept from us. At least it eliminated Esmé Barnes from the picture.

With a sigh, Kitty said, "Leighton's just a great big rich silly old goat. But he's my old goat. So you see, I like to keep an eye on him whenever I can."

"Why, Kitty! You really do love him, don't you?" It slipped out before I could stop it.

She arched a surprised black eyebrow at me. "Well, of course I do, Claire. What did you think?"

26

Just before Dan and I reached the safety of the elevator, we were ambushed by an Indian.

Sam Stormshadow looked haggard and totally miserable. "I've got to talk to you!" he groaned.

"Can't it wait until tomorrow morning?" Dan pleaded. "We've had a full day."

"If you could spare me a few minutes right now, I'd really appreciate it," Sam persisted.

Dan clapped him on the shoulder. "Okay. Sure," he said sympathetically. Giving me a resigned look, he reached into his breast pocket for the room key. "You run on, darlin'. I'll be up, soon as I can."

Sam put out a hand to restrain me. "Wait. What I really meant is that I need to talk to both of you."

For privacy, we retreated to a cluster of cordovan leather chairs near the center of the lobby. There were too many people we knew in the lounge, though Belinda was not among them.

They had, Sam informed us, been invited to a dinner party at the home of the man who'd purchased *Woman #1*. Since Sam refused to attend, Belinda had gone without him, taking Kyle Dalton, of all people, as her escort!

"God, my life is a mess!" The pain punctured Sam's voice like a sharp instrument in one of his detestable statues. "Just when I thought things were about to go right, for a change."

As I'd surmised, Sam had gotten very serious in a big hurry about Montaigne Duffosat, and he had every reason to believe the feeling was mutual.

"What a bizarre match, right? A two-drink Indian and a somme-lier!"

He'd been up front with her about that, though, when they were all alone down there in the wine cellar, sampling those bottles of Chilean red and Argentinean white she'd recommended for his exhibit.

Montaigne thanked him for the warning, saying she could easily call security from the cellar extension if things got out of control.

"But listen to this!" Sam said. "I had the equivalent of two-and-a-half glasses of wine with her, and nothing happened!"

"What do you mean by nothing?" Dan asked.

"Just what I said," replied Sam. "It was so weird. I didn't get drunk, I didn't black out. In fact, I barely felt a buzz! I accused her of ringing in non-alcoholic wine on me, and I wasn't joking!

"But she showed me the label, then opened another bottle and we both had some more. Now I'm up to four glasses—not just drinking, but savoring—and still acting like a normal human being!"

For Sam, it was nothing short of miraculous. Obviously, Montaigne was very good medicine for him. As if to prove it, not once when they'd had drinks together after that, did he get drunk, act crazy, or have one of his hideous blackouts.

Until last night.

Sam didn't remember a thing when he woke up in the tank this morning. After they let him out, Belinda was right there, ready and waiting to tell him what an asshole he'd been.

She'd finished by saying, "Get used to it, Sam. You're stuck with me for a long, long time. Who else would put up with you?"

Back at the hotel, Sam had rushed to find Montaigne, but she wouldn't talk to him. In place of the affection he'd grown accustomed to seeing in those fine dark eyes, had been total revulsion.

I felt terrible for him.

When Sam lapsed into morose silence, Dan remarked thoughtfully, "So what you're saying is last night, the minute Belinda broke up your tête-á-tête with Montaigne, you snapped and everything after that is a complete blank."

"Yeah, I guess so," Sam droned. "The last thing I remember, Montaigne and I were talking about where we'd live if we could live any place on earth. The next thing I know, some goon with a tattoo that said, 'Love Lump' was unbraiding my hair. Man, was I freaked!"

"And prior to your involvement with Belinda," Dan went on, "did you become violent during your blackouts?"

Sam shook his head. "I used to get a little nutty, but I never had blackouts—" he stopped suddenly. "My God, Dan! I never had blackouts, even after several drinks, until I met Belinda!"

He stared at us. "What does that mean?"

Dan hesitated. "I'm not sure, Sam. This ain't exactly my department. But I wonder if Belinda's mixed up in voodoo or the like."

"Oh, that." Sam shrugged. "Sure. She found some old prune in Santa Fe calls herself a 'wise woman.' Hell, the only thing wise about her is she knows how to milk money out of rich, gullible Anglos. And ever since I've known her, she's raved about somebody in the Quarter called Daddy Jake. Tried to get me to go with her once, before—well, you know what happened."

Dan and I looked at each other. Daddy Jake was a menacing-looking little black man who was said to be a witch doctor. I understood he claimed to receive messages from his variety of pet snakes, all of whom were poisonous and pampered in heated glass cages filled with artistically arranged rocks and bite-sized living creatures.

Sam sat up straighter. "Wait a minute! Do you think Belinda put some kind of hex on me?"

"I don't know," Dan said honestly. "But if I were you, I'd consult Reverend St. Dennis about your experiences. Coming from the Caribbean, he's very knowledgeable about that stuff. In the meantime, how can Claire and I help you, Sam?"

"Well, as I told you last night, before the disaster, I want to hire you to break my contract with Belinda. I'm going to call my secretary tomorrow morning and have her fax a copy here. Will you do it?"

Dan nodded. "I will certainly try. With pleasure."

"Thanks." Sam gave him a grateful smile, then turned to me. I sensed what was coming.

"Uh, Claire. Montaigne really likes you. Well . . . maybe if you kind of talked to her? At least get her to give me a half-hour. That's all I'm asking."

I looked a question at Dan. He rolled his eyes, but nodded.

"All right, Sam. Since I am an incurable romantic who always wants to see true love reign victorious in the end, I'll try."

"Oh, hey. That's great, Claire."

As we retraced our steps to the elevator, Sam straggled after us. "Well, I guess I'll go up and watch TV since I don't have anything better to do."

"Sam! Wait!" called a woman's voice.

He turned eagerly, hoping for Montaigne, but it was Fawn Gold-feather instead.

"Sam, I haven't seen you all day. I've been so worried about you," she told him.

"You were?" he asked, in disbelief.

Fawn went on. "Yes, Sam. I was kind of hoping we could talk for awhile, but maybe you're too tired."

Fawn looked exceptionally attractive tonight in a plain, dark, clingy wool dress that did far more for her figure than the conglomeration of artifacts she'd been sporting lately.

Sam eyed her with new interest. "Who said anything about being tired?"

It was only as the elevator doors snicked shut between us and them that I realized the direction from whence Fawn had materialized was a marble pillar very near to where we had been sitting.

A marble pillar, as I knew from personal experience, that provided excellent cover for an eavesdropper.

How much had Fawn Goldfeather heard?

27

Three women fled down a narrow alley that was nearly as badly lit and foul smelling as it had been two hundred years ago.

One of them slipped in something, but caught herself before she fell.

"Dammit!" fumed Kitty Blanchard. "I hope that wasn't doggie-poop. These are my brand new Donna Karan sneakers!"

We emerged breathless and giggling onto Chartres, threading between Jackson Square and the St. Louis Cathedral back to Napoleon House, from where we'd made an abrupt departure forty-five minutes before.

Our secluded table, which Kitty had tipped the waiter twenty dollars to hold, was now a bier for the corpses of Kitty's Pimm's Cup and Charlotte's and my sloe gin fizzes.

The waiter approached with a fresh round as soon as we'd fallen into our chairs. "I was beginning to think you broads had stiffed me," he complained, removing the dead soldiers.

"Not us!" declared Charlotte. "We're high-class broads!"

Kitty raised her drink. "To the boys in the Back Room!" she proclaimed, and Charlotte and I clinked rims with her.

Laughing and ridiculously pleased with ourselves, we relived our little adventure.

For me, it had begun at about a quarter to six when Dan, looking like a luscious chocolate bear in a cocoa brown wool suit, kissed me goodbye.

"I'll probably be back pretty late, darlin'," he said. "What are you going to do tonight?"

"Well, I still have some presents to wrap." Indicating my black velours sweatsuit, I added, "Actually, I was also thinking maybe I should work off some of that food I've been eating." That was true. I just didn't say how I planned to do it.

"As of yesterday, you looked pretty damn fine to me," he said.

"Thank you, darling," I murmured. "I'm so glad you enjoyed my . . . ah . . . performance. The feeling is mutual."

When he paused at the door for another kiss, I reminded him, "Honey, you're one of the hosts. Hadn't you better get going?"

Dan checked his watch. "It's only a ten-minute taxi ride. I'll be right on time." He gave me a squeeze. "Sure you'll be okay?"

"I'll be fine, Dan. You go and have fun now."

He couldn't've possibly suspected anything, yet he seemed oddly reluctant to leave. I watched from the door to make sure he boarded the elevator.

Back in the room, I did wrap presents. Stocking stuffers for him were an exquisite sterling cigar lighter and matching cutter. Each pair of double entendre underwear was in a separate package, coded for easy reference.

Dan's serious gift had used up almost my entire personal shopping budget, but was well worth it; a sleek sound system for his office, encased in burlwood, no bigger than the large humidor it resembled.

That done, I phoned Juanita to confirm everything was under control. She'd been at the house earlier to deliver the "bedtime snacks" of paté, Roquefort cheese, flatbread and large, ripe hothouse strawberries on long stems, injected with Grand Marnier and dipped in chocolate.

Dan had instructed Juanita to put a couple of bottles of our own Cristal '81 in the refrigerator. Although Foley some time ago had purchased a case of his own, planning to open the first bottle with

Charlotte on their wedding night, there had been a change of location and this was a precautionary measure.

Juanita and Carlos were going to the wedding, and she had bought a new dress for the occasion. Excitedly, she described it to me as long and electric blue, with spaghetti straps.

I winced. Not only is Juanita endowed with breasts like prize watermelons, she doesn't shave her armpits.

Tactfully, I inquired whether it had a matching jacket in case she got too cold?

Juanita thought this was hilarious. "No, *niña!* When Carlos and I dance, we heat up *muy pronto!*"

Well, next to the bride herself, I knew who'd be getting the most attention.

Ambrose Xavier's phone had been reconnected when I called. Yes, the painting was ready. I arranged for him to deliver it to the house at eight o'clock the next morning. Dan and I would hang it after he left.

At around twenty minutes till seven, I caught a taxi to Napoleon House, where I rendezvoused with Kitty and Charlotte.

As promised, Griffin Jones had called, and we proceeded to our destination.

"If any of the guys find out about this, I'm ruined!" he moaned, hustling us through the fire exit and into a catch-all room jammed with metal filing cabinets and shelves of paper towels, toilet tissue and cleaning supplies, cases of hard liquor, soft drinks, and a stack of sound equipment.

From beneath a closed door on our left seeped a melange of tobacco smoke, beer, jukebox music and boisterous male voices.

Kitty inhaled the nicotine fumes voraciously, while Charlotte and I coughed.

"Hey! Pipe down!" ordered Griffin.

"Well, you should've warned us to bring oxygen masks," Charlotte retorted. "Claire and I can hardly breathe."

Griffin folded beefy, freckled arms and looked injured. "It's the best I could do," he huffed. "I guess you don't appreciate what a big risk I'm taking here."

Shooting us a warning glance, Kitty said soothingly, "Yes we do, Griffin. We'll be fine."

Mollified, Griffin explained in a low voice that the "entertainment" was already positioned on the Back Room's small stage, just on the other side of that closed door. After he got his cue to punch on the CD music for the act, he would crack the door open about six inches, affording us an oblique view of the stage and a few ringside tables, among them the one around which Foley, Dan and Leighton were seated.

"Six inches isn't going to give us much scope, Griffin. And we'll be kind of crowded," objected Kitty.

"Tough nuts, baby," Griffin said flatly. "What you're forgetting is, if you can see them, they could see you too, if that door's open any wider. Six inches, take it or leave it," he added, grinning as the double meaning belatedly struck him.

"Ha, ha, Griffin," Kitty returned sarcastically.

"SSSH!" Griffin cautioned, cocking an ear.

The jukebox music had faded into the screeching of a live microphone. Griffin snapped off the overhead light. "Hang on, ladies. Here we go!" he muttered, turning the knob and easing the door open.

I was the shortest, so I got to stand in front. The crack widened to reveal an enormous wooden cake. Beyond it, Dan, in rolled up shirt sleeves, suspenders, and loosened tie, stood before the microphone.

He removed a cigar from his mouth and grinned down at the audience.

"You boys having fun yet?" he bellowed.

This was greeted with an affirmative roar.

With mock solemnity, Dan intoned, "We have gathered together to celebrate the last night of our brother Foley Callant's bachelorhood. Stand up, brother Foley!"

Beaming and disheveled, Foley rose to field a round of rowdy comments and catcalls before resuming his seat.

"We have consumed a variety of nutritionally deficient fried foods, accompanied by raw onions, without the slightest concern about offensive mouth odor!" Dan declared.

Enthusiastic applause.

"We have imbibed vast quantities of fine micro brews with no regard for road safety because all drinkers were required to surrender their car keys at the door to our designated drivers."

Cheers.

Dan frowned as if puzzled. "And yet, I have the nagging feeling something's missing. What could it be?"

"The stripper!" yelled somebody. "Yeah! Where's the stripper?" demanded another voice.

The word buzzed around the room until it became a chant. "Stripperstripperstripperstripper!"

Dan raised his hands for silence. "Okay, okay! Down, guys!" He laughed. "I'm gonna tell you right up front, though. There ain't gonna be no lap dancing here tonight."

Groans of protest.

"See, I promised my wife I wouldn't participate in anything I wouldn't want her to do in a roomful of strange men."

Charlotte poked me in the ribs as Dan paused. "Stop and think real hard about that one for a minute, boys. Or, as Reverend St. Dennis would say, '*Selah*, my brethren!'"

"But don't worry. We have something truly unique in store for you right now, and I guarantee you won't be disappointed.

"Lawyers and gentlemen, may I present—*The Case of Della's Dilemma!*"

The houselights dimmed; there was a stir of anticipation. We drew back as Dan half-turned in our direction. "Music, maestro! Please!"

Alternating blue and pink spotlights began to pulsate gently onto the giant cake. Griffin pushed a button on the CD player, then opened the door wider. Though it was darker now, we could still see Dan, Foley and Leighton pretty well.

Leighton was sitting on the edge of his seat, looking stodgily expectant.

Daaa-daaa, da-da! Daaa-daaa, da-da-da!

The familiar sustained intro to the *Perry Mason* theme burst suddenly into the silence, eliciting surprised laughter.

This musical phrase was repeated. Slowly, the top of the cake opened. There appeared a long, shapely leg in a 1950s-style seamed stocking, wearing a black high-heel pump on its foot.

Again, the introduction sounded. The leg hooked over the edge of the cake, sliding and kicking sensuously back and forth, taking on an identity of its own.

An eddy of murmurs signaled the crowd was getting interested.

As the notes rang out one final time, a second leg materialized to an outburst of applause. This leg joined the first in its coy routine.

Abruptly, both legs disappeared back inside the cake.

There was a brief silence.

All at once, the theme song proper (or, in this case, improper) blared out at top volume. From the cake arose a Della Street look-alike so perfect, she could've been lifted by virtual reality straight from an episode of the show.

She was wearing an exact replica of one of Della's suits. Only Della had never swung her booty around in it quite like this before.

As she came bumping and grinding her way down the layers of cake that served as steps, the men, including our three, leaped to their feet, whistling and applauding.

"Go, Della honey!" shouted Leighton, waggling his own wide hips responsively.

Behind me, Kitty chortled helplessly.

The dancer descended into the audience, slithering expertly out of clumsy grasps until she reached Foley.

"Uh-oh!" I recognized Fenton's voice. "She's got him now!"

Della seized Foley by his tie and drug him back with her on stage. The men howled.

She gyrated around, trying to coax him into dancing with her. Foley resisted for awhile, but finally gave in, responding with a slow version of the Twist.

"Get down, Foley!" bawled one of the Callant cousins.

Charlotte writhed in silent laughter.

Suddenly, the music broke off. Della looked alarmed. A confused buzz rippled through the audience.

Then, the theme introduction shattered the silence.

The cake opened again.

"Too, too priceless!" gasped Kitty, when out popped Perry Mason!

As the sonorous notes continued to drone, Perry, clutching a briefcase, stomped angrily down the cake and yanked Della away from Foley.

Foley retreated to his table, receiving a standing ovation.

The theme music started throbbing again. Perry flung aside his briefcase, and pulled Della roughly into his arms. They began to dance steamily.

He twirled her around, and her suit jacket suddenly fell off to reveal an old-fashioned concentrically stitched brassiere!

There was scarcely time to absorb this before realizing that Perry's torso was now magically, magnificently bare.

Soon, Della had been stripped of all but her bra, and a vintage girdle with garters that held up the sexy seamed stockings, and Perry was down to his socks and white boxer shorts.

Then, the couple began dancing in earnest.

Guys were pounding the tables and standing on chairs. Leighton got so carried away, he almost fell off of his. Dan and Foley, who were laughing at least as hard as we were, managed to catch him just in time.

Without warning, the music again skidded to a halt. The intro notes blared again. From inside the cake came a "shave-and-a-haircut" knock.

"Oh, no!" Charlotte croaked, holding her sides, as a debonair Paul Drake emerged and sashayed down to break it up between Perry and Della.

The piano music pounded into action again. In an attempt to lure Della away from Perry, Paul peeled down to his Jockey briefs. Poor Della just couldn't make up her mind. Hence the title, *Della's Dilemma.*

When the music grew louder and the action speeded up, Griffin Jones barked, "Come on, girls. This deal ends in about ten seconds!"

He rushed us to the door we'd come in, deactivated the fire alarm, and shoved us out into the alley.

Now, Charlotte noisily slurped up the last of her sloe gin fizz through a straw. "Well, I can truthfully say I have never seen anything like that in my entire life!"

"Nor I," I said. "And I must admit, the whole performance was pretty tasteful, all things considered. And funny."

"I always wondered about Della, Perry and Paul," Charlotte mused. "Anyway, I'd say our fellas acquitted themselves, if you'll pardon the legal pun, very well on the whole."

An indelicate snort of laughter escaped along with the cigarette smoke through Kitty's elegant nostrils. "Did you ever see anything so hilarious as my big old Leighton trying to balance on that flimsy chair?

I wonder what tale he would've concocted if he'd come home with an injury?"

"Hey, Claire!" Charlotte exclaimed suddenly, pointing to her watch. "You better hurry and get back to the hotel before Dan does."

I hadn't realized how long we'd dallied over our drinks. We exchanged quick hugs and I dashed out, hoping Dan wouldn't already be riding in the cab I tried to flag down.

Fortunately, I found an available taxi almost at once, which hurtled me at top speed back to Riverside Manor. I barged through the revolving doors and was halfway across the lobby when I heard a male voice urgently calling my name.

I froze like a guilty thing surprised and looked over my shoulder, fully expecting that Dan had found me out.

"Claire, I've been ringing you off and on all night!" the man said accusingly.

It was Mo Tulley.

28

"Mo! I was wondering what happened to you!" I exclaimed.

"I've been on hold, Claire. As usual. But finally, things are starting to move. Do you have a minute?"

I really didn't, Dan would be along soon. But I'd developed a soft spot for Maumus Tulley.

"A minute is about my limit, Mo. What's going on?"

"Is there someplace we can sit down and talk?" he asked.

He was puzzled when I selected an uncomfortable-looking bench against a wall near the bank of elevators. I didn't explain it was the only seating not in close proximity to a marble pillar.

While Reggie was out whooping it up at Foley's bachelor party, Mo and Cecille had dinner together, to plan what to do next.

"I advised her to put the divorce scheme on the back burner for now, and focus instead on changing her will." Score one for Dan.

"She still can't figure out what went awry with her original plan." Mo chuckled.

Much to his surprise I said, "Well, it sure wasn't Reggie's fault. He was doing his dead-level best to help Cecille, without realizing it. But

Fawn showed up too late, I don't know why. Maybe she was trying to make a power play. Whatever, it screwed up the timing."

I proceeded to explain Dan's theory that Reggie had been prepared to use Fawn to get Cecille to make a move, not knowing Cecille had the same idea.

"Dan is positive, and I'm now inclined to agree, that Reggie thought his one stone would kill two birds. To cut loose from Cecille and Fawn at the same time."

"But that's sheer suicide!" Mo protested. "He'd wind up with nothing!"

"Only if you consider Belinda Callant nothing," I pointed out.

His crinkly eyes shriveled to slits as he considered this angle. "You know, that's the only thing that makes any sense at all." He nodded. "Yes, yes. I can see it now."

Mo had no trouble grasping, as I initially had, the convoluted reasoning that would prevent Cecille from handing Reggie over to somebody like Belinda, as opposed to a nobody like Fawn.

Mo laughed. "Reggie's cleverer than I've given him credit for. Belinda Callant would be a perfect match for him. She's got money and power in the art world. And he's got the knack for spotting real talent, I'll grant him that. Like I told you, the purchases he's made on Cecille's behalf have skyrocketed in value."

I chose my next words very carefully. "Perhaps more than you realize, Mo."

He looked at me curiously. "What are you suggesting, Claire?"

I gazed at the ceiling. "Maybe Reggie is even cleverer than your recent upgrade, Mo. Maybe he inflated purchase prices to give himself a little extra pocket money. And, just maybe, he knows how to give a profit margin such a smooth shave, you'd never realize he'd been there with a razor."

Mo jumped up excitedly. "Claire, do you realize this could be the exact wedge I've been looking for? I won't ask you how you know this."

"I only said *maybe*," I reminded him.

He sat down again. "I'll catch an airport taxi right away. I won't even go back to the Lakefront first. If you're right, I've got to get hold of those books as soon as possible, and go over them with Cecille's accountant and a fine-tooth comb."

With a grin, Mo added, "Now my conscience won't bother me when I draw up that new will giving Reggie the shaft. Then, if he refuses to go quietly, I'll just threaten to turn over evidence of his fraud and embezzlement to the Feds."

"Provided you find any," I cautioned.

"Oh," he stated confidently, "now that I know what I'm looking for, I'll find it."

A new mantle of authority seemed to have settled around Mo's shoulders, transforming him from Cecille's passive lapdog into a man of action.

"Don't tell her where I've gone, Claire," he instructed. "I want to make sure I've got hard evidence first. I'm also going to have to get our insurance company to investigate this. We've got to find out whether those paintings were insured based on a higher value than they're actually worth."

"Not Lloyd's of London, I hope," I remarked facetiously.

Mo squinted at me suspiciously. "How did you know, Claire? Or was that just a lucky guess?"

"Neither," I hastened to assure him. "It's just that Belinda owns a half-interest in some paintings by a deceased Indian artist that have unaccountably vanished. She said they were insured by Lloyd's and that their investigator was useless because he couldn't locate the art."

"That's not been my experience with the company," Mo said. "I'll ask my guy there whether he knows anything about the case."

He grinned a crinkly grin. "If Belinda Callant's going to be supporting Reggie Worth from now on, we want to make sure she gets all the money she's entitled to. She'll need it."

"Ahem!"

Dan's irritable throat-clearing cut into our laughter.

Immediately, I felt furtive, but not because he'd discovered me in close conversation with another man.

Covertly, I inspected my husband. He certainly looked a whole lot neater than when I'd last seen him. Evidently, he'd taken time to comb his hair and freshen up before departing from the Legal Limit. He still retained an ambience of beer and smoke, however.

I summoned my poise. "Oh, hello, darling!" I greeted him blithely. "Did you have a good time?"

"Uh-huh," he grunted, looking askance at Mo.

"Dan, remember I was telling you about Maumus Tulley, Cecille's lawyer?"

As the two men shook hands, Mo said, "Sorry I can't stick around to get acquainted, Dan. But I sure owe you two a big one. Your wife will explain."

He thanked us both, then loped off toward the revolving doors.

Dan pushed the elevator button. "Okay, wife. Explain," he invited.

Balancing on the ledge of my strict policy of never lying, especially to Dan, I merely replied that after I'd done all the gift wrapping and telephoned Juanita and Ambrose ("By the way, Dan. We've got to meet Ax at eight o'clock tomorrow morning.") I decided to come downstairs and have a drink. (I didn't say where I'd had the drink.) I was just about to get on the elevator back to our room (after an unspecified interval of time), when Mo spotted me and wanted to talk.

" . . . and then you showed up." I finished, in synch with the arrival of the elevator.

During our ascent, I filled him in on that conversation, which had galvanized Mo into making tracks for the airport.

Dan whistled when I mentioned the insurance angle. "I never even considered that! Oh, yeah. They could conceivably nail Reggie not only for embezzlement, but also for insurance fraud."

"Mo doesn't want to do that, though," I told him. "He's only going to try to find enough evidence to convince Reggie it would be in his own best interests to fade gracefully out of the picture, as it were, and into Belinda's waiting arms."

"Into Belinda's waiting clutches is more like it," Dan observed, steering me from the elevator toward our door. "Reggie may very well wish he'd chosen prison before it's all over."

29

Foley and Charlotte's wedding day dawned very early for us.

At shortly past seven o'clock, we were driving up St. Charles Avenue, which was still swathed in cold morning mist.

Dan, looking a little bleary, but otherwise in good spirits, divided his attention between the traffic and a large Mocha Melt he'd sent me to fetch from Beanie's while he waited, motor idling, at the curb.

Basically, as many male tenants of the twenty-first floor as possible were being evicted from 10:00 A.M. to 4:00 P.M., because we girls would need as much space as we could get for our hair and makeup marathon.

Huey Dalton's room, vacant since Friday night when he'd disappeared from the barbeque, was no longer available. He'd turned up sometime late yesterday afternoon, a shadow of his former self.

After refusing to answer any questions, Huey had retired to his quarters, posting a DO NOT DISTURB sign. He hadn't even made it to the bachelor party. Presumably, he would emerge in time to serve in his capacity as usher tonight.

Now, Dan was to pick up his tuxedo and accessories at our house, then spend the rest of the day with Foley in his temporary residence, a snazzy furnished condo on the river. A limousine would deliver them to Riverside Manor for the wedding.

Charlotte and I would dress together in Dan's and my suite after I'd done her hair.

"Hey, darlin'. Does this house look familiar?" Dan teased, as we pulled into our driveway.

"Just barely," I replied, half-seriously. "It feels like we've been away much longer than we actually have."

Upstairs, it was evident that Juanita had been hard at work yesterday. Woodwork gleamed, tile sparkled, the paint smell was gone, and the fresh flowers I miraculously remembered to order in time were expertly arranged in tall vases.

She had even left a detailed list for the newlyweds, explaining where to find everything.

What, oh what, would I do without that precious woman? Hairy armpits and all, her price was far above rubies.

It wasn't until Dan went around switching on lamps that we saw what we'd missed when we walked in. A trail of rose petals had been scattered from the front door, leading to the guestroom!

Dan shook his head. "Can you beat that? I guess we're going to have to give her a raise."

Avoiding trampling the petals as best he could, he went through our bedroom into his dressing area to collect his formal attire.

Hearing a car pull up, I walked out onto the balcony and looked down. It was Ambrose's dark green Dodge minivan, bought for cash during one of his flush periods. In his philosophy, a van was a wise investment for any artist since you could always live in it if things got really bad.

Ambrose climbed out, then looked up and saw me. "Where y'aat, doilin'?" He yelled cheerfully. "Merry Christmas, and all. Listen, I got a friend to help me carry the feather chick down my stairs. But I'm going to need some major assistance getting her up there. That big mother frame's got to weigh over a hundred pounds, all by itself!"

"Dan will be right there," I called back.

I ran inside to find him. "Dan Louis! Ambrose is already here with the painting, but you've got to help him bring it up."

"You seem mighty excited about this," he commented, leisurely zipping the protective cover, stamped "Rubenstein Brothers" around his tuxedo.

I prodded him toward the door. "That's because I've seen it, and I can't wait until you do. Hurry!"

After he'd gone downstairs, I made out a check to Ambrose for the balance, adding a little extra, then put it with his wrapped Christmas gift.

I heard them struggling upstairs, and ran to the door. "Be careful!" I shouted.

Ambrose rounded the curve first. He was backing his way up as Dan guided him. "You got four more steps . . . three more . . . "

I felt much calmer when the painting was lying safely on our living room floor. It was wrapped in opaque plastic and string.

"Well, bring us some scissors, woman!" Dan ordered. "You got me all worked up over this thing now."

I scurried out to the kitchen, then flew back with a pair of shears, which I handed to Ambrose.

I held my breath as he cut the cord, then gently peeled the plastic aside.

Dan's reaction was all Ambrose could have wished. "Holy moly!" he breathed. His eyes widened into big blue marbles.

Ambrose smiled shyly. "Hey, I'm real jazzed you like it and everything, man."

"That doesn't even begin to cover it, Ax," Dan's voice sounded far away.

While he was thus transfixed, I drew Ambrose aside to complete our business.

"Intermission, Claire!" he protested when he saw the amount of the check I'd written.

"The laborer is worthy of his hire, Ambrose," I told him. "You earned this, and you'll take it if I have to stuff it into your ear."

Then, I extended the package. "This, however, is a gift. You didn't earn it. So the only thing you can do is receive it."

After engaging in a silent struggle, Ambrose reached out and accepted the small bright parcel from my hand. "You're good people and all, doilin'," he mumbled.

After bidding a final, wordless farewell to his creation, Ambrose made an emotional exit down the stairs.

Between us, Dan and I managed to get Charlotte's portrait safely into the guest room and up onto the mantlepiece. We made the happy discovery it was sufficiently broad and textured to anchor the painting securely, thus eliminating the cumbersome necessity of hanging it.

Before leaving, we stood at the door and gazed at Ambrose's masterpiece. Dan said quietly, "Well, I always thought he was good, but I never realized he was this good."

"I don't think Ambrose knew it himself," I told Dan.

When we pulled up in front of Foley's place, I said, "In a way, I'm almost as excited for Charlotte as I was when we got married, Dan. Do you feel like that about Foley?"

"Yeah," he agreed. "But beyond all that, I'm becoming more and more aware this marriage stuff is very serious business."

He gave me a sweet, lingering kiss. "I'll be waiting for you at the altar, baby!"

30

Morning tea was being served in the Court Lounge when I returned to Riverside Manor. The delectable scent of freshly-baked scones and crumpets bade me to partake.

While I yet wavered, Big Ben struck nine, deciding the issue. Marcel had decreed ten o'clock as the hour he and his entourage would arrive to begin transforming us into Cinderellas with facials, manicures, pedicures and hairstyles.

It wasn't often I had the luxury of being pampered from head to toe, all in one day, and I was definitely planning to make the most of it.

In the meantime, I ordered a pot of Ceylon tea and a crumpet with Canadian bacon and prepared to relax.

This proved unexpectedly difficult, because I kept seeing people I was curious about.

Reggie Worth, for instance. Natty in a blue blazer, he sat alone at a table across the room, peacefully immersed in the *Wall Street Journal*. Fawn Goldfeather's arrival put an end to his solitude. I couldn't imagine why she'd come at teatime, feeling as she did about the beverage.

When Fawn made as if to sit down, Reggie stopped her. At first, she looked angry, but his ensuing explanation—or lie—seemed to appease her, and she allowed a waitress to direct her to a table in the back, out of my viewing range.

The room began to fill rapidly and there was nowhere left to sit when Pearl and Topaz arrived. They spotted me before I could pretend I hadn't seen them. Sighing, I beckoned the aunts to join me. What else could I do?

"So charming of you to share your table with us, Claire," Pearl tweeted, settling herself with a flounce of printed silk.

"You, Miss! Over here, please!" Topaz yodeled to a passing waitress, startling the girl so, she nearly dropped her loaded tray.

When they'd ordered scones, marmalade, clotted cream and a double pot of China tea, Topaz fumbled in her large handbag and produced a padded brown envelope.

"I bet you can't guess what's in here, Claire!" She waggled it enticingly. The envelope had already been opened, and there was a bulge in the middle.

"Not more Aunt Sally's pralines!" Just in time, I remembered I wasn't supposed to know about the money.

The sisters exchanged secretive looks.

"Now, dear. We would hardly order those from"—Pearl lowered her voice dramatically—"Hong Kong!"

Topaz polished off a scone. "I can see you're not exactly on the ball today, Claire. Too much partying, no doubt." With incongruous daintiness, she licked marmalade from her fingers, then proceeded to re-open the envelope.

She peered cautiously in either direction before extracting a hinged box covered in worn blue velvet with a domed lid.

Pearl leaned forward, all her attention riveted on the container.

Then I knew.

"You found Marcel a sapphire ring like the one you were telling him about!"

Pearl's eyes were still glued to the jewel box. "No, dear," she corrected me through lips that barely moved. "There's not another ring like that one."

"What Pearl meant," Topaz interpreted, "is that yes, we did find Marcel a Kashmir blue sapphire ring. But it isn't *like* the ring we described to Marcel—"

"It *is* the ring! The very same ring!" Pearl broke in, unable to contain herself any longer.

"But, how?" I demanded.

Pearl's eyes began to fill. "Oh, it was the most amazing thing, Claire. Such an elementary idea, and so simple, it would scarcely seem to answer such a monumental endeavor."

Topaz picked up the narrative. During the past week, she and Pearl had literally left no stone unturned. They'd rented an e-mail address at a local computer store, and spent many hours surfing the web for leads, none of which had panned out.

Until yesterday morning, it never occurred to them to launch a search for Patek himself. Strictly as a last resort, they had posted a query, not expecting anything to come of it.

Two hours later, they were absolutely astounded to find an e-mail from Patek! He currently resided in Hong Kong, and would be pleased if they would telephone promptly.

"Patek made a killing in construction before the commies took over," Topaz said.

"However, his millions mean so little to him since his dear wife passed on. After learning of her death, I must say I felt a bit awkward about mentioning the ring, but I needn't have," Pearl added.

Patek was touched that their quest for a Kashmir sapphire had been inspired by their childhood memories of him, and romantic enough to believe his love for his wife would live on through the ring in Marcel and Nectarine.

Without further ado, an agreement had been reached. And now, via special courier, here it was, less than twenty-four hours later!

Gently, Topaz opened the frayed container to reveal the most beautiful blue stone I'd ever seen, surrounded by diamonds and set into a substantial platinum band.

Though the ring had been created for another bride long ago, it was unthinkable that anyone but Nectarine Savoy should wear it now. The sapphire was exactly the color of her eyes.

Closing the box with reverence, Topaz put it back in the envelope and returned it to her bag.

Pearl poured her sister a fresh cup of tea.

"Does Marcel know?" I asked.

"Not yet," Topaz admitted. "It only just arrived, you see. And frankly, we wanted to enjoy it ourselves first."

"I can understand that," I agreed. "You know, I think it's totally of God how that particular ring virtually flew to you two like a homing pigeon."

"Praise Jesus for the Internet!" Topaz declared, quaffing her tea and reaching for another scone.

Pearl had been observing the comings and goings of the well-dressed crowd with benign, baby-blue eyes. Suddenly, they sharpened to focus on someone behind me.

Swiveling in my chair, I saw Belinda Callant, looking fresh and vibrant in a Chanel suit of tangerine mohair. She affected not to notice us as the maitre d' escorted her to Reggie's table.

Reggie stood as she approached. They really were a perfectly matched set.

Pearl spoke with dogged determination. "One ring down, and one to go."

A few minutes later they abandoned me to savor the loot in the privacy of their room, before surrendering it to Marcel.

I felt too comfortable to leave, so I ordered another pot of tea, which I didn't want, to justify my continued occupancy of the table.

I sneaked a look at Reggie and Belinda. They were deep in conversation. For the first time, it consciously registered that Belinda never behaved aggressively coarse and vulgar around Reggie like she did other men. Instead she conducted herself in a ladylike manner that would've fooled me if I didn't know better.

But surely, Reggie wasn't fooled. Nor Belinda. It takes one to know one. Perhaps part of the attraction was that they could just be themselves. And possibly, even bring something better out in each other.

They drew apart when Kyle Dalton stopped by their table. His broad back blocked my view. It was frustrating not to be able to see their faces or hear what they were saying.

Eavesdropping, I was discovering, can be habit-forming.

Whatever transpired between the three of them, Kyle didn't linger. When he passed by my table, I was relieved to see he had himself under control.

Poor Kyle! Hopefully, he realized Belinda was a lost cause.

The couple resumed their tête-á-tête, too deeply engrossed to notice that Cecille had materialized and was watching them coldly from behind the brass railing separating the lounge from the lobby.

Thinking this was my chance to pump her, I waved, planning to offer to share my table. But either she didn't see me, or pretended not to, and walked away, which left me with my hand stuck in the air, feeling foolish.

The clock bonged out the quarter hour. Marcel's beauty squad was due in fifteen minutes, and I hadn't accomplished much in the way of detective work.

Hardly surprising, since I'm not a detective.

Ordinarily, neither Dan nor I would get involved in this raunchy soap opera: Cecille's warped marriage to Reggie, who was cheating on her financially and sexually; Belinda's three-way split between Sam, Kyle and Reggie; Kyle's unnatural obsession with Belinda and his hair-trigger temper; the Jekyll and Hyde effect of alcohol upon Sam; and Fawn's corrosive bitterness that refused to be pacified.

But given the abnormal number of potentially explosive situations swirling around Foley and Charlotte's wedding, we felt responsible to ensure that it came off without any hitch except the one pronouncing them man and wife.

Preparing to leave, I saw Montaigne Duffosat enter the storage room behind the bar. When the waitress brought my check, I told her I'd pay it at the bar register.

Montaigne was polite but distant.

"Listen," I said, "can we talk for a few minutes?"

She waved a vague hand. "I'm really very busy right now," she demurred.

"Please?" I coaxed.

"Okay," Montaigne looked resigned as she raised the mahogany bar flap. "Come through, we can talk in the storeroom."

I followed her into a similar space to our spyhole at the Legal Limit, only this one was much fancier. It was stocked with mammoth containers of olives, pickles, pretzels and nuts, along with cases of wine, liquor and assorted mixers.

"It's about Sam," I began.

Montaigne's face closed. "End of conversation."

I caught her arm. "No, wait. Please listen. All he wants is a chance to talk to you," I said. "Just thirty minutes to explain, and then it's up to you."

She looked down at her hands. "What shocked me, Claire, was how instantly and completely he changed, from sweet and gentle to violent. There wasn't even a transition period."

"He told us he tried to warn you."

"Yes, he did," she admitted. "But I'm afraid I thought he was exaggerating. He wasn't."

"Look, this may sound farfetched," I said, "but—never mind."

"What?" Montaigne prodded curiously.

"Well, Sam swore nothing like that had ever happened to him before he got mixed up with Belinda. Then he mentioned she was very involved with Daddy Jake, and—"

"Oh, please!" Montaigne exclaimed angrily. "I know all about Sam's destructive relationship with Belinda, and I was serious enough about him to deal with that whole can of worms.

"But now he's trying to claim she hoo-dooed him? Well, that's all I need, isn't it? Some weird little devil boy to light up my life!"

She shook her cloudy dark hair furiously. "No thanks! Tell him we'll talk—after he's been exorcised!"

Montaigne strode out of the pantry.

As I straggled after her, I noticed that Reggie and Belinda's table was now occupied by others.

It was horrible timing, plain and simple, that Sam happened to be at the maitre d's desk waiting for a table, but Montaigne naturally thought she'd been set up.

Flashing scornful eyes at me over one shoulder, she blew by Sam like a gust of Arctic air, the heavy silver cellar keys clanking a dirge to his hopes.

Sam made as if to follow her, but I restrained him. "Trust me, I wouldn't do that if I were you. The discussion did not go well at all."

"Shit, Claire! What did you say to her? What did she say to you?"

"Hey don't take that tone with me, Sam!" I shot back. "I didn't want to get in the middle of this in the first place, but you pleaded. I did my best, but she's not ready to talk to you yet."

He gave me a haggard look. "I'm sorry. It just feels like everything's caving in on me at once."

I tried to lighten things a bit. "Maybe you'll feel better after some tea and crumpets."

"Naah." He smiled faintly. "I think I just lost my appetite. Besides, there aren't any tables."

Fawn Goldfeather approached us. "I've got a table, Sam."

She explained she'd seen him waiting and offered, "Why don't you come sit with me?"

"I've already eaten, thank you," I said, as if she'd invited me, too. I was talking to air.

While Sam hesitated, Fawn had taken charge and was leading him off to her table. He sat down, looking bewildered as to how he'd gotten there, but clearly flattered. After all, he'd just been rejected by Montaigne, and Fawn, even with a chip on each shoulder, was a very attractive woman. He relaxed and let his wounded ego soak up the balm.

But once again, Sam's timing was disastrous. Maybe he really was under a curse!

Mercifully, though, he was unaware when Montaigne Duffosat reappeared, her heart having softened slightly in delayed response to my intercession for Sam. She had come back with every intention of giving him the opportunity to speak his piece, only to find him cozying up with Fawn over the menu.

Montaigne noted the twosome exchange a chuckle with their waitress. "Well, that's a load off my mind. The poor boy's not likely to die of grief." Caustically, she added, "Just don't try to convince me this one put a hex on him, too, Claire."

31

The twenty-first floor was in a state of cheerful pandemonium.

Nails were being done in Jolene and Bobette's room; facials in Daphne and Emory's; makeup in Imogene's; and hair was divided between Cecille and Reggie's room and our own.

Gradually, the stress and tension that had been building for days had mellowed into an atmosphere of festive anticipation and sisterhood as Marcel's elite wedding brigade herded us efficiently from treatment to treatment.

Since he would be doing Nectarine's and my hair last, I was trying to keep a low profile. He had an irritating habit, left over from the days when I was his personal assistant, of pressing me into service.

Eugenie, one of the two facialists, skillfully arranged me on her portable table without disturbing my still-damp fingers and toes. The manicurist had suggested what she called a "French Tiptoe" pedicure to match my French manicure, and I was glad I'd complied. It was a very sexy look.

Eugenie's speciality was the Epicuren facial, which I had become addicted to. I braced myself as she applied the cinnamon-scented glycolic masque, guaranteed to jumpstart your heart.

Through the several layers of products that followed, I let my mind drift, thinking how wonderful that in a few short hours, Foley and Charlotte would be getting married . . . wishing everybody could be happy . . . wouldn't it be fantastic if Imogene and Purcell reunited half a century later . . . wondering if Mo had unearthed any proof of Reggie's fraud already . . . hoping Montaigne and Sam could get back on track . . . which man Fawn really wanted, Reggie or Sam. Or neither one . . . whether Belinda was actually as serious about Reggie as she seemed . . . what Cecille would do if she was . . . what Reggie would do if she wasn't . . . whether Mo's dream of marrying Cecille was finally about to come true . . . what he'd do if it didn't . . . how thrilled Nectarine would be with her very special ring . . . if Belinda really intended to relinquish the black opal . . . *nobody better try to put something over on me or take anything that belongs to me, or else . . .*

"Okay, Claire. You're done," Eugenie said. She packed my face in a thick layer of colostrum cream. When it absorbed, my face would be taut, satiny and ready for makeup.

The hair had to come first, though. Marcel wasn't ready for me yet, so I wandered in and out of the other rooms, admiring Imogene's Gibson Girl pompadour, Daphne's sleek chignon, Alicia's biggish swirl.

I almost didn't recognize Mamie, she looked so different—not to mention ten years younger—with her customary top-heavy short cut sleeked straight back. No one thing went as far as a different hairstyle to totally change a person's looks.

"Why, Mamma! You look downright citified!" Bobette exclaimed.

"Hey, Bobette! She's been a Society Dalton all along and we never knew!" marveled Jolene. "Mamma, you ought to keep it like that for awhile," she advised.

Mamie was pleased but temporized, "We'll see how your daddy likes it."

The girls themselves were adorable in their ribbon-threaded braid coronets.

They saw me and slunk forward in exaggerated model glides.

"Look at us, Claire!" cried Jolene. "We're swan-yay!"

Bobette demanded, "Do you think we're ready to catch us a couple of those high-class New Orleans uptown men?"

"If they don't catch you first!" I laughed.

Lambie and I met in the hallway as she proceeded from nails to facial. All the bridesmaids were wearing red polish to match their dresses.

"How are . . . things?" I asked significantly.

She smiled. "I'd say T.J.'s beginning to get a real revelation."

I just bet he was.

Marcel and an assistant named Pepe were working on Cecille's hair in her room. Nectarine sat by watching.

"Hello, Claire. Goodness, your face is glowing!" she exclaimed.

"Thanks. It's partly excitement, partly the Epicuren," I replied.

"Wait a minute! They're not actually giving Epicuren facials in there? If I'd known that, I wouldn't've just been sitting here being mesmerized by Marcel's nimble fingers."

"You get a choice," mumbled Cecille, keeping her head bent as Marcel dictated. "I prefer the aromatherapy one. It's more relaxing."

Without looking up from his painstaking work, Marcel said, "My darling, while I am naturally delighted to be the focus of your attention, my self-esteem will certainly survive should you choose to avail yourself of Eugenie's services. I myself intend to do so before we leave to array ourselves in wedding garments."

Pepe looked confused. *"Como?"*

Nectarine was already on her feet. "In that case, catch you later, daddy. Toodles."

Pepe's brow furrowed with anxiety. He'd thought his English was improving.

I wanted to find out whether Marcel knew about the ring yet, but without giving anything away if he didn't.

"Have you seen Pearl and Topaz today?" I asked.

"Indeed I have not," Marcel replied. "They have unaccountably vanished."

"They're not the only ones," Cecille complained. "Remember Mo Tulley, my attorney, Claire? The friends he was staying with said he never came home last night. They were frantic, until he remembered to call and let them know he'd flown back to Atlanta."

She sounded royally pissed off, and a little uncertain, too, because he hadn't checked with her first. Which could be very good for Mo.

"Must've been a pressing legal matter," I suggested.

Cecille made a noise. "Mo's most pressing legal matters consist almost exclusively of my own. There's absolutely no excuse whatever for him flying off, right in the midst of revising my w—"

"Well, hello Fawn!" I exclaimed loudly, cutting Cecille off. With her head bent, she hadn't seen Fawn come in.

The last thing Cecille needed was for Fawn to relay the news of an imminent will change to Reggie. It wouldn't be hard to guess who was about to get the short end.

Fawn gave no sign of having heard. Instead, she was watching with interest as Marcel and Pepe intricately wove the braids into Cecille's own hair.

"This is what I was talking about the other day," I reminded her.

"It sure looks like a lot of trouble," Fawn commented.

"It's a pain in the neck, literally," snapped Cecille. She appealed to Marcel. "May I please raise my head now?"

"Certainly." Cecille straightened and wriggled her shoulders. But when she caught a glimpse of herself in the mirror, she froze in shock. The long dark plaits hung from her head as if they'd magically sprouted there.

"My God! I look more like an Indian than you do!" she told Fawn.

Fawn, in turn, looked almost as stunned as Cecille at the transformation.

Pepe brightened. This he understood. "*Si*, Indian! Woowooowoowooo!"

Fawn's hackles rose and she glared.

"Have you had an interesting day?" I asked quickly, to distract her.

"Actually, I have." She sounded mildly surprised. "Sam Stormshadow took me to see his exhibit again."

Now I was surprised. Sam had adamantly said he couldn't bear the sight of it. I failed to imagine him going there voluntarily.

Fawn's next sentence confirmed it. "He had to meet Mrs. Callant— Belinda—and the man who wants the new statue. So I went along to keep him company."

Ah, now the truth was out!

Marcel and Pepe began to join the braids together on top of Cecille's head. Her eyes met mine in the mirror ironically. Fawn's sole purpose had been to see Belinda.

"Speaking of *Mrs. Callant*," Cecille stressed the name, "didn't *my husband* tell me you finally have a meeting with her to show your portfolio?"

Fawn nodded. "Yes. Later this evening. We firmed it up today at the gallery. *Reggie* thinks there's a very good chance she'll represent me."

Cecille's gaze sharpened acquisitively. "Just remember which two paintings are spoken for."

"Reggie said he mentioned an advance deposit," was Fawn's rejoinder.

"It's extremely high." Cecille grimaced. "Particularly for an unknown."

"Well, that's the price." Fawn shrugged. "It doesn't matter. Belinda may not want me to reserve anything, even if somebody else offers a deposit."

Cecille said hastily. "I'll discuss it with Reggie again." Obviously, she really did crave those paintings.

"Suit yourself," Fawn said carelessly. A minute later, she left.

Cecille was still fretting over wanting the artwork and not wanting to pay so much for it, when Marcel and Pepe finished the coronet. She looked absolutely beautiful. As Jolene and Bobette would put it, "Real swan-yay."

With a crochet hook, Marcel deftly wove a piece of scarlet velvet ribbon through the braids, then passed Cecille the hand mirror.

"You know, it does make me look very interesting," Cecille admitted. "Almost like a different person."

"But now, no more Indian," mourned Pepe.

Champagne Buffet

December 24
5:30-6:30 P.M.
The Crystal Ballroom Corridor

Oysters on the half-shell.
Beluga Caviar served with sour cream
and sieved egg yolks.

Grilled Buster Crabs served with jalapeño sauce.
Chilled Gulf shrimp.

Relish tray of Portobello mushrooms, Kalemata olives,
baby artichokes and hearts of palm.

Perugina chocolate assortment.

Perrier Jouet Champagne 1987

32

The challenge of decorating for a yuletide wedding is to capture the warmth and sparkle of the season, yet avoid winding up with something that looks like the *Nutcracker Suite*.

Trevor of Fashion Bouquet had sidestepped this pitfall by confining himself to a color scheme of green, gold and white, filling the Crystal Ballroom with muted splendor.

Three hundred mundane folding chairs had been transformed by white muslin slipcovers, knotted in the back with green and gold tassels, and the dark green runner leading from entrance to altar had been stenciled with gold leaves.

A while back, Charlotte joked that Trevor might try to make her carry a partridge in a pear tree down the aisle. She had greatly underestimated his scope. Instead, he had surrounded the entire seating area with white stone planters containing tall ficus trees, adorned with pears of golden wood.

The altar was sheltered by a curved arbor entwined with white-frosted English ivy, mistletoe, and tassels of green and gold like those fastening the slipcovers. Semi-circular white wrought iron candlesticks held towering golden tapers.

The plethora of crystal chandeliers, whence the ballroom derived its name, were dimmed to cast a glow of perfection over all.

Strains of Renaissance music played upon harp and harpsichord by a female duo billing themselves "The Harpies" reached into the vestibule while Mrs. Cahoon gave her bridesmaids a final inspection. Then Sally Holt took over, reminding us to "lift from the diaphragm" as we walked.

Pushing one of the swinging doors open a crack, Sally expertly gauged the proceedings. All the guests had been seated now. Trevor's "pear trees" served both as stunning decor, and an effective screen from the audience.

Sally backed away when the door swung outward. Buddy Gaines, Charlotte's longtime friend and cameraman, exited with his elaborate video recorder trained on us.

"Y'all say something cute to Charlotte and Foley," he instructed, passing down the line.

When Charlotte had asked Buddy to recommend a video production company for her wedding, he was outraged and offended. "You don't really think I'm gonna let somebody else shoot this thing, after all we've been through together!"

Others at WBGZ felt the same way. Consequently, there was a team of three additional videographers under Buddy's direction tonight. Afterwards, they would edit and mix it at their own expense as a wedding gift to Charlotte.

After I delivered my little nugget to the camera, Buddy moved on to Nectarine. He was always a little skittish around her, because he'd gone out a couple of times with Officer Cates, a striking blonde rookie. Cates, however, was not nearly as enthusiastic as he would have liked. Buddy suspected she had confided her true feelings about him to Nectarine, but he didn't dare ask. And Nectarine gave him no hint.

The instruments faded softly out, Huey and Kyle's cue to swing open the double doors for us.

I was glad to see that Huey had recovered to the extent of being able to perform his usherly duties. He looked a little drained, but otherwise presentable.

His erratic son Kyle was, for the moment, mellow, flashing a smile of masculine appreciation at the sight of me and Nectarine in our slithery green velvet and feathers, and Lambie, Cecille, Jolene and Bobette in their strapless red grosgrain and coronets.

The bridesmaids' gowns and bouquets of scarlet sweetheart roses were the only red in the entire tableau, like a dash of cayenne for zing.

Oh, yes. And Charlotte's rubies. Her necklace and earrings had been delivered by messenger to our room while we were dressing. She immediately fell apart and I'd had to retouch her makeup.

We were all wearing our gold bracelets with the heart-shaped charms Charlotte had given us at the bridesmaids' luncheon.

All at once, the rich, pure harmonies of a French madrigal sung by an a capella quintet rung like bells into the silence. Two tall young black men in white tuxedos and clerical collars approached from either side of the altar and began lighting the gilded candles in the white iron holders. Meeting in the middle, they passed by each other and exited in opposite directions.

Next on the scene was Saint, majestic in a flowing white robe trimmed with gold. He carried a shiny black Bible, and looked ready for action.

A few beats after Saint came Foley. Tears stung my eyes at the sight of him, substantial and handsome in his wedding clothes. Dan was right behind him, so gorgeous I instantly felt lightheaded. He rested an encouraging hand on Foley's shoulder. Both men exuded that fresh, prosperous glow imparted by steam bath, massage and luxurious barbering from Pierre of Distingué.

Marcel, Leighton, Tucker John, Woody and Wes filed on in rapid succession. Behind me, a tiny hum of pleasure escaped Nectarine when she saw Marcel looking so fine.

As one, the bridegroom and his attendants turned in our direction.

"Okay, ladies. This is it!" Sally stage-whispered. "Remember, count seven before following the person ahead of you."

My heart starting racing, and I clutched my fragrant bouquet of gardenias. If not for the short, sexy little green panne gloves that matched my dress, my hands would've been damp.

For the thousandth time, I touched the reassuring bulge inside the palm of my left glove, Foley's wedding ring. He'd told Charlotte he wanted a band as wide as Dan's, and Mr. Sidney, from whom I'd purchased it, had found the perfect ring for Foley as well.

Like Dan's band, this was also an Italian antique of 18K gold, with deep, narrow, overlapping vertical pleats all around. It was a very masculine and impressive piece of jewelry. No one would ever guess that *Foley-pie* was engraved within.

A new madrigal began. "Claire, go!" hissed Sally.

I stepped out onto the green carpet scattered with golden leaves. There was a hushed little wave of admiration from the onlookers as I emerged into view.

From the corner of my eye, I spotted Juanita and Carlos Valle. Thank goodness she was at least wearing a shawl during the ceremony.

Dan observed my sedate progress with loving pride so strong, I could feel it pulling me toward him. When I reached the front, he closed one blue eye in a slow wink. I was now near enough to Saint to see he was wearing a big gold button on his white robe proclaiming, "Jesus is the Reason for the Season!"

Foley smiled, but I doubt he actually saw me, or any of the other bridesmaids that followed. He was saving his eyes for the bride.

The quintet finished their madrigal, and once more the room grew still. Anticipation began to build again. I had to admit, Sally Holt's sense of timing was superb.

The harpsichordist slid onto the bench of a small organ and plunged into "The Wedding March."

When Foley caught the first glimpse of his bride in her wedding gown, his knees literally buckled, she was so lovely. Dan unobtrusively grabbed his elbow before he could go crashing down. Not that anybody else noticed because they were standing in honor of Charlotte, entering on her father's arm.

The plumes of her headdress wafted gently. Rubies and diamonds flashed at her ears and throat. Her bouquet was a masterpiece of feathery white peonies that Trevor had had flown in from somewhere far away. Once he'd seen the plumes, no other flower would do.

Somehow, Foley managed to remain upright when Emory delivered Charlotte to him. Charlotte was pretty shaky herself. When she passed her bouquet to me, her trembling hand brushed my inner arm. It was ice-cold.

"Dearly beloved . . . "

Saint guided us through the traditional ceremony. Dan and I were able to transfer the rings when required with a minimum amount of awkwardness.

During Holy Communion, Saint explained the ancient symbolism of cutting a blood covenant with another person.

"In it they were saying, 'My life for your life. What I have is yours. What you have is mine. Your friends are my friends. Your enemies are my enemies.'

"They would cut the fingers or wrists and mingle their blood together, then rub a dye into the wound to always carry the mark of the covenant. And that is what the ring of the marriage covenant symbolizes, my brothers and sisters.

"Tonight, Foley and Charlotte kneel to partake of Holy Communion, which is in itself a mark of covenant between Almighty God and mankind, in the presence of the Father, Son and Holy Spirit, and you witnesses, as a testimony they will never break covenant with each other."

The candle lighting ceremony was accompanied by the madrigal singers. Foley and Charlotte lit their individual candles, then joined the flames to light a new candle, signifying two lives joined together as one.

" . . . and the two shall become one flesh," Saint concluded.

Then at last came the words Foley and Charlotte had waited so long to hear.

"I now pronounce you husband and wife. You may kiss your bride." Foley did so, with gusto.

"Ladies and gentlemen, I present to you Mr. and Mrs. Foley Preston Callant."

A storm of applause burst forth as the recessional march rang out and the radiant couple made their way up the aisle.

After a count of seven, it was our turn. The groomsmen actually all remembered to bow to their ladies.

I clung tightly to Dan's arm, feeling as if we were being transported on a wave of love and joy so glorious, it should have been powerful enough to sweep every evil thing completely away.

The reason it failed to do so is because human beings are free-will creations with the terrible power to choose between life and death, blessings and cursings.

Reverend Percival St. Dennis had taught us that marriage was a blood covenant.

But so was murder.

Reception Banquet

for
Mr. and Mrs. Foley Preston Callant, Jr.

December 24
The River Queen Club
Riverside Manor Hotel
New Orleans, Louisiana

Menu
Paté de Salmon
Consommé de Gibier
Supremés de Pintade Sautés
Nouillles Truffleés
Fenouil à la Vinagrette
Mousse au Pralin

Wedding Cake

33

The wedding party had just finished posing for what felt like several hundred formal photographs. My pupils were still strobing from all those flashes when we walked into the River Queen Club. There, we were greeted with an equally dazzling display.

After creating an elegantly restrained medieval chapel for the ceremony, Trevor had let himself go wild for the reception.

From the ceiling, luminous stars, snowflakes and mirror balls hung suspended from invisible wires. On each table stood a medium-sized rosemary bush clipped to the shape of a perfect Christmas tree, strung with tiny, twinkling blue lights.

Tall blue aluminum Christmas trees, trimmed with blue ornaments and big, old-fashioned blue bulbs lined the rear of the stage, providing a dramatic backdrop for the musicians imported from New York, Valerie Romanoff and the Starlite Orchestra. Charlotte had recently attended a wedding in New Jersey where the group was playing, and decided none other would suffice.

As we took our seats at the table on the dais, they were doing a medley of Cole Porter tunes.

I very much liked that dinner was being served one course at a time with dancing between, instead of buffet style.

Dan, as best man, led off with the first champagne toast to the couple, followed by Leighton, who pontificated at great length, then Marcel, ditto.

For Foley and Charlotte's first dance, the girl singer, à la 1940s big band with a smooth blonde pageboy and elbow-length gloves, crooned "Embraceable You." Foley gazed down adoringly at Charlotte, his dream come true.

Her now defeathered hairdo was holding its own very nicely, thank you.

Next to join them were Daphne and Emory, then Imogene and Purcell. After that, Dan and I led the rest of the wedding attendants onto the floor to finish out the dance together.

The orchestra segued into a set of classic ballads, and Dan and I exchanged partners with the bride and groom.

Foley held out his hand for me to admire his wedding ring, then spun me around energetically a few times before commencing some serious footwork on "Tea for Two."

"Well, I'm glad to see you got your landlegs back," I remarked.

He grinned. "Spotted that, did you? Honey, when I saw that gorgeous woman heading my way, my bones turned to rubber. For a minute there, I thought I was going to have to yell, 'Timber!' I never expected anything like that to happen. Thank God Danbo was on the case."

"That's what a best man is for," I said.

Foley held me tight. "You are *both* the best, Claire. If it weren't for you and Dan, I wouldn't have Charlotte. Do you realize the four of us will be together for the rest of our lives?"

He passed me on to Marcel, who said, "My beloved and I are receiving many inspirations for our own exchange of vows, Claire.

"However, while one acknowledges the unparalleled convenience of a hotel ceremony, we shall most likely select the St. Louis Cathedral. Aside from the distinct spiritual atmosphere wherein we prefer to begin our lives together, I must confess to a more unworthy motive; I have always cherished a secret wish to have policemen diverting traffic away from Jackson Square, solely on my account!"

Saint, dark face beaming ethereally, white robes billowing, swept by with Charlotte in an elegant meringué.

Leighton handled me with ponderous delicacy, as if fearing I might break. When I remembered him bawdily shaking his hips at "Della Street" and nearly falling off his chair, I began to giggle.

"Now, what's so funny, young lady?" Leighton asked. "Share the joke with your Uncle Leighton."

This set me off again. "Oh, but I couldn't!" I managed to say. "I mean, it's just that everything seems so marvelous and funny to me tonight. Can't you feel it, too?"

Leighton gave this his serious consideration. "No I can't say that I do," he replied finally.

That did it. I sensed a major fit of hilarity threatening to erupt. Leighton was looking at me strangely, which made it even funnier. Fortunately, I spotted Kitty standing with some other people, watching the dancing.

"Oh, look! I think Kitty wants to cut in on us, Leighton."

Flattered, he edged us in her direction.

"Okay, he's all yours!" I told a puzzled Kitty, and retreated.

"Dance, Claire?"

Kyle Dalton caught me by surprise, and I couldn't think of a nice way to say no. At least he was still sober and knew my name wasn't Darby.

"Uh, Claire? Remember the other night when . . . Belinda wanted me to tell Dan about a couple of my ideas?"

I nodded. "They sounded very interesting and potentially very profitable. Colored canvas primers and natural-born blue cotton, right?"

"Right. Well, Dan said he'd talk to me after the wedding if I liked. Did he really mean that?"

"Kyle, my husband never offers to do something he doesn't intend to honor. But I think what he had in mind was a meeting at his office next week."

"I know, but—well, something's come up. I've got to have legal advice in a hurry," said Kyle.

He looked so bleak, I took pity on him. "All right, Kyle. I'll tell Dan you need to see him soon as possible."

"Thanks, Claire," he said, in a relieved voice. "But tomorrow or the next day's fine. Nothing's going to happen tonight, anyway."

Famous last words.

Shortly thereafter, Dan found me and we returned to our table in time for the appetizer. All the food was rich and delicious, as befits Christmas fare. We laughed over the praline mousse, speculating that perhaps Pearl and Topaz had managed to ditch their truckload of Aunt Sally's with the chef. They certainly couldn't eat them all, no matter how well they kept in the freezer.

Between courses, we danced, table-hopped and gossiped. Everybody seemed to be having a wonderful time.

Jolene and Bobette had recaptured the young Blanchard, Smithson attorneys they'd met at the barbeque. The youths appeared dazzled by their exuberant personalities and their equally exuberant bosoms, forcibly gusseted into submission by Mrs. Cahoon.

Speaking of submission, Huey Dalton whirled by in the iron grip of Sally Holt. He must have been emitting some sort of signal audible only to dominatrixes. Else, how did they keep finding him?

As I'd predicted, Juanita was attracting a lot of attention. She had piled her hiplength hair high for the occasion, which made her appear even taller than Carlos than she actually was. The couple was jitterbugging to "Boogie Woogie Bugle Boy."

Above the low-cut blue gown, Juanita's traffic-stopping cleavage, which made even Jolene and Bobette look like they needed training bras, was misted with perspiration. It trickled down that satiny olive chasm, never to be seen again.

Each time Juanita lifted her arms, the eyes of every man nearby zeroed in on those dark, damp patches of hair.

Dan and I had the next two or three dances together, during which we teased each other with hints about our Christmas presents.

I saw Reggie skillfully maneuvering Cecille around the floor, but his eyes were scanning the crowd as if in search of someone else.

A musical riff preceded the announcement that the cake was about to be cut. Guests began gravitating forward as two white-coated waiters wheeled in the cart bearing a five-tiered wedding cake, uniquely frosted in white icing piped to look like hobnailed milk glass. The bride and groom figures on the topmost layer both had red hair.

When Foley carefully guided Charlotte's hand to make the first slice, it created a sensation. Inside, instead of traditional white, the cake was red!

Imogene preened at the reaction. "Well, can you think of a more fitting cake for a Christmas wedding than Red Velvet? I ask you!"

She'd gotten the recipe from a friend who'd gotten it from a nurse in Pensacola named, oddly enough, Opal. Imogene had had great fun surprising people with its unexpected red color and chocolate taste over the years. When Charlotte was trying to think of something spectacular for her wedding cake, she remembered her grandmother's Red Velvet, and requested the recipe be FedExed forthwith.

The bakery, Cakewalk, had no trouble calibrating ingredients for multiple layers. The only difference between this and the original was the icing.

I've never seen wedding cake go faster than Charlotte's Red Velvet.

It was getting close to the time for throwing the garter and bouquet. A few minutes later, as far as anyone knew, Foley and Charlotte would be on their way upstairs to the honeymoon suite.

What would actually happen was that Darren, the desk clerk, our co-conspirator, would be waiting to lock off the elevator from stopping on any other floor and whisk the couple right back down to the garage.

There, Blanchard, Smithson's Mercedes limo, driven by the enigmatic Rex, would rush them to our house.

It was such a simple scheme, yet we'd had to involve Juanita (which included Carlos), Darren, the bellboy who'd originally brought up Belinda and Sam's luggage, and now Rex, which meant tips galore.

Never mind. It was worth whatever it cost to give Foley and Charlotte the necessary privacy for a romantic wedding night, without offending Uncle Purcell and the rest of the Shiveree Boys.

There was a three-way tie for Charlotte's bouquet, between Lambie, Jolene and Bobette. But when Tucker John caught the garter, the other two girls good-naturedly conceded the flowers to Lambie.

The orchestra struck up "Making Whoopee," as a laughing Foley and Charlotte ran the gauntlet of rice-throwers to make their escape.

And an escape is exactly what it was, in more ways than one.

34

"They're stuck! I can't get them off! I can't get them off!"

Her panic-stricken cry ruptured the silence of the ladies' room, which had been deserted when I came in. She sounded like she was dying.

As quickly as possible, I flew out of my stall to discover Cecille, in a frenzy, trying to rip the braids from her head.

"Help me, Claire!" she pleaded.

"Sssh. It's okay, Cecille," I soothed, trying to gauge the situation.

Twenty minutes earlier, she'd been doing an impressive Hustle with one of Foley's cousins during the Starlite's disco set. Maybe she'd had too much to drink and it was hitting her all at once.

For whatever reason, Cecille had taken a sudden and violent dislike to her braids. I surveyed the havoc she'd wreaked and sighed. Obviously, she couldn't go back to the party looking like this.

Pushing her gently down onto a stool at the dressing table, I reminded her, "You're not supposed to be able to get them off, Cecille. That was the whole point."

She clung to me. "I want looong hair. Like yours, Claire. Like Beelzebub's."

"Who? Oh, you mean Belinda?"

"That's right," Cecille agreed. "Belinda, a daughter of Belial, son of Beelzebub."

"Hold still," I told her. I'd gotten the braids detached from each other at the top. The real job would be to unravel the tediously-woven extensions from her own hair.

"Do you have a comb?" I asked.

She flung a hand toward her long, narrow vintage evening bag. "In there."

"This may hurt," I warned.

"Everything hurts, Claire," Cecille droned. "It truly does."

"I thought you and Belinda were friends," I remarked casually, inserting the comb.

"Ouch! Not since I found out she wants Reggie. For keeps, I mean. Not just a loaner."

"So what?" I said, freeing another knot. "You don't want him anymore, do you?"

"That's not the point," Cecille snapped. "He's mine, and I should be the one to decide who gets him.

"Belialinda is out there dancing with him right now," she added.

I dropped the comb. "What? You mean she crashed the reception?"

Cecille went on darkly. "I know they're plotting to get together later. Well, I won't have it!"

"Have you talked to Mo?" I asked, changing the subject.

She grew haughty. "I have not! But he had the front desk page me several times today."

I felt excited. This could mean he'd found proof of Reggie's treachery.

"But I won't take his calls," Cecille continued. "He's got to learn he can't just pick up and go somewhere without telling me first."

"Is that really the kind of man you want, Cecille? Again?"

She maintained a stubborn silence.

At last, one of the braids came off, falling into Cecille's lap. She took it and tucked it comically beneath her nose like a mustache.

"Boy, do I need a lip wax!" she laughed.

"By the way, how much money does Fawn Goldfeather want up front to reserve those two paintings you like so much?" I inquired.

She glared at me suspiciously. "Why do you ask? Are you going to try and buy them yourself?"

"Not at all!" I stated emphatically. "I was just being nosy."

"Oh. Well, in that case, I'll tell you. Two hundred and fifty thousand down. One and a quarter grand apiece."

"Wait a minute!" I was shocked. "That's a half-million dollars for both. Aren't those pretty steep numbers for an unknown artist to demand?"

Cecille looked smug and sly. "If you tell her I said this, I'll deny it, but they are definitely worth it. More, probably."

The second braid came off in my hand. She took it from me, and tied it to the other with the red ribbon. I used water to reactivate the hair gel and spray, then did the best I could to make her coiffure presentable.

Cecille went on chattering about Fawn's work. "Reggie says once she begins exhibiting, they'll most likely double in value overnight. And that's his most conservative estimate.

"So you see, it's in my own best interest to pay a big price, because it makes a statement that this is a major league game from the get-go. And anyway, I adore Fawn's pictures."

Reflectively, she twirled the amputated braids. "I hate her, however."

Back in the River Queen Club, the emphasis had shifted from Society to Swamp.

Valerie and the Starlite Orchestra had called it a night. Now, Uncle Purcell and the Shiveree Boys were warming up for their big event by belting out a set of hillbilly classics; "Hey, Goodlookin'," "Just Because," "Don't Let the Stars Get in Your Eyes."

They sounded great. Their harmonies were slick and professional, yet with that haunting, just slightly off-note that typified the original country groups before country was cool.

Mamie, who'd declared she wanted no part of the actual shiveree itself, made up for it with a solo turn on "Don't Go Courtin' In a Hotrod," accompanying herself on the mandolin.

Blue was evidently Kyle Dalton's color, going from blue cotton to performing a moody version of Elvis's "Blue Christmas." He had a silvery voice, tarnished enough to be interesting. Together with his looks, he could probably have a successful recording career, if he half-tried.

Another change in the dynamics was an increasing number of strangers among the wedding guests, a signal that the gaming area had opened for play.

Foley and Charlotte only had exclusive use of the room until eleven-thirty, and it wasn't called the River Queen Club for nothing.

Dan and I danced some more, then walked around and visited with people we hadn't seen in a while. We noticed Reggie Worth enmeshed in an intense-looking poker game. Belinda, wearing a black dress and a wide diamond choker in place of a scarf to cover her throat, was standing behind him. She leaned over, murmured something, tapped her watch, and sauntered off.

Lambie and Tucker John had also been watching the poker players. Belinda paused briefly beside the couple, and made a remark that caused T.J. to flush. Lambie, hands curled into miniature fists, watched the other woman depart.

"If another woman tried to take T.J., I think I'd kill her."

But Belinda didn't get very far. Kyle, still wearing his banjo after a strenuous set of "pickin' and grinnin' " with Purcell that would've put Buck Owens and Roy Clark to shame, intercepted her.

It was too noisy for us to hear what they were saying, but Kyle was unmistakably furious. And when Belinda first drew a vertical line in the air, then held up seven fingers, waving them in his face, it was touch and go whether he would rip off his instrument and bash her senseless with it.

Instead, he stormed past her out of the club.

"If I'm interpreting the semaphore correctly, looks like she duped the boy into signing a straight-down-the-middle, fifty-fifty contract for seven years," Dan remarked.

"What does she do, have Kinko's run them off by the gross?" I snarled. I felt outraged for Kyle. No wonder he was so anxious to see Dan.

When I told Dan about my conversation with Kyle, he shook his head. "How the hell did I get to be the Belinda contract-breaking specialist all of a sudden?"

Belinda resumed her leisurely stroll to the exit, but was again thwarted. By Cecille, this time.

Cecille looked absolutely bizarre. She was clutching an open, white-flowered bottle of Perrier Jouet, and her hair, which I'd tried to tame, had erupted into wild little clumps.

In this case, we could hear all too clearly what was said.

"You rotten, conniving daughter of Belial!" shrieked Cecille. "You're not going to get my husband, my art, or one nickel of my money! I'll see you dead first, you bitch!"

A knot of spectators began to gather.

Cecille put her thumb over the bottle opening and shook it hard.

Belinda, realizing what was coming a few beats too late, attempted to run, but Cecille caught her with a solid spray of champagne all over her black sliver of an Isaac Mizrah dress.

Howling with laughter, Cecille was getting ready to aim another blast at her fleeing target, but Woody and Wes showed up just in time to stop her.

"Come on now, Cece," said one, taking her arm gently. "Nothing's worth carrying on like this."

"That's right," agreed the other. "We're supposed to be having a good time. Hey, listen. Mamma and Daddy are waiting for you at our table. They saved you a big piece of Charlotte's wedding cake."

"Cake?" Cecille dropped the bottle, and it smashed and fizzed several feet in every direction across the floor. "That red cake? Oh, it's beautiful!"

"It tastes even better than it looks, Sis. Hurry up though, before Daddy eats the whole thing."

"You know," Cecille said dreamily, as her two little brothers escorted her away, "when I get married again, I want a red cake, too. Only bigger. Much bigger. Seven tiers . . . "

Apparently, any drunken Dalton, whether Swamp or Society, could be lured away from violent behavior by the promise of dessert. We had witnessed Lambie and T.J. work it on Kyle the night of Belinda's dinner at Antoine's.

"Dan, what on earth is a daughter of Belial?"

"Well, let's see. If memory serves, the sons of Belial were a gang of perverts in Sodom and Gommorah who tried to break down Lot's door in order to rape the angels God sent to get him and his family out before the place was toast. So, I guess a daughter of Belial would be their sister."

"Hmmm." I couldn't quite see the analogy, but it apparently made sense to Cecille.

The excitement was over and still, no hotel janitor had arrived to mop up.

It was a very busy night at Riverside Manor, and they were clearly shorthanded. For instance, even though the uneaten wedding cake had been boxed up and stored safely away, the cart it was wheeled in on still stood in the same spot. All that remained was a stack of smeary plates and silver, and the cake knife, its blade congealed in red crumbs and white icing.

Surely someone was seeing to the knife, which was Imogene's. She'd lent it to Charlotte for her "something old." Cecille had loudly complained that Imogene had promised it to her.

Now, people were forced to carefully navigate through the expensive mess on the floor as best they could.

Two of these were Pearl and Topaz.

"You-hoo! Claire! Dan!" Topaz bellowed. "Guess what?"

"Don't be silly, dear. How can they guess?" Pearl chided.

To us, she said, "At long last, our beloved sister's ring shall return to the bosom of its family tonight. Belinda has agreed to sell!"

Topaz snorted. "And high time, too! Anyway, we're going up to our room now to wait for her call." She looked at her watch. "12:25. She didn't have much on so it shouldn't take her very long to dry off. Wasn't that a hoot?"

"Such a wonderful Christmas present!" Pearl exclaimed happily, not specifying whether she meant the ring's return, or Belinda's humiliation.

"And to all a good night!" Dan muttered with a smile, as we waved goodbye.

"Speaking of Christmas, Dan Louis. Shouldn't all good little girls and boys be nestled snug in their beds, right about now?"

He gave me a squeeze. "In about twenty minutes or so, darlin'. I have to see Saint and present him with Foley's honorarium check first. And if you notice, he's still eating and debating theology with Charlotte's folks. But, listen. Long as we're waiting, let's go and watch the suckers."

Our detour around the champagne mud puddle took us past the foyer. It was filled with people either waiting for an elevator down, or being disgorged from an arriving car. Two of the debarking passengers were Montaigne Duffosat and Sam Stormshadow. She was walking fast, but he grabbed her by the shoulder.

I caught the flash of danger in her eyes as she whirled around. "How many times do I have to say it, Sam?" she demanded. "Until you're completely loose from that woman, I won't—I can't—have anything to do with you. Now, let go of me or I swear, Sam—I'll call security."

He dropped his hand and watched as she about-faced and plunged into a crowded, lobby-bound elevator just as the doors were closing.

Simultaneously, a casually-dressed Fawn Goldfeather who had decided to give the wedding a miss, came pushing her way upstream through the bottleneck in front of the elevators toward Sam. Her cheeks were flushed and her eyes glittered.

Sam gave one last look at the closed elevator door, then hailed Fawn. "Hey! Just who I was waiting for!"

They didn't notice Cecille's wreckage on their way to the dance floor. Fawn slipped and almost fell.

"Damn!" Sam exclaimed, catching her. "What happened here?"

"Boy, did you miss a fight, pal!" answered a stocky man who looked like a tourist. He was relishing his role as commentator. "Two broads from some big wedding. One was a real looker—long hair, black dress. The other broad threatened her with a bottle of champagne, can you believe? Careful, you'll cut yourself," he warned Fawn. "Somebody's supposed to be here in a minute to clean up."

At the games, two or three people were on a roll, but Reggie Worth definitely wasn't one of them. As we approached the poker table, a suave, tuxedoed gentleman bent and spoke discreetly into Reggie's ear.

Reggie folded his final losing hand and, with dignity, rose from the table and accompanied the man. Turning a corner, they disappeared.

Dan whistled softly.

"Mercy! That looks serious."

It was.

35

During our absence, a bottle of Perrier Jouet and a box of Perugina chocolates, compliments of Mr. and Mrs. Foley P. Callant, had been delivered to our room.

We also found an emotional, garbled voicemail message from the aforementioned Callants, attempting to express the impact of Charlotte's portrait upon them, and raves for their delightful little love nest.

I noticed the gifts scattered beneath the Christmas tree had multiplied slightly. A narrow gold box trailing silver ribbons caught my eye.

"Looks like Santa Claus has been busy up here," Dan remarked.

When he bent over to plug in the tree lights, I couldn't resist stepping over to caress his fine Southern behind before he got a chance to straighten up.

"I just hope Santa's not too worn out to get busy again," I said, deciding it would be lots of fun to see him in the skimpy briefs with two great big jingle bells attached—one red, one green.

"He'll be fresh as a daisy, darlin'," Dan promised. "Just give him a minute to slip into something comfortable."

"In that case," I said, fishing the correct package out from among the others, "how about trying these on for size? Although I must confess, your comfort wasn't exactly uppermost in my mind when I purchased them."

The parcel jangled faintly as Dan shook it. "Sounds like a pair of spurs," he said.

I laughed. "No, darling. Mommy didn't know ums wanted a cowboy outfit! This is more like, well—a Shiveree Boy outfit."

"Hell, I'd forgotten about that! When is the thing supposed to start?"

"It's after one o'clock, so probably any time now. Which works out fine. You'll blend right in!"

Dan pointed a finger at me. "Listen here, Claire. Somehow, you seem to have gotten the notion I'm your love slave." He grinned. "And you're absolutely right!"

He began to tear off the wrapping paper.

"Stop!" I ordered suddenly.

Dan paused. "Now, what? Do I have to submerge it in water first so it won't explode?"

"Nothing like that," I assured him, spotting another intriguing new box—shiny black with a pink net bow—while rummaging through the gifts again. "I just think we should start slow and build up to that one."

I got him to trade in the original package for the package containing the black silk boxers that read, *Your real present comes later!* "Here. I think Santa will find these very comfy indeed."

He carried it off with him, unopened, into the bathroom to change. I could hear the paper being ripped off. Then I heard him laugh. "Not that much later, darlin'!" he called through the closed door.

And it wasn't.

That's why the sudden, strident clanging of a bell caught us completely by surprise. At first, Dan thought it was the fire alarm. Then we remembered.

Flopping back against the pillows, he laughed. "Well, here's a chance to test Marcel's theory about this ritual being an aphrodisiac."

"Marcel's theory is that everything's an aphrodisiac," I reminded Dan. "It's the secret of his strength."

The chuckwagon-style dinner bell was joined by dully clanking cowbells and a tambourine or two, but not merely in random cacophony. There was a distinct rhythm pattern. I had to admit, it was kind of sexy at that.

Perhaps now would be the perfect moment to ring those jingle bells.

Telling Dan I'd be right back, I went into the sitting room to retrieve that first package.

Just then, the banjo and guitar kicked in, and the Shiveree Boys began to sing.

Two hearts throbbing as one
Form a union more sweet
Yon lovers must mate
To the shiveree beat

It was an eerily beautiful melody, chosen, I recalled, for Imogene and Purcell's wedding night that never happened. I pictured Imogene lying in her bed right now, and wondered how she must be feeling.

Dan howled when he opened the present. "Oh, this time you've gone too far, Evangeline Claire!"

"Goody. That was my intention," I confessed.

He held up the slice of Spandex from which the two suggestive bells depended. "And you actually expect me to put this—these—on?"

"You are my love slave. Remember?"

Dan laughed again. "I must be since I'm actually considering doing it. Well, okay. Your wish is my command. But if I'm going to act this crazy, I want to make a grand entrance."

He left and I buried my face in the pillow to muffle my mirth. Silly, sexy fun was just what we needed after all the stress and tension of these last weeks.

The Shiveree Boys sounded closer. No singing now, just instruments, but the pace had picked up. I gathered they were walking back and forth through the corridor, building volume and speed until they judged the moment was ripe to lay siege to the bridal chamber.

My mental image of Belinda's reaction, not to mention whoever happened to be in there with her, struck me as so hilarious, I had to drum my heels on the mattress.

In the immediate vicinity, another set of bells heralded Dan's return before he actually came into view.

"Wow!" I yelped, at the sight of him. What started out as just a goofy caper had taken on an entirely new aspect.

He slid melodiously into bed beside me, my own big old personal Shiveree Boy in the luscious flesh.

"Is this what you had in mind, darlin'?" he inquired.

"No, sir. It's way, way better," I told him.

Propping himself up against the headboard, he produced the black box tied up in pink net I'd noticed earlier.

"I know you prefer to open your presents on Christmas morning, baby. But I just can't wait that long to give you this one."

The shiveree music sounded at once louder and farther away. They were moving in for the kill.

I reached out for the present, but Dan held it back. "No. Come sit on my lap and open it."

"But I don't want to crush your, um . . . bells," I demurred.

Suffice it to say, I have never had a more rewarding experience unwrapping a present. It's just as well I didn't realize it was the last one I'd be opening for awhile.

Inside the box was a gold Tiffany Tessoro watch. I was rendered speechless. Quick, silent tears rolled down my cheeks as Dan fastened it around my wrist.

The shiveree was growing louder and faster.

"This is the best way I know to tell you how much I treasure every moment I spend with you, Claire," he said softly.

Ironically, moments were all we'd have before tragedy struck.

Just when the shiveree had reached maximum decibel and tempo, it broke off abruptly. An earsplitting crash followed. Then, blessed silence.

"There went the door!" Dan chuckled. "I bet Belinda is boiling!"

"You are confusing me with someone who cares," I informed him. "I shall now demonstrate how much I treasure every moment with you, Dan Louis."

But it was not to be.

Into the stillness erupted a bloodcurdling, masculine shriek, succeeded by loud shouting.

"That does it!" fumed Dan, jumping out of bed. He grabbed his bathrobe from a chair and sashed it. "I'm going down there and put a stop to this right now."

"Wait! I'm coming too," I said, not wanting to miss out on the fun. Little did I know.

I trotted alongside Dan, who was oblivious to the fact he was jingling all the way, surprised that not one person had been curious enough to open their door.

I figured they were either passed out, or had simply endured the ceremony and were now preparing for sleep.

When we arrived at the honeymoon suite, Kyle was on his knees in the hallway, wailing like an injured wolf.

"Poor guy's drunker than six skunks," was Dan's snap diagnosis.

The remaining Shiveree Boys milled uncertainly outside the splintered door, which had been kicked open according to tradition.

"Okay, everybody!" Dan called out. "Enough is enough. Break it up. Now!"

Nobody responded.

Dan scowled. "Claire, these people are crazy!" he muttered. "Hey, Emory! Fenton, Purcell! What's the matter with you guys?" he demanded, as we came up behind the group.

Only then did we see that Woody or Wes was vomiting.

Purcell turned his head slowly to look at Dan, and I was shocked. His usually affable face was grim and grey.

"Take a look and see for yourself, son. What we got here is murder most vile. Step aside boys," he added to the others.

Silently, they parted to give us a clear view.

Dan grabbed my head and pressed my face tightly against his chest.

"Don't look, Claire!" he said, in a choked voice.

But it was too late.

I had already seen the body.

It was a naked woman.

She had been stabbed numerous times. Two knife handles and a long, thick shard of green glass protruded variously from her throat, her heart and her womb.

A raw, crescent-shaped patch above her forehead revealed she had been scalped. The severed hank of hair lay several feet away on the carpet beside her, along with two crumpled green objects that were nothing but oddly familiar blurs to me at the time.

She was arranged in a contorted position, and red roses had been flung down upon her body.

It was an awkward, grisly parody of one of Sam Stormshadow's blood-drenched sculptures of Belinda.

It was, in fact, Belinda.

36

My beautiful new watch said it was exactly twenty-three minutes after two on Christmas morning.

I kept my eyes fastened on the dial, because no place else was safe to look.

It's not easy to project an air of authority while wearing nothing but a bathrobe and a pair of naughty, noisy underwear, but Dan managed it, instructing Purcell and his motley shiveree band to return to their own rooms.

Between them, Huey and Tucker John hauled Kyle to his feet and led him away. Purcell trailed stiffly behind them, carrying an armload of percussion instruments scattered by the others.

Whichever twin had been throwing up lapsed into an occasional dry heave. His brother gently mopped his face with a handkerchief, then they walked off together, leaning on each other for support.

Emory looked like a zombie. "I thought . . . at first . . . Charlotte," he mumbled. "Where's Charlotte? Where's my little girl?"

"Don't worry, Emory. She's fine," Dan assured him. "They sneaked away. Understand?"

A little color seeped back into Emory's face as he caught the gist. "Thank God," he breathed faintly, and shuffled down the corridor toward his and Daphne's room.

Fenton started to follow Emory, but Dan stopped him. "How are you holding up, Fenton?"

The other man shrugged, causing the guitar slung over one shoulder to rise. "Good as you might expect after seeing that in there." He jerked a thumb toward the honeymoon suite. "A little rickety, maybe, but I ain't about to cave, if that's what you mean."

"Good," said Dan, "because we need you to stand guard while we go contact the police. Don't let anybody in, no matter who it is, no matter what they say."

"You got it, compadre!" Fenton saluted, looking perkier.

Dan put his hand in his bathrobe pocket and gingerly pulled the ruined door to by its knob. "Another thing, Fenton. Don't touch the doorknob."

"Didn't in the first place," Fenton reminded him. "Ain't likely to now."

We left him propped against the wall on the opposite side from the vomit-spattered carpet, strumming moody chords on his guitar.

Back in our room, while Dan tossed the jingling briefs aside in favor of conventional Calvins, jeans and a cable knit sweater, we discussed how best to approach Detective Sergeant Nectarine Savoy.

Regardless of the fact that Belinda Callant lay brutally murdered, our primary concern—rightly or wrongly—was that Foley and Charlotte take off on their honeymoon in a few short hours, unimpeded by a criminal investigation, and unburdened with any knowledge of the crime.

When they returned to New Orleans would be soon enough to face all the emotional ramifications of Belinda's death.

We knew the murder had been committed outside Nectarine's district, but hopefully, she could grease a few wheels to ensure maximum efficiency and minimum publicity.

I looked up Savoy's home number for Dan in my calendar book, realizing I'd neglected to buy a new set of pages for the coming year. Belinda most likely had already done so, because her business required so much advance planning.

I wondered if she'd experienced the slightest premonition, when she paid for that cellophane-wrapped package of days, that she'd never live to see one of them? Evidently, neither her so-called "wise-woman" in New Mexico, nor Daddy Jake had predicted this eventuality, since Belinda was seriously considering marriage to Reggie Worth. According to Cecille, anyway.

I duplicated Dan's attire of jeans and sweater, keeping an ear trained on his end of the conversation with Nectarine.

"Uh . . . Nectarine? This is Dan. Listen, I'm real sorry to wake you up, but the fact is, well, there's been a murder . . . yes, you heard right, I'm afraid . . . Belinda Callant . . . here in the hotel . . . the honeymoon suite . . . " He grimaced and held the phone away from his ear.

"It's a long story . . . yes, Fenton's guarding the door . . . so how do you recommend we proceed . . . uh-huh . . . will do . . . thanks."

Hanging up, Dan reported that Nectarine had ordered us to sit tight and do nothing while she made a few phone calls.

I went into the kitchenette to start a pot of coffee, then joined Dan on the sofa. He was lost in thought, staring unseeingly at the Christmas tree lights, which twinkled every bit as cheerily as they had before.

He automatically reached down to stroke my hair when I put my head in his lap, but since it was still done up in wedding mode, any comfort to be derived was limited.

Without warning, an image of Belinda's long, severed hank of hair, still attached to its piece of scalp, popped into my mind. I began to shiver in delayed reaction.

Dan realized what was happening. "Hang on, baby. I'll get you some coffee."

He returned quickly with a steaming mug that sported Riverside Manor's logo. He'd added a couple spoons of sugar to the coffee, and after a few sips, I began to feel warm again.

"Dan, that grotesque parody of a Stormshadow sculpture! Who could have ever calculated such a hideous way to kill Belinda?"

He looked at me sadly. "Claire, based on what we know, I'm sorry to say the most likely person to think of doing it like that would be Sam Stormshadow himself."

It was some consolation to learn the investigation would be in competent hands. And a big surprise when we discovered to whom those hands belonged.

"How did you get yourself assigned to this?" Dan demanded of Nectarine Savoy, when she came to our room after starting the ball rolling.

Nectarine ticked off points on her fingers. "One. I got transferred. Two. It's not quite dawn on Christmas Day. And three, Captain Carruth thinks he's punishing me."

I remembered after the bridesmaids' luncheon, Nectarine had been late for her dress fitting, mentioning that something had gone down at headquarters.

At the time, I frankly hadn't been interested, figuring she'd meant skirmishes with the usual felons, but no. Orders had descended from on high that Detective Sergeant Nectarine Savoy was to be transferred to the Eighth District, forthwith.

Few were happy about this.

Not Nectarine, who had toiled laboriously to hone her people into top-notch investigators.

Not Captain Russo of the Second District, who didn't wish to lose Nectarine. Least of all, Captain Carruth of the Eighth District, who did not wish Nectarine to fill the prize slot he'd had his eye on for his own handpicked protégé.

In career terms, though, it was a good diagonal move for Nectarine, because the post carried a slightly higher increment of authority. And a fortunate one for us, since Riverside Manor was located in the Eighth District.

"But enough about me." Nectarine's manner shifted abruptly.

"Obviously, there's been a whole lot going on around here I didn't know about, so I expect you two to fill in the blanks for me. Let's begin with why Belinda Callant was in the honeymoon suite instead of Foley and Charlotte."

When Dan started off by reminding her of Belinda's original reservations snafu with Riverside Manor, she nodded impatiently.

"Yes, yes. But Marcel and I left to hold the table at Bayonna before the situation was resolved. And we never really discussed it afterwards."

Dan explained how the necessity of accommodating Belinda and Sam dovetailed with Foley and Charlotte's desire to escape the shiveree, yet avoid offending Uncle Purcell and the band.

"So, since they wouldn't be using the suite for several more days anyhow, it seemed like the perfect solution," Dan concluded.

"The only catch was that Belinda and Sam had to promise not to let anyone else on the twenty-first floor know they were in the honeymoon suite, which would've defeated the whole purpose."

"And do you think they lived up to their side of the bargain?" Nectarine inquired.

Dan gestured in the direction of the murder room. "Doesn't much look like it."

"No," she agreed. Pulling out her familiar brown leather notebook and gold pen from her designer tote, she started writing. I noticed she wasn't wearing the sapphire ring. Either Pearl and Topaz were still selfishly holding out on Marcel, or he planned to give it to Nectarine later today.

If so, he was going to have a long wait.

I stole a look at my watch. After four. So far, so good. Nectarine hadn't yet asked where Foley and Charlotte were now. In four more hours, we could truthfully answer we didn't know.

Meanwhile, Nectarine continued to quiz us regarding Belinda.

Reluctantly, we told of her management padlock on Sam's career, how she'd possibly duped Kyle Dalton into signing away half of something that hadn't yet materialized for seven years, and her alleged intention to not only take Reggie Worth from Cecille, but to cut her out of the Fawn Goldfeather art deal as well.

Nectarine raised her eyebrow when we described the separate physical attacks by Kyle, Sam and Cecille against Belinda.

"Obviously a woman who inspired strong feelings, either positive or negative," she commented. "I notice, though, you neglected to mention the victim's fight with Charlotte."

"Belinda started it!" I shrilled childishly. "She goaded Charlotte about Foley, then pushed her. Charlotte just finally popped. But she's the one who got the worst of it, having her stomach pumped and all."

"Be that as it may," Nectarine replied firmly, "it has to go into the report."

She scribbled some more in her notebook, then cleared her throat.

"Okay. Let's recap. Belinda Callant's ex-husband provided lodging for her and her lover, Sam Stormshadow, with the proviso they would not reveal which room they were occupying to any of the wedding guests.

"Naturally, Mr. Callant expected the couple to confine themselves to their own devices and business. Instead, Mrs. Callant actually sought out opportunities to mingle with various members of Mr. Callant's party in residence at the hotel.

"On two separate occasions, Mrs. Callant crashed events intended exclusively for invited guests, and was physically attacked each time. The first incident involved Mr. Callant's then-fiancée, Charlotte Dalton. The second, Cecille Worth, wife of Reggie Worth, with whom the victim allegedly intended to enter into a business and personal partnership.

"On another occasion, Mrs. Callant was attacked twice. First, by Kyle Dalton, whom she allegedly duped into a disadvantageous contract by using sex. Second, by Sam Stormshadow, also involved in a disadvantageous contract with the victim."

Nectarine paused. "Does this track so far?"

"You got all that just from what we told you?" I marveled, impressed by her synopsis.

"Mostly," Nectarine said, then concluded her narrative.

"Victim at this point was last seen alive leaving the River Queen Club after being accosted by Cecille Worth with a bottle of champagne. Her body was discovered at approximately 2:15 A.M. on December 25, in the honeymoon suite originally designated for the overnight use of Mr. Callant and his new bride. Victim was apparently murdered in such a manner as to emulate one of Mr. Stormshadow's sculptures of her."

Nectarine started to close her notebook, then paused. "Is there anything else I should know before I began questioning the other guests on this floor?"

Dan replied he couldn't think of anything at the moment, while I resolutely omitted Lambie's empty (I was certain) threat to kill any woman who tried to take Tucker John away from her.

Also, there was another source of enmity I definitely didn't want to bring up—the one between Pearl, Topaz and Belinda. Because I had just flashed on Belinda's pathetic corpse again, and remembered something I'd subconsciously noticed at the time. She was no longer wearing the black opal ring!

Which meant the aunts had possibly been the last people to see her alive. Except the killer, of course. Unless they . . . no! They wouldn't have. The only thing they wanted was the ring, and Belinda had promised it to them. Or so they said . . .

This time, Nectarine did close the notebook.

"What strikes me as odd is how many people on this floor Belinda was involved with, in one way or another," she remarked.

"Not when you remember she already knew Pearl and Topaz, and Foley's cousins from when she was married to Foley," Dan pointed out.

Nectarine nodded. "Yes. But I was thinking more about the ones she didn't know before—Kyle, Reggie, Cecille. And, because of Reggie, Fawn."

A pounding on the door interrupted us.

"Sergeant Savoy!" bellowed a man. "Are you in there?"

Nectarine made a wry face. "You should see what Carruth assigned me to work with. Now *that's* punishment. I'd give anything for that old grouch Leo Wickes, right about now."

Dan opened the door to admit two plainclothes detectives.

One was tall, fair-haired and pink-faced; the other short, chubby, jet black and bald. They looked askance at Dan and me, trying to remember where they'd seen us before.

Dan and I exchanged glances. We recognized them, all right.

Nectarine performed the introductions. "Mr. and Mrs. Claiborne will be helping us out. They've worked with the police before."

"Sergeant, we already got this case sewed up tighter'n a chicken butt," declared Jim Cletus, the chubby officer.

"Is that right?" Nectarine murmured.

"Yeah!" said the other, Officer Wayne Harp. "Just a couple days ago, her boyfriend beat her up. We arrested him, but she refused to press charges."

"I recognized the signs," Cletus said dolefully. "I warned her, but she wouldn't listen."

Harp tsk-tsked. "And now just look at her. The poor broad."

"Anyway, Sergeant," Cletus finished. "You find the Indian, you got your killer and we can all go home to our Christmas turkey."

38

Our Christmas tree lights had to be unplugged in order to prevent a power surge when a techie-type officer arrived from the station to set up his computer.

Nectarine had not consulted us before requisitioning our suite as a temporary base of operations. Now, NOPD personnel were ebbing and flowing through the door, which stood propped open with a wrought iron stool from the kitchenette counter.

While we weren't ordered to stay in our boudoir, there was nowhere else to go. Thankfully, a small powder room located just inside the entrance was adequate to answer any police calls of nature, allowing us to retain some shred of privacy because they wouldn't be barging through to use our bathroom.

But, much as Dan and I wanted to close ourselves off and pull the covers over our heads, we were also unwillingly drawn by the all-too-familiar swirl of energy surrounding a homicide investigation emanating from the living area. Cell phones whirred, beepers went off, computer keys clicked, voices rose and fell.

We wound up drinking coffee at the small round table intended for romantic bedside dining, and kept our door ajar, the better to hear what was going on. Like Sergeant Savoy, gently but firmly setting Officers Cletus and Harp straight about who was in charge of this case.

The two men were frustrated because she wouldn't allow them to churlishly rout everybody from their beds at once, then force them to anxiously await their turn for questioning.

Nectarine's strategy was just the opposite.

She reminded them that this killer had very recently committed a particularly gruesome murder, which he knew was likely to be discovered by the Shiveree Boys.

If still on the premises, he would be anticipating and prepared for exactly what Cletus and Harp were proposing—a wholesale roundup to announce there'd been a murder. In the emotional bedlam that followed, he would be able to legitimately release some of his pent up tension without serious danger of giving himself away.

However, if they approached and questioned each single guest or couple on this floor separately, with as little fanfare as possible, it would keep the killer isolated from any viable emotional outlet, and in a state of suspense as to what was going on. Which just might be enough to throw him off balance and provoke some word or deed of self-betrayal.

The officers were extremely disgruntled by what they considered to be an unnecessarily oblique angle, but had no choice other than to comply.

It was now 5:30 A.M. In one hour, Foley and Charlotte should be on their way to Moisant airport, blissfully unaware of what had happened to Belinda.

When our own phone rang, Dan quickly started to pick up the extension on the nightstand, just in case it was the newlyweds, but Nectarine had already answered in the living room. A dark shadow of annoyance surfaced to mingle with his unshaven growth of beard, making him look surly and unkempt.

Under his breath, he growled that she could've at least had the courtesy to request permission before having her official calls forwarded to our room, and I agreed.

Through the door we heard her say, "Oh. Hello, D.L . . . .yes, it's Nectarine . . . no, not a party . . . well, Merry Christmas to you, too . . . and to you, Rae Ellen . . . yes, I've heard the Ingleside Inn is wonderful . . . uh-huh . . . just a minute . . ."

Nectarine appeared on the threshold, looking slightly apologetic.

"Dan, your parents are calling from Palm Springs. I'm sorry, but I've got to ask you not to tie up the line any longer than absolutely necessary."

Dan reached for the extension. "Can I tell them about Belinda?" he inquired.

Nectarine thought about it, then nodded. "Just make sure they don't repeat it to anybody else," she said, and left.

Lifting the receiver, Dan greeted his father. "Merry Christmas! But why are you two up at this hour? What time is it out there anyway? Three-thirty, something like that?"

Dave Louis reported that he and Rae Ellen were preparing to take a swim and Jacuzzi before embarking upon an invigorating four-hour "Desert Dawn" hike through the Indian Canyons. Hence the early Christmas greeting.

It was Rae Ellen's opinion that Dan sounded sluggish, and would benefit greatly from the marvelous colonic hydrotherapist they'd discovered. Why didn't we fly in and join them this coming weekend?

Despite his weariness and preoccupation, Dan laughed. "I'm afraid Claire and I couldn't keep up with you folks. Y'all's lifestyle sounds way too intense for us." His tone grew sober. "Things are already intense enough around here, as it is."

He then proceeded to break the news of Belinda's bizarre demise.

After their initial shock, both his parents were full of questions. We took turns answering as best we could, recounting the salient events since Belinda and Sam's arrival at Riverside Manor to find no room at the inn.

"That poor, doomed girl!" Rae Ellen lamented. "Nobody ever knew what to do with her, and she was so rich, nobody even bothered to try." She sighed. "Of course precious Foley did the best he could, but he was completely out of his depth."

"Hell, the girl needed a keeper," Dave Louis stated flatly. "I'm frankly surprised somebody didn't just pick up a gun and blow her away a long time ago. But I sure never would've expected one of her men to take his own sweet time and make such an artistic job out of it."

According to the coroner's preliminary examination, his current estimate was that Belinda Callant had died no earlier than 12:30 A.M., and no later than 2:30 A.M.

Based on that hypothesis, Officer Songy, Nectarine's young technocop, had constructed a computer timetable grid to coordinate everyone's movements from midnight through 2:30 A.M.

Our data was the first to be entered, based on what we'd told Nectarine earlier.

Now, while Cletus and Harp watched critically, she made us sit down and go over the whole thing again with Officer Songy.

It came out looking something like this.

CLAIRE AND DAN CLAIBORNE	
12 Midnight	River Queen Club
12:15 A.M.	Witness altercation between victim and Kyle Dalton
12:20 A.M.	Witness altercation between victim and Cecille D. Worth
12:23 A.M.	Witness victim leave River Queen Club
12:45 A.M.	Claibornes leave River Queen Club

CLAIRE AND DAN CLAIBORNE	
12:48 A.M.	Return to hotel room (2100)
1:45 A.M.	Shiveree begins
2:20 A.M.	Hear screams (Kyle Dalton)
2:23 A.M.	Arrive at honeymoon suite (2117) to find victim dead
Also present: Kyle Dalton, Emory Dalton, Huey Dalton, Purcell Dalton, Fenton Dalton, Woodrow Dalton, Wesley Dalton, Tucker J. Dalton Note: All times approximate	

It was just after seven when we were done. Through the windows, I saw a thread of silver light weaving a division between water and sky. In less than fifty-eight minutes, Foley and Charlotte would be airborne.

Cletus and Harp were chomping at the bit to begin knocking on doors, but Nectarine felt it was still too early. "Let them stew a little longer," she said. "Nobody concerned can try to leave the hotel now without our knowing about it. And if they've already gone, well—why bother to lock the barn door?"

She studied a diagram of Riverside Manor's twenty-first floor provided by the manager. "The good thing about this Z-formation is that people in the middle rooms can sense something happening on both ends, but they can't tell what without actually coming to investigate. It will be interesting to see if anybody does."

Nectarine then dispatched the restless officers to the crime scene. "Bring me everything they've bagged so far," she instructed.

After they'd gone, Dan told Nectarine, "Look. I'm getting cabin fever just sitting around here. Now it's daylight, more or less, I'm going to take Claire out for a walk."

She studied the carpet pattern, tiny grey pindots inside diamonds of darker grey. "Actually, I have something to discuss with you both, right now."

Casting a glance toward the open door, she lowered her voice and added, "Quick. Before Cletus and Harp get back."

We followed her into our bedroom. I perched on the foot of the bed, while she and Dan took the two chairs at the table.

"Okay. Here's how it is," said Nectarine, drumming her fingernails on the glass surface. "You see, in a way this case is punishment for me. But I knew what I was getting into when I asked for it."

It was a well-known fact that Captain Carruth resented Uptown in general, and the cops who worked the Second District in particular.

Specifically, she'd heard through the grapevine that Captain Carruth had vowed, since he was stuck with Sergeant Nectarine Savoy, he was going to break her of her "uppity high yellow ways."

She laughed at our expressions. "That's nothing. Carruth's no more of a racist than Brother Jim Cletus, who feels exactly the same about me."

When Dan had awakened Nectarine with the news about Belinda, she instantly saw how she could use Carruth's prejudice to her advantage, as well as ours.

Calling Carruth at his home, Nectarine reported the crime and explained why she was the first to know about it, stressing the "Uptown" and "society" aspects of the wedding.

She'd pleaded with him to put his very best available detective on the case, saying that, though of course she wouldn't be directly involved in the investigation due to her personal acquaintance with a number of the suspects, whoever he assigned to handle the case should feel free to call on her for assistance at any time.

Dan chuckled. "Oh, Br'er Fox! Please, *please* don't throw me in dat briarpatch!"

"You got it," Nectarine agreed, with a smile.

The same simple reverse psychology that worked for Br'er Rabbit on Br'er Fox, worked on Captain Carruth.

He had exploded.

"Oh. So he should feel free to call on you at any time?" Carruth echoed sarcastically. "Well, that's mighty big of you, Sergeant Savoy. And we both know why you're being so generous, don't we? It wouldn't do for your high and mighty Uptown friends to have you personally poking your proud nose into their dirty linen, would it?

"Okay. Since you were such a big famous fashion model, try this on for size. As of right now, *you* are the detective in charge of this case."

Thinking he'd scored, Carruth had laughed heartily.

"Merry Christmas, Sergeant Savoy! And welcome to the Eighth District. We'll make a real cop out of you yet!"

"So, *voilà!* Here I am in the briarpatch," Nectarine finished.

"As the old saying goes, I'm beginning as I mean to continue. Carruth has no idea yet what a messy, complicated—not to mention tabloid fodder—situation we've got here. By the time he does, I intend to have the killer trussed, stuffed with evidence and ready to roast, like that Christmas turkey Cletus can't wait to get home to."

Dan's bristly cheek rasped as he scratched it. "So you don't necessarily subscribe to that old adage, *chercher le Indian.*"

Nectarine shrugged. "At this point, I'm not about to jump to a conclusion, no matter how obvious, and make an arrest without, as I just said, solid evidence to back up the charge. All we need is for a bunch of Navajo activists to show up and stage a protest outside Eighth District headquarters." She grinned. "Although it might be worth it, just to watch Carruth bust a gut!

"But seriously. I'm not ruling out anybody yet, except you and Claire, and Foley and Charlotte, naturally. Why do you think I haven't asked you where they are?"

I started to speak, but she lifted a cautionary hand. "Don't say a word. Because when Carruth finds out about that cat fight between Charlotte and Belinda, it's just the kind of thing he'll jump on, accuse me of trying to protect my 'society friends'."

Nectarine cocked an ear toward the door, which she'd left open a crack. "Hark, my knights extremely errant return. Anyway, the reason I'm unloading like this is because I am counting on you two to be my extra eyes and ears."

"What do you want us to do?" Dan asked.

"Hang out. Ask questions. Listen. And"—she fixed her brilliant eyes on us sternly—"tell me *everything.*"

"Yo, Sergeant! You in there?" Harp bellowed.

"Coming, Officer," Nectarine called back.

Cletus and Harp were each carrying several plastic bags. "Where do you want this stuff, Sergeant Savoy?" asked Cletus.

I suggested the kitchenette counter, since it was the only flat surface free from police paraphernalia.

"Good idea, Claire," Nectarine approved. "Okay, officers. Spread it out and let's see what we've got here."

The moment Cletus and Harp began carefully laying out the bags, I felt a distinct heaviness settle into the atmosphere.

The first bag contained a wide, sharp, bloody dagger, its hilt of hammered silver inlaid with turquoise. I recognized it as similar to those used by Sam in his *Beautiful Woman* statues.

The second held another knife, with a long handle of intricately cut lead crystal. Its blade was also caked with blood, and . . . cake?

My head whirled.

It was Imogene's "something old" knife, which Foley and Charlotte had used to slice their Red Velvet wedding cake.

Next was a bag holding a long, curved shard of thick green glass, embossed with a blob of white, spattered with dark brown droplets.

"There were a bunch of these, but we just brought one," Harp said, laying down a bag which contained three red roses.

The sight of Belinda's long, bronze trademark comma of hair, encased in plastic, made me too queasy to explore my impression that something didn't look quite right about it.

But it was what was in the last bag that really did me in. Two shimmery, glimmery green things that I'd vaguely noticed on the floor near Belinda's body.

They were gloves.

My matron-of-honor gloves.

The pindot/diamond design in the carpet came rushing to meet me.

40

"I took them off as soon as we got to our table when we finished posing for pictures," I told Nectarine, who was sitting next to me on the edge of the bed. "After that, I never gave them another thought."

If nothing else, we now knew whoever had originally taken the gloves was at the wedding reception. This did not, however, prove the person did so with the idea of using them to commit murder, or that they were the guilty party. Furthermore, someone else could've lifted the gloves from the initial light-fingered guest.

Nor would any prosecutor be attempting an O.J.-type demonstration with those gloves. The stretchy little numbers were one-size-fits-all.

At first, this seemed good for Sam. He hadn't been at the reception, and only showed up after Belinda had been routed from the River Queen Club with champagne by Cecille.

But Nectarine, who'd departed with Marcel right after the cake was cut, reminded me I'd told her there were still plenty of stragglers left over from the wedding at that time.

"Your Mr. Stormshadow sounds unusually resourceful at coping with rejection," observed Nectarine. "First you say he comes charging off the elevator in hot pursuit of Montaigne Duffosat.

"But right after she gives him an ultimatum and splits, he's trotting Fawn Goldfeather around the dance floor. Who knows who he latched onto after that? I'm very curious to discover where he eventually wound up spending the night. Because whether he killed Belinda or not, he certainly didn't spend it in the honeymoon suite."

"For true," I said.

Nectarine patted my cheek fondly. "I think you'd better try to take a little nap, Claire," she advised, and returned to the living room, shutting the door behind her.

I closed my eyes, listening to the comforting noises of Dan in the bathroom.

When I fainted, he'd carried me to the bed. Then, after making sure I was okay, had announced if he didn't get a shower and a shave, he wouldn't be responsible.

Now, I pondered the mystery of where—and with whom—Sam Stormshadow had spent the night. Unless he'd picked up a local girl and they'd gone to her house, he was still in the hotel. Provided, of course, he hadn't immediately hopped on a plane after butchering Belinda.

Among the wedding party itself, there weren't that many possibilities. Cecille, in her deranged state, was a definite maybe. Although in that case, where had Reggie been? Getting fitted for cement shoes by the River Queen Club's pit boss?

But other than Cecille, who was left?

Jolene and Bobette? Not likely. Lambie, to teach T.J. a final lesson? She'd still been angry at him because of Belinda, but surely not enough to do something so tacky.

Pearl and Topaz might've taken pity on Sam and let him use their sofa; Imogene wouldn't have dreamed of it.

There was always the possibility that he'd connected with a single woman staying at Riverside Manor.

Or, he could've even gone on one of his rampages and started hunting for Montaigne again, despite her previous warning.

I hoped he had, and she'd locked him in the wine cellar. At least he'd have an alibi.

Dan emerged from the bathroom, still tired but somewhat refreshed. He climbed into the same jeans and sweater he'd worn earlier, and suggested a hot shower would do me good.

I didn't budge. "Dan, please, please, tell me none of this is happening," I begged.

He came over and sat down next to me. "If it could change anything baby, I would. But we've got to face facts. Belinda was murdered at the other end of this floor, possibly"—he swallowed hard—"no *probably* along about the time we were having big fun with a pair of loony underwear and a Christmas present."

"That would make it during the shiveree!" I sat up. "Which is why, even if she screamed her head off, nobody would've heard a thing."

Dan thought. "In that case, all the Shiveree Boys are in the clear. Even Kyle. Unless he did it earlier, knowing if he managed to keep himself together until they broke down the door, he could freak out without arousing undue suspicion."

"Dan, you're right. Kyle stormed out of the River Queen after arguing with Belinda, but before Cecille hosed her down with bubbly. What if he simply came up here and lay in wait until she opened the door, then pounced and drug her inside?"

Sadly, it fit with what we knew of Kyle's nature. Even that clumsy imitation of a Sam Stormshadow art piece was a classic example of acting out jealousy and rage against Belinda, while attempting to implicate the other man—one of the other men—who'd been her lover.

Dan concurred with this line of reasoning, pointing out Kyle had access to my gloves during the reception. Unless he was a closet queen, he wouldn't have bothered to take them if he hadn't been premeditating violence.

Once he'd gained entrance to Belinda's room, he may then have spotted the silver knife, and come up with the idea of framing Sam. I recalled how he'd been staring at the mutilated Belindas at the exhibit.

It was sounding bleak for Kyle, until I remembered something. "Wait, Dan. That doesn't explain Imogene's cake knife. Kyle and Belinda had already gone when I noticed it lying on the serving trolley."

"Hey, you are a sharp-eyed little thing!" Dan exclaimed. "I never even saw that knife. But it doesn't really let Kyle off the hook. There was conceivably time for him to ride back up to the River Queen, take Imogene's family heirloom (which he would've known about) return to this floor and . . . perform the *coup de grâce*.

"Or, he might have even used the stairs. We're only one floor down from the club, remember."

I felt nauseated.

"You mean, he went off and left her half-dead and—and—cut up, to go get another weapon to finish her off? Oh, no. Not Kyle. Yes, I can see him getting inspired, if we can call it that, as to how to frame Sam in the heat of the moment. But this other thing—no. It's too cold-blooded and calculated for a hothead like Kyle."

Dan grimaced. "You may be right, darlin'. But just suppose that's what happened. It would also explain where he acquired a big, long piece of Perrier Jouet glass, from when Cecille smashed it on the floor. The cleanup crew still hadn't gotten to it when we left, remember."

His words conjured up an image of the thick, green shard jutting from Belinda's naked throat. Another burst of nausea hit me.

Yes, either Sam Stormshadow or Kyle Dalton could star in Dan's scenario. They were both physically strong, and emotionally unstable. Both had been sexually used—and artistically abused—by Belinda Callant.

Each man had compelling motive, access to the same means, and, as far as we knew, an equal opportunity for eliminating Belinda.

Even allowing for adjustments and refinements, Dan's rough chronology of how the crime could've been committed explained so much.

Except for one thing.

Those briarless red sweetheart roses strewn across Belinda's body.

Roses that could have only come from one of the bridesmaids' bouquets.

Wedding Breakfast Buffet

For Mr. and Mrs. Foley P. Callant and party
December 25

Menu
Turkey Hash
Popovers
Crab Quiche
Corn Muffins
Fried Grit Patties
Scrambled Eggs
Applesmoked Bacon

41

I stood beneath the shower and let hot water pound onto my head, wishing it could penetrate my skull and wash away all the confusion.

It was now after four o'clock in the afternoon on a Christmas Day that had been chock-full of very un-merry surprises.

The fact that everybody, with the exception of Riverside Manor's horrendously overworked staff, had forgotten about the wedding breakfast buffet only served to heighten the surreal madness.

At about ten-thirty this morning, the telephone had rung in 2117 (formerly known as the honeymoon suite) and was answered by an investigator collecting forensic evidence.

On the line had been Jaime in catering, wondering why Mr. and Mrs. Callant and their guests had failed to show up in the Conservatory for breakfast.

There was a luncheon scheduled for noon in that facility. What were they to do?

"Have them bring it up here," decided Nectarine, when presented with this question. "There's plenty of room right in front of the elevators. That way, we can legitimately detain everybody until we're through questioning them, and avoid getting interrupted by room service."

"Golly! It'll be just like a big old party!" Cletus exclaimed sarcastically.

Nevertheless, he'd put away a large percentage of the turkey hash all by himself.

I lathered some Phyto Panama shampoo into my hair, inhaling its clean, tangy fragrance as if it could purge my spirit of the sordidness I'd been exposed to.

Nectarine had finally unleashed her two bloodhounds upon the witnesses at about eight o'clock.

Stafford and Alicia Dalton, who occupied 2101, the room next to us, had been first.

Stafford, head of accounting at Peach Island, was like a sepia version of his technicolor brother, Emory. Alicia, though nice enough, was remote and brooding. Her otherwise attractive features relaxed too easily into lines of discontent.

They claimed to have had no direct interaction at all with Belinda Callant. Yes, they were aware their daughter Cecille had developed a sudden aversion to her, but had no idea how serious it was until Woody and Wes brought her to their table after she'd attacked Belinda.

But when they'd tried to take Cecille back to her room she became noisy and resistant. Nobody could do a thing with her, until she'd spotted Fawn Goldfeather.

"I want my lil' Indian artist pal!" Cecille demanded loudly. "C'mere, lil' Indian artist pal!"

Perhaps Fawn had been flattered, because she'd obligingly rallied to Cecille's aid, helping find her things—which were scattered from dais to dance floor—then saw her safely to her room. When? Oh, maybe about one o'clock or so. They didn't really notice.

The Stafford Daltons were followed by Grandma Imogene, across the hall in 2102. For the first time, she came close to looking her true age, which Charlotte revealed was somewhere on the shady side of seventy.

Certainly Imogene knew Belinda was Foley's ex-wife, but the nearest she'd ever been to her was that fateful night when the former Mrs. Callant and Charlotte had taken a spill into the Mississippi.

Though exhausted by wedding activities, Imogene had purposely stayed awake to listen to the shiveree.

Yes, she had heard a loud scream, but simply assumed it was part of the hoedown. After that, things got quiet and she'd almost immediately fallen asleep.

Imogene was absolutely devastated to learn her cake knife had been one of the murder weapons. "I need to go lie down. Please," she whispered, when Nectarine asked her to identify it.

The three Callant cousins and their wives, in the trio of rooms next to Stafford and Alicia, were useless.

The six had eaten, drunken and been merry until after midnight, when they'd staggered to their respective nests to find champagne and chocolates from the newlyweds awaiting their pleasure.

All of them said their original intention was to stay up and drink champagne while waiting for the shiveree to start—maybe even join it—but none of them managed to retain consciousness long enough.

Naturally, they all knew Belinda from when she was married to Foley; none of them admitted to having seen her for the last four or five years until a few days ago.

It was at this point that Nectarine murmured to Officer Harp to collect the champagne bottles from everyone she'd interviewed so far.

Purcell, when his turn came, looked even more ravaged than he had earlier. He said he felt terrible because the shiveree noise had provided a perfect coverup for any sounds of murder.

Yes, the door was definitely locked when they kicked it in. He'd checked especially.

"See, sometimes they leave it ajar, just to save the wood," he explained, with a wan smile.

Mamie and Daphne said they were so worn out, they'd ridden down from the River Queen Club together and fallen straight into their beds, while their respective husbands were organizing for the shiveree.

Both women stated they never heard a peep until the door crashed open and somebody screamed. Neither realized anything was wrong until Emory and Fenton had come back bearing the dreadful news.

Their husbands had little to add.

Emory was still reeling from the shock of thinking his new son-in-law had gone inexplicably berserk and murdered his daughter.

Fenton said his first reaction was that Foley and Charlotte had played a practical joke by putting one of "that nutty Indian feller's" statues on the floor to scare them.

Lambie, who seemed to have rolled herself into a tight little ball, admitted she couldn't stand Belinda. Her hair was still in its coronet, but fuzzy with a halo of little blonde escapee tendrils.

"That woman said nasty, suggestive things to T.J., right in front of me. But I can understand why Sam Stormshadow, and poor Kyle and Reggie, and, oh, lots of other men fell for her. She was like . . . a beautiful piece of chocolate with poison in the center."

Lambie swore she hadn't seen Belinda after that outlandish contretemps with Cecille.

She and Tucker John had argued (yes, about Belinda) then she left and went directly down to her room while T.J. had stayed to hook up with the other Shiveree Boys around the bandstand.

"About what time was that, Miss Dalton?" Nectarine asked suddenly.

Lambie looked startled at the formality.

"Well, um. I'm not real sure. Maybe twelve-thirty, a quarter to one? T.J. might remember."

Nectarine tapped her gold pen rapidly against the notebook.

"Miss Dalton. Where is the bouquet of roses you carried in your sister's wedding?"

42

Lambie had no idea where her red roses were.

Following Jolene and Bobette's forfeiting Charlotte's bridal bouquet to her, she promptly forgot all about her own.

When Lambie returned to her room, she had removed a pile of overpriced snacks from the mini-fridge to make space for Charlotte's peonies. But as for the roses, presumably they'd been thrown out with the rest of last night's debris from the River Queen Club.

"Find out which dumpster that stuff went into and get somebody on it right away," Nectarine ordered Cletus.

He started to exit, but she called, "Wait a minute!" and crossed the room to add something inaudible to the rest of us.

When Cletus had gone, Nectarine refocused her attention on Lambie. "All right, Miss Dalton. Did you see anyone in the hallway when you went back to your room?"

Lambie frowned. "No. I did hear a couple of doors slam. And—" she broke off.

"Yes?" Nectarine prodded alertly.

"Well," Lambie was reluctant, "there were some loud thuds. Like somebody bumping against the walls in the corridor? Then I heard all this laughing and—I guess you could call it chanting—about Indians. And I realized it was Cecille."

"You didn't open the door to verify your impression?" asked Nectarine.

"No. I didn't want to embarrass her by sticking my head out to look," Lambie explained. "But I'm very sure it was Cecille."

Lambie couldn't say what time that had been. At least one o'clock, probably a little later, she thought.

Nectarine let her go, then went to look over Officer Songy's shoulder at the computer screen as he typed Lambie's movements into the time grid. From what I could tell, Lambie's story confirmed Cecille's parents' estimate of when Fawn Goldfeather assisted their drunken daughter to her room.

Dan brought back a couple plates of food from the buffet. "Come on, eat something, honey," he urged, setting them down on the bedside table.

I protested that I couldn't, but in fact consumed an entire popover and everything but the crust of a piece of quiche.

We tried to figure out where Nectarine was going with this. She didn't appear to be calling those she interviewed in any particular order.

Huey Dalton was fetched next, providing us with one of the few light moments in the whole dismal day.

Because Huey did not arrive alone. With him was a peevish Sally Holt, dressed in last night's wilted wedding finery, only marginally embarrassed at being discovered in Huey's room.

Sally had appointed herself spokesperson for them both. Huey had, she said, invited her down to see his view, shortly after midnight. While she was busy picking out all the Baccis from the Perugina chocolates sent by Foley and Charlotte, Huey had opened the white-flowered bottle of champagne and poured them each a glass.

Later, fifteen or twenty minutes after one, perhaps, Huey received a phone call he said was from his father, Purcell, and left to join the Shiveree Boys in the River Queen Club.

Sally had settled down with the remaining chocolates and champagne to await his return. "And a good thing, too!" she averred stoutly. "Finding that poor woman dead took all the starch out of him, didn't it

Huey honey? If I hadn't been there to whip him back into shape, he might've completely collapsed!"

Nectarine didn't touch that one, instead asking whether Sally had noticed any red rose bridal bouquets lying around at the reception.

Sally stated it was her business to notice such things and yes, she had seen one standing upside down on a corner of the stage. "My first thought was that it was such a waste. But then, the wedding was over and the flowers were already dead anyway, so what difference did it make?" Sally concluded.

With a flourish, she conducted the docile Huey away for some breakfast, with a ponderous joke about real men eating quiche.

"Geez, Louise!" sneered Harp disgustedly.

The twins were next.

Woody said he was the one who had thrown up. He insisted people who knew them could tell him and Wes apart by his right eyebrow, which was noticeably higher than his left.

They concurred with their parents and Lambie about the time Fawn brought Cecille down to the twenty-first floor.

"Gosh! We were having a lot of fun until poor old Cece went apeshit," Wes said.

Though at the promise of cake, Cecille let them lead her away to her parents' table, she yelled at them to leave her alone when they tried to take her downstairs.

"Yeah," said Woody. "Then Fawn came by and Cecille just glommed onto her. We know nobody in our family likes Fawn, but she was the only one who could handle Cecille last night."

Relieved of their burden, the boys had gone in search of the two lovely local young ladies they'd met, and the four of them had danced until Uncle Purcell came to round up his two youngest Shiveree Boys.

"Since it was already running so late, we were kind of hoping they weren't going to have it after all," Woody said.

Nectarine looked up quickly. "You mean the shiveree was running late?"

Woody nodded. I think it was Woody. I had lost track of them again and I couldn't see both his eyebrows.

"Uh-huh. We were all supposed to meet at the bandstand by twelve-thirty. Only Kyle didn't come. So Uncle Purcell said for everybody to go and enjoy themselves until he came and found us."

"And when did Uncle Purcell find you?" Nectarine asked quietly, but I could hear the throb of tension in her voice.

"I think it wasn't quite one-thirty," said one, and his twin agreed.

After they'd gone off to raid the buffet, Nectarine began pacing the carpet. "I think we're getting somewhere!" she declared.

Harp was dubious. "How do you figure, Sergeant?"

"Because, Officer Harp, until just now, we didn't know there'd been a more or less set time for the shiveree. We have just learned it started nearly an hour later than scheduled, because Kyle Dalton didn't show up."

Dan looked at me significantly. This development tied in with his scenario that Kyle could've done it earlier, then glued himself back together until he broke down when the ghastly corpse was discovered.

Except for one thing.

When we saw Kyle quarreling with Belinda, he had just come from performing onstage, where Sally Holt spotted the abandoned red roses.

Nevertheless, even if they had been the ones used to decorate Belinda's body, Kyle Dalton was definitely not carrying a bridesmaid's bouquet when he left.

But where had he been from twelve forty-five until one-twenty?

43

"I came down here to wait for Belinda," Kyle admitted readily.

He looked extremely pale and washed out, like a watercolor of himself.

"So you knew which room she was staying in?" Nectarine asked rhetorically.

"No," responded Kyle. "Not then. She—she had always been very cagey about that. I couldn't think why, unless it was because of Sam. We used to . . . meet in my room," he added stoically.

"Anyhow, I waited by the elevator for a minute, then I had to, uh, go to the bathroom. So I just went on along to my room. Mine and T.J.'s, actually."

Afterward, as he was opening his door to go back up to the River Queen, he saw Belinda coming down the hallway. "I didn't want to jump out and scare her," Kyle explained. "So I shut the door except for just a crack so I could tell when she passed by."

But instead of calling her name, Kyle decided, on the spur of the moment, he claimed, to follow her instead. That's how he found out she was in the honeymoon suite.

In fact, he thought she was trying to sneak in and ruin things for Foley and Charlotte, so he'd leaped forward (so much for not scaring her) and grabbed her arm, noticing as he did so that she was soaking wet.

Belinda had had to let Kyle in to prove to him that Foley and Charlotte weren't there. She told him what she believed to be true, that they had taken our room and we had gone home, then ordered him to get out because she had important business to tend to.

Kyle instantly assumed she was expecting another man, and Belinda had laughed.

"If I am, Kyle, it's nothing to do with you. Like I told you before, we had a little fun, and you're going to make me a whole lot of money. If and when I change my mind, I'll let you know. Anything's possible. After all, darling, we're going to be partners seven whole years!"

Then Belinda told him if he didn't get out immediately, she would call hotel security.

Kyle had gone quietly, because he'd suddenly realized Belinda knew nothing about the shiveree. It was his ace in the hole, a way to get revenge on Belinda and whatever man she was "tending to business" with.

To fortify himself, he'd returned to his room and drunk most of the bottle of champagne he'd found waiting in an ice bucket with a card from Foley and Charlotte, and watched part of *It's a Wonderful Life.* Then he'd gone up to the River Queen Club to report for shiveree duty.

The whole time Kyle had been roaming the corridor with the others, a-singing and a-playing, he was revving himself up for that delicious retribution.

Only Kyle had known they would find Belinda behind that door, instead of Foley and Charlotte.

But when the moment came at last, and there Belinda had lain mutilated on the floor, he had collapsed in agony.

"I loved her, no matter what!" he sobbed now. "I even asked her to marry me!"

44

"I'd lock him up, I was you, Sergeant," grunted Officer Harp. "He's a wacko. He could've done it, all right."

Nectarine looked puzzled. "Oh? I thought you and Officer Cletus were positive 'the Indian' did it."

Harp scowled. "Well, he probably did. But this guy—I dunno. He sounds even screwier than the Indian."

Nectarine studied Songy's updated grid. "Well, we'll see, won't we?"

Tucker John Dalton came in right after Kyle. As far as I was concerned, his major crime since before he even left Peach Island for New Orleans was Pure D ignorance in the Ways of Women.

He said he should've never let Reggie talk him into hiring Fawn Goldfeather. She'd done nothing but cause trouble for him business-wise with the other textile artists, and personally.

T.J.'s account of his actions during the critical time period was straightforward and uncomplicated.

He'd been with Lambie the whole evening, until they quarreled about something raunchy Belinda said to him. "Like it was my fault!" T.J. complained, spreading his hands helplessly.

Anyway, after Lambie left, he had tried to call her in her room, but she'd hung up on him.

Mainly though, he'd been singing and playing with the others, until Kyle finally turned up and they got the shiveree rolling.

"In fact, we were so behind getting started that in all the rush, I forgot to bring the roses."

Nectarine grew still. "What roses, Mr. Dalton?"

T.J. laughed self-consciously. "Oh, it's kind of an old hillbilly version of a knight carrying a glove or something belonging to his lady during a tournament. An engaged Shiveree Boy sometimes wears a token belonging to his fiancée during somebody else's shiveree. In this case, I was going to hang Lambie's wedding bouquet from my belt. Silly huh? Only I forgot it."

T.J. thought the flowers were still on the bandstand when he left, but couldn't swear to it.

Reggie and Cecille, according to Harp, had taken some rousing before they appeared in our room to face Nectarine Savoy.

Side by side on the loveseat, which was seeing big action as a witness chair, dark hair and eyes contrasting harshly with their extreme pallor, the couple looked like a dysfunctional Morticia and Gomez Addams.

And yet, despite her hangover and her unwashed hair—which today resembled inferior fake fur—Cecille seemed oddly smug and sure of herself. I wondered why; certainly no mirror would've backed her up.

Cecille at first tried to dismiss her encounter with Belinda as the equivalent of a sorority prank, but Nectarine wasn't buying it.

"Mrs. Worth, there were many eyewitnesses to the incident. You were overheard to tell the victim you'd see her dead before you allowed her to take your husband, your art, or your money."

Reggie twitched at the recital.

Nectarine continued. "The woman you threatened was murdered shortly afterward."

Tossing her spiky head, Cecille retorted, "So? I didn't do it!"

All things considered, Cecille's account of her movements during the vital time period was fairly lucid.

After her impersonation of a champagne fountain, Woody and Wes led her over to her parents' table where she remembered eating red cake that tasted like chocolate.

The next thing to happen was Fawn Goldfeather helping her down to her room. Cecille had decided to join forces with Fawn, calling her, "the devil she knew," infinitely preferable to that web-spinning Daughter of Belial.

"Fawn was going to make me a lot of money," Cecille said, "but Beelzebub got greedy. She wanted to cut me out of everything. It wasn't fair."

Cecille recalled when she and Fawn got off the elevator, she had pointed out her own strong Indian features to Fawn in the big mirror on the wall opposite. Then, the two of them skipped hand-in-hand down the hallway singing, "One little, two little Indian gur-rils . . . "

Fawn came into the room with her to make sure Cecille was going to be okay. She even helped her get out of the bridesmaid's dress, and into a nightgown.

After that, Cecille claimed to have fallen asleep until Reggie had come in, when he tripped over something and made a lot of noise. Oh, definitely after two o'clock.

"Of course then I couldn't get back to sleep until after that god-awful shiveree racket stopped," Cecille concluded.

Questioned about her bouquet, Cecille stated positively she'd taken it down to her room earlier, along with the braids I'd removed from her. There, she discovered the bottle of champagne from Foley and Charlotte, and had carried it back up with her on the elevator to the River Queen Club.

The very bottle, in fact, she'd used to drench Belinda.

When Nectarine told her that would be all for the moment, Cecille rose and headed for the door, saying she was going to take a shower.

"I'll save you some hot water, Reggie-ums!" she caroled over her shoulder.

Reggie-ums Worth, who'd remained silent and listless during Cecille's performance, became slightly more animated upon her departure.

"I'm afraid it's been a very unhappy Christmas for us, all the way 'round," he said. The tremor in his voice belied this somewhat flip understatement.

Reggie's story was tawdry, but concise.

Yes, it was true. He and Belinda Callant had almost immediately recognized that they would make a formidable team in the art world. Both understood this meant marriage. Reggie had no problem with that. He'd been trying to find a way to break with Cecille for a long time.

He'd been up front with Belinda about his gambling addiction. She'd responded that it was only money. She had plenty, and they were going to make much, much more together.

However, she felt in order to show good faith, Reggie should eliminate Cecille from the Fawn Goldfeather project, keeping it between the two of them on a 50-50 basis. This before she had even seen Fawn's work, telling Reggie she knew enough about what he'd accomplished for Cecille to trust his judgment.

Reggie had balked at the proposition, on the basis it would be adding insult to injury to poor old Cecille, who had her heart set on two of Fawn's paintings. He told Belinda he felt obligated to inform Cecille of this, and had done so at the reception.

Reggie said he hadn't expected for Cecille to react by physically assaulting Belinda. Moreover, he hadn't heard about the incident until later.

"It was a hell of a night at the tables," he confided. "I dropped quite a bundle."

The manager of the River Queen Club had called Reggie into his office and cut off his credit until he paid up. Afterwards, Reggie sat drinking scotch in the club bar until 2:00 A.M. or so, trying to figure out how to lay his hands on some immediate cash.

"The only solution I could come up with was to hit good old Cece for one last bailout. Kind of a goodbye present, as it were."

Poor old Cecille. Good old Cece. The man really was despicable.

But in the end, Reggie broke down and buried his head in his hands. "Belinda gave me a whole new lease on life," he groaned in a muffled voice. "I really do believe we could've made a go of it. But now"—he raised a stricken face—"nothing's ever going to change."

45

Pearl and Topaz came in balancing cups of coffee and plates of scrambled eggs, fried grits patties and bacon.

"Such a terrible, terrible thing," Pearl clucked, daintily forking up a crispy square of grits.

Topaz, decimating a strip of bacon between her strong white teeth, agreed. "No matter she was a thoroughly rotten bitch. One wouldn't have wanted to see her go like that."

Officer Harp stared at the two older ladies like they were from another planet. Too bad his pal Cletus was still down doing dumpster detail. They could've been having a ball.

Pearl went on. "And I'm sure she had no inkling, not the slightest! Why, when she came to our room to get the ring cut off, she seemed most excited about something!"

"But angry, too!" Topaz spoke around a mouthful of egg. "Said she finally found something she'd been looking for, and she was going to throw the book at somebody. Then she stopped and laughed. 'That's exactly what I'm going to do. Throw the book'."

If Nectarine had a whistle, she'd've blown it. "Whoa! Hold on a minute, ladies! When did all this happen?"

Pearl's coffee cup hovered in midair. "Why, dear. Didn't we say? Last night. Well, this morning, actually."

When Dan and I had exchanged goodnights with the aunts, they'd proceeded to their room to prepare for Belinda's visit.

"She told us she'd call after twelve-thirty, and we wanted to be ready," Topaz said.

Knowing Belinda, they were almost surprised when she actually followed through, ringing them at about twelve forty-five.

When Belinda showed up at their door, she was carrying a black briefcase. "But we told her we had a much safer place to keep the money," Pearl giggled, and the sisters explained about the Aunt Sally's praline boxes.

Harp couldn't stand it. "You mean you two were keeping $35,000 cash money just laying around your room? In *candy* boxes?"

Topaz stared down her nose. "My dear man, unless someone who had an unnatural affection for pralines had broken into our suite, the money was perfectly safe."

As Topaz had carefully clipped their sister's precious opal ring from Belinda's finger, she told them to call her Santa Claus, because if she hadn't needed the cash right away, they'd be out of luck.

When the deed was done, Pearl and Topaz transferred the four Aunt Sally's shopping bags to Belinda, who crammed the briefcase into one of them, making a remark about keeping all her valuables together.

Then, Topaz said, Belinda noticed the time, one-fifteen on the dot by the digital bedside clock and said she needed to go call a man on the east coast. That she had some news that would really wake him up.

"Floyd somebody, dear," Pearl reminded her.

Topaz waved a hand. "Whoever. Some man, of course."

And that was the last the aunts ever saw of Belinda.

When they'd departed, Nectarine sent Harp down to the crime scene to collect the bags of money, then sat back and perused Songy's latest printout of the time grid. Now we knew Belinda was alive and well as late as one-fifteen.

Jolene and Bobette provided the next surprise, in the form of Bradley Ford and Andrew Petit, the two young Blanchard, Smithson attorneys they'd smuggled into their room to spy on a real live hillbilly shiveree.

The four youngsters were frightened and chastened, having spent the last few hours miserably huddled in the girls' room, 2116.

When Brad and Andrew saw Dan, they were very nearly petrified on the spot.

2116 happened to be the last mini-suite in the corridor, right around the bend from 2117.

When the shiveree started, they had all crowded around the door, taking turns at peeking out to watch the goings-on.

"Well, I mean it was interesting at first. But then it got boring after awhile," Bobette said.

They had temporarily turned their attention to the contents of the mini-fridge ("Can you believe they charge four dollars for one little bitty can of smoked almonds?" Jolene complained indignantly) and to the bottle of champagne, until such time as things in the hallway sounded like they were getting more exciting. Then, they'd resumed their rotating vigil at the doorway.

"Only we couldn't always see them because the hall lights are so dim. And sometimes the boys were way down at the other end by this room—Claire and Dan's—or around the corner at what we thought was Charlotte and Foley's."

The upshot was that when the Shiveree Boys kicked the door open, Jolene, Bobette, Bradley and Andrew had slipped out to watch from around the corner, giggling and breathless with anticipation.

And though, mercifully, none of them had been able to glimpse the body from their hiding place, they'd seen and heard enough to realize someone in that room was dead.

Jolene began crying. "We thought something just awful had happened to Charlotte. So we hurried back to our room and shut the door. None of us knew what to do. Bradley and Andrew couldn't leave, because Daddy might catch 'em and make us marry them or something."

At this statement, Bradley and Andrew looked both relieved and chagrined.

"Until Mamma called awhile ago and told us, we didn't even know who it was that died," Bobette added. "And like Jolene said last night, the way she treated him, it's amazing he didn't finish her off sooner."

"Who?" Nectarine straightened up. "Who are you talking about?" she repeated.

"Why, Sam Stormshadow, of course," Bobette replied. "Who else?"

"Oh." Nectarine lost interest. "There's no actual evidence to suggest Mr. Stormshadow is guilty."

Bobette was scornful. "Are you kidding? After the way that woman was killed, and all? Just like one of his creepy statues of her?" she waved a hand at the grisly counter display.

"And anyhow, Jolene saw him."

Nectarine swivelled her head to look at Jolene. "You saw him *what*?" she snapped.

Jolene wiped her swollen eyes. "Well, once I looked out and couldn't see the boys. I could hear them though, so I figured they were back down at this end. And then, I saw Sam tip-toeing around the corner, toward Charlotte and Foley's honeymoon room.

"At the time, I just thought Uncle Purcell and Daddy and the others had roped him into playing a shiveree trick on them. Foley and Charlotte, that is."

"What time was this? Do you know?" Nectarine asked tersely.

Jolene said she did know because she checked the ubiquitous bedside clock before looking out. They hadn't expected the shiveree to begin so late, or last so long.

"It was five minutes till two, just before I peeked out the door and saw Sam," Jolene stated positively.

"And you can swear it was Sam Stormshadow you saw?" persisted Nectarine.

Jolene blew her nose and looked sulky. "I didn't see his face, if that's what you mean. But I saw him from the back. Nobody else around here has long black braids."

She stopped suddenly, and looked sick. "Oh, my Lord! I just realized! He was carrying some roses, just like in our bridesmaid's bouquets. That's why I thought it was all some kind of joke."

Just then, Officer Harp loped in. "Sergeant! Sergeant!" he panted.

"We turned 2117 inside out. And there's no candy boxes full of money anywhere in that room!"

46

"But she couldn't have seen Sam!" protested Fawn Goldfeather. "He was with me the whole time!"

As Fawn solved the mystery of where Sam Stormshadow spent the night, the bleary-eyed man himself sat hunched to one side of the loveseat. His copper skin had turned dull and rusty.

Fawn, on the other hand, looked more beautiful than I'd ever seen her. She was glowing like any other woman who'd experienced a satisfying night of long-play love.

Ironically, Sam could only summon fuzzy recollections of those early morning hours.

Fawn said she'd felt it best not to attend the wedding. She really didn't belong, and would've written the whole trip off as a big mistake, if Belinda Callant hadn't turned up.

Belinda was supposed to come to Fawn's room at twelve-thirty to look at the photographs of her paintings, but had instead called and asked her to come to 2117, because she'd been delayed.

"She said Cecille had sprayed her with expensive champagne," Fawn related, smiling slightly.

Their meeting had been brief—not quite ten minutes—but profitable. "Belinda loved my work!" Fawn crowed. "She said she wanted to represent me, but there were a couple of details to iron out with Reggie, first. I was so jazzed, I decided to ride up to the River Queen Club. I thought Reggie might still be there, and I couldn't wait to tell him."

Only Fawn had gotten sidetracked by Sam Stormshadow, on the rebound from Montaigne Duffosat. They'd had two or three dances. Fawn even let him talk her into breaking her rule of not partaking of the white man's firewater, and sharing Sam's margarita to celebrate.

Belatedly recalling she'd intended to find Reggie, Fawn told Sam she might be back in a little while. Then she left him at the bar and headed for the gambling area.

This time, however, she'd been roped into babysitting Cecille.

After that, about 1:10 or 1:20, she'd come back to the River Queen Club, but there was no sign of Reggie.

Sam, however, was still at the bar, and she'd taken a few sips of his current margarita.

Fawn looked rueful. "I almost never touch alcohol on general principles, but when a guy you're, well, attracted to says, 'Please share this with me,' it's kind of hard to resist."

Shortly thereafter, she'd invited him to her room, where a bottle of Perrier Jouet, addressed to Tucker John, awaited.

Fawn decided that, since she'd already had several swallows of margarita, it would prove nothing to boycott the champagne.

"Sam popped it, and I guess we drank the whole bottle. I remember Sam throwing it at the fireplace. Only, there wasn't any fireplace! It seemed hilarious at the time!"

They had the stereo turned up pretty loud, so weren't aware when the shiveree started, though Fawn said she caught gusts of it from time to time.

Being so unused to drinking, she didn't have a clue when they actually went to sleep (passed out) and Sam acted like he wasn't even sure whether he was fully conscious yet.

Nectarine asked if he had anything else to add to Fawn's account.

He shook his head slightly. "Nah. Sounds about right to me. From what I remember."

Folding her arms, Nectarine leaned back against the sofa cushions, looking from one to the other.

"You are aware Mrs. Callant was murdered in such a way as to mimic one of Mr. Stormshadow's statues of her."

Fawn flared angrily. "That's right! Blame it on the Indians. My God, somebody sure went out of their way this time, didn't they?"

Nectarine waited until she subsided, then requested Sam to take a look at the bagged evidence.

Fawn protectively accompanied him to the kitchenette counter.

The cake knife he said he'd never seen before, but unhesitatingly admitted the silver and turquoise dagger was one of many a Zuni silversmith friend in Flagstaff designed especially for use in Sam's statues.

"In fact, it's the one I took from the sold statue the other day at the Thorton Gallery," he confessed. "They're all a little different, and this was my favorite. So I pulled a switch when nobody was looking with the dagger I usually carry in my boot sheath."

Officer Harp's eyes bulged as Sam hitched up the right leg of his jeans to reveal an empty scabbard in the top of his Luchese cowboy boot.

"We got him for carrying a concealed weapon Sergeant Savoy!" Harp said triumphantly.

"Officer Harp. There is no weapon in that boot at the moment," Nectarine pointed out gently.

Sam said nothing. He'd already betrayed the fact the murder knife had been in his boot sheath.

At that juncture, a dirty, unhappy and wet Officer Cletus returned, carrying a green plastic garbage bag.

"We found the stuff just when it started to rain," he griped, upending the bag on the remaining counter space.

Out fell a clear plastic bag containing a shriveled bouquet of red sweetheart roses, its once festive ribbons gummy with filth.

The second bag was weighted with what looked like five pounds of shattered green glass, dotted with white flowers. The biggest piece was where it had broken off at the neck.

"There's probably more, but if the busboy hadn't just shoveled it into a box, we wouldn't have had this much."

Nectarine smiled. "Thank you, Officer Cletus. I believe we have all we're going to need of that particular bottle."

Cletus noticed Sam. "Oh, there he is. You arrested him yet, Sergeant?"

Predictably, this set Fawn off again. "Just another typical racist cop!" she shrieked accusingly.

Outrage flooded Cletus's dark face. "Who the hell are you calling a racist?" he shouted.

Harp was about to weigh in when Nectarine intervened. "That'll be enough of that, please."

Turning to Fawn, Nectarine added, "Miss Goldfeather, we've been collecting the champagne bottles delivered to everybody on this floor." She indicated the row of classic white-flowered bottles, some empty, a few unopened, the one delivered by Cletus crushed. "Just for the record, we'd like to have the one from your room."

"But why?" asked Fawn. She hadn't yet noticed the bag with the big deadly shard. "It's broken, like I told you."

"We need it anyway," Nectarine answered. "Could Officer Harp have your key, please?"

With a shrug, Fawn produced it from the pocket of her black leather jacket. "Sure."

Harp pulled a pair of latex gloves from a box that looked like it should hold Kleenex, and picked up a fresh plastic bag. "Back in a minute," he said.

Sam had slumped onto the loveseat again. Cletus stood in the open doorway, watching him like a hawk.

Fawn paced. "I don't understand what all this is about!" she fretted. "Sam had nothing to do with this. Somebody's trying to frame him. There are plenty of other people who hated Belinda as much as he did. Why pick on Sam?"

"Calm down, Miss Goldfeather," Nectarine advised. "We're investigating every possibility."

"Hah!" Fawn laughed grimly. "I'll just bet you are. Not."

Cletus stepped aside to allow his partner to enter.

Harp was holding the plastic bag aloft with his prize—a Perrier Jouet champagne bottle in several large, long pieces.

Cletus grinned.

"Bring it over to the counter please, Officer Harp," Nectarine directed.

Harp obeyed, laying it, without waiting to be told, next to the bag containing the piece taken from Belinda's throat.

"Mr. Stormshadow, Miss Goldfeather. Would you please come here and look at this?" Nectarine asked politely.

With a groan, Sam heaved himself to his feet, and trudged over to the counter. Fawn stalked defiantly to join him.

Dan took my arm and propelled me forward to look over their shoulders.

Even without an official reconstruction it was clear that the jagged piece of glass, almost the entire length of a bottle, had come from this very vessel.

Sam seemed to have turned to stone.

At last, Fawn took a deep, shuddering breath and turned to look at Sam. Angry, painful tears welled in her eyes.

"Oh, my God!" she screamed. "Oh, my God."

47

Officer Songy had done a masterful job on the time grid, including a separate breakdown for each individual, plus an elaborate combined schedule of all of the above.

Nectarine gave Dan and me a copy of the printout to study while she huddled with Officers Cletus and Harp over another set.

I didn't see the point; Sam Stormshadow, though not under arrest, was being "detained for questioning" at the Eighth District.

Besides, trying to assimilate a sense of continuity amid all the asterisks and footnotes made my head hurt.

Stripped of its streamlined presentation, what it boiled down to was that, unless Dracula himself had flown in through Belinda's French doors opening onto the terrace, nobody but Sam Stormshadow could have killed her.

I felt very depressed. I hadn't wanted it to be him.

"Neither did I, darlin'," Dan commiserated. "And if it makes you feel any better, Nectarine was hoping for another answer. "Anyway, he's the only one besides Belinda who had a key to that room. Sure, somebody could've taken it, but Jolene saw him, honey. Carrying flowers and sneaking around the corner. And this business of 'I don't remember. I must've had another blackout,' just ain't gonna cut the mustard."

That's when I'd decided to escape into the shower. And, I realized suddenly, the water therapy was working.

There was still a very important unanswered question: What had become of that $35,000 cash in the Aunt Sally's praline boxes?

We knew it wasn't in Fawn's room, so Sam didn't take it after he'd killed her.

Stepping from the stall, I shuddered at the thought of how poor Montaigne must be feeling right now. I wrapped my wet hair in a towel, then burrowed into Dan's big terrycloth bathrobe, for comfort more than warmth.

Back to the money.

Nobody who wasn't aware that a) Belinda had recently acquired $35,000 in cash, or b) it was packed into candy boxes from a famous local praline factory, would've even known it was there, or where to look for it.

None of the Shiveree Boys took the money at the time the murder was discovered; there were too many witnesses.

And the only one of them who could've conceivably known anything about those candy boxes was Kyle. He was still down on this floor when Belinda went to Pearl and Topaz's room. She would've had to pass his door both times.

But, even if he'd seen her carrying the shopping bags back to 2117, he'd never have guessed what was really in them. Unless Belinda herself told him.

Maybe she did.

Maybe they'd had another encounter Kyle didn't mention.

I toweled my hair, thinking hard. Yes, it might've happened just like that.

We knew Kyle didn't get down to the bandstand until nearly one-thirty. He'd been drinking alone in his room.

What if he'd started to leave around one-fifteen, as Belinda was coming back up the hall from Pearl and Topaz's room with the money?

It would be just like Belinda to tease Kyle with it. By then, he was drunker than before. Maybe he grabbed the bags from her.

I dropped the towel. He might've chased Belinda to her room, then attacked her. He would have just had time to kill her, figure out how to frame Sam, and make it back to the River Queen Club to confab for the shiveree.

No, it wouldn't work.

Sam admitted the dagger had been in his boot, last he knew, and there was no opportunity for Kyle to have acquired it.

He also would've had to have the cake knife, the flowers and the gloves ready, which would eliminate a spontaneous action.

And of course, the champagne bottle found in Fawn's room hadn't even been broken yet.

I sighed. I really didn't want it to be Kyle Dalton either.

Sam had come to the River Queen Club long before the cleanup crew arrived, which, according to the manager, wasn't until after 2:00 A.M.

We only had Sam's word for it that he didn't return to this floor between when he'd first danced with Fawn, and the time she found him in the bar.

He could've collected any number of discarded items for his perverted plan; my gloves, Imogene's cake knife, Cecille's flowers.

Because Cecille's bouquet was the only one missing. She insisted she'd brought it down on that first visit to her room, but nobody gave the story much credence, considering her known condition at that time.

She'd already been in pretty bad shape when I unraveled her braids.

Seeing the broken champagne bottle on the dance floor possibly triggered that deadly inspiration in Sam's soul.

My gloves were easy enough to hide. The cake knife he might've slid down inside his other boot.

But where had he put the flowers?

In my mind's eye, I saw the large, elegant trash container that stood in the elevator alcove. Resembling a Calder sculpture more than anything, it was exactly the hiding place likely to appeal to Sam.

Even if I could understand his tormented spirit taking this last, desperate measure to be free of Belinda Callant, I was disappointed he'd involved Fawn Goldfeather as his alibi.

Sam's goal was evidently to get her started drinking, knowing she would definitely crash at some point, yet still think he'd been there all along. Which meant Fawn had imbibed far more than she realized, while he himself had drunk very little. Otherwise, he could've never carried out such an elaborate scheme.

I remembered his almost aggressive approach to Fawn when she suddenly appeared in the River Queen, right after Montaigne fled.

I'd thought he was simply grabbing at a straw to ease the pain of rejection.

Now, it looked like he'd been thinking, "Well hello, sucker!"

I turned the blow dryer on, reveling, as I always did, in the luxurious sensation of freshly-washed hair billowing softly around my head.

Hair, hair, everywhere. So much of it in this case.

Lambie's baby blonde fleece . . . Jolene and Bobette's pumpkin pie colors . . . Nectarine's burnished gold curls . . . Belinda's long, bronze comma on a raw patch of scalp . . . something funny about that . . . little red-headed bride and groom dolls on the cake . . . Sam's purple-black braids . . .

Speaking of braids. I hoped that top section of my hair which had been braided wouldn't display residual crinkles after having been up all this time.

Braids, braids, braids. The word kept ricocheting around my head. I switched off the blower and stared into the mirror, willing that woman in there who always looked like she knew so much more than I did to tell me what I was missing.

There's a touch of the tomahawk . . . one Indian at a time should be enough . . . My God! I look more like an Indian than you do . . . two little Indian gur-rils . . .

I gripped the edge of the sink to keep upright. Of course! It explained the flowers, the gloves, the cake knife, and why Jolene thought she'd seen Sam Stormshadow creeping along to the honeymoon suite.

It also explained why Cecille Dalton had looked like the cat who'd swallowed the canary this morning.

48

"Run that by me again, will you, Claire?" Nectarine requested with a frown.

She and Dan and I were the only three people in our suite now. Officers Cletus, Harp and Songy were taking well-deserved three-hour dinner breaks. Cletus had hightailed it home to Gentilly, where he planned to get outside as much of his wife's roast turkey with oyster dressing as possible.

Dan reached over and stroked my cheek. "I think you're onto something, darlin'," he said, with a note of pride.

"Well, it makes as much sense as the Sam theory, anyway," I said modestly.

"Okay. I think Cecille did it. She definitely had a motive, plus the means and the opportunity."

My scenario went like this. As Cecille said, after I removed her braids, she took them to her room, along with her bridesmaid's bouquet.

Upon her return to the River Queen Club, Reggie told her that Belinda wanted to cut her out of the Fawn Goldfeather deal. This news, on top of knowing that Reggie had found bigger fish to fry in the person of Belinda Callant, had sent her over the edge.

In her unbalanced state, Cecille started planning to kill Belinda, and make it look like Sam Stormshadow did it. She already had the disguise; but she needed weapons.

She knew exactly where to find one of them. Imogene's cake knife, still congealing in white icing and Red Velvet cake crumbs on the serving trolley. She was carrying an extra-long narrow, vintage evening bag, I reminded Nectarine.

"I'll bet you'll find it's pretty sticky inside."

Cecille had spotted my gloves lying on the bridal party's dais table where I'd left them, handy as could be for a killer who didn't want to leave fingerprints.

Then she'd staged that drunken brawl with Belinda, afterwards docilely allowing her brothers to lead her away.

At her parents' table, she'd waited for just the right situation to get her back downstairs and provide her alibi.

Poor Fawn Goldfeather must've had a big "Kick Me" sign stuck to her back that night.

As soon as Cecille saw her, she'd started carrying on about her "lil' Indian pal."

Fawn would've welcomed the opportunity to tell Cecille her good news about Belinda wanting to represent her, not knowing Belinda intended to eliminate Cecille from the equation. Fawn had undoubtedly mentioned she'd met with Belinda in the honeymoon suite—a tidbit like that was too good to keep.

In so doing, she'd driven the final nail into Belinda's coffin.

When Fawn and Cecille got downstairs to her room, she pretended to pass out, thus acquiring an alibi.

After Fawn left, Cecille began to disguise herself as Sam Stormshadow, pinning on the long, dark braids and letting them hang. And of course, everybody had a black leather jacket.

"She knew the shiveree would promenade for awhile, so there'd be plenty of chances to sneak out. And if anybody saw her, they'd think it was Sam Stormshadow. Just as Jolene did."

Dan shook his head. "Sorry, baby. On this go-round, it doesn't wash."

"Why not?" I asked.

Nectarine answered. "Because you haven't explained how she managed to get into Fawn's room and take Sam's dagger, and that piece of broken glass, all without disturbing Fawn and Sam, no matter how drunk they were."

"Hmm. Well, T.J. used to also be in that room remember? Cecille could've gotten hold of his key somehow."

"That won't work either, Claire," Dan objected. "Even if she had T.J.'s key, she couldn't have known Fawn was going to bring Sam to her room. But suppose Cecille did see them go in together. She had no guarantee they would conveniently pass out so she could waltz in and take the dagger and the piece of glass."

As an afterthought he added, "Nor does it explain what happened to the money."

"Plus," Nectarine delivered the final blow to my theory, "she would've positively had to know Sam was in the habit of wearing a dagger in his boot."

I felt deflated. "You're right," I sighed. "But, gosh! It seemed to make so much sense when I first thought of it."

Nectarine smiled. "Actually, you have given me something new to mull over, Claire."

"Then tell me!" I begged. "Maybe I won't feel so inept."

"Well, think about this," Nectarine said. "You projected your case against Cecille on the basis of her motive, and that she had access to the flowers, the gloves and the cake knife. Oh, yes. And the means to disguise herself as Sam Stormshadow. Right?"

I nodded.

Nectarine went on. "We—the police—have projected our case against Sam on the basis of his motive, his access to the dagger, the cake knife, and the piece of broken glass. And the eyewitness who saw someone resembling Sam disappearing around the corner to Belinda's room."

"I think I see where you're going," Dan interjected. "If I may?"

Nectarine bowed. "Say on, Lawyer Dan."

Dan got up and walked over to our blacked-out Christmas tree with the still-unopened presents beneath. Jiggling a fat little angel ornament on one branch, he said, "There's something missing in both cases. Cecille had no opportunity to acquire the dagger and broken glass. If

Cecille indeed brought her bouquet to her room as she claims, Sam had no way of accessing it."

"Unless Cecille really was fried and never brought the thing down here at all, and Sam found it in the River Queen and stashed it in the trash can," I broke in.

Dan justifiably ignored the interruption.

"So," he concluded, "no matter who we've constructed a hypothesis against—Kyle, Cecille, or even Sam—each with a very juicy motive to kill Belinda—there's always some quirk that makes it pretty damn impossible for any one of them to have gotten hold of all the pieces of evidence."

I laughed. "Then maybe they *all* did it. Like *Murder on the Orient Express*."

"Uh-uh," Nectarine disagreed. "No. Somehow, I can't see such wildly diverse characters getting into the necessary harmony long enough to pull off such an intricate caper. But, strictly for argument's sake, let's say they did.

"*Where is the money?*"

49

Well, if we hadn't been trying to get so deep and Sherlockian—or even Christie-ish—about it, the answer to that question was staring us right in the face.

Only one person in the whole gang really needed money—and lots of it—right away.

Fortunately for Detective Sergeant Nectarine Savoy, newest member of the Eighth District NOPD, things began moving very quickly the next morning.

Nectarine, who was in a race against time, had managed to keep a tight lid on things thus far. Yesterday, being Christmas, made it easier. But rumors were bound to start leaking out about the strange doings on Riverside Manor's deluxe twenty-first floor. Rumors that would quickly reach the irritable ears of Captain Carruth. And when they did, Nectarine intended to have a solid case built up against the prime suspect—whoever it might be.

That's why she'd allowed Cletus and Harp to read Sam his rights and hold him for forty-eight hours on suspicion. It would provide a bone for Carruth to gnaw on, and keep him out of Nectarine's hair. If Sam were truly guilty, then she would be a jump ahead.

If he were actually innocent, well, tough. Especially if "Love Lump" was still in custody.

But Sam's absence in that case just might lure the real killer into the light.

Last evening, Nectarine rang Officers Cletus, Harp and Songy during their dinner breaks, and ordered them to take the night off with her blessing. She had then driven home for a shower and some fresh clothes and called Marcel to explain the situation, before coming back to the hotel, where she'd slept on our sofa.

Now, at a little after 8:00 A.M. on December 26, she was bright-eyed and bushy-tailed, ready for battle. This was primarily thanks to the advent of Maumus Tulley, who, being unable to reach Cecille for the last two days, became alarmed and hopped another off-hours flight from Atlanta to New Orleans.

Mo hadn't bothered to ring from downstairs, simply charged up to twenty-one, where he was intercepted by a uniformed officer as he stepped from the elevator, and delivered forthwith to Nectarine. He sat on the loveseat in rumpled but expensive corduroy outdoor gear by a famous American designer, and reiterated what he'd already told Nectarine for Officer Songy's benefit.

Songy's fingers clattered nimbly over the keyboard as Mo spoke.

"Well, like I mentioned to Claire the other night," he began, crinkling his eyes at me, "I rushed back to Atlanta specifically to look for evidence that Reggie had consistently been bilking Cecille on what she was paying for art acquisitions. And, I found it!"

Mo had spent hours on the phone, tracking down the artists, not always the simple task it sounded as I knew from my dealings with Ambrose.

Once he'd made contact, Mo inquired how much they were paid for specific paintings or sculptures, referring to an inventory list obtained from Cecille's accountant. In almost every instance, the artist had received up to $5,000 less than Reggie claimed to have paid for the artwork!

Then, Mo compared notes with the insurance agent from Lloyd's of London. Again, in every case, Reggie had insured the art based on the falsified sales documents.

Mo rubbed his hands together. "We've got him over a barrel now!" he said gleefully. "It's just as well I didn't connect with Cecille earlier, because I wasn't able to get everything down in black and white until late last night." He patted the briefcase as fondly as if it were Cecille's bony little rump.

"May I say something, please?" I asked Nectarine, and she nodded.

"Then Fawn Goldfeather is an accessory, because she knew all about what Reggie was doing. In fact, I . . . overheard her kind of threaten him about it."

I related the conversation I'd eavesdropped on, and Nectarine made a few notes.

"This is all very interesting," she commented, "but I'm afraid it's a side issue that has no bearing on the murder."

Mo shrugged. "Well, it seems we all have our work cut out for us, don't we, Sergeant?"

He picked up his briefcase from the floor, preparing to depart, then relaxed back against the cushions.

"Oh. There was one more thing I found out that could mean something. Claire, remember you told me Belinda Callant said the Lloyd's of London investigator assigned to her case was useless because he couldn't find a stash of missing paintings by a deceased Native American artist?

"Well, I tried to call him, but we played phone tag until after I left. However, this morning on the plane, something kept nagging at me to try him again. I didn't really want to, I hate using those stupid seat phones, but I did it anyway."

This time, from thousands of feet in the air, Mo finally made contact with the guy. And what he learned was about to change everything.

The investigator told Mo that the missing art insured by Belinda had been created by a young Indian woman named Jean Trainor, who had died about a year ago. Contended he'd followed every possible line of inquiry; her little studio in a downtown Atlanta loft held nothing but stiff brushes and used tubes of paint.

None of the girl's remaining relatives knew what could've happened to all those paintings. Or so they said.

But when the man checked his answering machine at the office on Christmas morning, there had been a message from Belinda, telling him to call her at the hotel immediately, because she had a good idea where he should look for the paintings.

He'd tried to reach her, but by then the switchboard had been instructed not to put any calls through to 2117.

"Not Floyd. Lloyd's!" exclaimed Dan.

Nectarine looked at him blankly.

"Remember?" Dan persisted. "Topaz told us Belinda left at 1:15 to call somebody on the East Coast. She said the news would really wake him up."

Songy was already scrolling back to the interview. "Here it is, Sergeant!" he piped. "Shall I read it back?"

"Absolutely," Nectarine said.

Songy rehearsed Topaz's verbatim statement that Dan had referred to.

"Then Mrs. Pearl Key said, 'Floyd somebody, dear'."

"Thank you, Officer Songy," Nectarine replied absently. Her blue eyes were turned inward.

"Oh. And thank you very much, Mr. Tulley," she added. "This could be vital information."

Mo inclined his head and crinkled at her. I felt a little jealous.

"My pleasure, Sergeant. Now, what's the drill with my client, Mrs. Worth? Am I allowed to see her? I mean, she's not under suspicion of murdering that woman or anything!"

Nectarine replied, with all apparent candor, "We already have a suspect in custody, Mr. Tulley. Now, obviously I'm in no position to prevent you from meeting with your own client. However, I am seriously going to request that you not attempt to contact her for the next few hours. It could mean all the difference to us."

Mo stood. "As you wish, Sergeant," he said, with a courtly bow.

"I saw some people checking out as I came in a little while ago. Perhaps I could best serve all our interests if I were able to secure a room in the hotel and take a nap."

Nectarine drummed her gold pen. "One more thing before you go, Mr. Tulley."

"Yes?" Mo paused politely.

"Would you," Nectarine mused, "say that Reggie Worth is capable of murder?"

Mo grinned. "Oh, how I wish I could answer yes, Sergeant Savoy," he said regretfully. "But no. You see, Reggie's own father was murdered, though of course he had only himself to thank for it.

"Our Reginald has a horror of physical violence. And I cannot imagine him inflicting such hideous mutilation as you described upon a beautiful woman he had great expectations from.

"Mind you," Mo wagged his index finger professorially, "if it had been a matter of theft, in any way, shape or form, anywhere, anytime or any place, I'd bet the ranch on Reggie Worth as the culprit.

"Once a thief, always a thief."

50

After Mo departed, Nectarine played Dan's hunch and tracked down the River Queen Club's night manager, reaching him at his home in Metairie.

Initially, the man had been unforthcoming, stating only that Mr. Worth's accounts had been satisfactorily settled.

But after Nectarine snarled at him she was conducting a murder investigation and expected specific answers to specific questions, he'd finally divulged the following information.

On Christmas Eve, Mr. Worth's losses were extremely heavy. Added to his previous run of ill fortune, the total came to something over twenty thousand dollars.

Nectarine whistled softly.

Upon being summoned to the manager's office, Mr. Worth assured him that the debt would be paid in full within twenty-four hours.

Understandably, the manager was exceedingly skeptical of this declaration, having heard it many times before. However, at around three o'clock of that same morning, Mr. Worth delivered a briefcase containing the exact amount—$22,500—in one-hundred dollar bills.

To Nectarine's query, the manager huffily retorted he certainly had not asked Mr. Worth to disclose where he'd obtained such a large amount so quickly.

Nectarine then asked if he'd noticed anything unusual about the money.

After a short silence, the manager replied yes, indeed. It had smelled very sweet. Like cookies. Or candy, perhaps.

Where was the money now? Why in the vault, naturally. Yes, still in the briefcase, as a matter of fact.

"Sir," Nectarine snapped, "that money is evidence in a murder case. I'm officially asking you to report to your place of business immediately, and I will meet you with a court order to collect the briefcase."

The manager hastily assured her that he would be at Riverside Manor within the hour.

"Right!" Nectarine hung up and pounced like a tigress upon Officers Cletus and Harp, who'd just come in looking chipper and refreshed.

"Go to Room 2110 and bring me Mr. Worth right away," she commanded. "Alone. Without his wife."

51

"All right. Yes, I took the money!" Reggie Worth announced defiantly. "But it was mine, dammit!"

"Really? Why don't you tell me all about it?" Nectarine invited cozily.

He and Belinda had come to an agreement that she would pay off his gambling debts before they were married, claimed Reggie. There were a couple of pressing matters demanding his attention back home. But more seriously, he had already run up quite a tab at the River Queen Club.

Belinda said she knew where she could get hold of $35,000 immediately, and it wouldn't cost anything except that relic piece of jewelry Foley's aunts were always nagging her about.

Then, laughing, she revealed that the two sisters had hidden the money in praline boxes.

On Christmas Eve, when Belinda showed up at the reception, she told Reggie that the deal with Pearl and Topaz would go through that night, and to wait in the club bar for her call.

Meanwhile Reggie, like every other deluded gambler, started feeling like he was hot, and decided to try his luck. And if he lost, what the hell? Belinda was going to take care of it.

He hadn't counted on losing quite so big, however.

Following that sticky scene in the manager's office, Reggie parked himself on a stool at the bar as instructed, and waited. And waited. He was becoming alarmed. What was taking her so long? Had she changed her mind?

Finally, at seven minutes to two, Belinda called, telling him she had the money and to come on up. She'd be waiting for him in bed.

"How were you supposed to get in then?" Nectarine asked.

Reggie extracted a narrow strip of plastic from his breast pocket. "With this. Belinda had an extra key to 2117 because Foley gave her his own when he said she and Sam could use the suite."

Belinda, in turn, had awarded the surplus key to Reggie, who'd used it several times already.

And naturally, in all the confusion surrounding that particular arrangement, poor little desk clerk Darren would've automatically handed over two keys without hesitation.

Reggie smoothed his mustache with a trembling pinky.

"So I finished my drink and went down. It was a few minutes after two o'clock by then. And almost walked bang into the middle of the shiveree, which I'd forgotten about. Fortunately, I managed to conceal myself in the elevator alcove until they rounded the corner to parade in front of this room, then nipped on to Belinda's."

But once inside 2117, he discovered, instead of a beautiful naked woman awaiting him in bed, a butchered one sprawled on the floor.

Reggie's first clear thought after that initial shock was (surprise, surprise) about the money.

He spotted the Aunt Sally's shopping bags and grabbed them, then sprinted back up the corridor, reaching his and Cecille's room in the nick of time. The door had barely shut behind him when he heard the Shiveree Boys coming in that direction. In the darkness, he tripped and fell over Cecille's red bridesmaid's gown, which she'd left lying in a heap on the floor.

I was glad Mrs. Cahoon wasn't present to hear that part.

His tumble awakened Cecille, who proceeded to wrest the whole story out of him.

"At first, she actually thought I killed Belinda for her sake!" Reggie marveled.

Once convinced he had not, Cecille pointed out that nobody must learn he'd been in the room with Belinda's corpse, or he would be a major suspect. Together, they'd concocted a story that sailed so close to the truth, it might possibly have remained undetectable, if Reggie hadn't taken the money.

Cecille advised him to go and settle up with the River Queen Club right away, and that's what he'd done.

Obviously, they weren't thinking too straight because it never occurred to them that Pearl and Topaz would mention the money, or that the sweet smell from Aunt Sally's kitchen would betray what Reggie had done.

"Where is the remaining $12,500, Mr. Worth?" demanded Nectarine.

Reggie winced. "In our room," he mumbled. "Oh, but see here! I already explained Belinda meant it for me. Surely you don't intend to take it!"

"We surely do!" Nectarine contradicted blithely. "And, Mr. Worth. I am requesting you not to leave the hotel premises today. Should you do so for any reason, I expect you to notify me. You are of course free to consult an attorney if you wish, but I imagine he'll advise you to cooperate with the police."

52

Shortly thereafter, the River Queen Club's night manager delivered Reggie's briefcase containing $22,500 in cash to Nectarine at his office.

Now, she placed it on the coffee table next to three Aunt Sally's boxes packed with hundred dollar bills, and gazed at the arrangement in perplexity.

"We know she had the money by one-fifteen. Why, since she intended to give it to Reggie, did she wait almost forty-five minutes to ring him at the bar?"

"You only got his word for it she was gonna give him the loot," Cletus offered, from his perch on the counter stool propping the door open.

Nectarine shook her head. "No, officer. We've also got this"—she held up the third key to 2117—"and the fact that Mr. Worth is much too fond of Mr. Worth to murder his next meal ticket."

"Well, she made a phone call," Harp reminded her.

"But we know about that one," Nectarine replied. "It was to—" she stopped abruptly and frowned. "If she made one call, she might've made others, too!"

She smacked her forehead in self-reproach. "Officer Harp! Go get me the phone records from December 24 and December 25 for 2117. Now, please!"

Harp straightened alertly. "Yes, ma'am!" he barked obediently, to Cletus's open-mouthed astonishment.

Looking faintly surprised himself, Harp sped off to do her bidding.

In fifteen minutes, he'd returned with a printout of telephone calls made from 2117, between midnight of December 24 and 2:00 A.M. of December 25.

At 12:32 A.M., there'd been an intra-hotel call to Fawn Goldfeather in 2115.

At 12:49 A.M.—another intra-hotel call to 2104—Pearl and Topaz Key. Then, nothing more until 1:17 A.M., to Atlanta, Georgia.

Officer Songy accessed the Atlanta phone book on the Internet, and Nectarine read out the number.

"Lloyd's of London, Sergeant," he confirmed.

Nectarine studied the sheet. "Well, now. Isn't this interesting? Officer Songy, let's not leave Georgia just yet."

Following her call to Lloyd's, Belinda had dialed 555-1212 for Georgia information three times. Once to area code 404; twice to area code 770.

"Looking for somebody," Cletus remarked.

"Wasn't she just?" Nectarine murmured, turning to Songy. "Where's 770, Officer?"

Songy scrolled. "Mainly Duluth, Sergeant."

"Then this next number she called is in Duluth," said Nectarine.

"And yes, last is her call to Reggie at the bar. Just like he told us. 1:53.

"I don't suppose, Officer Songy, a person can enter the telephone number and match it to a name?"

Songy said, with a superior little smirk, "Oh, *certain* persons can, Sergeant. It'll take me a minute or two, though."

Nectarine feigned impatience. "That long, eh?"

The Duluth number belong to a J. Trainor.

Muttering, "Bingo!" Nectarine picked up the receiver and punched in the digits, only to experience an anticlimax when the line remained continually busy.

Dan, playing host, asked if anybody wanted a soda or some Evian. Nectarine said she'd stick with coffee. Cletus and Harp opted for Cokes, scoffing at Songy, who selected Evian.

While Dan was tending to the pouring, I slouched aimlessly around, looking out the window at the rain, which had just begun to fall, and wondering when—or if—we'd ever be in the mood to open our Christmas presents.

"You want a Coke, darlin'?" Dan called.

"Thank you. I'll come get it," I told him.

On my way into the kitchenette, I glanced over at the barren countertop, former "evidence room." Everything had been cleared away and transferred to headquarters the night before to preserve its integrity.

We already knew the cake knife handle had been wiped clean of prints.

The only fingerprints on the Zuni turquoise and silver knife, however, belonged to Sam Stormshadow, though they were somewhat smudged. Which could mean someone wearing gloves had used it.

Sort of good news/bad news for Sam.

Again, I thought about Belinda's scalping. They had found traces of blood and hair on the Zuni blade, indicating it had been used in that heartless ritual.

I couldn't imagine anyone being so cold-blooded. Had Belinda been alive when it happened? I prayed not.

I closed my eyes to erase the image of that amputated lock of hair. Instead, it only loomed more clearly, as if I were staring right at it.

And then I saw what my hairdresser's eye had subconsciously registered right away.

And now, I knew that I knew who had done this terrible thing.

"Claire! I've been standing here holding this drink for you, darlin'. You want it or not?"

Dan's voice swept me back with a jolt. "Oh, I'm sorry, Dan. Just leave it by the sink."

I hurried back into the sitting room to tell Nectarine, but she had at last contacted J. Trainor in Duluth and waved me to silence.

"Mr. Trainor? Hello, I'm calling from New Orleans . . . Um, it's raining right now . . . anyway, I . . . well, yes. You could say I'm calling for Mrs. Callant . . . she what? I see . . . I'm sure it's hard to find a fax place open on Christmas Day, but . . . uh-huh . . . you were? Just a minute, Mr. Trainor."

Covering the mouthpiece, Nectarine hissed, "Officer Songy! Can you receive a fax on that thing?"

Songy looked superior again. "Just call me Mr. Modem," he bragged. "Would you prefer color, or black and white?"

Nectarine spoke into the phone again. "Mr. Trainor? Let me give you a better number to fax those things to . . . " she read out the number Songy had scrawled down on a piece of paper, " . . . in about fifteen minutes, you think . . . thank you very much, sir . . . goodbye . . . *who?*" Nectarine shot straight up from the sofa in surprise.

"Oh, I will definitely do that, Mr. Trainor," Nectarine promised. "Yes, I'm sure you do. Goodbye."

Nectarine flopped back onto the sofa. "Oh, wow! Am I ever glad Marcel and I went to midnight mass at St. Louis Cathedral on Christmas Eve!"

So that's why they'd slipped away so soon. Which was totally irrelevant at the moment.

"Nectarine," I said. "You've got to get that piece of Belinda's hair back right away." And then I told her why.

She jumped up again. "Yes, yes, yes! It fits, Claire. You were right all along. Only in reverse."

Cletus and Harp stood side by side, turning befuddled faces toward Savoy like two big dogs trying to understand what their mistress expected of them.

She didn't keep them in suspense.

"Officer Cletus. I want you to retrieve Mrs. Callant's hair sample and bring it back here ten minutes ago."

Cletus bustled out.

"Officer Harp, fetch Mr. Tucker John Dalton to me immediately, please. Then find out if Mr. Maumus Tulley is registered here and get me his room number. After that, I'm going to want to see Reggie Worth again."

When Harp left, Nectarine began strutting around the room like a saucy waitress, holding an imaginary serving tray aloft.

"Watch it, y'all! Hot turkey, comin' through!"

53

Rain was still falling softly at six o'clock that evening as Nectarine stood by the fireplace, observing the arrival of her invited "guests." Which was everybody currently inhabiting this floor, with the exception of the three Callant cousins and their wives.

Ironically, the only room large enough to assemble everyone at the same time was 2117.

The honeymoon suite.

The murder scene.

Because of the humidity, it was too warm for the central heating, yet far too cool for air conditioning. Nectarine had dealt with the problem by having Cletus start a pleasantly crackling blaze in the fireplace, and allowing the French doors to the narrow terrace overlooking the river to stand open for some fresh air.

In addition to its substantially larger square footage, the terrace was the major difference between this suite and ours.

Cletus and Harp sat unobtrusively near the hall door, still splintered from the feet of Shiveree Boys. The officers looked more doggy than ever. Doggies that Nectarine had trained to eat out of her hand in less than forty-eight hours.

Jolene and Bobette were the first to enter.

"Oh, Nectarine! This is just like something out of Agatha Christie!" Bobette exclaimed excitedly.

"Only they almost always had high tea or cocktails at the time," Jolene pointed out.

"Sorry, girls," Nectarine laughed. "No refreshments at this here denouement."

"Daynewmon?" Bobette echoed, mystified. "Is that French? Like swan-yay?"

Everybody else was subdued as they filed in and found seats.

I looked around at the faces that had grown so familiar—some even dear—in such a short time: Imogene, Daphne, Emory, Lambie, Stafford, Alicia, Woody, Wes, Pearl, Topaz, Mamie, Fenton, Huey, Purcell, Kyle, Tucker John, Cecille, Reggie, Fawn and Mo.

Last, but not least, the surprise guest, Sam Stormshadow entered.

There was a stir and murmur as a uniformed officer escorted him in.

Fawn turned away, looking sick.

Sam, for his part, was wearing that impassive cigar store Indian expression again as he twirled a dining chair backward and straddled it to face Nectarine Savoy.

The room gradually grew quiet, except for the snap of burning logs and the patter of rain against the windows.

Nectarine allowed the silence to lengthen before she finally spoke.

"I realize this must seem pretty dramatic. A gathering in the murder chamber, so to speak. Kind of like Agatha Christie, as Bobette said. But don't worry, I have no intention of pontificating like Hercule Poirot, or moralizing like Miss Marple.

"You see, we know who killed Belinda Callant."

Sam studied the toes of his boots.

"This," Nectarine went on, "is just the fastest way to verify the facts, and tie up a few loose ends. So if something doesn't sound quite right to anyone, please feel free to interrupt."

Nectarine picked up a file folder from the mantelpiece and opened it. Whether by accident or design, the plastic bag containing Belinda's hair slid out and fell to the floor.

Not everyone could see it from where they sat.

"Excuse me." Unhurriedly, Nectarine stooped gracefully and recovered the bag. Straightening, she held it up.

"This, by the way, is the lock of hair that was scalped from Mrs. Callant's forehead."

Jolene squealed and clamped her hand over her mouth.

"It's a very important piece of evidence, because of what it tells us about the murderer. Which isn't as obvious as you might think. But we'll get to that later."

Then, Nectarine began summing up the case in her patented style, referring occasionally to the notes before her.

"My investigators—Officers Cletus and Harp—and I have positively confirmed that Belinda Callant was killed at some point between 1:54 and 2:08 A.M.—approximately—a timeline of less than fifteen minutes.

"There were only three people who appeared to have the motive, opportunity, and access to at least some of the means. I won't take time to elaborate further, except to say that we narrowed it down to Sam Stormshadow.

"We had eyewitness evidence from Miss Jolene Dalton, who claimed to have seen Mr. Stormshadow from the rear, heading in the direction of 2117, at around 1:55 A.M."

Jolene squirmed.

"Of the suspects, Mr. Stormshadow alone had access to a key to Room 2117, and all the weapons used to attack Mrs. Callant. The only thing not immediately clear was how he came by the roses from Mrs. Cecille Worth's bouquet scattered across Mrs. Callant's body. But we acted on the basis that Mrs. Worth was mistaken about returning them to her room, having instead left them in the River Queen Club, where Mr. Stormshadow acquired them."

Cecille started to say something, but Mo quelled her with a look.

Nectarine added, "Mr. Stormshadow, incidentally, does not deny the charges, explaining that he is prone to blackout periods when he drinks a certain amount of liquor.

"Miss Goldfeather, who initially provided Mr. Stormshadow with an alibi, saying that he spent the night with her"—Fawn hunched, embarrassed, as startled eyes sprung in her direction—"is herself unused to drinking alcohol, and consequently passed out.

"She therefore was unable to testify that Mr. Stormshadow was indeed with her during the critical time period, and was forced to retract her alibi."

Nectarine closed the folder. "And that would seem to be that. Except, as I mentioned, for a few loose ends.

"We have learned that Mrs. Callant recently discovered the whereabouts of a large number of paintings she alleged were stolen from her."

Reggie grew alert.

"This afternoon, I received some colored photographs of the missing artwork via fax. The quality isn't very good, but it should be sufficient for identification purposes."

Nectarine removed several flimsy fax sheets from the file folder.

"Mrs. Worth! If you'll be good enough to step forward and take a look at these?"

Cecille was caught by surprise. "Me? Why me?" she shrilled. "What would I know about any paintings stolen from Belinda Callant?"

"Just do it, Cecille," Mo urged quietly.

"You come with me then," Cecille snapped at him petulantly.

While Mo stood by, Cecille began looking through the photographs.

"But"—she stared at them in confusion—"this is—"

"Thank you, Mrs. Worth," Nectarine interrupted, then turned suddenly to Fawn.

"Miss Goldfeather. Where is your art portfolio?"

"Well-I-I don't know," Fawn stammered. "I left it with Belinda. Did you find it?"

"No. But I did," Reggie said, producing the leather case. Fawn looked utterly baffled.

Topaz honked, "Why, that looks like the briefcase Belinda brought to our room to put the money in! Only she didn't need it. Not that it would've ever fit in there."

"She did say she wanted to keep her valuable things together," Pearl recalled.

Nectarine looked at Reggie. "Mr. Worth, would you please bring that portfolio up here and let your wife examine it?"

Reggie approached and passed the leather case to Cecille, who looked at him curiously before unzipping it.

Cecille flipped through the acetate pages, getting more upset with each turn. "I don't understand!" she wailed.

Mo patted her shoulder "Patience, darling. All will be revealed."

"But when—I mean, how—did Reggie get my portfolio from Belinda?" Fawn wondered.

"Oh, he didn't know he was getting it, Miss Goldfeather," Nectarine explained. "When he went into Room 2117 and discovered Belinda dead, all he wanted was the money she promised him.

"Money that was packed into praline boxes in Aunt Sally shopping bags. You'll be delighted to know Belinda considered your work so valuable, she even took it with her to a meeting in Pearl and Topaz Key's room. Why was that, I wonder?

"At any rate, she put the case in one of the shopping bags to carry back to her room. Which is why, Miss Goldfeather, you couldn't find it after you murdered her!"

An excited babble erupted.

"No!" Fawn cried.

Nectarine was relentless. "Yes, Miss Goldfeather. It was the shock of your life when Belinda looked at 'your' portfolio and recognized it as the work of your dead half-sister, Jean Trainor.

"Oh, by the way. I spoke to your stepfather, Jim Trainor? He said to be sure and tell Fawnie to please come see him. He misses her."

"Stop it! Stop it!" Fawn put her hands over her ears.

Nectarine didn't stop. "Neither you nor Reggie had any idea Belinda Callant had already discovered your sister, and planned to make her a big star. But Belinda had an odd way of doing business. Her standard contract was 50-50, right down the middle, for seven years. Belinda already owned half of Jean's art. And she was prepared to make a deal with Jean's legal heir, her father, for the other half. Only the work mysteriously disappeared."

Nectarine moved closer to Fawn. "You hated your sister. You even admitted it to me, remember?"

"She stole my mother!" Fawn sobbed, "She stole my talent!"

Nectarine shook her head. "I'm sorry, Miss Goldfeather. You had no talent to steal. A fairly competent graphics designer is what you are."

Pivoting to T.J. she said, "Mr. Dalton. Will you tell us what you did this afternoon?"

T.J. struggled to his feet, avoiding Fawn's eyes.

As Vice-President of Peach Island Textiles, he'd called and ordered the electronic security device removed from Fawn's office door. Inside, they had found nothing but a wastebasket overflowing with aborted sketches. Oh, yes. And three wooden crates containing sixty oil paintings of various dimensions.

"I could've been a great artist, now that Jean is dead," Fawn moaned. "She wasn't even a real Indian. It wasn't fair. I just needed more time."

"My God! You stupid bitch!" Reggie expostulated. "I kept trying to tell you you couldn't paint worth a gnat's ass! It was a perfectly splendid scam as it was.

"Sell off a painting or two to Cecille and a few others, whet their appetites. Then, a big successful exhibit. You'd be famous. Get revenge on your dead sister. We could've eaten out on that for years to come before anyone expected you to produce another such body of work.

"Then, Belinda came along, and it seemed like too good an opportunity to miss. With Belinda Callant behind you, the pot would be even bigger."

Only Reggie had fallen for Belinda. What masqueraded as his conscience began to bother him. He was glad that the meeting between Fawn and Belinda kept getting postponed.

When Belinda called Reggie at the bar, she told him Fawn was trying to pull a fast one, and she was going to nail her to the wall. She had no idea Reggie already knew the work was Jean Trainor's.

Then, minutes later, Reggie found Belinda dead. In the terror of the moment, it never occurred to him Fawn was responsible. He'd barely summoned the presence of mind to take the money. He hadn't even thought about Fawn's book, and was amazed to find it shoved into one of the shopping bags.

"She said she was going to throw the book at somebody!" Pearl twittered.

"Oh, she definitely was," Nectarine agreed. "Jean Trainor's book. Belinda Callant had a reputation for never letting anybody do her out of anything."

She turned to Fawn again. "You could have survived the shame of exposure, Miss Goldfeather. But not prosecution and certain imprisonment for fraud and grand larceny, while your sister was being acclaimed and praised posthumously by the art world. Which is what Belinda threatened you with. And that's why you killed her."

Fawn had regained her composure. "You can't prove a thing," she scoffed.

"Oh, I'm pretty sure we can," Nectarine said. "Here's how I think it went down."

Fawn had been in a panic after Belinda threw her out. She'd gone up to the River Queen Club to look for Reggie to warn him, and figure out what to do.

Instead, Sam, still smarting from Montaigne's rejection, had intercepted her.

Again she'd tried to find Reggie, but a drunken Cecille latched onto her. While Cecille was circling the room, trying to find her things, she spotted the cake knife. Saying Imogene promised it to her, she jammed it into her purse.

"That's right," Cecille confirmed. "Well, you *did* promise it to me a long time ago, Aunt Imogene!" she said, in response to Imogene's stricken look.

Nectarine went on. "And that's when you started to hatch your very nasty plan to kill Belinda, Miss Goldfeather. You're the one who saw Claire's gloves and took them, just in case."

Then she'd gotten Cecille back to her room and there were the braids.

"I believe you decided right then and there to frame Sam Stormshadow."

Obligingly, Cecille had quickly passed out. It was almost too easy for Fawn to take the braids, the knife, the flowers, and Cecille's room key.

"It was important for you to return the braids to Cecille," Nectarine said. "You couldn't keep them. And to leave them at the scene of the crime would have screamed impersonation."

Fawn had put everything in her room, then gone down to find Sam, who was still sitting in the bar, drinking and mooning over that half-breed Montaigne Duffosat.

Sam had been easily persuaded to come to her room, to open the champagne bottle, to smash it.

"That glass was just a little extra *artistic* touch, wasn't it, Miss Goldfeather?" Nectarine needled.

Once Sam had crashed, Fawn took his key to 2117 and the Zuni knife from his boot, put on her black leather jacket, and pinned the braids to her own hair.

Then she slid on the gloves, gathered up the flowers, the cake knife, and the green glass. And went off to murder Belinda Callant while the shiveree rolled on.

"Belinda must've been very surprised when you suddenly appeared in her room, dressed like Sam and carrying roses, Miss Goldfeather. Which is what gave you the advantage.

"You scalped her with the Zuni knife before you plunged it into her uterus. You knew nobody could hear her, no matter how loud she screamed, over all that racket.

"Afterwards, you only had a few minutes to look for your portfolio. But as we know, you couldn't find it."

The next moments were critical for Fawn, because she needed to return the braids and key to Cecille's room, then get back to her own without being seen by the Shiveree Boys.

Fawn was rigid. "You're crazy. You've got no proof."

"No?" Nectarine picked up the plastic bag containing Belinda's hair and waved it in front of Fawn. "This is Belinda Callant's trademark, a long, smooth, sweeping lock, perfectly tapered to fall just so.

"But Claire Claiborne, a professional hairstylist, noticed something peculiar about it. Instead of coming to the necessary angle at the end, there's a blunt gap where about two inches or so has been roughly hacked off.

"I must advise you, Miss Goldfeather, I obtained a warrant to search your room while you've been here. Officer Cletus! Have you got anything to show us?"

Cletus stepped forward, holding yet another plastic bag. This one contained a short, bristly bronze nubbin of hair, bound tightly in a rubber band. "Find the Indian and you got your killer," he'd told Nectarine. He had been right. It was simply a matter of which Indian.

Nectarine dangled the bag before Fawn's eyes "Behold! The hair of your enemy, Fawn Goldfeather!"

Without warning, Fawn leaped from her chair and headed toward Nectarine.

Cletus grabbed at her arm, but she slipped easily from his grasp and kept going.

But instead of attacking Nectarine, Fawn snatched up the portfolio and held it to her breast.

"Put your hands up, lady!" yelled Harp from the doorway. He had his gun trained on Fawn.

Fawn seemed not to have heard. She just stood there, clinging tightly to the leather case and catching her breath in deep, shuddering gasps.

Harp came closer. "Drop the satchel and put your hands up," he ordered.

Fawn sighed, and her shoulders slumped. Harp returned the gun to his shoulder holster.

"All right, Miss Goldfeather. Let's go," Nectarine said coldly, moving in.

The instant she did, Fawn's muscles tensed.

"Watch her! Watch her!" Dan shouted, just as Fawn began running.

He threw himself forward in a football tackle, managing to catch hold of her ankle. But he was too far away, and she had too much momentum. He lost his grip.

Fawn lunged out onto the terrace, into the rain.

When Fawn hitched herself to the top of the low stone wall, Bobette shrieked, "Stop her, somebody! She's going to jump!"

"Oh no, she's not!" declared Nectarine.

In a heartbeat, she'd wrestled Fawn face down to the terrace, ordering, "Cuff her, Officer Cletus."

"Yes, ma'am!" Cletus bounded forward to do his duty.

When Harp finished reading Fawn her rights, Cletus hauled her up from the floor.

As they walked her forward between them, Nectarine yelled, "Watch it, y'all! Hot turkey, comin' through!"

Red Velvet Cake

2-1/2 cups plain flour
1/2 cup shortening or unsalted butter
2 eggs
1 teaspoon salt
1 teaspoon vanilla
2 Tablespoons cocoa
1 cup buttermilk
1 teaspoon soda
1 Tablespoon white vinegar
1-1/2 cups sugar
2 ounces red food color

1. Cream shortening, sugar and vanilla. Add eggs, one at a time, beating well.

2. Make a paste of cocoa, food color and vinegar. Set aside.

3. Mix buttermilk, flour, salt and soda. Set aside.

4. *Now!* Mix numbers 1, 2 and 3 together. Blend until batter is smooth.

5. Pour into 2 nine-inch pans or 3 eight-inch pans. Bake at 350 degrees F. for 40 minutes.

Original Icing

1 cup whole milk
5 Tablespoons flour
2 sticks salted butter
1 teaspoon vanilla
1 cup sugar

Cook milk and flour until thick in double boiler. Let cool. Cream sugar and butter. Add vanilla and blend until fluffy. Add milk and flour mixture. Beat well.